PRAISE FOR TOOTHLESS

"Despite the title, this gritty supernatural historical has plenty of bite. Compelling and well told...this is an unusual mapping of familiar fantasy territory. Toothless himself is an introspective, complex protagonist, and his quest to recover what he can of his past is by turns moving, intriguing, and highly entertaining."
—Publishers Weekly

"Powerfully written, TOOTHLESS plunges the reader into the heart of a gripping, sometimes brutal, wonderful tale of what it truly means to be alive. Not to be missed!"
—Ed Greenwood, creator of the Forgotten Realms® fantasy world and bestselling author of *Elminster Must Die!*

"Toothless is compelling, intriguing and above all, utterly original. At last, something new!"
—Peadar Ó Guilín, author of *The Inferior*

"Toothless is...brutal, and it is utterly brilliant. Moore wraps his words around your ears like a fog, swirling to reveal the dying world in awful, sorrowful slivers."
—The Podagogue

"What a wonderful book. The story is fresh, well thought out, and superbly told."
—Podiobook Reviews by Craig Robertson

TOOTHLESS

A NOVEL BY J. P. MOORE

Dragon Moon Press

www.dragonmoonpress.com

Toothless

TOOTHLESS

A NOVEL BY J. P. MOORE

ACKNOWLEDGMENTS

My last moments with *Toothless* have been happy moments. I have received many good wishes and congratulations on signing with Dragon Moon Press, but waited a while before taking that quiet hour to express my thanks. Writers look forward to that, because we are generally unassuming people who need an excuse to express ourselves in understandable ways to the people around us. We also dread that moment, because we have to acknowledge how difficult it must be to deal with us when we are at any other point but this last, quiet hour.

So, I have to thank family and friends, especially my wife. Writers are needy and selfish. The people who stand by us deserve better. But we are not anywhere near our best, anything close to what they deserve, without their love and support. If *Toothless* is about anything, it is about a wife who inspires, children whose love redeems, and the power of friendship.

Gabrielle Harbowy and Gwen Gades at Dragon Moon Press saw something special in *Toothless*, and were not afraid to give an unconventional project a seat at the table. Gabrielle is a terrific editor. The book is better because of her. I am proud to be working with her and all of the other good folks at Dragon Moon Press.

Scott Purdy provided illustrations that make me wonder if he understands the book better than I do. His work makes me want to write.

Toothless gathered thousands of fans as a podcasted audiobook. I have to thank Evo Terra and the other wizards at Podiobooks.com for providing a platform for authors to share their work.

And the fans—without you, there would never have been that next chapter, or the one after that. You gave me this last, quiet, happy hour. I am very grateful.

For Sean,

who would have liked it.

And for Ian and Madeline,

who always make me smile.

Most of all, for Meghan,

my Aine, who does so much more

than just inspire me.

Book I: Fallen, Arise

France, 1180 AD

Chapter I

He remembered his name.

He could not remember a family name, only a single word. "Martin."

Martin lay on the ground. His left leg was straight, his right bent beneath it. His arms were outstretched, palms to the gray sky. The hilt of his greatsword, the silvery angel's face there, touched his right fingertips. Its round, smooth cheeks were like a baby girl's.

He was conscious of the battle, of his wounds, of the loss. The notion of a loss, however, retreated through a shimmering barrier at the edge of his consciousness. There, a colonnade, a stand of bright trees, marked the border between the living and the gone. Memories fled to this wall, passed through and dissolved. In all of the heroic tales, dying soldiers saw their lives pass before their eyes. No, Martin realized. The memories were just running like rats from a sinking ship, down the ropes only to drown. He watched the backs of their heads.

There was Aine, his wife. She carried Emer, only thirteen months old. The girl had been an early talker, having mastered "mama" and "papa," and even experimenting with the dog's name. "Goonka," she would say, pointing a fat finger at the young bitch Kennocha and laughing with lust and a deep chest. The dog enjoyed this and would jump among the sheep so much as to startle them into a stampede.

"Just making more work for herself," Aine would say.

Aine, dark hair braided, was beautiful like the dusky spring hills. Walking away from him, neither she nor Emer showed the bruises of the plague. First, the black moss appeared on the trees. Then, animals fell ill. Kennocha died, pink froth blooming out of her mouth. Then, Aine pointed out her first bruise. It was purple and deep beneath her skin. Within days, both she and Emer were dead.

The Black Yew had arrived.

The plague infected life itself. It closed the market. It shut the heavy chapel doors and silenced the monks in their cells. Aine was not surprised. She had always acted as if something would happen, as if something would go wrong. Martin could barely remember Aine's face, just gray eyes that always betrayed a cold cynicism, even when she was happy. He had forsaken another life to be with her. He had broken vows and abandoned comrades for her. It infuriated him that she would remain so suspicious.

Though she was right in the end, she refused to say it. She gave him that.

It did not matter now. She was just another ghost in the long retreat. But one figure stood apart—Tuan. The master Templar was short and wore a tonsure in the old Irish style. The front of his head was bald, but his hair fell to his shoulders in the rear. For a man who had seen so much, who limped and ached each day but who could best any of the initiates he had trained, he had a soft, grandfatherly face. Laughter had worn lines and grooves into his forehead, into the corners of his eyes and mouth. Tuan was a font of myth and understanding, a scribe, a teacher. He was also a warrior. Tuan, standing apart and looking back—Martin would not have predicted it, but he was not at all surprised.

Tuan was speaking. Martin heard the words from memory.

"If they kill you, resist them."

"I don't understand," Martin had replied. "If I am dead, then I am dead."

The Yew had only begun its march. Reports reached France from the edge of Scandinavia, which had quickly become a black wasteland. Martin did not yet know of the plague, or the fate of those who fell in battle against the Yew's demons.

He and Tuan sat in the scriptorium, a place consecrated by the great Irish Saint Columbcille. It was a magical room. The monks concocted ciphers in this room, and buried them deep into glorious manuscripts. It was empty but for Martin and Tuan. Still, the room echoed with the monks' quills against the vellum. The sound was now part of the soft wood grain of their desks and buried in the cold stone of the walls.

"They will promise everlasting life," Tuan said. "Power and glory. These are false prizes."

"I still don't—"

"Go. Protect us. Keep your vigil. Know that if you perish, we will honor you, your wife and your daughter, as long as we have breath. As long as we remember them, they live."

Tuan's voice receded beneath a curious string of numbers, meaningless arithmetic that floated over Martin in his own voice.

"Three plus three times twenty..."

It faded into the smoke.

A breeze touched upon the roof of Martin's mouth. His teeth and lower jaw were gone. The slice had come from a demon. Martin could still taste the blue steel blade of the scythe deep in his open throat, upon the root of his tongue. Fading, perhaps dead, he felt no pain. He could see it, though. The pain hovered around him, a green cloud of mist that clotted like his blood about the broken edges of his skin and the thick black hair at the back of his head.

The battle was distant and muffled, as if coming to him through water. Men made plans for battles. When armies followed these plans, they made music. They were a king's symphony. Every man, every horse, every joint of armor was a string or a breath through a reed. In defeat, the army was a primitive, amateur ensemble. Its voices were untrained, its instruments broken or bumped out of tune.

Martin heard the enemy. Leather slammed into dirt, thousands of feet marching in order so precise as to be a single thing walking. The Black Yew's wagon creaked. Clumps of dirt, sticky with vile sap, plopped to the ground. Fibrous ropes, their threads straining, twanged in the smoke.

The marching dead shed their memories with every step, leaving them behind to be taken by the black roots, drunk by the Yew's needles and sighed as a raspy voice, a whisper carried through smoke and stench by buzzing insects fat with carrion.

"Fallen, arise."

Martin had heard it through the entire battle, but was conscious of it only now. It was the Yew.

"Fallen, arise."

Creatures surrounded him. Spriggan—they were bred from frogs or salamanders. The monks were not sure. The imps were no taller than a man's knees. They waved long, awkward arms and had bulging eyes without pupils. They scurried in packs over the battlefield, their noses to the air and their pointed ears against the earth. This was their role, to find and harvest the dead, to carry them to the Yew. Martin had heard them. They spoke like the fat frogs that, upon discovery, belched in warbling protest before flopping into the water.

Tuan closed his eyes and turned, joining the refugee memories.

Martin was moving. A pair of spriggan pulled him by the wrists. His back scraped against stones. Another pair straightened his right leg and took his ankles. The four chanted. Their song went into his chest, separating his soul from his heart as a butcher separates fat from meat. The memories were now all gone. Still, Martin could see and hear. He could think.

The Yew spoke again.

"You will live forever."

They lashed his wrists and ankles to a post as if he were prey. The spriggan, the pair at the front and the pair at the rear, carried him through a gully. They slipped, dropping him in mud. Beside, a stream ran red. They lifted him.

The spriggan moved along a tree line, seemingly bickering. Their voices ran high and low, fast. They slapped one another and threw stones at their comrades, who carried others from the battlefield.

Martin's head fell back and bobbed, dragging through dirt and twigs. He could barely see. A gray green mist framed the world. This haze grew larger and larger, threatening to choke off the center altogether.

He was dying.

His feelings, his very consciousness, seemed to break further with each of the spriggan's steps. Like his memories, his own being fled his body. Yet something remained. That voice, that strange rustle of sound that was the Black Yew, gripped certain bits of him and held them fast. His spirit, incomplete, tore away and drifted. It was an empty, listing ship to be swallowed by the sea.

Now, Martin thought, he should be floating above the lifeless corpse that had been a warrior. He should see his wounds, his fibrous muscle and tendons. His heavenly gaze would mark that ground as hallowed ground. Instead, his head bobbing, he saw the rumps of the spriggan that carried him.

"Fallen, arise."

They entered the forest. Brush and bracken whipped Martin's face. Brier tore at his dead hide. The spriggan kicked up dirt and leaves that clumped in the gore on his neck. The forest leaned over the creatures, surrounding them in darkness. The trees themselves were poisoned, wearing the plague moss that bred tumors in their bark. Their limbs snaked around one another. Leaves, where there were leaves, were thin and brown or had been eaten into mere sketches of leaves by tiny insects that swarmed in buzzing, choking clouds. This had been a living forest.

The Yew had brought the plague from the north. It had brought demons and spirits. It had freed ancient slumbering things that now possessed the woods. Shouts and cries, screams of witches—even the spriggan moved slowly. Their shivering steps seemed full of fear.

A light danced into view, answering the cries of the spriggan. The orb bounced and bobbed. A wisp. It shot forward, lighting the path ahead, overshooting and coming back, then darting off again like a puppy. The spriggan followed, yelling at it, throwing sticks that missed it every time.

The path led downward, sloping into a clearing. The wisp darted into the canopy, its light lost in smoke. Corpses, though they were not dead, sat and stood upon the moss. These were the mindless shamblers, the fodder thholeat the Yew threw into battle.

Some of the dead, however, stood apart. They were sentient, almost human. One of these stood in command. Little more than bones, he wore a tattered purple cape and bronze armor that had gone green. He shouted and the shamblers gathered in formation. This captain turned his sunken eyes at Martin. The dead captain stepped forward, crossing the clearing with strength in his stride that would have been uncommon in a living man.

The wisp fell and flew through the opposite wall of the clearing. Its light exploded among the trees, casting twisted, bony shadows onto the marching dead. Groups of spriggan gathered into a line, bringing Martin and many others. The captain followed.

The forest fell into a field of stumps. Demons the height of four men felled the trees with their bare hands and broke them upon their thighs. They burned these trunks in giant piles. The smoke filled the sky, announcing the coming of the Yew to the next army foolish enough to stand against it. Priests in black robes chanted. The flames took a green hue and danced in rhythm with the song. Spriggan heaved some of the dead, the unsuitable dead, into these flames. Swallowing each of these corpses, the flames swirled with playful glee.

The smoke billowed. Martin could not smell, but he remembered the sickly-sweet of burning flesh. The lord who owned his farms had wisely, though to great controversy, ordered the cremation of the victims. So had Emer and Aine left the world, drifting on the wind. And fire was fire. Those flames had danced like these.

Countless dead gathered around a copse of trees at the bottom of the slope. The wisp bobbed once, then shot back over the heads of the spriggan, back to the battlefield.

It was not a grove, but a single tree. It was the Black Yew. Tortured beasts, tangled in ropy vines, pulled its massive wooden cart just inches with each struggling step. They were mammoth, deformed beings with muscular legs and shoulders. Their faces twisted in pain and their mouths opened in silent roars. The Yew's roots spilled from the sides of the cart and shot through the ground in all directions. Its needles and branches breathed. Deep within its canopy, a greenish orange light shone, the phosphorescence of insects lured from subterranean darkness to feed on the black tar that seeped through the cracks in its bark. The creaking of the massive wheels, the marching of the dead, the sighs of the branches—this was the melody of the victor's symphony.

The spriggan carried him forward through the crowd of the dead, past the tangled demons, to the edge of the cart.

"Fallen, arise. Now."

Martin was not the first. There were several ahead of him. A demon stood at the Yew's twisted trunks. His gray skin was riddled with white scars and his left eye was missing. A single horn, broken at the root, grew to the side of the center of his bald head. He wore nothing but a dented silver girdle over his groin. He held an unrolled, mildew-stained parchment and a black quill.

The corpse ahead of Martin now lay in a heap.

"Breakneck," the demon bellowed. "Who will take him?"

The captain from the clearing stood forward, his arms crossed over his breastplate.

"I will," he declared, his voice little more than a whisper. "And the next one."

"Longinus claims Breakneck, and the next."

None challenged the claim. The demon squinted, then made two marks on the parchment. Breakneck unfolded himself and stood, his head falling to one side. He stepped down the stairs, toward the captain.

The spriggan cut Martin's bonds. He lay in the glistening mud at the demon's feet. The ogre peered at him, perhaps wondering if this corpse were too damaged, if Martin were better suited for the bonfire than the field. Finally, he looked at his parchment, as if realizing that he had already made the mark, and said: "Toothless."

On the second snaky syllable, Martin's body flooded with prickling energy. His limbs jerked, pulling him to stand. He felt no pain, only a cold tingling. Pins and needles. He began to walk without thinking, as unsteady and stiff as a newborn foal. He remembered his daughter walking her first steps, as if her feet knew what they were doing but had failed to alert the rest of her body. His shoulders threatened to drop him, but he soon found his center. A column of life, some sort of soul, rammed up through his body. He clung to it, a mast in a storm. He walked more smoothly, but not adeptly, down the stairs and across the mud, to Longinus.

"You," the captain said, his voice a breath of dry air through the bleached, exposed bone of his jaw. "Choose your arms."

A mound of loot lay on the field beyond them. Toothless and Breakneck wandered to the edge of that pile, gaining confidence with each step. They did not look at one another. They did not speak, or even know how to speak. Toothless could not even conceive of how to force air from his lungs, and remembered that he had no tongue or jaw to form words. He concentrated on staying abreast of his companion. So, he learned to walk.

Swords, axes, shields, armor. Toothless still wore his chain mail and, though it was forbidden to a married man, even a widower, the white surcoat and mantle of the Knights Templar. The red cross on his surcoat, however, was stained with his own blood.

A familiar hilt, an angel's face—Toothless reached for it. His hand was shriveled and gray.

"Resist them," Tuan had said.

The Yew spoke to him, now.

"You shall live forever."

Toothless gripped the sword, Martin's sword. Its steel sang as it slid from the heap, filling him with glorious rage.

Chapter II

To be dead was to be less than an animal. His organs were silent. His stomach was an empty sack that wanted nothing. His heart was a dried gourd. Toothless now had, he realized, the stare that he had seen when he fought the dead of the Yew. It was a stare that looked past the living, past homes and fields, past even the horizon, to the depths of the west where memories had fled and souls lived forever.

There was something of humanity in that gaze. He knew it now. The black magic of the Yew filled his limbs and carried his body forward into battle. He felt power and limberness when he killed. The Yew tapped into the training he had received as a man. He would be an effective warrior for the Yew. He could feel the Yew recognizing that, surrounding what was left of his mind, the pieces torn away from his soul. In that gaze, however, a dull ember of longing burned. He was looking for his memories. Always. Toothless spent every waking moment, even those in battle, trying desperately to remember the faces of his wife and daughter, the smells of the cooking pot, the warmth of the fire.

He remembered in sleep.

The rhythm of war was no different now than when he had been alive. Most of the time, they marched. When the sun went down, they slept. When the sun rose, they woke. He felt neither tired nor refreshed. Sleep simply happened, a habit of the body. It seemed a frustration to Longinus, who would have marched them through the night were sleep not written into their bones.

Sleep did not restore them, but Toothless dreamed. They were simple dreams. The dog, hiding in the field and crouching low in the barley. His wife, shedding clothes before the fire. His daughter, pulling herself up and taking two timid steps, then falling down to all fours. These were recent events, the last memories. Each disappeared as soon as he remembered it. They were late morning pockets of fog waiting for the sun to burn them from gullies, to send them back into the sky.

Not all of the dead dreamed. The shamblers, as far as he could tell, could only stare toward their lost memories. Degrees of humanity thus separated the Yew's dead. Most were shamblers, but there were others who could act almost human. Breakneck was one. His head bobbed to the side and his voice had an inhuman quality, a rake across stones. Still, he spewed bawdy jokes and then laughed at them, acting as if he were not dead at all.

Did lifelessness, Toothless wondered, make one more or less useful to the Yew? The Yew seemed to prize, in its captains, a certain amount of humanity. Though Longinus was little more than a skeleton, his orders carried such force that even troublemakers like Breakneck would fall into line. Part of it was the captain's mere presence. He still bore within him the spirit of a Roman. Perhaps the Yew had long ago struck a bargain for Longinus with some pagan god of the dead.

And there were black priests. They were human, or close to it. They ate and pissed. They chanted over fires and watched the stars, when stars were visible through the smoke. They ranked higher than the captains, a fact that was lost to Toothless until he saw one barking orders at Longinus. The priests were old, bent, twisted. But there were acolytes who scurried after them. The acolytes were younger, stronger, though scrawny and gray-skinned. Toothless wondered what they had done, in life, to earn the role.

Priests lorded over captains, captains over the marching dead in the cohorts, the Yew over them all. Under Longinus, Toothless, Breakneck, another sentient named Curdle, and countless shamblers were the Cohort of Ruin. Each of the Yew's cohorts bore the name of a demon summoned from Hell to act as a beast of burden, a champion, a force with which to be reckoned. Ruin was a creature the height of three men. A loincloth of skin, perhaps human, covered his penis, though pumpkin-sized testicles dangled below the edge of the garment. His skin was reddish orange and sprouted tufts of coarse black hair. Ruin's head, however, was bald. He carried a tree limb with a steel blade lashed crudely to one end, something of a scythe, which he swung before them, carving swathes in the ranks of any advancing enemy.

Toothless knew that blade. It had killed him.

The priests had carried on, summoning what energy was left in their broken, spent frames to demand food and water. Longinus thus ordered Toothless, Breakneck, Curdle and five shamblers to follow the demon Ruin to a mill in the wilderness. This mill sat between a stream and a thin path, both of which led to a market town, walled and abandoned. The stream, fed from a warm spring, would be a steaming ribbon through the icy dirt.

It was to be a simple march.

The nine of them broke from the forest and stepped into a field. November rain had fallen and frozen. The hard ground was harvested and unplowed, waiting for winter and then a new season of planting that would never come. The Yew was far behind them, but its roots already stretched before them, breaking the ground in stony clumps that tripped up Breakneck's feet. Curdle, named for the blistered burns on his skin that had been deflated in dry death, picked his way across the field. Toothless jumped over furrows and ridges. His heavy greatsword pounded on his back.

Ruin, ahead of them, walked over it all. The giant grunted. His stomach growled. He was hungry, which meant that his temper was foul. Toothless kept himself some distance behind the beast. He had seen Ruin strike at the Yew's own, the soldiers of other cohorts and once at a number of his own shamblers. Ruin had never acted so in front of Longinus. Rather, like a dog, like Kennocha, he waited for lapses in supervision to misbehave.

The Yew's voice filled Toothless' head, louder with each step.

"Advance," it said, as it did in any battle, though none of them expected to fight this day.

Ruin reached the opposite treeline and waited. Not far into those woods, Toothless guessed, the mill's wheel turned in the water, its grindstone disconnected still, but soon to grind looted seed for the loaves of the black priests. He could hear the water. Somewhere, falls crashed upon glistening stone, washing lichen that was still green and would remain so through the winter.

Toothless could smell nothing, though air moved through his dry nostrils. He breathed, though his lungs were full of holes and the muscle beneath them was like a slab of dry beef. Yet, he had no need of food. He could hear and see, but could not smell. Whatever magic was conjured by the Yew and channeled by the priests to keep him moving, was imperfect. Or, perhaps they knew what they were doing in limiting his senses and needs.

Ruin lifted his loincloth and pissed upon the trunks, twisting his hips back and forth as if he were addressing a massive forest fire. Clouds of stinking vapor rose from his urine.

Toothless turned. Smoke billowed over the trees behind them—the advance of the Yew, signaling the living to retreat. Soon, there would be nowhere for them to go. The Yew's army would push them over the sea, into the deserts. The smoke floated in a giant bank that blotted the sunrise, though pink fingers of clouds shot south.

The market town seemed of some importance. Longinus took command as a high captain over several cohorts to occupy it. It was certainly empty, like all of the places they had taken. There would be no dead to gather, no men to fight, no women or children to slaughter. The plague had come before them. The hairy black moss was thick on the trees, and bloated corpses of cattle dotted the field.

While a man, Toothless had once defended a place like this. He had waited in a forest as an army of bandits crossed a field. The Yew had created, in the earliest days of its advance, a movement of refugees. At first, they were peaceful. Then, they turned on one another. Bandit warlords rose to prominence among them. It must have been the Yew's strategy to cause the living to fight among themselves, to produce dead without the Yew having to spend any of its own resources. Then, the spriggan would come to collect whatever was left.

The living realized it all too late.

On that day, in a field like this, bandits were confident that they would cross unopposed. They sheathed their swords and began to joke with another. They lacked discipline. They lacked fear. They were opportunists, and so could not conceive of any strategy but opportunism. They did not understand patience.

Toothless had been a Templar. If he had learned anything, he had learned patience.

"Martin," his men implored. "Strike the bandits now. Meet them in the open ground."

There was no opportunity to flank from the long stand of trees.

"Patience," he said.

As the first bandits struggled through the brambles, losing sight of what was before them as they squinted against the brush and swatted the insects, Martin gripped his greatsword and leaped forward, killing three at once. And so the bandits fell. At least on that day.

Ruin surveyed the forest before him, peered left and right and then began parting the trees as if they were curtains. He left Toothless and the others to navigate the treacherous path, to climb and duck around the split trunks and broken branches. Ruin would stop, laughing, waiting for them. The beast would push the first who reached him to the ground. Ruin was bored. But the dead did not oblige. And Toothless, more so—he refused to take the fore, refused to sate the demon's masochistic appetite.

"You all right?" Breakneck asked Curdle, who had begun to slow.

"My joints seize in the cold."

Toothless nodded, clenching his fist. The cold played havoc on all of their joints.

"Perhaps we can make a fire," Breakneck said.

Toothless shook his head and pointed at Ruin, who barreled through the trees. The demon stumbled, then, into the clearing of the mill.

"No matter," Curdle said. "We will be back to the Yew before too long. Then I will feel as if I am roasting."

"Feel," of course, just meant a different kind of numbness. Though there was some unpleasantness in the heat, and some pain to injury, touch was another sense that was all but completely dead. Prickling, at times, as the skin woke in patches only to realize, perhaps, that it had expired. Or, it was the magic of the Yew, stretching and gathering across the body. Perhaps, though, it was just death. It was ghosts of feeling, scraps of soul, itching.

The mill was a tower and a side building sitting beside the babbling misty stream. The tower seemed the remnants of an older thing, a keep or a monastic hermitage. It was ruined, broken at the top, taller than the demon. Ruin approached the tower and straddled it. He hugged it, cackling, pretending that the tower was his penis. Then he rubbed against it. Toothless shook his head. Breakneck smiled, which looked quite strange on his tilted face.

Toothless closed his eyes as the cold caught him and gathered around his knees and shoulders. He stretched, more out of habit than any relief, for it did nothing but cause his skin to crack.

Ruin screamed. The sound of it shattered the cold air. Trees shook. The ground buckled. Toothless opened his eyes. Ruin grabbed at a thick shaft protruding from his thigh. He was drawing in a breath, preparing to scream again.

Men emerged from the far edge of the clearing. They pushed a ballista. They had shot the demon in the leg, but they had made a mistake. There seemed to be only a handful of them. They were simple village folk or bandits who had found themselves in possession of a powerful weapon. They had not planned their next steps.

The demon writhed.

"Attack." The voice of the Yew filled Toothless' head. "Attack."

"Let's go!" Breakneck shouted.

He hefted his ax, a heavy thing that had been new in the loot pile but was now nicked with use. Curdle drew a wide blade with a short hilt, a sword forged in the old Norse style.

Ruin screamed again. The ground rumbled.

Curdle and Breakneck stepped forward, the shamblers behind them. Toothless extended his arm over their path. The Yew continued to order their advance.

"Attack."

Toothless shook his head and pointed along the edge of the clearing.

"We must advance," Curdle said.

To attack, to step into that clearing with Ruin so angered, beginning to pound and flail, and with the disorganized ambushers advancing to face the demon—Toothless saw his own end in that chaotic scene. Though he might have welcomed it, a strong instinct resisted.

Toothless stepped across the path, through the trees, more quickly than he thought possible. The Yew's energy filled him, but he used it now with his own judgment to take his own course. Breakneck and Curdle seemed to understand. They followed him. The shamblers, perhaps unsure of what to do, perhaps not thinking at all, advanced straight on the mill.

Toothless watched them as he rounded the clearing. Ruin stomped them into dust as he thrashed and spun, trying to reach the giant arrow lodged in his thigh. The men ducked and scrambled, trying to get closer to the demon. They wielded tools—one had a hoe, one a spade—or swords that were rusting or loose in their hilts.

Something like pity, but then hunger. Hate. Toothless could not fight this. The Yew's voice ceased. Toothless felt its attention upon him. The Yew not only tolerated his humanity, but seemed curious at what it might create.

The three sentient dead had traveled the whole edge of the clearing, and now stood behind the crossbow. They waited.

Ruin was on his knees, grabbing at the men. The living broke and ran. Ruin slumped against the tower. The men crashed into the forest, stumbling over the ballista and bumping into one another in their haste.

Toothless stepped into their path, holding his greatsword before him. A breeze moved his tunic, the red Templar's cross. The men showed no fear. Perhaps they had fought the dead. If so, they were lucky to be alive.

Perhaps these were looters, picking over the market town for trinkets, melting holy implements from its church into links and bars for a short-lived wealth in a world that was about to die. They could not even escape their greed.

They advanced, eight in a tight group. Curdle and Breakneck stepped out of the woods behind them. Toothless nodded, and his comrades attacked. Three chops from Breakneck's ax felled two of the men, their sides split. Grievous wounds, but the corpses would still be useful. Curdle killed three others, swinging his sword in wide arcs. Wounds to the center, to the chest and the heart, just as they had learned. Those corpses would rise for the Yew.

Toothless killed two with one swing, slicing their bellies.

One last man. Toothless looked into his eyes and saw the plea. The man dropped his weapon and fell to his knees, hands clasping in prayer.

Something. Pity. Remorse. Something sparked. Toothless swung wide, cutting the man's head and left arm from his trunk.

Curdle and Breakneck froze. The Yew's voice reared. Toothless heard the rustling breath. He expected to be vanquished for rendering a corpse useless.

"Attack," though there was nothing left to attack.

Then, the Yew was silent.

Toothless walked between Curdle and Breakneck. Ruin sat against the tower, vile ichor streaming down his leg. Curdle said nothing, looking at Toothless with surprise. Breakneck shook his head, as if shaking away sleep or a bad thought.

"Don't go in there," Breakneck said.

Toothless stopped.

"Ruin is crazy. He'll trample you. Wait for Longinus."

Breakneck looked at the eight corpses.

"Seven more for the Yew," he said. "And one for the dirt."

"Not bad," Curdle said, turning to Toothless and pointing at the cross on his chest. "You were a Templar."

Toothless nodded.

"You know how to fight. I will follow you."

"I, too," Breakneck said.

✠

The monks, the workers, the craftsmen, the farmers—they had all abandoned the market town. Its walls were strong and thick. Its buildings were all pristine. The living had kept this place, taken oaths to protect it, considered its church and monastery sacred. Then, they left it to brigands and, ultimately, to the Yew.

Toothless and Breakneck entered first. They opened the main gate and walked in as if they had just returned from the Crusades, triumphant and expectant of celebration. The long gravel road climbed a short rise as it went between workshops and homes, their doors open and their chambers empty but for whatever the living could not carry. Beyond, in the church enclosure, cells of wattle and daub littered the ground between the chapel, the scriptorium and other structures. The chapel's bell tower rose into a sky that had already begun to swirl with the Black Yew's approach. Ravens shouted. Pigs snorted at the tinge of smoke in the air as they rooted through the remains of life. Weeds and wild grass had already begun to grow out of control.

Breakneck seemed melancholy as he picked through the implements of the blacksmiths. He flicked over a mug of ale on one counter, and sliced a bag of grain beneath another with his ax. He watched the seeds spill for a long moment, perhaps waiting for them to dry and rot right before his eyes.

They passed through the monks' gates and over the chapel graves. Toothless looked at the stones beneath his feet. Names and dates. Some had died recently, but the lichen was already blooming. Now, there was no one to remember them. He blinked. The words and numbers went blurry and shifted. He blinked again, and they settled for a moment.

The breeze moved his black hair. He imagined the smell of a wood fire, and thought he even heard it—the crackle of green wet logs and the sizzle of meat. He did not feel hunger, of course, but tried to imagine the feeling. Next was to imagine the taste of meat, to imagine it upon a tongue that was now surely rotted into the dirt of a battlefield not so far behind them. The tongue lay, a leathery strap, with his jaw and his teeth in a gully or nestled in a footprint left by one of his retreating memories.

"I think I made horseshoes for monks," Breakneck said.

Toothless arched a prickly eyebrow.

"I think I made horseshoes. Then swords."

Toothless pointed at the ground.

"No," Breakneck said. "I don't think I was here. I can't be sure, though."

Ruin, now bandaged, smashed the main gate from its hinges, bringing down a portion of the wall. He roared, slamming into the first home, and then the second, reducing them to rubble. Curdle came next, followed by Longinus. The shamblers poured in behind, their marching shaking the ground. The clouds blotted out the midday sun as the host approached.

The shamblers went structure by structure, carting away stone and taking metal to be melted into even more weapons and armor. Toothless turned from their frenzy and walked toward the scriptorium.

"Where are you going?" Breakneck shouted.

Toothless entered, closing the door behind him. Dim light fell through a hole in the thatch. Crows, perhaps, had picked at the ceiling. It had rained. Puddles had formed on the floor and tables beneath the hole. A manuscript, left half finished, was soaked, its colors running. It may have been a masterful illumination. It was now a swirl of pinks, oranges and blacks. The rain had painted a reflection of a sunset.

The desks were old, their wood soft and their joints loose and creaking at the slightest pressure. They bore countless scratches—knives and quills. In one corner, a monk had carved his name in what must have been a rebellious fit of self-awareness, no doubt snuffed by a regimen of penance. In another corner, near the back in shadow, a woman spread her legs in a lewd drawing.

The monks imbibed in humanity, as well, reveling in it in whatever moments they could steal to sneak a sip.

There were more signs of the practice of their craft. Manuscripts with mistakes, illuminations improperly colored, practice sheets with endless repetitions—some of these sheets were spread over tables, while others were rolled and stacked like discarded firewood. Toothless heard the voices, then, the chaos of their retreat. The room was not meant to handle such noise.

I am dead, he thought. And I hear ghosts.

These monks were probably not dead. No, they had likely been the first to go, heeding the warning from some other monastery, perhaps even the one that he had failed to protect.

"The Yew is coming!" He could hear their shouts.

They left the men, women and children who had kept them alive. Perhaps these monks now filled the ranks in some other community. Or, they boarded a ship to Rome, to Jerusalem. Or, as the Irish did, they floated themselves to the mercy of the sea in White Martyrdom to land on some unknown shore.

It was all pointless. The Yew would find them all.

Toothless turned and shuddered at the sight of a figure. He reached to his back for the hilt of his sword. It was his own reflection in a mirror that leaned against the wall. He let his hands fall. His armor, his mantle, even his boots and gloves were still in decent shape. There were some holes, and some patching in his mail. He stepped forward into the light, and saw the gaping, dried wound that was his face. He had eaten, spoken, kissed and cursed with that mouth.

He stepped from the light and wrenched the door back open, unsure of why he had entered the scriptorium in the first place. A loose memory of Tuan, of a speech in such a room, flared and then was gone. Outside, the shamblers had already reached the chapel. Lime and plaster had fallen away from the stones, leaving gray wounds in the facade. One ran almost the full length of the tower, which climbed along the front of the building. Toothless saw the shamblers in the windows, climbing the stairs in one long line. At the top, two worked at the rope that held the bell, a gleaming bronze globe set in the center of a large window that was like an open black eye. The rope snapped then, and the bell clanged and banged down the stairs, muffled at points by the shamblers that it crushed, and settled in a cloud of dust in the entrance.

Ruin took three great strides from the center of the village, arriving in seconds at the foot of the tower. He took the bell and, after ripping the clapper from its hook, placed the bronze globe over his head. His laughter echoed within, sounding like a thousand demons. He ran off, crushing shamblers beneath his feet. Then, like a charging bull, he lowered his head and ran forward, crashing into whatever first came into his way. He did this four times before slumping to the ground, moaning in pain. Again, a thousand demons moaning. He struggled to pop the bell from his head.

Breakneck was still there. He shook his head.

"Longinus has been looking for you," he said. "He's in the chapel."

✠

The chapel was modest, though it had a high vaulted ceiling. It was dark at its heights, but dropped a gleaming chain that brought an iron candelabra to what seemed the exact center of the space. The dead were all about the place. Some seemed more alive, like him, but wearing the purple of Longinus' retinue. The shamblers had found ladders in the work houses and used these to strip tapestries and metal sconces from the walls. Under the direction of a black priest, a group of shamblers had even erected a sloppy base of stones and stacked pews to get at the hanging candelabra. The ladder that they leaned against this column was unsteady, and fell as soon as they stepped onto the first rung.

Toothless wandered through this scene, past the altar, which was just a slab of stone. A curtain fell, revealing a doorway to the sacristy. There was a dim glow there. Toothless entered, finding Longinus, Curdle and more of the captain's retinue. They stared at empty coffers, open cabinets and one empty hole in the floor beneath a paver that had split. A single candle lit the room. The relics were gone.

Curdle seemed not to care, though his face was incapable of much expression. Three dead in purple, as skeletal as Longinus, gestured at the empty spaces and shook their heads. Longinus turned and, noticing Toothless, issued a command in his thin voice that nonetheless filled the small chamber.

"Leave me to speak with this one."

Toothless stood still. He could feel the tingle in his feet as the black roots spread through the soil below him.

"I remember you," Longinus said, stepping closer. His joints creaked and his bones clicked in his boots. The torn sheets of skin that still clung to his mouth did not stretch, but rather unfolded as he spoke. His voice had a magical twang, the sound of one yelling through an alchemist's glass. Perhaps it was the echo of his empty chest, his bare bones. His voice bounced upon the back of his breastplate instead of living fat and flesh. Or, perhaps the Yew gave him a voice. Whereas the throats of the shamblers had rotted away, and Toothless' wound left him speechless, Longinus may have received the benefit of some extra magic, spun by the black priests for their favorite captain.

"I remember you. You destroyed many of us. What is your loss? What drove you to fight with such madness when you knew that you would die?"

Toothless could do little but shrug, and realized immediately how weak the gesture must have seemed.

"Tell me," Longinus said. "Where did they keep the relics?"

Toothless shook his head.

"Have you ever been to this place?"

Toothless shook his head again, though he was less sure.

"A Templar. A guardian of places and people. A keeper of secrets. And yet, you do not know. Perhaps it has all slipped away. I do not think so."

Longinus reached up, grabbing Toothless by the cheekbones. One of the captain's deflated eyes twitched as his twigs of fingertips hooked into the leathery scraps at the edge of Toothless' wound. Toothless wondered, what could the captain see? Or was it the Yew seeing and speaking?

"I remember you," the captain said again, releasing his grip. "You led men. When they fell, you stood your ground. You fought hordes of us. It was Ruin who finally killed you. Now, you fight the living with the same strength and the same brilliance. The Yew tells you to advance, but you flank. Why?"

Toothless had an answer. It left his mind and went to his mouth, where it fell to the floor.

"Because I remember," he would have said.

"Because you are a warrior," Longinus said. "You know no other way."

The captain turned and walked away from Toothless. Silence fell between them, broken only by the candle that guttered and sizzled. Then, Longinus stopped and spoke once more. It was a simple but profoundly confusing statement that fell down Toothless' spine, one bone after the other, landing in his gut with a loud clang that roused a gnawing.

"Find some ale," Longinus said.

Chapter III

They found the kitchens behind the scriptorium. They entered at dusk, Breakneck and Curdle flanking the doorway, Toothless kicking it in, as if there would be a fight. Rats scurried away from stinking scraps and ripped bags of grain. The pale evening glow was a column in the air, falling from the smoke hole to the dead fire pit. Flies buzzed over a side of mutton that lay on the butcher block. There was a cleaver jammed in the ribs. A bloody apron was a heap in the corner, discarded. The kitchen was stocked—sacks of grain, jars, barrels of pickling vegetables, baskets of fruit.

"It is a shame we do not eat," Curdle said.

"They left in a hurry," Breakneck added. "They weren't prepared to leave. You think they would've known."

Toothless examined the cleaver. He wrenched it from the meat and held it in his hand. It had a good weight. This had been a good chef, or at least a chef with good tools. How many times had he whacked this cleaver into dead flesh, or to cut vegetables from their woody roots? Without thinking, Toothless flung the thing at the door. It flew end over end, describing perfect circles, embedding its top corner into the wood with a satisfying thwack.

"Impressive," Breakneck said.

"They took nothing with them," Curdle said, looking still about the room. "The bandits have not yet been here."

"That's what I mean," Breakneck answered. "They left in a hurry. We got here before the bandits. The black priests will be pleased."

Toothless moved about the room, examining barrels and opening clay pots. No ale—he found only vinegars, oils, jellied fruits. An iron cauldron sat beside the fire pit. It held soup, which was now cold. A thick skin of fat gelled at the surface.

"I understand," Breakneck said. "They had no room for both the ale and the food. So, they took the ale."

Toothless kicked a bag of grain. One last rat scampered down a stairway cut into one wall. Toothless bound down the slippery stones, nearly falling. A heavy door at the bottom, heavier than the door to the outside—he opened it and thrust himself into the dark chamber. A cellar. Rats feasted on meat piled high. They paid him no heed. Mushrooms, potatoes, carrots. In the back, half in the dim light, a single barrel stood. There must have been others, for the floor showed rings in the dust and muck.

He tried to move the barrel, but could not. It was full. A cork poked from the bung. Toothless twisted and pulled. It threatened to snap in half before giving way, squeaking. Red and gold gushed to the floor and frothed.

Ale.

The sound of its thick body slopping against the stones filled him with a strange sensation.

Thirst.

Toothless could taste it. He could feel it on his tongue, though his tongue was gone.

He pushed the cork back into barrel and ran back to the cellar door. Breakneck and Curdle had resorted to breaking things, dropping vessels and pots on the floor one by one to see their contents. After each, they announced to one another.

"Peaches."

"Pickles."

"Some sort of meat. In fat."

Toothless climbed the stairs and, with a flourish, invited them into the cellar. Both Curdle and Breakneck smiled, took three flagons from a rack and, passing one to Toothless, rushed down the stairs and through the doorway.

✠

He tipped the flagon against his open throat and, leaning back, let the ale fall into his body. He expected it to leak all over the floor. Instead, it filled him. It awakened every surface it touched.

He could taste it in every corner of his body. Apples. Grass. Smoke. Hops. It was good ale.

For a long time, four pints worth of time, Curdle and Breakneck were silent. The three of them sat in the darkening cellar and drank.

Toothless had his back against the barrel. Breakneck and Curdle leaned against sacks of potatoes.

After three pints, Toothless had felt cold. With the fourth, however, his face bloomed in heat. The contrast made him shiver. Curdle and Breakneck shivered, as well. A familiar ache struck the broken joints of his jaw. Whenever he drank, he felt it there. It had always been his signal that the drink was having an effect. It had always been a sign to stop. Every bit of human left in him now, however, pushed him to drink more.

The Yew's voice was silent.

The shreds, the dry sinew, every fiber released its reserves of memories, flooding one on top of the other with no connection. Kennocha as a puppy. Martin and Aine had taken a break from threshing to eat and make love. When they returned, the dog was rolling in the chaff, covered in a fine yellow dust.

The year before, Martin met Aine. He was only an initiate, studying under Tuan. He had followed the Templar master from Languedoc on a mission to Ireland to deliver manuscripts. Dublin, not far from the monastery in Tallaght, lived and worked beneath a particularly somber cloud as the first reports of the Yew's stirrings reached the world from the frozen north. Though under Norman rule, Dublin was still a very Norse town.

He went with Tuan to a fair, an Irish celebration of spring. They called it Imbolc, and it was similar to the market fairs that once flourished in Normandy. The Irish festival was more than a market fair. Men did business and made laws. Children played at annual sport, their results determining much of the joy or grief that their peers would heap on them for the remainder of the season. Women floated between, attending to husbands or looking to land one. Tuan looked for weapons. He and Martin discussed the coming war. Tuan was worried that the Templar ranks swelled too quickly, that the order's strength and vision would dissolve.

"It is important," he said. "It is important that you learn the tenets. You must study and train. Each Templar is a work of art, an angel of war. To rush that, to field banner upon banner in a time of crisis, in the time that will soon be upon us—you would be no better than the peasants who take up sickles and hoes. Worse, for your foe is no peasant."

"I do not see it happening," Martin said. "I do study and train."

"Because you study with me. My brothers—some of them would have sent you to the battlefield three times over in the year that you have trained with me. All of those knights will be dead. Or worse. You will see."

Martin was so conscious of that moment, of the stillness of the air and the crunch of dead straw beneath the horses' hooves, of the deep rich smell of the stew in the cauldrons, that he was unable to answer. He would look back and understand Tuan's premonition.

The revelers lavished gifts upon a goat. It wore a maiden's dress, and regarded the whole affair with frightened confusion.

"A shame," Tuan said. "He probably does not know that he is to be boiled and eaten."

There was Aine. She moved through the fair with the lightness of a spirit, as if her feet did not touch the ground. So, she was a mythical creature. All of the light, all of the sound of the place seemed to avoid her and, in so doing, seemed to point toward her. She was not tall. Average height, if not shorter. She was not dressed in riches. The goat wore more finery. Her face, however—her dark hair, her gray eyes that seemed to see through to the back of everything, her full lips parted over pearls—set a fire deep in his spine.

Tuan spotted her.

"We will go this way," the teacher said, pulling his horse toward a depression in the plain, where tents and smoke marked the makeshift, week-long town of the tradesmen. Ireland had few towns other than those that glommed onto monasteries and forts, or those that sprang from the grass at festivals. Settlements like Dublin were exceptions.

Martin's horse followed, though the initiate strained his neck to see her crossing behind them. She was not a soft woman. The lines of her face were hard and smart. She walked with purpose. But there was grace in that purpose, and sureness of motion that was as studied as his exercises with the greatsword.

No, her feet did not touch the ground. She did not touch the dirt.

The woman infected him. He carried a sickness, a fever away from the fair that day. He took excuses, small tasks and deliveries typically reserved for initiates far less advanced than he, to leave Tallaght in search of her. He traveled farms and pastures, into Dublin, to churches on mass days to find her. One day, he rode atop an esker into the west to deliver a message to a warlord squatting in an ancient fort atop a hill in the Irish midlands. She came toward him, escorted only by a wolfhound and a flock of sheep. She was, he learned, the warlord's stepdaughter. They conceived Emer out of wedlock.

Tuan ranted and raved, but the Grandmasters in Iona and Scotland gave their blessing to Martin's departure from the order. The Yew had conquered much of Scandinavia. In these times, the Grandmasters said, families were as valuable as armies, healthy children as valuable as soldiers. Martin would go to a farm in France. He would make a fine father. They were certain.

A long night over ale, much like the ale that Toothless drank with Curdle and Breakneck, and a deep conversation that ended badly with Tuan declaring that he would retire, or die, or set himself adrift in White Martyrdom.

"You were to be my last! And you go to father children!"

"Sons," Martin said. "Soldiers. As many as we can."

"It will not matter. The plague will likely get you before that happens. Die at your hearth, or threshing your grain. Die a simple, anonymous man. Perhaps it is better that way."

"I will continue to train."

"It will not matter."

After a moment watching the head of his beer dissolve into a lace of foam clinging to the side of his clay mug, Martin spoke.

"I need to fight for something more. More than relics. More than dead things and stones. I need to fight for the living."

"So you take a wife only to give yourself something to die for? It does not seem quite fair to her, does it?"

Martin shrugged.

"It is the first time in a year," he said, "that I have heard anyone extol the fairness of things."

He settled in his chair, and faced his mentor with fear that he hoped did not show.

"I am called to marry her, as surely as I was called to train with you."

Tuan's eyes narrowed as he studied Martin. The teacher then stood, and without another word, departed the tavern.

There were no sons, only the glorious, beautiful daughter who was every bit her mother. And there was the dog, who was the first to die.

Another memory, then. Numbers. Arithmetic.

"Four times twenty plus five..."

Toothless tried to focus, tried to see the numbers. They had come before, when he lay on the battlefield. When he had died. He tried, wishing that he had a jaw to gnash. He had recited the numbers. He knew it. He had recited them over and over. He tried to recapture them but they receded, disappearing behind the fog of the ale.

"Are you Irish?" Breakneck asked.

"He is not listening," Curdle said.

"Toothless! Are you Irish? Maybe a Scot?"

Toothless shook his head, and pointed to his right with his thumb.

"Dane?"

"East," Curdle said. "East is right on a map. Danes are north."

"France?" Breakneck said. "You're from here?"

Toothless nodded.

"A Templar from France," Breakneck said. "Defending the churches. Is this the first time that you were allowed to drink their ale?"

Toothless tried to smile. He wondered if it made any impression upon his face.

"Probably not the first time he stole it," Curdle said, squinting at the ceiling.

"So there's magic in ale," Breakneck said, looking at his mug. His was a fine flagon, with intricate carvings. Toothless and Curdle had received much simpler specimens.

"Life," Curdle said.

There was a science to it. Toothless knew something of the process. It involved yeasts and flowers. The ale invaded them, a different kind of plague that unlocked memories and let them fly. These memories were otherwise timid creatures, coming out only at night, to return to their dark, musty spaces during the day.

Toothless thought of Longinus, then. The captain must have been here, basking in the life of ale.

As if Breakneck sensed these thoughts, he asked, "Why would Longinus want us to feel this way?"

"To remember," Curdle said. "There is value in this. Look at Toothless. He cannot say a word, but he is the most human of us all. He wins battles for it. He...he thinks. It takes all that I have just to follow you, Toothless. I usually cannot conceive of making my own decisions."

"We're different from the shamblers," Breakneck said.

Toothless nodded. Curdle and Breakneck were not as simple as he had thought. Breakneck, a blacksmith or some other tradesman, had a thoughtful streak. Curdle was another type altogether. He seemed to be a learned man, a man with some sense of poetry or philosophy. Perhaps he had been a monk. Both of them discussed but did not quite articulate the paradox that Toothless now considered. The Yew seemed to wish the end of all humanity, but also seemed to need humanity to accomplish its goal.

The unavoidable question, then, was why Toothless chose to comply at all. The pull of the Yew's voice was significant, but he had no trouble steering away from it in battle. He made his own decisions for self-preservation, for glory, for something else. He chose to fight for the extinction of his kind. He wondered if it would be different if his wife and daughter were still alive. What would happen if he were to enter a village and find them? He was not sure that it would make any difference. That was the fragility, the brittleness of humanity. The Yew pressed lightly and it crumbled. Men became bandits. They lost all sense of law. Monks left their wards. The bells, the croziers, the tapestries, the learning—they left it behind as they fled.

"It is the end," Curdle said.

As an initiate, Martin had memorized the Irish epics. The lists and numbers were ciphers leading to the secret sacristies. He remembered one flourish, a passage that was perhaps a frivolous addition. A battle had ended in victory yet one goddess, Macha, foretold the end of the world. It seemed so Irish to see the tragedy in the victory.

I shall not see a world
Which will be dear to me:
Summer without blossoms,
Cattle will be without milk,
Women without modesty,
Men without valor.
Conquests without a king...
Woods without mast.
Sea without produce.
False judgments of old men.
False precedents of lawyers,

Every man a betrayer.
Every son a reaver.

The worthy had died. Their spirits wandered to the western shores, to cross the sea and live forever. Now, only the punished remained. All of the victories, the glories, the accomplishments led to Toothless, Breakneck, and Curdle.

Toothless nodded as he tilted his head back, draining his flagon. The room spun. Clouds, stars, a canopy of leaves careened around a zenith. Certainly, he imagined that. Eight fat fingers with broken yellow nails then pierced the sky, prying it apart, creating a hole like the mouth of a grave. It opened onto shoots of pink and purple mixing with the Yew's smoke. It was dawn.

Then, Ruin. There was a look of confusion in the demon's eyes. Then a smile spread across his face. His teeth were clotted with gore. Shamblers appeared around the rim of the hole. Their empty gazes betrayed nothing of their thoughts, if they even had thoughts. The demon and the dead looked upon them a moment longer before Ruin bounded away, his heavy footfalls shaking the cellar. The shamblers followed him.

"We did not sleep," Curdle said.

"Is the ale gone?" Breakneck asked.

Toothless tipped the barrel. A third left. They had been drinking for hours. It had leaked out of them and puddled on the floor all around them. They sat in the mixture of mud, drink, and sediment from their own organs.

"I wonder if we can take it with us," Breakneck said.

Toothless shook his head.

"We will find more," Curdle said.

The western wall of the town opened onto a plain. In the distance, a forest appeared through the thickening smoke as little more than a gray ribbon. The dawn had yet to touch the far western horizon. The moon, a hazy yellow smudge, hung low. From the right, from the north, shamblers and spriggan poured into view. Their formations nearly carpeted the entire plain. Following them, cohorts—there was

Pestilence, its namesake demon a gray skinned, muscular beast as tall as Ruin, but with four arms jutting from its torso and tentacles flailing from its mouth. Squalor came next. They pulled their demon, a giant eye, upon a wooden cart similar to the Yew's. The eye's gaze could turn men to stone, so a metal panel covered the pupil. Other cohorts, other demons, came. There were hundreds of dead in each, most shamblers but some like Toothless—thinking, remembering, making a choice. Then, the tortured beasts pulled the Yew. Their cries filled the air, the smoke passing the noise from one grimy, greasy particle to the next.

The Black Yew was but a silhouette. A giant thing, like a tree that Toothless remembered from childhood that stood in the middle of a barley field in a village that may not have been far from this place. The Yew crept across the field. Cohort after cohort moved past, heading south.

"We bring judgment."

Toothless turned. It was Longinus. The captain was alone, standing just a yard or inches more behind him.

"We bring judgment. Punishment. We bring immortality."

Toothless blinked.

"The living have ruined this world," Longinus said. "They have squandered its magic, spent its gifts. The Yew has seen the future. We hasten an end that is inevitable. We inflict suffering and sickness, but the best of them join us. If it were not for us, they would inflict suffering and sickness upon themselves."

Toothless turned back to the army. The Yew had reached the middle of the plain. Shamblers, cohorts, spriggan, demons flooded ahead and behind the tree, like waving barley. Toothless remembered the tales of Templars returning from the Crusades. They watched enemies from hidden outposts. It took some of those armies an hour or more to pass a single point. The Yew's army was smaller than that. But it had the plague. It had fear and desperation. It had demons. With each victory, it grew.

"You will feel the ale another hour or more," Longinus said. "Then, you will take Breakneck and Curdle, a detachment of shamblers and spriggan, to the southeast, just beyond the Yew's reach. Bandits camp there. An important man leads them. It does not matter if he lives or dies. If you must kill him, he must be suitable for resurrection. He must be able to speak."

Toothless waited, then nodded.

"Bring back whatever fresh corpses you can. If our own fall, leave them." Longinus stepped forward, toward the army.

"Bring Curdle and Breakneck to me no later than mid-morning," he said over his shoulder. "Be ready to depart."

Several minutes passed. Toothless watched the captain disappear into the mist. The last cohort crossed the plain, which was now mud and soot. Toothless turned.

We bring judgment, he thought.

Chapter IV

Toothless, Breakneck and Curdle marched with twenty-four spriggan and twenty-four shamblers. They crossed a frozen rain-glassed plain, climbed over the low broken walls of abandoned farms, and picked through a thick, wild wood. They left the smoke behind them. The sky was clear but for high strands of clouds that took on the pinks and oranges of the setting sun. It was a fury of fire in the western sky.

He thought that he would find the sight of a sunset refreshing, but it was flat. He could not smell the clean, sweet air. He could not feel the cool breath of the evening breeze. It was but a tapestry of a sunset to him.

Oddly enough, the Yew's voice intensified as they left the reach of its roots. Toothless wondered if the shamblers were vessels, mere echo chambers. At least they moved ably enough. These seemed a grade higher than the mindless ones who sacrificed their immortality in great numbers against city walls. These moved with some dexterity and speed. Perhaps they were the young of the shamblers, the newly-emptied.

"That's us," Breakneck said. "How long? Who knows?"

Toothless was thinking the same thing. No matter how much ale they drank, they would become shamblers.

"Not you, Toothless," Curdle said. "You will lead a cohort. Us, though..."

Toothless shook his head as Curdle abandoned the thought.

The spriggan had minds of their own. Toothless wondered what bargain kept them in line. They, like the demons of each cohort, had come from some depth, some slumber, to serve the Yew. Two dozen was a small number. They clotted by the thousands in crags and holes, shadowy corners of camps and conquered cities, teeming like rats. Now, they marched in a tight group—six rows of four, abreast. Each held two daggers, thin and irregular like icicles. They led the way, pounding the undergrowth into the dirt. Such discipline for such a small role, to glean the dead who might still serve the Yew.

Two dozen spriggan could perhaps carry six men back to the Yew.

Longinus, however, had been clear. Only one mattered, and he was a Templar. Guillaume. Longinus knew only his first name. Toothless had trained with the Templars at a time when the great houses were dissolved, the teachers sent to monasteries across Europe to train solitary warriors to do what damage they could. The days of the lances, whole armies of knights, had gone with the order's retreat from the Holy Land, just after the Yew's arrival. The few Templars left in Jerusalem, receiving no or confusing news from the West, fell to opportunistic tribes of brigands. It was not Saladin. It was not the great armies of Mohammad. Brigands slaughtered the knights. The Yew, then, stole the Holy Land from Christendom without even laying a single root in that sand. Kings emptied the Templar coffers. Some used these funds to fight. Others used them to flee.

So Toothless had not known many Templars. Guillaume had organized bandits into an army of sorts, squatting in a town to the southeast. They harassed all who fled, particularly priests. Longinus had smirked, remarking that the man had lost a sense of his mission. Toothless wondered if this Guillaume knew more of the state of affairs than the average man. The fact that he targeted clergy said something about this Templar's interpretation of events. Perhaps he saw himself bringing judgment, as well.

In any event, Longinus had reason to believe that Guillaume knew more about the relics. The relics, it seemed, were very important to the Yew. There were countless bits of bone, slivers of wood and thorns. But Longinus looked for one, in particular.

"It is a cloth," Longinus said. "It is the bloodstained robe of Mary, mother of Jesus. It is the robe she wore while giving birth to him."

"We have not slept for these past two nights," Curdle later said.

Toothless shook his head.

"Why?" Curdle asked. "Do you think it is the ale?"

Toothless shrugged and jammed a thumb toward the spriggan, who had gathered in a pile on one side of the clearing. The spriggan were tired. The shamblers had simply dropped where they halted, sitting and staring forward at nothing or at the backs of the heads of those in front of them. Their eyes were open, though they were empty. It was not sleep, like Toothless and the other sentient dead experienced.

Toothless felt unsafe in the open. It was true each night, when he, Curdle, and Breakneck sought shelter. Perhaps it was more than the fear of ambush. Perhaps he believed that a wall between him and the Yew would prevent the Yew from seeing his dreams, stealing his memories. There was guilt, then, in dreaming. The sentient of other cohorts behaved exactly the same.

"The Yew wants us to be awake," Breakneck said. "We'll stand guard all night."

"You think it is not safe?" Curdle spat. "It is not safe to send all three of us on this task. Longinus would lose his best warriors at once."

Toothless squinted between the trees. The forest darkened around them. A thick mist rose. This was a tranquil wood. Their very presence, however, blackened the bark and coaxed ghosts and worse from the knots and tangles. Ravens filled the trees around them, cackling as if a storm were on its way. It was. The Yew was only two or fewer days' march to the west.

"We are expendable," Breakneck said. "That's why we are ordered to take care with Guillaume, and why there are spriggan here. At the end of this, Longinus will have six more like us. If we make it through this, we'll be shamblers before we know it."

Toothless shook his head. Longinus had told him to bring Curdle and Breakneck to the ale. There was something in that. Why he had sent them all on this mission—it was a valid question. The thought of his self-preservation sent a peal of thunder through his skull, as if he had broken a rule written into his body. He thought it again, and heard the roar again.

He brought his hands to the edges of his severed jaw. He could feel the wound with his fingertips, but his face felt nothing from the touch.

Then, there was another sensation. It rose through his chest, into the back of his throat. It filled his head and then fell into his gut.

It was panic.

Frantic, burning panic.

He tried to stifle it. He looked left and right. Was Guillaume there? Was there an ambush? There was nothing in the forest, which was now black. The sun had set. Stars shone through streaks of thin clouds.

Toothless moved to the edge of the clearing and gripped a tree limb tightly, so tightly that he heard the dry skin of his fingers crack.

Curdle and Breakneck seemed unaffected. They sat on a fallen log. Curdle regarded his foot. He picked mud from the bottom of his broken boot with a stick. Breakneck stared.

Toothless wondered: how could they be so still?

The panic gathered in his chest, where in life it would have set his heart pounding. Now, it was a glaring, burning itch around the empty chambers. He wanted to scream.

The shamblers began howling, then. One in the back released a frightening scream, followed by the rest. It was a mindless wail, a pointless chorus. The shamblers did this each night. Curdle shook his head. Breakneck flinched. Curdle rose and approached Toothless.

"We should take positions around the clearing," he said. "If that does not attract our enemies, then nothing will."

The spriggan tossed sticks and clumps of mud at the shamblers, who howled until their voices were raw and hoarse. Toothless was frightened. He felt something, an urgency. He felt the howl welling up within him. He wanted to join them. He wanted the noise to echo through his body, to fill his emptiness. He wanted to hear something in his head, something that was not the Yew and that was not dead. With each scream, he sighed in release. Then, however, the panic flared again, waiting for the next of the dead to wail at the stars.

Toothless found that walking calmed him, calmed the itching in his chest and his gut. He wandered the edge of the clearing, around and around, until Breakneck finally spoke to him.

"Relax. No one will attack us."

Toothless squinted at Breakneck. He wondered why he was different from Breakneck and Curdle, why he was pulled to scream. It meant, no doubt, that he was closer to becoming a shambler. Was it his inability to speak? Did the exercise of voice, then, preserve humanity?

The shamblers' screaming rose and fell. At times, they seemed close to stopping. Then, suddenly, one would begin anew and spark the rest into a cacophony that threatened to shatter the chill, fragile night.

Without a gesture, without a look to his companions, Toothless left the clearing. The further he went, the less he could hear the screams over the din of the forest—croaking frogs, clicking insects. There were odd cries, as well. They were evil-sounding shouts and bays that came from those creatures beaten out of the ground like worms by the Yew's booming advance. To be on the edge of the

Yew's control reminded him of his last months as a living man. He remembered these sounds and sights of the land that was soon to be dead, soon to be wasteland.

Deep into the forest, he thought he could hear Curdle calling his name. Toothless continued until the shamblers were indistinguishable from the forest, just another sound on the breath of the night. He nearly fell into a gully. He followed the rut down a slope as if it were a path. The trees here did not show any signs of the Yew's plague, though they seemed to darken as he passed. Everything living, he had noticed, glowed with a phosphorescence, a fairy-pale blue glow that he had never seen. Now, it outlined the brush and the grass, the weeds and the leaves of the trees. There was no moon, and a thickening haze blotted out the stars. The light of life was all that guided him.

The gully opened into another clearing. Shapes, forms dancing in a circle—Toothless ducked behind a tree at the edge and, his hands reaching for the angel hilt of his greatsword, peered into the clearing. The forms did not move. They were ancient standing stones. Ivy, glowing blue and shivering in a breeze that dipped from the open canopy, adorned many of them like glinting armor.

Toothless stepped into the clearing. The forgotten builders had left these stones, and nothing else. He had seen these stones in France, in Ireland. This is what the world would be. Discarded. Overgrown. This was the sum of judgment. Such works of the living would remain as the only testament to hubris and fall. Nothing more. The stones spoke of little but failure.

He broke the circle and walked along the inside faces of the stones. Some bore decorations, pockmarks and swirls like stars. Others crumbled beneath a skin of white lichen. Others were pillars of ivy, and Toothless wondered if there were stones at all behind the choking vines. He stepped into the center. The clouds moved quickly now. The haze parted. Starlight shone again, lacing the cloud edges with silver.

The sight reminded him of the monastery kitchen, of looking up from his ale to the stone and dirt of the cellar roof that looked like a sky. Premonition? He had heard of no such thing among the dead. It seemed possible that he, sentient perhaps forever, would lose chronology altogether, would become divorced from time. Thus, he would live through memories as well as premonitions. A man would make quite a living foretelling the future, if he were always correct. Oh, to be alive with this skill.

The stars moved. He blinked.

They shimmered. He looked at his hands, the stones. Everything was still. He looked back to the sky. The stars were all lazy comets, bouncing and leaving trails, growing large. Pinpricks at first, they were now soft puffs like giant, ponderous snowflakes. One landed on his hand. It sat there. It was a firefly. The yellow green light of its tail was so bright that Toothless squinted. Then, another touched upon his shoulder. Several landed on his arms. They clotted about his face, obscuring his vision.

He stepped back, full of fear. The flies gathered and twisted in the center of the clearing. They formed a tempest of light that cast wild shadows from the stones. They spun, faster and faster. The stones seemed to lean into this storm. The world seemed to alter its spin to match.

Toothless blinked. They were gone.

He heard nothing. Moving to the center of the circle, he looked at the ground. They had left nothing. Above, the haze had thickened again below the stars. The wind howled over the tops of the trees and, dipping into the clearing, whistled between the stones.

✣

"We'll go as we planned, then," Breakneck said.

Toothless nodded.

They had marched only three hours. The pinks and blues of the morning had faded into gray. Fat raindrops now tapped onto the fallen leaves. Steam rose from their bodies.

Toothless had halted the march at a stream that curved with the foot of a slope. Toothless bounded over the stream and climbed the slope, gesturing for Breakneck to follow him. Curdle shrugged and sighed, resigned to watching the shamblers once more.

Forty yards on, through thin, gray trunks growing from a waist-high tangle of shrubbery, the forest ended. A country road, two ruts in the mud, ran through a pasture. A ransacked cart sat in the ruts, its bags spilling. It was mostly grain, and Toothless had the image of it sprouting, covering the road so that all that remained would be two low lines amongst the tall heads of barley.

The cart bore a red cross, a Templar's cross. It was not a banner or a device. Someone had painted the cross crudely onto the wood to claim the crime. The rain had all but washed it onto the road, into a reddish puddle occupied by four corpses in priestly garb. Their hands were crossed over their chests, and they lay abreast of one another. Either the murderers had moved the dead monks, or had killed them in execution. The horses—if there ever had been horses—were gone, most likely already chopped into hunks of tough meat, braising in a stew.

Toothless held Breakneck back, for the latter had almost vaulted from the forest to search the cart. But Toothless had seen, across the pasture in the far tree line, the gray of mail amidst the dying green of a laurel bush. He counted others, at least five. Guillaume's men.

It was a trap.

"The timing will be difficult," Breakneck said.

The shamblers, after all, would do what the Yew ordered them to do. Toothless crouched at the edge of the forest. Breakneck took a position some yards behind him, but still in sight. He, in turn, could see Curdle down at the bank of the brook. Toothless heard nothing from the far treeline. Thunder rolled far to the north. Birds cackled at the approach of the storm. The brook tumbling over rocks—a fine sound like the random ringing of countless handbells that, through some magic, formed a beautiful music—sounded over the carpet of ferns, around the rain-softened and swollen bark of trees.

Toothless raised his right hand and touched his thumb to his two middle fingers, pointing his last and index fingers into the air—the head of small creature. Breakneck repeated this gesture.

At first, there seemed to be no result. A growing rushing, however, signaled the approach of the spriggan. Toothless could not see them, but did notice the shiver and wave in the ferns. He stood. Then, the bald domed heads were at his feet. Their eyes lit the wet mulch beneath the fronds. They drew their evil little daggers and entered the pasture. Seconds passed, and they were upon the monks' corpses. The demons examined each and seemed, then, to determine that three of the four were suitable. The spriggan broke, four to each of these corpses, and began to carry them back to the forest. Twelve spriggan remained at the wagon, three at each corner.

Guillaume's men did not wait. Crossbow bolts whistled from the far treeline. Most missed their mark. One, however, caught a spriggan in the leg. The creature made an awful noise, a screech that seemed capable of breaking glass. The spriggan fell, writhing in pain and grabbing its shattered leg. The corpse that it carried fell to the ground, the three others failing to correct for the shift in weight. The rest of the spriggan dropped their burdens and joined the twelve behind the wagon. They peered below it and around its edges, waiting for the bolts to stop. The iron projectiles were no storm. They came in small numbers, in uneven volleys.

The Yew had not yet begun to speak. Toothless knew, however, that the shamblers would come soon. Curdle and Breakneck would not be able to contain them. Toothless realized, then, that his plan counted on the shamblers. It counted on the men. It broke every precept of strategy by entertaining too many questions: its outcomes, its decisions, its timing were all uncertain. Breakneck had seen it, but Toothless had ignored him. Though he had selected this ground, the entire plan was ill-conceived. He was fighting a Templar, not bandits.

These were doubts, and he could not make room for them. The bolts had stopped. The men rose from the treeline and began to cross the field toward the cart. He counted thirteen. They wore bits and pieces of rusted armor, though they carried solid weapons of all sorts. They were true soldiers, not farmers.

There was Guillaume. He did not wear the mantle of the red cross, but wore a familiar mail hauberk and closed helmet. Leather riding gloves, worn but thick, protected his hands. His high black boots splashed gray water from the muddy grass. Toothless knew it all, each piece of the ensemble. He was sure, however, that he did not know this man. He had never seen so impressive a form among the Templar ranks. Guillaume was tall, with powerful arms and legs that were unencumbered by the heavy mail. The armor itself was flawless and polished to a gleam even beneath the clouds. Toothless moved to glance at his own gray, patched links before catching himself. And Guillaume's voice—it filled the air like thunder, bringing with it a wind that swayed the tall grass, sent ripples across puddles, and seemed to force even the foolishly fearless spriggan to pause.

The demons, however, were quick to recover. They were sly, standing on one another's shoulders and stabbing again and again in a rapid drumbeat. Their daggers pierced the enemy's armor with ease.

Success, however, did not come without a price. The men swung their weapons as if scything grain. Where they could not hit the quick spriggan with weapons, they resorted to stomping their boots into the mud, onto the demons' heads, smashing them as if they were gourds. Several spriggan fell. With those casualties, the Yew's voice began to weave through the breeze, through the rustle of wet leaves and ferns.

"Attack."

Toothless had trouble resisting it. He felt it in his legs as if the voice, rather than any will of his own, moved them forward. He held a tree limb to steady himself.

I am slipping away, he thought.

But there was no time for those thoughts.

"They are coming!" Curdle shouted.

Breakneck, arms outstretched in helplessness, turned to Toothless. The shamblers were coming. Not an enormous number, but their footfalls rattled the ground.

Several of the spriggan were dead, their heads smashed into orange and white slime that spread into the mud. Toothless raised his feet, waited a moment, watched as the lead spriggan, a fatter and sourer character, stabbed a man in the leg and then turned. With that turn, something changed. Toothless could sense their break, perhaps in the way that their legs tensed or in some new character to their glances to the forest. Any second.

The shamblers were now almost upon him. Curdle jogged forward, unsheathing his sword. Breakneck brought his ax to his shoulder.

The spriggan retreated into the forest. The men were not far behind, and Toothless smiled. He braced as the spriggan passed him. He could hear the shamblers only yards behind him. Curdle and Breakneck were nearly at his side.

The men entered the forest. Two, then five.

"Attack," the Yew said.

Toothless swung. The release was orgasmic. The Yew filled his limbs. He leaped in the air, over the heads of the men, swinging his sword upon them. Breakneck and Curdle were now among them. In an instant, half of the living were dead.

Guillaume was not more than a half dozen yards from the forest. A Templar would never run, but Guillaume had renounced his vows.

Toothless had once done the same, and felt a pang of remorse as he landed with a squelch in the mud. The Yew chased the feeling from his empty veins, bringing his sword forward and missing the Templar by mere inches.

Guillaume and his men split into two groups. Some ran north. Guillaume and three others turned south. Toothless nodded at the choice, for it was the best chance for some of them to live. The northern group did not get far before finding themselves in mud. The shamblers made short work of them.

Toothless ran, not feeling or thinking a thing, hearing only the voice. "Attack."

Breakneck and Curdle were close behind him. Ahead, Guillaume and his men swerved onto dry ground. They could not go fast or far enough. One trailed, tiring. Toothless ran him through the chest, the greatsword piercing the mail as if a lance. That man would rise again. Toothless pulled to free the sword, but it held fast. He released the angel hilt and the man fell, propped by the blade that protruded through his shattered breastbone. Breakneck threw his ax. It spun end over end, cleaving the air, before thwacking between the shoulder blades of another. The third man slipped and fell. Before he could do anything, Curdle took off the man's head. That one was gone. He had found peace. Toothless was surprised that Curdle had destroyed him.

It was just Guillaume then, running. The Templar did not slow, but was not gaining any ground. Toothless willed his legs farther and faster, and they obliged. His kills had filled him with raw energy, like cold water filling his throat on a hot, dry day. The Yew's voice lessened then. Toothless was upon the Templar. With his right hand, Toothless grabbed Guillaume's shoulder and pulled. The man twisted toward him, as if they were dancing partners, and then fell to the ground. Toothless faced Guillaume.

The man was on his knees, his arms at his side and his head bowed. He looked at Toothless' feet, brought his gaze through the bloody mantle, the stained Templar cross, and then stared into Toothless' eyes. He knew that he was done—or, rather, that he was just beginning. He did not seem altogether opposed to the idea. He had, after all, been exacting his own judgment. This would be no different, though perhaps it would last longer than his own crusade.

Still, Toothless saw a bitter frustration in Guillaume's eyes. The man's left eye squinted, its lid quivering.

"Hello, Brother," Guillaume said, removing his helmet. He was older than Toothless had been, perhaps by five or six years. He had a stronger build, which carried through his thick neck and into his square face. He wore a short beard that, like his hair, was a shocking, bright red despite the wrinkles at the edges of his eyes. Freckles peppered his cheeks.

"Do what you must."

Toothless stood for a moment. Curdle and Breakneck looked on, doubt playing on their faces. Toothless, as a man, had taken a vow. This was a brother. It did not matter, though, and Toothless sensed that Guillaume understood. They had taken a vow before a church that had failed, that had fled.

"Strike me down," Guillaume said. "Do what you must."

"Do it," Breakneck said. It was almost a whisper. "Before I do."

Curdle offered the hilt of his sword. Toothless took it. The blade was light. It felt like air in his hand, moving almost on its own, straight through Guillaume's mail, through his heart. The man's expression did not change, not even with the slightest grimace. The spriggan were already there, lifting Guillaume.

Toothless wandered to the other corpse, to his greatsword. Bracing his foot against the dead man's back, he ripped the blade free. The Yew was silent. The energy from the kills flickered and was gone. Toothless had not slept in two days and felt, now, as if he would collapse.

He needed sleep. Or he needed ale. Forgetting Guillaume, he was determined to find one or the other.

Chapter V

Night fell on their march back to the Yew. The sun had extinguished itself in the sea to the west, sending pillars of pink and purple steam into the sky. Then, black clouds descended. The wind rose, sending rain sideways against a low stone wall that crumbled along the side of the road.

The spriggan, which Toothless had not bothered to count but which seemed at roughly half their original strength, carried three corpses—Guillaume and two of his followers. The corpses were stiff and white like marble statues left by the Romans. They had bled all that they would. Their wounds were now just pink and gray gashes. The bodies, thankfully, had given up the last of their steam. There had been something disconcerting in that, as if they were not fully dead. Like himself, when the Yew claimed him.

Toothless decided to stop for the night. An abandoned farmhouse yielded wine rather than ale. Toothless thought it would be enough. It was not. Despite wine's storied history, and the fact that it had its own gods, it put a tingle in his fingertips but that was all. It must not have been a good wine, he thought, though he could not taste it. It filled thin glass bottles that felt as if they would break from simple handling. The vintners had stopped the bottles with wads of cloth. They had left it all behind. Perhaps it was not even wine. Maybe it had fermented itself into vinegar. Though seemingly affected, and happier to have the wine than Toothless was, even Breakneck remarked that it was not as good as ale.

Toothless had ordered the spriggan and the shamblers to nest in the stables on the far edge of the property. With the wind and the rain slamming against the stone, Toothless would not hear the shamblers screaming at the night. This, he guessed, would allow him to sleep. The bodies, though—Guillaume and his men—Toothless kept close. The three lay in the center of the room, frozen in the positions in which the spriggan carried them. Breakneck and Curdle sat on the opposite side of the room, against the far wall. Toothless was near the door. The floor was stone, of a different character than the walls. Perhaps this had been a Roman building, a villa's outbuilding or a gatehouse. At some point, inhabitants of this region might have dismantled the rest of the property to build the wall along the road. And, here, farmers had later dug stones from the nearby Loire to reconstruct a rough structure atop a more expertly-built Roman foundation. They bundled thatch for its roof, which failed to keep out the rain. It did, however, channel the storm into slides of water that must have drained for decades onto the very same three stones of the floor.

His precautions notwithstanding, Toothless still felt an urge to run into the night and bray at the sky like the shamblers until his lungs filled with rain water. He wanted to ask Breakneck and Curdle. Did they feel the urge as well? But he could not see them. They were silent, caught in the sleep of the walking dead. He wanted to know that they worried. He looked about the room nervously, noticing the light retreating until the space was all but pitch black. He could barely see the bodies of Guillaume and his men, their life glow gone.

The worry ended up keeping him awake. Stress, worry...these were human feelings. Perhaps, then, the wine was working after all. He stared into the darkness, looking for memories. None came. They were like slippery eels. He would pinch the tail of one, and it would slip into the water.

There was a memory in that very image. As a child, he witnessed his uncle pulling eels from a river and skinning them as they squirmed.

"They taste better when you skin them alive."

For a moment, he saw his uncle's rough face. There was the broken, bulbous nose with enormous pores, and the bushy gray eyebrows. Then, it was all gone.

The rain pounded the stone walls so hard that Toothless could hear it, as if armies of crossbowmen shot their quarrels at the place. The thought of it brought a concern. The three of them were vulnerable alone. He reached for his sword and, finding the hilt, moved to bring the blade to his lap. It scraped against the stone floor. He paused and listened, hoping that he had not roused Breakneck and Curdle.

Toothless wished that he could sleep. It had been several nights. Sleeping, dreaming, was to inhabit memories rather than just to see them. To dream was, paradoxically, to walk in a wakeful, living body.

The greatsword in his lap was unique. Toothless touched the angel's face. Tuan had presented it to him.

There he was. Tuan's face—round, soft, full of deep lines, with a gaze and mouth all creeping toward the tip of his long nose. The master presented the sword pommel first, angel first, to the young Templar.

"You are proficient with many weapons, Brother Martin. This is most elegant in your hands."

The sword had come with a story. A German knight had seen such blades in the hands of devilish mercenaries in the Holy Land. So, he instructed a blacksmith to forge one for him. It was, simply, a large arming sword. The blade was lighter than Martin had expected. It came to an abrupt but serviceable point that could, with sufficient strength and the correct angle, pierce mail. It had been much more difficult in life. Toothless wondered now, with the Yew's strength, if he might force the blade through the stone wall.

When he first practiced with it, it took him several swings to find its center. But this he found very quickly, and he went from the novice's concentration on the wrists and shoulders to an almost spiritual joining with the blade, as if the angel on its pommel breathed blessings into his forearms. He and the sword, then, moved as if he had been born with it in his hands. The force of his feet, his neck, his legs moved the blade in great, graceful arcs. Many dismissed the sword as useless but for chopping the ends from lances and pikes. In Martin's hands, however, it was an artful weapon.

Now, his cold dead hands on its wet leather grip, he was still able to make it fly and dance. Sitting there, he moved it in the air before him with the finesse of a scribe moving a pen.

He had not sharpened it since his death, but it had cut well today. It had cut well at the mill.

Some weapons interested him. Swords interested him. Axes did not. Breakneck's ax, for instance, was a tool. It had other uses. A sword had no other use. It existed for but one purpose, conceived by men who wanted nothing but to find a better way to kill other men. A crossbow was a similar, if less intimate, weapon.

Another memory. He opened to it as if welcoming an embrace. His wife had found the long trunk of his Templar gear—his armor, his mantle, the sword. It lay in a corner of their barn, forgotten until then. She opened the trunk just as he entered. The sword sat diagonally in the box, corner to opposite corner, so tightly jammed that she could not lift it free without bracing her foot against the side of the crate. Once she had it, however, she gawked at the thing in her hands as if it were a foreign and disgusting, though somehow beguiling thing. Her hands went instinctively to the hilt and she held the blade, its tip pointing up to the dust and cobwebs of the dark rafters. It was a tall thing in her tiny hands.

"That is dangerous," he said.

Without turning or showing alarm, she asked, "What is the face carved in the bottom?"

"An angel."

"Why?" It was not a judgment. "Why carve an angel's face in the bottom of a sword?"

"Pommel," he corrected, though only to stall, for he had no answer to her question.

The most ancient blades, those pulled from rivers and dried lake beds, bent and crusted with accretion, still bore decoration. Though it was simple—a faceted knob, for example—it was decoration. They were all sturdy, solid enough to jam into a man's skull. The question remained for her: why decorate a sword?

"It has no purpose but to kill," she said. "Why decorate it?"

"Men are vain, perhaps."

Then she uttered the question that fell even into this time and place, borne of a peal of thunder and crashing through the thatch onto the Roman stone floor, onto the bare space amidst the three corpses.

"An angel," she said. "Does this sword bring judgment?"

"Of a certain sort," Martin answered, without thinking.

"What does that mean?"

He shrugged. He had left the Templars to marry her, to bring their daughter into the doomed world. It had been a painful, selfish choice. He did not want to discuss the sword with her. Martin stepped around her, stripping the blade from her hands as he did. He pushed it into the trunk and slammed the lid.

"Maybe it will save your life one day," he said. "For now, forget that it is here."

"It has killed many," she said. "I can feel it. Something in the angel's look."

"I judged no one. I did as I was ordered to do."

Something caught his eye, then. A tiny light blinked in the right corner of his vision—tiny, but strong. It floated over the stone floor, dodging the spilling water and casting a green yellow glow over the broken shelves, empty bottles, and even as far as the corpses in the center of the room. It was a firefly, blinking in and out like the memories that he pursued.

Had it followed him from the stone circle? Certainly, this was not their season. These were summer creatures. His wife would have spoken of them as a bad omen. And, with that, the firefly dipped. Another memory, he feared, was remembered and now gone.

But the memory unfolded. She would have called it an omen that such a creature appeared after he had seen so many at the ancient monument. He remembered killing one as a child, scraping it with his foot against a stone. The powdery glow of its body lingered. In death, in mutilation, it continued to glow for a brief moment. Its consciousness cut, it nonetheless lived.

Toothless blinked.

The door burst open with a suddenness that made him jump. Two men rushed in—actual men, not shamblers or dead, but men. They brought a lantern and its false light filled the room with a feeble orange. The firefly disappeared. Breakneck and Curdle remained still.

"Guillaume's not here," one said.

"There," the other replied, pointing. "He is there."

The first leaped forward, drawing his sword.

"Do it," the other said.

Toothless watched them. They knew the vulnerability of the Yew's dead. They knew that, once asleep, the dead would not stir. They would mutilate the corpse, Toothless realized.

"But he wants to serve," Toothless wanted to say. "He wants to serve."

For a moment, he did nothing. He watched, the first approaching the corpse with a look of concern. There was fear, as well. A corpse, stiff with open wounds. White and bloodless skin. Every one of the man's instincts must have told him to stand back, to keep distance from the dead. The hesitation gave Toothless a moment of thought, enough time to jut his leg forward into the man's shin.

Guillaume's would-be savior tipped and rolled forward, landing splayed before Toothless. Toothless could strike the man, now. He could easily reach across the man's gut and create another soldier for the Yew.

Or, a little to the left, across the neck, he could rob the man of immortality.

Was it a privilege to serve the Yew?

The question floated into his mind—too slow, it seemed, to arrive before the situation would evolve out of his control. Another man still stood by the door, twisting his lantern to get a view on the scene. Soon, the orange light would reveal Toothless.

It was a privilege to serve. Guillaume had wanted to serve.

Toothless twisted the sword from his lap and, using its own weight, let the blade fall across the man's neck. He pulled it free, straight, slicing. The victim gurgled. Blood bubbled in a silent scream as his chest fell. Toothless raised the sword and let it fall again, and a third time. The head rolled into the light.

The Yew's voice rose, now.

"Attack."

It was the same as in every other battle, yet it carried an edge, an annoyance, as if it were aware of the transgression. Toothless had robbed the Yew of another soldier. The Yew, however, had left Toothless with his thoughts, had benefited from his humanity. It was a pleasure to serve, and the Yew had allowed Toothless the power to decide who had earned the privilege. It was a calculable and tolerable loss, much the way losses due to theft and spoilage were considered by a shopkeeper.

Toothless stood, awash in the power of the life he had taken. Breakneck and Curdle did not wake. Guillaume stared straight at the thatch, locked in the limbo between marching for the Yew and disappearing. Of the pair who had come to rescue him from that march, one lay spouting blood onto the floor from his neck. The other stood in the doorway, his jaw agape. He had not even drawn his sword.

The light fell upon Toothless. Then the lantern dropped, its wick extinguishing. The man turned and, after slipping in the blood, stumbled into the rain, into the darkness.

Toothless leaped through the door. Breakneck and Curdle stirred. Breakneck would no doubt be sour from the interruption. Curdle would spend the day trying to recapture whatever memory had been robbed from him. He would talk of it until Breakneck threatened to cut off his jaw, make him as silent as Toothless.

Toothless, however, did not need them. He was already to the road, gaining on the man with every step. The Yew's power grew in his legs with each crash of his boots into the mud. Each footfall, and his legs pumped harder and harder. His strides were longer than he thought possible.

He slapped the flat of his blade into the man's head. It was the Yew placing the strike. Kill the man, but do not maim him. The man fell to the mud. Toothless stood over him, turning the sword and pointing it straight into the man's chest.

"No," he thought. "He will not serve at my side."

He tried, but could not move the sword. He tried again, and with incredible effort was able to bring the point to the man's neck. The Yew spoke. A single word, an interesting word.

"Obey."

Toothless blinked, then flexed his grip.

Obey?

It was a plea. There was weakness in the voice. It had lost him, and it sensed it. Toothless pushed again, and nearly fell forward as the Yew released him. The man peered from behind his hands, perhaps wondering at the delay.

Toothless raised his arms and slammed the point into the man's face. He lifted the sword again, brought it down again and again, until his victim's head was indistinguishable from the mud in the road.

Toothless was tense. He let his shoulders fall. The sword felt less a part of him, less comfortable in his hands. But that was judgment. To make decisions. The Yew had allowed it. It was what Longinus had meant. Together, Toothless, Longinus, the other sentients—they were judgment. The Yew would take anyone. It would swallow relics into its mud and rid the world of men as if they were vermin. But true judgment came from those who decided who would serve, and who would careen into the void, through the shimmering wall, and find their end. No rites, no gods, no kingdom or heaven. Just nothing.

That was judgment. That was the end of the world.

Toothless stood in the rain. He could not feel its cold, but he could feel it tapping against his skull. He shed his memories like a snake's skin. Perhaps he would become a shambler. Until he did, he would decide. Of those who crossed his path, who would endure to serve beside him and who would not? That was what Longinus had wanted him to realize. He was sure of it.

✠

They stood in formation, row upon row behind Longinus and his retinue. The three sentients stood at the fore. The scores of shamblers behind them neither fidgeted nor howled. They were still, their dry eyes unblinking. The demon Ruin stood in the center, his feet planted within the ranks. He folded his arms over his chest and shifted his weight, for his bandaged leg seemed still unable to bear his frame for any long stretch. When he shifted, his giant testicles swayed. Longinus was resolute, his hands clasped behind his back. His cohort had missed a large victory on the western flank, some fortress destroyed. Judged. Spriggan from other cohorts had culled hundreds of dead, bound to serve other captains for as long as shreds of memory remained.

No matter. Longinus carried centuries of victory. He had perhaps fought in some of the greatest battles remembered through the writing of his people's greatest historians. He may have participated in countless more battles that men had forgotten, or had lost to the vandal flames that had engulfed ancient libraries. And, this night, he claimed Guillaume. Toothless had delivered the Templar. The Cohort of Ruin, though dry of victims' blood through most of the day, stood in a place of honor at the foot of the muddy steps leading to the trunk of the Yew.

This was the resurrection. Toothless had seen no other, apart from his own.

Spriggan carried the dead on poles, just as they had carried Toothless. The line stretched deep into the formations and beyond them, to the fires where demons disposed of the worthless dead. The smoke was a roiling, frantic backdrop all around them. The worthless dead were uncountable, they were so numerous.

Toothless watched as, one by one, the spriggan dropped the lifeless dolls into the slick muck at the Yew's roots. The demon who named, who seemed fused into the mud itself, scratched on his parchment announcing each new soldier. A captain would stand forward for each, to claim him. The newly named and claimed struggled to walk. They moved straight to the great pile of arms and armor. Some became sentients. Most became shamblers, and would lose their names as soon as they joined the nameless rabble.

The greatsword, the face of the angel on its pommel—Toothless touched that face in a nervous gesture, as if to make sure it was still there, as if one of the shamblers would steal it. But they knew nothing but to gaze into the distance or fight.

Guillaume appeared. Strips of black and red cloth flowed from his pole. No other pole carried such decoration. Those frayed edge flags marked him. He belonged to Longinus. Guillaume was stiff, his head level rather than lolling. There was no fanfare, no music. There was, however, a growing rhythm. At first, Toothless believed it to be the fires, as if they had forged themselves into some pumping furnace. But it was marching. The shamblers lifted their feet and stomped in place.

Why were they marching? Did they know something? Or was it the twitch of some instinct in their guts?

Breakneck stood beside Toothless. Curdle stood on Breakneck's other side. Toothless gripped Breakneck's shoulder, shook, and pointed to the shamblers.

"I don't know what they're doing," Breakneck said, shrugging. He looked to Curdle, who seemed to know. He had seen other namings, for he had been with Longinus longer than Toothless and Breakneck. Curdle said something, but Toothless could not hear. Breakneck nodded. The less Toothless knew about the shamblers, he guessed, the better. Otherwise, he would look for the signs.

Guillaume was at the steps. The spriggan tried to untie his cords, but they could not untangle the flags from the knot. One spriggan produced a blade and sliced at the knots until Guillaume fell into the mulch and mud, his arms and legs straight as if he were still tied.

The demon paused, then did something that he had not done to any others. He reached down and turned Guillaume's corpse so that he could see the Templar's face. The demon stared with his one good eye.

The line halted. The spriggan looked up and ahead, but with neither alarm nor surprise. The sentients all around looked at one another. Longinus and his guard remained still.

Guillaume looked just like a man. A pale man, indeed, but a whole man, with no trauma of battle. Toothless looked at Breakneck.

The skin about the latter's neck was still purple and bruised. Curdle's empty pustules puckered all over his skin. And there was Longinus, who was little more than bones. Certainly dead. And Toothless—his jaw was gone. As for the shamblers, they each represented a text on some stage of decomposition, as if one might arrange them into a description of the progression of rot.

None, shambler or sentient, were so pure as Guillaume.

Sentients liked to breed other sentients. They marked their progeny. Several of the corpses in line bore symbols carved in their cheeks. Others were missing ears or noses. One, like Toothless, had even lost his jaw. The demon had named him "Hairlip." Toothless had not yet learned to participate in this marking. He was still proud to be able to decide, something he was not sure occurred to other sentients. As surely as his memories comforted him, so too did the ability to judge.

Now, Toothless regretted the clean kill. He could not even conceive of what would have happened to him, though, had he maimed the Templar. Toothless had not yet discovered what punishments the Yew could levy against the dead. Perhaps it did nothing. Perhaps it did not need to, for the dead would slip away, become shamblers, after some time. Perhaps the Yew decided when one remembered his last memory.

Guillaume would join Ruin. He would become Longinus' favorite. Toothless could have let Guillaume run. Guillaume, though, seemed as if he had wanted to die. And Toothless would have been worthless if he had not returned with the Templar.

The demon smiled. It was not an uncontrollable expression of childish mischief, like Ruin's. Rather, the naming demon showed some understanding, as if it saw the future of this one and found it interesting. It seemed to consider the name, turning several around in its mind, cocking its head to discard each of them as imperfect. There was more to describe here than a simple physical trait.

The demon beneath the Yew's needles, beneath its branches, beneath the hum and bristle of its fibers, the moaning of its laborers, the creaking of its cart, the marching of the spriggan and the crackling roar of the fires, said a single word after a long pause. He named Guillaume.

Breakneck asked, "Did you hear it?"

Toothless had seen the lips. He knew the name.

"Spoiler?" Curdle asked.

Toothless nodded.

As the body softened, as Guillaume stood, the name carried across the sentients in the fore of each cohort. From the great beast of Squalor to the left, the eye that turned all to stone, to the right, where Pestilence felt the air, perhaps felt the dead name of Guillaume, with tentacles snaking about his mouth, the name rose as if from the very dirt and ash beneath their feet. The crowd chanted.

"Spoiler."

This new champion, this Templar who caused fear to burn in Toothless' gut, did not walk to the pile of arms. He did not wait for direction. Rather, he turned to Longinus and walked straight to the captain. The shamblers quickened their pace, shaking the ground with such force that the Yew's needles shook in their rhythm. Spoiler stood before Longinus.

"I am ready to serve," the Templar said.

Chapter VI

Breakneck and Curdle were like boys at the end of a summer festival.

"Come with us," Breakneck said. "We're going to find some ale."

Toothless shook his head. There were nothing but ancient ruins in the woods. An abandoned priory brooded at the top of a hill not far away, but it seemed to have been the sad and severe place of silent ascetics. There would be no ale, if even kitchens or cellars. Toothless was certain that no other sentients would give up ale if they had it, so he guessed that a crusade for ale would end in frustration. Besides, he needed sleep. He felt it more acutely than at any point since his resurrection. His eyelids were heavy. He labored to walk.

The shamblers slept. They sat, facing one another in haphazard order. The spriggan slept, clotted beneath a willow. Toothless wanted and needed to sleep. The power that had filled him since the mill, since the fight with Guillaume and the attack at the farmhouse, had drained.

He closed his eyes and thought about Longinus. Perhaps the Roman had been a fair leader, a good father, committed to finer principles of war and honor. How did such a man, centuries ago, become enmeshed in such a movement as this? Or, did the black priests dig him up from some ancient battlefield and lay his bones at the Yew's roots? He could see the priests, a quiet and secret procession, carting the bones over flagstone Roman roads from the heart of the eternal city itself, to meet the Yew in the barbarian north. Toothless imagined this, and recognized the very act of imagination with some hope. Indeed, he had been slipping into sleep. He had begun to dream. Excitement over the existence of his imagination woke him.

Something like a sigh pushed up from the bags of his lungs, through the ragged end of his windpipe. He settled in, shifted his weight, and closed his eyes again.

"Awaken."

It was the voice of the Yew.

Knocking against his foot—he did not feel it on his boot so much as vibrating through his leg.

Two of Longinus' guards stood before him, kicking his soles. Their bright chain twinkled in the firelight. The purple of their robes looked black.

"Longinus will see you," one said. His voice, wind through bones and bleached brittle teeth, was as rough as the captain's. The other did not speak at all. He stood still, one hand upon the hilt of his sword and the other hanging limp at his side.

Toothless stood, then followed them across the clearing, up a slope. The woods were black with smoke and night. Dead vines cracked away from his legs. Light ahead—the first floor of the ruined priory. The second floor had but one wall. Vines, looking like snakes or tentacles, ran through a window, threatening to tear down the facade.

They walked the edge of the clearing to the front of the structure, to a choked path that led through a cemetery to the entrance. The memorial stones had all fallen. Two black priests directed spriggan in an excavation. Bones rose in a pile. The priests sought relics, but teams of spriggan presented only muddied cloth and splintered wood.

Longinus was inside, one of a group of perhaps a dozen. All were like Longinus, skeletal and adorned richly. These were the captains. They stood about a heavy table, upon which a large map described cities and roads, strongholds of France, the Angevin possessions, even the kingdoms of Northern Spain. Crude lines moved from the north. Four of the black priests, their pale faces shadowed beneath their hoods, stood at the head of the table, furthest from the door. Their lead had stepped forward and gripped the thick wood of the table at both sides. A silver cross in the Irish style—an ornately carved ring about the shafts—dangled on a thick chain around his neck. The cross twinkled, throwing spots of white light onto the walls.

Toothless wondered why Longinus had summoned him. Longinus' soldiers led him forward, to his captain. He was now quite near the black priests. It was the closest that Toothless had ever been to the strange clerics of the Black Yew. They ate, breathed, and lived, but he wondered if they were entirely alive. Perhaps they were opposites of the sentients. If so, they were slightly dead, rather than slightly alive.

The lead cleric lifted his gaze from the map and looked at Toothless. The priest had milky eyes with black pupils, yet the gaze nonetheless pierced. Toothless would not have been surprised if that gaze could snuff candles or cause glowing embers in a fire to sizzle and darken.

The captains argued. The black priests and their leader were silent through this. Then their leader spoke to Longinus.

"This is the other Templar."

Longinus nodded.

A captain across the table, his skull adorned with tiny flakes of translucent white skin, belched a lusty, roaring laugh. He wore furs and a helmet with cracked horns.

"Can he even speak?" he asked.

Toothless ignored him. He looked at the map. This was strategy. The campaign moved south. He could see it marked on the map. But there were twists and turns. They were chasing something. Longinus had said as much before sending Toothless off to fetch Guillaume. The Yew wanted the Marian Cloth, the bloodied birthing clothes worn by the mother of Jesus. Still, Toothless did not know why the relics were important. Indeed, in life he had come to regard them as false, even though he had sworn to protect them. They were traps to ensnare the wealth of rich pilgrims who slummed in the countryside on springtime weekends to make penance for weekdays of torturing their tenants.

The swirls on the map—the Yew seemed intent on finding the relics. And the living were intent on hiding them. They removed them from the sacristies and ran with them. The relics had some value beyond the fraud. Toothless realized then that the whole system—the Templars, the mysticism, the secrets—may have borne at its deepest, darkest roots a glimmer of truth.

Everyone was looking at Toothless. The room was almost silent, the last murmuring conversation settling as those captains turned to listen.

Longinus pointed at the map. In the marginalia, Templars guarded the edges of the Earth, beating back demons and monsters. Ornate script announced the name of each Templar. Toothless thought that he recognized one of the names. He thought that it might have been Tuan. The illustrator seemed to have possessed some skill and...yes, the face did resemble Tuan's. The map itself was sparse of any place names. Terrain appeared as fine lines and arcs. And numbers—numbers appeared all over the map as if tossed like so much sawdust.

One of the captains heaved an iron circle onto the map, where it landed with a thud. It was the size of a small shield and it bore points along its edge. Toothless noticed receptacles in each point. Waxy residue, as well. Candles. There were hooks for lines. Toothless recognized the device, then. It was the candelabra that, days earlier, the shamblers had torn from the vaulted ceiling of the chapel.

He squinted. A candelabra. Numbers on a map. What could he possibly know about this?

The leader of the black priests spoke. His voice was deep and rough.

"Your brother, Guillaume." He looked to Longinus. "What is he called now?"

"Spoiler," Longinus said.

"He told us the question. He told us that you may have the answer."

Toothless squinted again, but resisted a shrug. The priest paused as if expecting Toothless to speak. The captain across the table, however, repeated his outburst.

"He cannot even speak! He is wasting our time!"

As if time meant anything.

"The question," Longinus said. He paused, spreading his arms, as if laying the question on the table, presenting a dish at a feast. "'What is the number of the slain?'"

The words hit Toothless. He heard them in Longinus' voice, but also Tuan's. He knew this question. Toothless stared at the map. The answer was in his skin and brittle bones. Tuan had come from an Irish order. He had trained his Templars in the answers. Toothless remembered the story of the battle, the tale that the monks had penned from oral histories. They had added lines. Ciphers.

"A brother will ask the question," Tuan had said, again and again. There were many such questions, many strange answers. But Toothless had trained in this answer, had memorized the ciphers in the Irish epic of that ancient battle, a tale otherwise useless to him. He had repeated it in meditation night after night for the entirety of his career. And after he had left the order, the numbers played in his mind each night as the moon rose to the center of the sky.

"A brother will ask the question," Tuan said. "'What is the number of the slain?'"

Tuan pointed a finger at the faded manuscript, at the numbers marching across the page. It was a key moment of the tale, a retelling of a great victory. And there, in the midst of it, the tale broke into a puzzling array of numbers.

"This is the answer, Martin."

Toothless remembered the fire cracking, the smell of smoke because the flue was blocked with tar. It was an unseasonably cool summer night. They swatted at flies. A man at arms coughed outside.

Spoiler had asked. They needed Toothless.

He looked about the table. There were several lumps of charred wood. The priest noticed Toothless' intention.

"Give that to him. Fetch a parchment."

Longinus received a roll of fine vellum and spread it before Toothless, who took up the charred wood and began to write the numbers. He did not even think of them, or think on how to construct them. Writing, numbers—these were things of the living. Yet they spilled from him onto the vellum from somewhere in the remnants of his memory. It felt like hours passed as he wrote, but he was sure that it could not have been that long.

It was not a single answer, not a single number. He stepped back and regarded the parchment. The numbers were rough at first, almost unreadable. But, as he wrote on, there was more discipline and control in the lines. Confidence. The thing covered the entire face of the parchment, but appeared in its differences from start to finish as if two separate hands had done the work. The charcoal had worn away into grit.

"3 + 3 x 20 + 50 x 100 + 20 x 100 + 3 x 50 + 9 x 5..."

And more, in a dizzying march of arithmetic.

Longinus took up the parchment and passed it to the priest, who looked at it for some moments. Then, the priest began to shout.

"Six!"

The captains scrambled. Some were on the table now, lifting the circle of iron so as not to scrape it across the map. Others pointed at the map, at a single corner. Six.

"Seventy!"

"One hundred and twenty!"

The priest's white lips curled higher and higher into a smile as each number passed through them. The captains adjusted the iron circle, shifting it, finding better matches. Soon, they were still, the numbers now matching along the edge of the circle on their own.

Finally, he spoke the last. He almost whispered. "Sixty-two."

The captains at once looked down to match the final point. They stared a moment longer.

Longinus whispered. Toothless leaned.

"Mont Saint Michel," Longinus said.

The fur-clad captain was standing on the table, pointing to a feature on the map between his feet. The captains shouted at once.

"Mont Saint Michel!"

He lifted the circle and threw it to the side. It was worth nothing now.

"March!" some said.

"Circle," others said.

"Divide the force."

"We cannot divide the army," the fur-clad captain shouted. "Who will march with the Yew?"

Longinus remained quiet, staring at the map.

"Enough!" the priests yelled. The room went silent.

"Longinus," the lead cleric said. "What do you see?"

"We must take the Marian Cloth," he said.

Mumbling rolled like thunder around the table. Some agreed.

"We must take the Marian Cloth," he said louder, "because we are here. We can have it tomorrow. Our ranks have swelled with hundreds. They must fight. They must have blood before we lay siege to Mont Saint Michel. They must have blood or they will be shamblers before we reach the fortress."

Toothless blinked. Sentience was related to killing, then. Indeed, he remembered the flood of power each time he killed, greater when he maimed to such a degree that the victim could not serve the Yew. It was not so simple an idea as absorbing another man's power. One did not gain heat for snuffing a candle, but was more powerful for commanding that much more night. But this did not explain why, at moments, he still felt as if he were slipping away, becoming a shambler much more quickly than Curdle or Breakneck.

The skeptics conceded, nodding or shrugging. They had not thought it through.

"The next village," Longinus continued. "What is left there? Old men? Girls? Spoiler tells us that the Marian Cloth is there. Find it, and then we march to Mont Saint Michel. With our newest sentients sated, we will be able to sustain a siege of the fortress."

"If they leave the fortress?" asked the fur-clad captain, who had descended back to his position across from Longinus. "If they take it all with them? They have the sea behind them."

Longinus looked to the priest who, without removing his gaze from the point on the map, shouted. "Enough!"

The room went silent.

"We shall lay waste to the villages about us," he continued. "Those spared by the plague now serve us, though most are shamblers. They need blood. I give the recovery of the Marian Cloth to the Cohort of Ruin. A reward."

He nodded to Longinus, who bowed his head, his helmet falling against the back of his hard white skull.

"The Yew's sap runs thick," the priest continued. "Its needles fall. It will need the Marian Cloth to summon the sea demons, and to conjure other beasts. Once we have the relic, we will cut Mont Saint Michel from the sea. Then, we march to recover the blood."

Blood, Toothless thought.

✠

Toothless descended the slope, planting his heels in the carpet of dead leaves. They cracked under his boots. The earth was dry and cold. He knew this season. He knew it well. He could imagine the smells—pine needles browning in the bone cold sun, the first whiffs of burning turf. It was dead spring, pent up beneath musky loam through summer, now sighing into the air at the edge of winter.

The light—its slant, its distance. It was the same orange sunrise as on a summer festival morning, but much more melancholy. The fields now frosted each morning. Lush softness had gone to stone, as if Squalor had cast his cold gaze upon the world.

The small village sat in the valley, its church much taller and larger than any other structure. Squat brown buildings, only one or two with frayed ropes of smoke rising from their chimneys, surrounded the church. A wall of timbers surrounded the whole mess. Corpses of livestock littered otherwise empty fields. The plague had run its course. A bank of mist sat atop fresh earth on the southern side of the village, beyond the barricade, on the other side of a still and shallow river. It was a mass grave.

The living had gotten it all wrong. Toothless remembered regarding the Yew's army as a force of destruction that had no goal, no object but the elimination of life. But they were wrong. The Yew wanted relics. The priests emptied their sacristies before abandoning their flocks, but perhaps out of avarice more than out of any sense of duty or danger. A relic was portable wealth. A priest could open up shop anywhere with a relic, and bring hordes of wealthy pilgrims like a sorcerer bending a river.

What will be left when we are gone? Toothless wondered.

This village below him, or the village behind where he had first tasted ale—plants would crawl over the walls and vines would split the stones. A wealthy merchant's home would become quarters to the likes of Longinus. A wine cellar in which a host would have pored over his collection of bottles to present to guests at a feast would now enjoy the raucous party of sentients, still flecked with the blood of the living whom they had just slaughtered.

As a living Templar, he had achieved a mystical, almost pagan understanding of place. Places lived their own lives. They reacted to everything that passed through them. Humans, the living, had no monopoly over shaping the land. It was the dead, the soldiers of the Yew, who would touch these places last and leave them in whatever shape they chose. Ruin pounded buildings into gravel. Breakneck tossed bottles into walls. Curdle pulled books from shelves, forgetting how to read them, leaving something on the pages that was close to sadness and thicker than dust. Toothless left fear and longing. And, if he could, judgment.

The streets were empty. He thought he saw movement in the mass grave, but it may have been a trick of the light in the mist.

"Do they even know we are here?" Breakneck asked.

Toothless was startled. He thought he was alone. Breakneck and Curdle took positions at his sides.

"It is not safe for you to be here by yourself," Curdle said. "We thought we would join you."

Toothless nodded.

"The rest of the cohort comes behind. Any moment."

Toothless turned and watched the summit. The smoke came first, and it was like the smoke that had once crested another hill, smoke that announced the end of his family and thrust him back into service as a Templar.

That moment had been the end of his life. His death on the battlefield was inconsequential.

Chapter VII

Spoiler came first, not Longinus. The Templar was every bit a living man. Glinting, unblemished chain reflected the stark white and almost desperate light of the morning sun. The sun knew that the Yew's smoke was coming, and its light trembled at Spoiler. He carried a longsword and a shield. His visor was open, framing his face in such a way as to lend even more hardness, more chisel to the lines of his jaw. The leather of his boots looked just tanned, as if they had not yet even seen the ground, let alone battle.

"Shall we kill this man so that he might serve the Yew?" Breakneck joked.

Toothless squinted. There was some stiffness in Spoiler's gait, though Toothless attributed this to the slope of the hill and the weight of the armor. No—restraint. Spoiler flexed every muscle in his body to keep it in check, to keep himself from whirling into a dervish that would singlehandedly destroy every village in the region.

"I will be ground to dust before I let him take all of the blood and ale for himself," Curdle said.

"And I," Breakneck added.

Toothless nodded. He wanted to be as alive as Spoiler. Perhaps the Templar was as dry and brittle as the others under his armor—a dusty husk like them. Toothless, however, bore the visible scars of several battles, particularly his last as a Templar. No doubt, he looked more like a shambler than a sentient to any who gave him a passing glance. Perhaps a helmet to cover his head...though he dismissed the thought. It would restrict his vision.

Breakneck and Curdle looked at Spoiler with hate in their eyes. Toothless noted it, and watched it burn for several seconds. It seemed a foreign thing in their skulls. It seemed as if it would have required ale.

Spriggan poured around them now, falling over one another down the hillside.

"I have a thought," Breakneck said. "Wouldn't it be something if he didn't make it out of this village?"

"I believe it is our job to protect him," Curdle protested.

Toothless shook his head.

It was his job to kill.

✠

They crossed a marshy strip between the foot of the hill and the town's northern fields. Ruin struggled, sinking to mid-shin. His failed efforts to free himself only fanned his anger. Toothless, however, was relieved that he would reach the village before the demon. And Ruin would be sufficiently angry to deal carnage to any trouble that might surprise them beyond the barricade.

But he would not arrive before Spoiler, who led the vanguard with a swarm of spriggan. Toothless had little trouble with the marsh, hopping from one grassy tuft to the other, but could not gain on the other Templar. Curdle was slightly more clumsy. Breakneck remained behind to assist him. The two were not very far behind Toothless.

Behind them all, coursing now down the hill, shamblers shook the earth with their flopping feet. Longinus and his retinue would be among them, but would likely enter the village last. They would stroll down the main avenue to the church, bust its heavy worn wooden doors from their hinges, smash the statues and bits of pedestrian bone hawked to pilgrims as relics, to find the bloodied cloth of the mother of Jesus behind the altar.

The village remained quiet as Toothless reached the fields. Flies buzzed in the mist over corpses of cattle. Rough weeds were thriving. They were ropy fibrous things that only grew in places that men ignored or abandoned, in seasons when nothing else would grow. No vermin would be able to swallow them without choking off its gullet.

Fresh logs, still moist and yellow at their rough hewn points, formed the barricade. The gate was open. Spoiler was already through, with the spriggan close behind him. Toothless, Breakneck, and Curdle were not more than a minute or two behind. The village was empty and silent. It was not yet a ruin, but the seeds of one.

Toothless stopped just inside the gate, in a wide plaza with hitching posts and a tavern. He noted that there would be ale there. He looked to Breakneck, who smiled. There were no people, no dogs, no pools of waste crowded with carrion-hungry black birds. It was as if the living had erected the place, used it for a week or less, and then left. There were no signs of abandonment, no piles of discarded wares that would not fit on the last wagon leaving. No breeze through loose shutters. No birdsong. Just the silent early morning sun.

Spriggan coursed around them now, and the shamblers were crossing the marsh. Ruin still struggled to pull his legs through the mud.

Then, a scream.

Toothless turned toward the noise, toward an open doorway down the street, on the left. A woman's scream—she yelled again, this time ahead of a crash of pots and pans, or so it sounded. She then appeared in the street, her long dress in tatters and stained with blood. She was not young, but not a crone. Her sons were old enough to die in battle, old enough to rot with other plague-dead in the cold soil of the mass grave, old enough to serve the Yew. They were certainly gone. She screamed, but there was something deeper than horror. It was rage. She ran not to save herself, but to find something to grab and swing at Spoiler, who strode out of the building behind her.

He took the practiced stance of a warrior, a perfect stance. He was not yet basking in the power of the Yew. He had not yet given himself to the wild abandon of the dead. This was interesting.

Toothless fixed his gaze harder and harder upon the woman.

"Why does he not kill her?" Curdle asked, perhaps sharing the compulsion, the blood lust.

Toothless nodded. It was a strong drive. He found himself walking forward. He looked beyond her to the horizon, to spirits and memories dancing in silhouette along the ridge line on the opposite side of the valley.

He shook his head. This was how shamblers fought.

Toothless drew the sword from his back. He walked slowly past Spoiler, whose joints relaxed as he watched. Toothless brought his sword high. The woman stopped screaming. She did not lunge at him. She did not leap. She did not sprint to the far side of the street, where a stack of carpenter's tools might have given her a chance. She stood, looked Toothless in the eyes, and squinted. Toothless let the sword fall. It struck the base of her neck and cleaved down into her chest. He pulled, jerking her split torso to the side, then to the ground. Blood rose in a fountain of red and steam.

The surge—it welled up within him. Yes, he realized. He lived to kill. He lived to render useless. That was the judgment, to bring the end. To preserve one for the Yew was less satisfying.

Spoiler shouted. There were no words, just a howl of anger as he saw Toothless bask in the glow.

They went door to door, cottage to cottage, competitors. They rooted out dozens of women and children, vying with one another to kill the most. The two were soon bathed in blood. Toothless, who killed more this day than he had in all of his service with the Yew, began to feel warm. His movements were ever more fluid. He began to feel the muscles of his arms soften and flex. The stiffness, the dry rustling, faded from his limbs. He began even to feel his lost jaw. His sword slipped in the blood-wet leather of his gloves so dangerously that he had to clasp tighter and tighter, fearing that he might impress his fingers into the grip.

There was an impressive house near the center of town, the home of a wealthy merchant. The wife of the house was possessed with the noble but foolish duty that grips society's betters when they have no time to consider the wisdom of their choices in the face of a catastrophe. Or, perhaps she worked to preserve some memory of his generosity, for he was certainly dead. She quartered children so that the place had become an orphanage. Boys and girls, too young to fight but old enough to know what was happening, watched in stone-still terror as, one by one, each fell to either Spoiler or Toothless.

In this, Toothless and Spoiler exchanged glances. It was hardly camaraderie, but it was not the rage of Spoiler's earlier howl. Indeed, Spoiler seemed to learn from Toothless by watching him. He learned to use the power of the Yew to spin and leap, to drive his arms.

Toothless, however, reveled in consciousness rather than abandon. With each step through slick gore, he felt less and less like a shambler. He was becoming one of the living. Each blow arose from a desperate hunger. Each one landed as a feast. The memories did not dance on the ridge or flee. They were not flitting with the fireflies. They were in him, in his training and passions, in his love and hate. Tuan had tried to teach him to use these things, to turn each into an opportunity to perfect his practice. He had left the order in part because of the impossibility of that in the face of such distracting love for Aine. Now, however, he dared to think that Tuan might even have been proud of his performance. Though Toothless slaughtered children, he did so with perfect detachment.

The sun, now hidden in smoke, had crested. It was past noon. They had been at this for hours. Shamblers now crawled through every door and window, over every stone, but found no one left to kill. Spriggan with nothing to do lounged in shadowy corners. Even Breakneck and Curdle were bloodied, perhaps having found one or two who had escaped the two Templars.

None entered the church.

Longinus marched with his guard down the central thoroughfare. They reached the still and silent pool at the town's center and turned to the church. Toothless followed. Spoiler, Breakneck, and Curdle were behind him. Smoke rose in the northern quarters. Ruin had begun to dismantle the place, stone by stone and timber by timber. What had greeted the sun this morning was gone. The night would find a ruin.

Longinus was in the church for just several minutes before appearing in the doorway, holding aloft a gray and dirty scrap—the Marian Cloth. Toothless was surprised at his own reaction. He stood, seeing it as he would see any flag, any cloth. He expected more. He expected that it would be hard to see, that it would repel his vision, bring nausea. But these would be living reactions.

Still, the shamblers, Breakneck and Curdle, even Spoiler, all lifted their voices to the sky. The cloth compelled their outburst, though it inspired nothing of the sort in Toothless. He stood, silent and still, thinking only that it was the last shout the town would hear.

The town, however, proved him wrong.

Near him, there was screaming. Another woman. He had missed one. This filled him, compelled him, more than the cloth. He was sated and felt more alive than he had as a Templar, even as a husband and a father. He was drenched in the blood of a score of lives.

Two. Two screams. A woman and a child. Nearby.

He leaped into an alley. Spoiler was behind him. They broke door after door, finally entering the end of a long stable. One empty stall after another until Toothless found them, crouching in dung and straw.

Toothless stopped.

He knew the hair. Black hair braided. And the girl, with a head of tight curls like lambswool. The air moaned as it escaped the ripped edges of his throat. Had he a jaw, had he lips and a tongue, he would have said their names.

Aine.

Emer.

Indeed, the woman was a double. Everything he had forgotten about her face since she had died in his arms, everything he had forgotten about how she looked before turning ashen gray and blotched from the plague, sat now before him. The child was not as close an image of his daughter, but close enough. There they were, in terror, facing death. Again.

Spoiler was there.

Toothless blocked him, trying to maneuver to keep the other from entering the stall. Toothless was not sure what he meant to do. Did he wish them to live? Was he to take them, to run away with them? None of these could happen, but they all crossed his mind.

"Move!" Spoiler shouted. He poked his sword into the stall through the gaps under Toothless' arms, between his legs, trying to get at them.

The hunger rose in Toothless, as well.

"Move!" Spoiler repeated.

The woman pulled her girl to her chest. She bit her bottom lip, then swallowed hard. The toddler shivered and cried.

"Just kill us," she spat.

As he was about to lower his hands, as he was about to turn and tackle Spoiler, the hunger spiked. It gripped him, both in his stomach and his throat. It filled his arms and legs. As his throat opened, he swung again and again—one swing, it seemed, for every life that he had taken that day. There were so many that Spoiler stepped back, leaning against the door of the opposite stall. The woman and her daughter were gone, now so much red and pink and bloodied cloth in the straw and dung.

Toothless stumbled, voices rising in his bones. It was not the voice of the Yew. Rather, they were the voices of all he had killed that day. And more—they were voices from his memories. Above it all, he heard the howling of his wife and the cries of his daughter at her birth. The cacophony became so loud that it bounced in his skull, like metal shot in a shaken vase. He gripped his head to keep his bones together.

Spoiler stepped forward, laughing. Toothless pushed him, surprised as the big Templar fell onto his rump.

Toothless stumbled into the daylight. The Yew's smoke was thick. Ruin was now standing atop the church, jumping up and down and punching the tower. It fell in on itself, dust and grit spewing from the open doorway.

The pain subsided as Toothless walked. He did not know where he went. Corpses lay all about him. He was wandering toward the gate. He could see the tavern, the roof and the walls still intact. Ruin knew to leave it alone, or Longinus had ordered him. Either way, Toothless was thankful.

Breakneck and Curdle stood in the street. Two of Longinus' guards stood at the door.

"The captain is inside," Breakneck said. Then, looking Toothless up and down, "You were busy today."

Toothless nodded.

"I cannot even see your cross," Breakneck said.

Curdle turned and peered at Toothless' chest. Indeed, Toothless saw, his white tunic was as red as the Templar cross, so that the cross itself had disappeared.

He could command with gestures. He could win battles without his voice. But how to convey that he had found his wife and daughter resurrected, and killed them? And only to best Spoiler?

"The captain wants you," Curdle said, pointing with his thumb.

Without even a gesture, Toothless turned. Longinus' guards, their purple robes clean of blood and dirt, nodded as he passed through the door.

✠

"Let me tell you why you are special," Longinus said.

With this, he lifted a clay mug of ale, tossing it back toward his mouth. The ale fell through his bones and splashed on the wooden planks of the floor.

"Sit," Longinus commanded.

The place was empty but for the two of them, though benches and chairs were strewn as if a fight had occurred. Embers still glowed in the pit, their smoke rising in lazy tendrils into the darkness between the rough-hewn joists. Plates had been cleared from the night before, but a joint or two of meat sat on a table or the floor, glistening.

The night before.

Toothless could he ar the singing, the fighting, the gaming, as if their very sound were nestled in the soft grain of the wooden tabletops.

"Tell me, Toothless. Do you hear its voice?"

Toothless' eyes narrowed.

"Does it command you?" Longinus continued. "Does it tell you to attack? To rise?"

Toothless nodded.

"Did you know that the others do not hear it? Yes, they are so compelled, but...to hear the voice? No."

Longinus fixed his gaze at some sad point beyond Toothless and paused. He was still staring as he spoke again.

"You have a unique connection to the Yew."

He looked at Toothless, who shivered at the ice in his captain's dull eyes.

"Every death you claim strengthens the Yew. The Yew always needs soldiers, but its roots feed on any corpse that you leave to rot in the dirt."

He pointed at the tabletop as if it were the ground and, as if just below, the black snakes of the Yew's roots were twisting about their legs.

"I have seen it in others, so I know it when I see it in you. The power you gain from killing fades quickly. You give it all to the Yew. But, when I sink the Marian Cloth into the Yew's mud, you will be more powerful than anyone. For a time."

He paused again, looking straight at Toothless.

"You and the Yew—you are tied together. I do not know why the Yew chooses whom it does, when it does. Each has an air of life. Each commands the loyalty and respect of those around him. Perhaps the priests understand."

He tossed his left hand over his shoulder, gesturing. The old priest from the ruined priory stepped forward, two acolytes on either side. He looked older and more haggard. His bone white skin was loose on his face. His eyes were empty. The priests beside him wore their cowls so low that their faces lay in shadows.

"We do not," the priest said. "The Yew is weak. It needs the Marian Cloth. It needs corpses and blood on the ground. As it needs these things, Toothless, so do you. So do I. So do the captains. We are all connected in ways that the shamblers and the other sentients are not. Your Templar brother is gifted, but he is not so connected as you or I. Indeed, we believe that you have a stronger bond with the Yew than any of us."

Toothless shifted his gaze between them. Longinus looked into the distance, his head lowered. The priest stepped forward, limping, leaning against a gray knotted staff. He gripped this staff, planted it in front of him, and then stepped weakly, his two acolytes advancing with him. With each step, his stiff black robes shivered. He fell into a chair beside Longinus and gripped the edge of the table.

The door creaked open. Toothless heard many footfalls and turned to see the purple-robed guards of Longinus. He counted eight before the door closed and shadows fell upon them. Distant thunder heralded a coming storm.

The priest groaned and winced as he leaned forward, clasping his hands on the table. He looked at them as he spoke, as if he spoke to some creature he had captured there.

"As the Yew strengthens, so will you. As the Yew weakens, so will you. When the Yew is strong enough to seize Mont Saint Michel, then you will be strong enough to lead us all."

Toothless' thoughts swirled. He had no way to understand this. Questions flew, and he half expected the Yew to respond. If not the Yew, then some memory—Tuan, or even Aine or Emer, whatever that would mean. All he could hear, however, were the same screams that paralyzed him in the stables. Yes, that woman and that child had fed his strength. But they had turned his ear toward a sound that he realized he had always heard in the air, in the rush of leaves beneath the army's marching boots, in the smoke of the fires. It was a sound at the very heart of the turning of the sky. It was the wail of the dead, of the tortured, of the lost.

He was certain that Breakneck and Curdle did not hear it, as they did not hear the Yew. But he could imagine the Yew swaying to its rhythm. And the shamblers. Here, Longinus and the priest spoke of the shamblers as lost to the Yew. But when they howled, they howled as members of a great chorus. They, like Toothless, heard the howls of their lovers and wives, their parents, their children. Aine and Emer. Why did shamblers join the chorus? Toothless did not know. To shout back? To send their voices to the other side, where these memories might hear? He blinked and stood, stumbling, knocking his chair onto its back.

"It is why we must destroy you," the priest said.

Chapter VIII

T oothless had no time to think. He needed to move, to drop. He gripped the angel hilt of his greatsword and slid the blade free from its straps as he fell to his knees. A pike whooshed over his head. The priest fell back in his chair. Longinus, now invigorated, leapt to his feet. Still, no time to consider. Toothless launched forward, tipping the table. Pike blades lodged in the floor where he had been. He spun to face the captain's guard. Two were in front of him. They were not startled, though this was not going as they had intended. Confidence filled Toothless. The power of the day's kills had not yet faded.

He swung his sword in a wide arc, faulting himself for a swing that drew strength from his forearms rather than his shoulders and chest. He was in an awkward position, leaning against the upturned underside of the table. Still, the greatsword's blade sang as it sliced through three pairs of shins. The three in purple fell.

Three more advanced from the door. Two more came from either side. The captain was behind him, as well. The priest was not a threat. His acolytes had fled for cover behind the bar.

Toothless jumped to his feet and turned on the guard to the right. He was the closest, and carried a short wide blade of an ancient style. Toothless planted his elbow into the guard's face. The guard stumbled, not yet out of the fight, but paused long enough to allow Toothless to swing at two of the three approaching from the door. Their heads lifted from their bodies, which fell like sacks to the floor. Toothless spun again to the right, driving his sword deep into the chest of the stumbling guard. Toothless yanked the blade free. Its pommel smashed the face of another behind.

One left, he thought.

He heard the whoosh. He ducked as the pike sailed above. Toothless rose, crashing into the last guard, who stumbled back under the Templar's weight. A dry crunch sounded from the guard's frame as Toothless crushed him against a pillar. When Toothless gave way, the guard's torso flopped down against his thighs. Toothless kicked him down.

Steel slid from a scabbard. Toothless turned. The priest and his acolytes were nowhere to be seen. Perhaps they had gone to fetch more soldiers, or Spoiler, or even the demon Ruin.

But there was Longinus. The captain was weak and did not have fresh blood soaking into his bones. Still, he swung his longsword over his head with speed and finesse. The attacks were deft and precise, but trailing in the followthrough. Toothless deflected the blade, but the swings came too fast for him to mount an attack of his own.

Toothless backed away, hefting himself over the banister and retreating up the stairs. With height he hoped to build a swing against the captain, but the wall was too near. He could only jab as the captain climbed the stairs. Longinus parried each of his thrusts.

Still, the captain was tiring. His joints creaked. His attacks slowed, allowing Toothless more and more time to power his own blade. Jabs became overhanded chops. Then, as they reached the top and Toothless stepped into an open space, he drew his blade in a full arc. He looked at Longinus, who seemed about to relent, about to raise his hand to ask Toothless for mercy.

The Templar swung.

As the sword traveled, he thought about the conversation that might have happened. Longinus might have offered him some position, some honor. Perhaps the captain may have even ceded leadership over the cohort. But it was all wrong. The quest for relics, the death—it was not judgment. It was only self-preservation. They had proven it. Toothless was a threat to them, and they meant to destroy him. What would happen when all of the blood was gone—when all of the relics were absorbed into the Yew? Would the dead finally die? Would their sentience fade away or just disappear, like stars collapsing into darkness or fireflies flitting out, there and then suddenly gone?

Yet, he faltered. His wrists turned, bringing the flat of the blade to bear rather than the edge. On a living man, it would have been a harsh wound, perhaps a debilitating wound, but not a mortal wound. But Longinus, bones and dry skin, was not a living man. Though magical, though charmed and favored by the Yew, Longinus was a brittle corpse.

The blade passed through the lower half of the captain's skull as if through powder. Longinus ceased to be. His mouth and teeth became a cloud of grit. The shudder of the strike sent cracks through the long bones of his arms, through the plates of his ancient armor, through the blades of his shoulders. His ribs broke from the backbone and fell with hollow clatters to the floor like so many sticks of driftwood. The captain's cloak, his Roman armor, his sword—these fell in a heap, knocking the legs down with them. It looked as if someone had pulled Longinus' bones from a barbarian forest floor, baked them in the sun, and dropped them at Toothless' feet.

Now, he thought, I am captain.

The door below burst open, swinging wide into the walls. The wood splintered from its hinges and dust fell from the rafters. The black priest strode into the center of the room, his march unsteady but full of confidence, ahead of a large band of shamblers. The vanquished captain's retinue—fewer than a dozen remained—brought up the rear. Perhaps Breakneck and Curdle were among them, as well. Toothless did not stay to see. Instead, as the priest's gaze climbed the stairs and leveled upon Toothless, upon the pile of cloth and bone dust at his feet, the Templar turned.

"There!" the priest cried.

Longinus' guard climbed the stairs. Toothless fled through a room—quarters for guests and whores—and through a rear window, the glass slicing at his bloodied tunic. He steadied himself on the roof of a porch and paused. The dead came behind him. Looking down, he saw broken cobblestone, barrels of trash, and the thatch roof of small shack, perhaps an outhouse.

Toothless dropped, smashing through the thatch and nearly into the commode. His sword had fallen from his grasp and clattered now beside him. He thrashed his arms to free himself of the dusty straw. He moved with such strength and violence that the planks of the walls cracked.

Noise outside. He went silent, wondering if he should fall into the muck below the commode. Two fat red fingers spread the thatch. Ruin smiled through the gap. The demon burst with a belly laugh that filled the town like the rumbling of a quake of thunder. The demon flicked the walls aside and grabbed the Templar in his right fist. Toothless managed to pinch his sword hilt and, tossing the blade into the air, caught it.

Ruin peered at Toothless like a boy peering at an insect. Pure glee filled the demon's grin, revealing yellow splintered teeth. Ruin was enjoying this. He had captured the Templar, and would most likely collect some reward. But Toothless had always suspected that the demon hated him, hated his power and presumption, hated him like a dog would hate its master if it had more of a brain. This hate laced the demon's grin, curving its corners into a malicious smirk. Ruin could turn him in, or end this with a simple squeeze of his fist.

Toothless was amazed at his luck, thankful for the demon's indecision. The captain's guard climbed onto the roof. Ruin was now distracted. Toothless squirmed, freeing his arms and flipping his sword over his head. He gripped the hilt with both hands, point down, and plunged the blade deep into the joint at Ruin's wrist. Gore bubbled up, mixing with the grit of Longinus' skull. The blade lodged into bone. The demon's hand sprung open and Ruin cried in pain, stomping and knocking the porch away from the inn. The captain's guard fell with the shattering planks. Ruin took a deep breath that seemed to stop all time and all movement, then yelled into the sky, his voice bouncing between the ridges and launching into the gathering rain clouds, rippling them.

The Templar landed and bolted, leaping over the low stone wall around the inn's yard. He ran wildly at first, taking random turns through alleys. After some moments he slowed, staying close to walls. He was heading deeper into the village. The dead pursued him. He could hear the hooting and howling of the shamblers as they joined the hunt.

He ducked through a gate and crouched against the inside of the wall. A cemetery spread before him. Lichen grew on the older stones. Beyond, the broken church rose still with some defiance into the mist, though the tower had fallen. There was a breach in the wall to his right. A path of broken graves led to the church, marking Ruin's earlier approach. The church commanded the space, the voice of its pulpit seeming to still reverberate through the stones and moss. Indeed, its outline described a man rising after having been battered to the ground. A fallen sorcerer, now spending the last of his power to summon a fury of a storm. Toothless could imagine the metallic smell of lightning. The storm's potential filled the air between the grimy droplets of fog.

Toothless moved to the breach and peered around the broken stones. The town's plaza lay there, the water of its pool flat and black. A knot of a dozen shamblers, perhaps twenty or thirty paces into the plaza, stood silent as three of the captain's guard bickered over the next best step in their search for Toothless. One pointed toward the church. Another gestured back in the direction from which they had marched. The third seemed to be the one they both hoped to convince.

The mist had gathered into a light rain that whispered over the stones of the plaza. He heard voices behind him, near the gate. More hunters. The rain was not yet loud enough to drown them out, but it strengthened. The church was fading behind its shroud.

Toothless reached for his sword. It was gone, of course, perhaps still buried in the demon's wrist. His shoulders fell. He looked about and grabbed a fist-sized stone that had fallen from the broken wall.

He leaned against the wall and heaved the stone over and behind him. Toothless reached for another stone, then waited. The first landed with a clatter, sounding as if it shattered clay jars.

"What was that?"

"I heard it. This way."

Toothless could feel the cohort's attention shifting. He could hear the voices moving away from the wall. He pushed himself from the stones and, still crouching low, sped over the graves. His feet sank into the loose wet dirt of the newer mounds. These were plague victims, no doubt, with the means to keep their bodies from the anonymity of the mass grave across the river. Still, in some cases, the stones were not yet erected. They no doubt sat in some abandoned workshop, epitaphs and biographies half-inscribed. Stones and graves—they were disconnected forever. The men and women they described had not escaped the dreaded fate of the poor, then. It was as if they had never existed. Toothless wondered, as he ran, if he might burrow into those graves, lie down, and die forever and forgotten, ceasing to be. He would join his wife, his daughter, and the others in the ghostly march west.

Toothless paused, leaning against the wall of a mausoleum close to the church's wall. He heard nothing but the rain, which was now steady and strong, its fat drops smacking against the stones and slapping into the dirt. It ran off the roof of the church in fast, thin streams that crashed against the ground and through the broken roof to the floor.

If he continued in a straight line, he would eventually reach the edge of the town.

Then what?

The Yew would march its dead to Mont Saint Michel. It might take an indirect route, either to mask its intent or to feed on whatever living lay near the track. It would have the Marian Cloth, and would be sated for some time.

So would he.

Toothless looked left and right. A crash sounded far behind him, far beyond the cemetery's wall. Ruin had joined the search, he guessed, and was perhaps lifting roofs from buildings. Toothless could imagine the demon, enraged, moving from one roof to the next, intent on pounding him into the cobblestones.

He stood and flattened himself against the wall of the church. He began moving, inch by inch, probing the wet stones with his dead, unfeeling fingertips. He would follow the wall, then dart into the yard and into the streets. Once he reached the town's barricade, he would flee.

So, then, he had decided to leave. He relegated any questions about what came after to the moment at which he could pause and consider them. Now, his priority was but to escape.

The sky was a grimy gray now—smoke mixing with the night and the clouds. The rain itself ran with ash. When it dried he imagined that everything would be gray, like the graves and the stones of the church, like the sky. It would fill his tracks. It would bury the memories of him, as it would bury all the world in a layer of grit. He would be one more among the anonymous beings, the former denizens of abandoned, weed-throttled ruins.

The corner of the church was but yards away from him. This was the wall of the sacristy, the window on the rising sun. The grass went into a gully here that ran out from the sharp corner. The gully was a soupy mess of rain and mud. He stepped into it. The water covered his foot. He shifted his weight to bring his other foot across.

Stone scraping on stone—a curious sound from below, he thought. Perhaps an ancient grave, or some natural pocket.

The ground opened.

The water, the mud, Toothless—they all fell. It was over in a second. He remained still for a moment. The noise had been tremendous. He had no doubt that it would attract his pursuers.

Darkness lay just beyond the column of light that fell with the rain from the hole above him. He was on all fours, staring at the cut stones of the floor. This was not a natural space.

There were other sounds around him. Shuffling and moving. He rose to his feet, feeling eyes upon him. He had fallen into a trap. He knew it. A den of shamblers—they would descend upon him.

Something else. He heard breathing.

Many, if not dozens, of chests rose and fell at his presence. A gasp. A woman or a child. Muffled voices, hands over their mouths.

He swirled about, again reaching for the hilt of the sword that was gone forever. He still saw nothing beyond the light, though the light dimmed by the second as the rain and the smoke thickened.

Some spirit of the church, of these catacombs, now alive. Or the tortured he had sent to their doom, crowding about him in this holy place. The army of the resistance, arisen through the power of the ruined facade above them.

No, these were living beings. Survivors.

The shuffling moved away from him. Some of the voices now broke from their silence.

"Go!"

"Quiet!"

The rain fell in torrents and poured down the edges of the hole. He stepped from this space into the darkness. The crowd moved away from him. Why did they retreat? Certainly, they could see that he was not armed. How many were they?

The light disappeared. His eyes welcomed the darkness. Glowing, living auras bloomed. He saw their ghostly silhouettes all around him—old men, women, children. There were so many that he could divine the shape of the space. These were catacombs with flying arches and niches.

Something brighter sat mere paces to his left. He could sense it as if it were brushing against his cheek. He could smell the iron warmth of its blood.

It was the Marian Cloth.

These survivors, who hoped like he hoped to be refugees as soon as they could escape, carried the relic. But what had Longinus waved over his head? A proxy? A fake? It must have been.

Here it was, both repellent and compelling to him. It set his bones to ache and made a buzzing that reverberated through his skull. He nearly laughed at the thought that the captain would mistake a scrap for this true thing, this powerful thing.

Toothless realized, then, that he saw the relic as the Yew would see it. Longinus could not see it with such depth, such knowing. Toothless saw the eons of veneration ground into its threads. It was not the blood of Mary that gave it power, but the innumerable prayers and tears shed to the sky over its crumbling fibers. The same acts that gave spirit to places also gave power to these relics. Anything, perhaps, could become such food for the Yew, anything that received so much love and desperation, hope and devotion. The priests had known it all along. It did not matter what the object actually was, only what people believed it to be.

The cloth was redemption. He could march it back to the Yew and claim leadership over the Cohort of Ruin. The question rose again: the same question that had puffed from the dust of Longinus' falling bones, the same question that stood like a second wall just beyond the town's barricade.

What then?

A roar and a rumble of stones rolled over the gathering as dim light fell into the far end of the chamber. A hole opened. Toothless saw the living with his earthly eyes. Women and children huddled all about him. A man in priestly garb carried the blood-splotched Marian Cloth draped over his wrists.

Ruin had opened the floor. Shamblers fell into the place. The slaughter began. The crowd forgot him, rushing past him in their panicked push toward the corners of the chamber. Some fought. Old men unleashed rusty blades. Some shamblers fell. Their numbers were overwhelming.

Ruin hooked his fingers in another corner of the ceiling and pulled. Yet more shamblers dropped into the crowd. Now, Toothless had few choices.

Behind him, a passage led into darkness. He turned. The last of the living who could escape slipped into that corridor. Toothless followed. He ran with them. More came behind. So, too, did the shamblers, cutting them down as they ran.

Toothless saw nothing but the ghostly forms in front of him. Soon, torches and lanterns flared ahead, guttering in the heavy rain. The sound of that rain filled the tunnel and, against its walls, became a deafening rush.

Out into open air. Toothless stood in gravel and mud. A bridge spanned above him. A river ran strong in front of him.

The rain was sheets on either side of the bridge. The living coursed around him as if he were not even there. Some waded across the river, fighting its current. Others climbed the muddy banks to the bridge and fled into the pastures. Children scrambled, unsure where to find their parents, as if there were still hope. Old men slid, struggled. One such man resigned to sitting on the bank to await a fate that perhaps he had never really believed he would avoid.

The relic was not here.

Toothless stepped into the water. It rushed around his feet as they sank into the loose pebbles. Thin stalactites, bony growths like Longinus' fingers, reached from the underside of the bridge and bled drops of milky water from their tips. On either side, the rain was making an impossible barricade of the banks. The living slid back into the river, moments away from slaughter.

Three young men stood just yards from Toothless. They were different from the rest, oblivious to them, calm, conversing with one another as they glanced at Toothless. They would go down fighting. One held a sword. Another carried a stone and the third pounded his palm with a club.

"Toothless!"

It came from behind. He knew the voice. He glanced once more at the young men, who began to approach. Toothless turned to the tunnel. Several torches died on the ground, casting light upon Breakneck and Curdle.

"Come back with us!" Breakneck shouted.

The young men were moving forward with clear determination.

"We will pledge to you," Curdle said. "We will follow you."

"You will be our captain!" Breakneck shouted. "Come back!"

The boys were almost upon him. The current frothed around their ankles, pushing them. He looked about, but saw nothing that would serve as a weapon.

Most of the crowd had wandered up or down the river. The old man still sat in the mud. The boys sneered. Breakneck and Curdle stood, waiting for some answer. The shamblers could not be far behind them. No more of the living exited the tunnel.

One of the boys, the one who wielded the stone, was fat. The boy with the club was as thin as a rail. Their leader, the one with the sword, was fit and strong.

They stopped. The fat boy peered over his shoulder.

Breakneck and Curdle were closer, descending the ramp. Breakneck drew his ax. It was dripping with blood. Curdle reached for the hilt of his blade.

Toothless remained still. He waited for the Yew to speak, for his training to direct him. He waited, but nothing told him how to act. He blinked.

Curdle motioned. Breakneck raised his ax.

A hellish roar rose above the rain. The boys scattered, the fat one toward Breakneck who felled him with one swing.

Curdle extended his hand toward Toothless. With the same look in his eyes as days before, over the steaming corpses of bandits at the mill, Curdle yelled. "We will follow you! Take my hand!"

The roar shook the stones of the bridge. Toothless turned. He could not make sense of what met his eyes. Froth and spray, faces frozen in horror, limbs stretched in all directions, fingers grasping at nothing.

A great wave. A flood.

Whether from the rain or some act of Ruin upon a dam, the river was now a terror. Toothless could only stare at the riot. He believed that it would wrap around him, that it would leave him still to make a decision, to answer his questions. It would leave him as a captain or a fugitive.

The bridge groaned. The wave pushed a wind that blew the stalactites from the stones. It took him, smashing him into the boys who had hoped to destroy him, into the old man who had sat in the mud, and who wore a calm countenance in the tumult of the flood, into the stones of the bridge that broke and now flowed with them. Black and gnarled roots that fed from the river gripped and tore at him. He scraped along the pebbles and the muddy bank.

After some moments, the river deepened and laid him in the gentle dark depths, in the silt. It forgot him as it ran above him. Vague shapes of corpses, tossed like dolls with limbs and hair in all directions, sped over him.

Toothless closed his eyes and waited for the mud to bury him once and for all.

But warmth surrounded him, gripped his ankles, and pulled.

BOOK II: LIL

Chapter IX

The western sky was pink and orange with thin clouds spreading like arms from the distant sea. Lil watched as the sunset faded to purple. Her gaze ran the length of the cliffs of southern Brittany. Angevin land. Roman, before that. And further, into days when men smeared paint on cave walls and erected the stones. The sun had seen it all.

The sea was calm and silent. The wind was slow. Yet, she gathered the slack of her hood about her chin, lest the hood fall away and reveal the bulge that ran along the left side of her deformed skull.

She was just fifteen. Girls her age, the daughters of craftsmen in this village that was now her home, were marriageable. They would have thrown themselves from the cliffs if they were so afflicted. Lil's deformity had been with her from birth. She did not hate it, but rather felt it to be the single source of anything special that she could do.

The plague had not yet reached this place. The Yew's army was far to the east. The Loire might have carried the plague, but so far did not. The village girls looked for husbands, undeterred by the events of the world. They had not lost hope, though Lil knew better. Their days were numbered.

In any other age, she would have died. The men of the village would have killed her. Wives would have stared into her asymmetrical eyes and spat the verdict, "Witch!"

But Father Peter, or rather his pulpit, protected her.

For now, she thought. Her pessimistic tendencies forced her to recognize that.

Lil turned from the cliffs. Patches of fluffy snow perched on blades of dying grass like wisps of milkweed. She thought she might blow them away with a breath.

The rest of the village had gathered beside a hillock. Father Peter was there, facing the Champion. Peter was thin and shivering, standing on the frozen ground with bare feet. He had been a monk from an ascetic order and he wore his hair in the old Irish style—bald in the front, long in the back—like Tuan and others who still clung to ways that Rome had long ago tortured from the priesthood. It was one of his few rebellious acts, and she suspected the he was proud of it, even if it made his wide forehead look even wider. Severity had not bred any more courage than that. Lil suspected that his shivering was from fear rather than the cold.

The knights, the noble, even the bishop had gone to fight the Yew. They had left months before, leaving the care of the village—practical and spiritual alike—to Father Peter. He was a kind man and a good teacher, but Lil did not trust his ability to face emergencies. He was a scholar and a hermit playing, now, at being a country priest. It took a very different type of man to care for people than it did to care for manuscripts and tomes.

But Peter had taken good care of her. Lil pursed her lips and sighed.

The latest emergency was dead, under the Champion's foot. It was something like a wolf, though it had gnarled joints and twisted black fur. Even in death, its lips curled away from yellow, jagged fangs. Steam twirled from wounds that were blue and red with gore.

The Champion tried to flick the beast's blood from his hands, but it was sticky like sap. The Champion was a foreigner. He had seemed excited about the prospect of a monster, but was now disappointed. Lil wondered if he had wanted the monster to kill him; if he were some desperately self-destructive and depressed hero. He had arrived the day before, walking ahead of a mule and a wagon. A mule was such a rare sight in these troubled times, and this one seemed fit and young. The wagon's load bulged beneath thick blankets. Pots clanked on hooks. Three men-at-arms walked beside the cart. They were fit and young, as well. All were armed and their armor, though patched and mismatched, seemed new. In all of this, they were men from a different time.

Lil did not trust the Champion. He claimed to have survived a battle against the Yew. She had never heard of that.

The Champion. She had forgotten his name, and the label seemed good enough. His face was hard and square, with a scar below his right eye that was brighter than his tanned skin. Eyes, gray-blue as the cold sea, were sharp beneath straight, short yellow hair.

He gestured at the wolf.

"That is your monster," he said, his tongue twisting on his accent.

"What do you think?" Father Peter said.

Lil shrugged and cleared her throat, though her voice would crack anyway. "The farmhands said they saw a beast standing like a man," she said. "It tore the sheep apart with hands. It had hands."

The Champion's men looked at one another, unable to hide the concern that they traded in their glances. But he shrugged it away. Contempt was clear on his face. He looked into Lil's eyes. His posture made her think that he was about to draw a weapon, though the shortest of his men still held his fine sword. The Champion had insisted on fighting the beast with his bare hands, though he had taken up a rock to finish the fight.

She looked past him. The corpse's shattered bones tore through broken skin. It still steamed, as if it were breathing through its wounds now.

The sky was darkening. Father Peter shivered again, harder. It went through his body like a wave.

"It is cold," the priest said.

"There's no wind," Lil replied. "But you're not wearing shoes."

The Champion looked at the priest, then back at Lil.

"Beasts like this run wild now," he said. "The Yew has stirred all manner of things. Did you know that sea creatures gather near Mont Saint Michel? When I fought this thing, it stood on its hind legs. It swatted at me with its paws. Its claws were like knives, like teeth. No doubt that is what the farmhands saw."

Lil guessed that his accent was Baltic, or German.

She shrugged again.

"Perhaps," she said.

She did not feel it, though. It was more than his tone, which was like a historian's, reshaping history for a king. "No doubt." It seemed meant to hide the truth at the same moment that it irrevocably refuted it. The farmhands had seen wolves. Grotesque ones, but just wolves.

No one spoke for a moment.

"What do you think?" Peter asked again.

"Can I go back to my room now?"

Peter shook his head at Lil. "You are a puzzle."

She was not listening to him, but rather thinking aloud.

"I wonder," she said, "how we came to be here."

The snow had not yet fallen. The Champion had not yet arrived. Lil stood with Father Peter on a hillside that sloped to the east, over the borders of Angevin land and into the ravage of the Yew. She saw none of that carnage, but just a pasture wandering into blue mist. A bank of clouds, far to the east, may have been smoke. She wondered. There was a breeze. Her hood had fallen. Her fine yellow hair flowed around her cheeks. A breeze from the far west, from the ocean—she did not smell the smoke. She had in days prior, when she and Father Peter had traveled from a monastery on the edge of the plague lands. They had collected important manuscripts to send to Iona and Ireland. There were no relics. The brothers had answered that question with tragic, deep frowns.

Instead of smoke, she smelled a hint of the sea and the taint of fading autumn. The ground was frozen. There was ice in the cracks of the jutting stones.

"What do you see?" Peter asked. He sat on a bump of stone and picked at the blooming lichen. He crossed his legs like a woman. His feet, as usual, were bare. Their soles were rough and cracked, thick with hard skin.

Lil waited. Birds crossed the sky, but their flight told her nothing. They fled. They were not interested in messages, or she could not read them. She had observed other seers capture birds, slice them down the front, and separate slimy brown and red parts. They studied those parts, and divined something from them.

Visions and dreams—these, she felt, lived in the long lump on her head. Nothing, now. Dry grass waved and rustled, its whisper telling her nothing.

Peter sighed and stared.

"They were still heading south," he said. He shifted his legs. "South to cross the Loire, perhaps. The brothers thought that they were chasing something. Priests are fleeing, taking the relics."

Lil blinked and looked though the mist, deep into the far bank of clouds. It was a flat slate thing with no lines, no shape at all. There was nothing to see there.

"They said the Pope has fled to Jerusalem," Peter continued. "Can you imagine that? They say Jerusalem has nonetheless fallen. The crusaders, the Templars, all gone. All here. Dying. And the Pope flees there? I've heard nothing of the lord and lady, or the bishop. The flock remains under my care indefinitely, I imagine. The weight of caring for all of these people is..."

Lil looked north and south for some animal running, some sign. Still, though, she saw nothing.

"I can look after their souls all right," Peter said. "But putting food in their mouths, especially now—that is a different thing altogether."

She dropped her gaze. Frustration stiffened her limbs and balled in her fists. She drew a long breath, then turned.

"I don't see anything," she said. "Maybe they go south. Maybe they turned west and are just beyond the mist. Maybe they are behind us, sacking the village as we sit here. I'm of no use."

"That is the thing about you seers," Peter said. "Your gift is fickle. It comes and goes. You are no charlatan. A fake would stand here and tell me something. Anything. When you do not know, you do not know. And for all of your gifts, you are humble and doubt yourself."

He paused. Lil blinked and sighed.

"Tuan was right about you," Peter continued.

Lil squinted at the name, then scrambled to change the subject.

"What did the farmhands tell you about this beast?"

Peter looked at the sky, then nearly shouted his reply.

"Ah, the beast! They say it kills the sheep in their pens. One of them saw it. He said it was like a man, and that it turned the sheep inside out with its bare hands. It did not consume the animal, but seemed more interested in the blood, or the mutilation. No tracks in the frozen ground, of course. The farmhands say they have no hope of figuring out what it was. It came two nights this past week. They live in fear. They tend the sheep in the day, and hope for the best at night."

"That's all they say?" she asked.

"That is all they say. I am sure I have a prayer for it. In these times, however, I doubt the prayers of a small parish priest about such a thing would rank all that highly among the other happenings of the day."

"You'd never tell them that," she said, sitting beside him. The stone was cold.

"Of course not."

She looked at her hands. They looked like old hands to her. Her mother called them witch's hands, as if the lump on Lil's head were not wicked enough. She needed devilish hands, as well. A kind woman, otherwise—she had the insight, at least, that the church should be enlisted in Lil's care rather than allowed to be curious and scared. The priest then—Lil forgot his name, for she was horrible with names—saw fit to send her to the Templars rather than tie her to a stake and burn her alive.

Witch's hands, wide at the joints, thin between, with thick veins and splotches. The hands were also too big for a girl her age. They looked almost like the elongated, wrinkled relics of a saint. Perhaps the Yew followed her now, hoping to take her hands into its soil. That was what Tuan had said, that its demons buried the relics in its dirt.

She sighed again and looked at her palms. She drew her fingers into fists and, absent-minded, turned her gaze back to the eastern horizon.

There it was. Clear as day. A vision.

It was not a single image, nor a single sound. It was the color, the clouds, the rustling of the grass, a flight of birds and of wind, the stars peeking now from behind the high dark canopy. It was the moon as an etching of thin, frail lines against the sky. It was all of these things. She felt the movement in her gut. The creaking of the tree and its wagon vibrated in her bones. The march of the dead pulsed in her skull, in the lumpy mass above her left ear.

The Yew, its army—they had found something. They were more powerful. They had turned. But their beat was hasty and careless.

She gasped.

"What is it?" Peter asked. As soon as he realized, he burst with excitement and stood. "You see something."

Her eyelids strained to open wider. She put her hands to her ears to stem the pounding that filled her skull. She felt as if a club were smacking her, over and over, harder each time.

All of the noise climbed to a whistle, reaching a peak and snapping. Normal sights and sounds floated down, fluttering from one another, drifting back into their place in the world.

"They march north," she said.

"Here?" Peter asked.

"I can't say. They know something. They have something. But not all is right with them. Something is wrong. There is some loss. Some desperation. But they are strong. Very strong. It is…very hard to understand." She shook her head.

Peter sat and wrapped his arm around her shoulder.

"Who do we need to tell?" he asked.

"I don't know who tell. I don't know who is left."

"Mont Saint Michel?" Peter blurted.

She turned to him.

"I'm telling you," she said. "Do whatever you want with it."

✠

Lil looked at the western sky. She and Father Peter walked the gravel road back to the village. The land rose and fell gently, but was generally flat. She could see the sky through the trees. The setting sun was an orange smudge. The clouds were a treacherous terrain, looking much like ground. She wondered if they were a mirror to the frozen dirt upon which she stood. The edges of those clouds were like a jagged, unnavigable coast.

Was that the land of the dead? Was that where souls went to live forever?

Behind her, to the east, the world had fallen to ash. The black moss of the plague consumed everything. To the west, hope and eternal life bloomed, just as the Irish had always said.

Here was...just here.

The sky went darker with each thought. The sun was falling behind the cold bare branches.

They had reached the stone walls of the sheep pens. The grass was cropped close. The shepherds wondered how they would feed the sheep. They had stockpiled little, and there was nothing in the way of trade.

No matter, she thought. There was a beast afoot. She understood Peter's concerns. The weight of rule was heavy.

A hush had fallen over the buildings at the edge of the village. Shutters slammed closed and fat grandmothers carried infants indoors.

"What's happening?" she asked.

"What do you mean?" Peter was oblivious, but seemed to understand after looking around them. "I do not know. This is strange."

The blacksmith was leaving town. He led an ancient, nearly dead donkey by the reins. The beast, in turn, pulled a cart with all of the smith's possessions. The smith would not uncover his head or look

Father Peter in the eyes. The priest had to move in front of him. It seemed as if the smith considered walking around Peter. The smith answered questions quickly, with nods or shakes of his head if he could manage it. Lil heard little of the conversation. She stood by the side of the road, kicking at a clump of frozen mud. She kept her head covered, though her deformity was no secret here.

Peter returned and motioned Lil to walk forward. He said nothing.

"What's happening?" she asked.

"Apparently," he said. "They will be arrayed against us."

"Who?"

"The townspeople." He laughed nervously. "They believe that I have invited evil upon them. They believe that this beast kills the sheep because I made our village amenable to its appetite."

"What does that mean?" she asked, though she knew the answer.

He shrugged.

"You mean," she said. "I brought the beast."

"Well—"

"You allowed me to live here, and they're blaming me for the beast."

Peter paused, stopped walking, then continued on as if he had been direct from the start of the conversation and found her reaction to be unreasonable.

"One day to the east," he said. "The dead rise. Plague kills. You fall off of the edge of the world. Here, a beast kills sheep and they are ready to burn you alive? I find it laughable."

"They are ready to what?"

"The smith. He will find out. He goes east, thinking that he will find work among the armies."

"Did you tell him that the Yew marches north? Did you tell him that the armies are gone?"

"I did not," Peter said. "But you are right. He should march to Mont Saint Michel."

She had been there, before Tuan sent her south on a mysterious task. She still did not know why, though it was certainly not to be burned alive by men who did not know the danger that faced their world only a short march from their quiet village.

"I have powerful friends," she said, though she regretted it. She liked to believe that she was capable on her own.

"I know," Peter said. "Understand, the villager's world is no wider than his village."

He gestured to the crumbling walls and thatch roofs around them.

"They are superstitious," he continued. "They believe in Christ, but they do not. Do you know what I mean?"

She knew what he meant.

"So what do we do?" Lil asked.

"I am hoping that I can protect you," Peter said.

A crowd had indeed formed on the closest edge of the village square. Lil recognized some of them, though she had not been in the village long enough to know their names. She had seen them in the fields. She heard them loving their wives at night, and yelling at their children during the day. Peter was right. They did not understand, but were more dangerous for it. They knew nothing of Templars or the walking dead.

"Father Peter," their leader declared. "We would have a word with you." He was tall and thin, and stood in front of the group. He was the only one to wear armor, though it was just padded cloth, tattered at the edges. He carried a weapon, a proper sword. The others bore whatever they had found—tools, rocks, branches cut into clubs. One held a bar stool, waving it as if wielding a stool was a practiced art of war. They were quiet. There was little frenzy. There were no more than a dozen of them, but it was perhaps the entire adult male population of the hamlet.

Lil blinked and looked at Peter, who had stopped right there, a dozen or so yards from the crowd.

"What is it?" Peter yelled. "I bring news from the east that is much more dire, much more important. It concerns all of us."

"The girl is evil. We don't want her in our village."

"Quite the contrary," Peter replied. "She wards it away. Do not tell me that the lump on her head—"

"The demon comes to eat our sheep. It came first on the same day that you allowed her to stay in the chapel. My cousin knows a priest in Lyonne. My cousin thinks the priest would agree."

"And you are an expert?" Peter asked.

Lil tried not to smile, but she was proud of him. He was a learned man among men whose hands were rough. He spoke every Sunday to men who barely understood a word he said. Now, he stood up to them, even mocked them, for her. If not for her, for her benefactors. The Templars were powerful, but they had lost much favor. To the east, church men had fled, leaving their flocks to die. Peter had stayed, but the village did not trust him. They must have thought that he would run at the first sign of danger.

But he was not running from her.

"My cousin's friend is an expert!"

The sun had nearly set. Lil looked up to see the edge between day and night. Dim stars peered through holes in the clouds.

"I have come from the east," Peter said. "We saw demons. Real ones."

They had not, but the look of horror on the faces of those who had was enough for Lil.

"We saw them marching with the risen dead," he continued. "The end is upon us, and she tells us where they will march next. She is on our side. She works for God."

Some of the men muttered. The leader's shoulders fell for a moment, but he regrouped.

"Why does a devil eat our sheep?" the man called.

"A devil?"

It was not Peter, but a booming voice behind them. Lil turned, exposing her back to the crowd. She wondered if it was wise of her, but the voice had surprised her.

The Champion.

He walked ahead of his companions, his chest bare and his arms wrapped around his helmet. His blade was sheathed on his back. The Champion's frame bulged with youthful muscles, but he was not a young man. His arms and chest were sketched with scars.

The pots and pans clanked against the side of his wagon.

"Then I am in the right place," he bellowed.

All went silent and weapons fell at his voice, the edges of which were as clean as the lines of his jaw, despite his accent.

The breeze stopped. The cold clung close to the ground. Even the sun seemed to halt its descent. Here, and in the cloudy land of the dead, all bent to listen.

"They said that there was a demon eating sheep," the Champion declared. "I have come to kill it, for that is what I do."

He drew his sword and flung it about in mock maneuvers that were fluid and graceful. It all seemed staged. She expected the troupe to break into a play, to declare that they were not warriors but actors. But the Champion plunged his sword into the frozen road and stood, leaning on its pommel.

"Feed my men tonight," he said. "By this time tomorrow, the demon will be dead."

He was serious. Lil squinted and looked to Peter, who smartly jumped on the opportunity.

"If he kills the thing," Peter said to the crowd. "Can we put our issue to rest?"

"I will kill it," the Champion said.

And that was that. The crowd dispersed, satisfied that they may yet see action but not have to take part in it. They would continue to enjoy a feisty anger that would take them through an evening of drinking. Peter sat with the Champion for long hours in the tavern, a tiny hovel of mud and thatch extending from the side of a widow's home. She cooked meager meals, and ladled a gritty, bitter ale into earthen mugs. The Champion seemed thankful for the food and the drink, for much laughter rose from that place.

Lil went to bed, curling beneath the blankets in a corner of a closet beside Peter's study.

Chapter X

The next night, the Champion and his entourage faced Peter, Lil, and the villagers. Lil squinted at the wolf's corpse in the dying light. It was not such an odd thing. It was a bit large. Its fur was more wiry and darker than was typical. Nothing remarkable. Some oddities to the appearance, but that was all. Like herself.

"I tracked the demon to this place," the Champion said.

He planted his foot into the beast's shoulder. Either he had not actually seen a demon, like those that rampaged to the east, or he was a stupid opportunist thinking that this village had something to offer him.

"It's just a wolf," she said, though she did not believe it. The dead thing had been a monster.

The Champion's gaze snapped to her. His eyes harbored such derision that she cringed.

"Who are you?" he asked. "This priest keeps consulting you, and you speak as if you have a free tongue. But you are a harmless girl. This thing would have torn out your stomach. Did you see the sheep it killed? I did. And you say it is just a wolf?"

"No," Lil replied. "In fact, I believe it to be a dog. A wild wolfhound, like they have in Ireland."

Peter nudged her with his elbow, but there was no stopping her now. Ire had risen up her spine and now governed her behavior. The Champion had anger to match, though, and he bared his teeth. He stepped toward Lil, leaving the wolf behind him, well in his past.

"I have killed bears," he said. "I have killed witches. I have killed men who were nine feet tall. I have fought the marching dead of the Yew, and lived to tell of it. I have grown fat and rich from killing monsters. I have smashed girls like you against trees. Do you see my men? They are better warriors than most and they follow me."

She looked him up and down. His facade did not withstand such close scrutiny. He was a wanderer, with patchwork armor. Still, there was some wealth. A fine gold bracelet on his wrist, studded with jade.

His breastplate bore lapis. Any warrior could wear such things. But, that he wore them openly indicated that he had more in some keep, or in a horde buried in a hillside. He had wrinkles in the corners of his eyes and, she noticed again, scars on his arms and his cheek. He was at the end of his career.

His men smiled.

"Uncover your head," he ordered. "Show me some respect."

"That is quite enough," Peter said.

The villagers seemed satisfied with the scene evolving before them. This was a best, if unforeseen end. The monster was dead, and now the witch might follow.

Lil could have scurried between his legs and around the hillock perhaps before he even noticed. But the plateau was wide. She would not make it very far. And, there was something impudent about baring her head, something quite attractive to her mood at the moment. The sight of her deformity would be like an unexpected counterattack.

She brought her hands to the edge of her hood and pulled it to the nape of her neck. The villagers gasped as if they had never seen her. The Champion's lips curled into disgust, but he said nothing. Peter put his hands on her shoulders, which may have been comforting at a different time. Now, she was too angry. Angry and now feeling somewhat foolish for not being afraid.

"Tell me," the Champion eventually said. "Did I kill your pet?"

He turned his face to Peter, but kept his gaze on Lil.

"Is this witch here with your blessing?" he asked the priest.

Peter nodded, then said, "And the blessing of powerful men."

The crowd sighed and booed. They were tired of hearing this.

"Who believes," the Champion addressed the crowd, "that this girl brings evil upon you?"

They all shouted. The Champion continued. "Who believes that the wolf belongs to her?"

More shouts.

The Champion stepped back, extending his right hand. One of his men-at-arms was there, the shortest one, placing a sword into the Champion's grip.

She wished, then, that the wolf belonged to her, that she could summon such things to protect her. It would rise from the dead and carry her to safety. Now she was scared. It filled her from the bottom of her stomach, up and down her entire body. She was scared and cold.

Peter held her shoulders tighter and stood behind her, perhaps ready to take any thrust into his body as well. It did not matter. He was a culprit, as well. He was a minion of powerful men, of Templars and a devilish church that had brought a witch to this village. He was at the center of all of their troubles—a failing harvest, the end of trade, war and plague to the east, a negligent God who had abandoned them all.

"I'm sorry," she said, hoping that Peter would hear.

"Will you fight me?" the Champion asked, smiling. His three companions took positions near him, but did not draw their weapons. "I have withstood witchcraft. Will you try yours? Or will you send wolves against me?"

He stepped closer, some caution in his stance.

"Come, Witch. Try your best. I will cleave that ill-formed head right from your shoulders and let its black magic spill onto the ground."

A shroud fell. The world blurred and darkened behind him, as if the night sky had fallen through a funnel to the ground at his heels. The villagers gasped. Lil raised an eyebrow. She could not see what it was. The Champion blocked her view. She guessed another wolf, but it was not so. Whatever it was threw the Champion aside and, twisting the man's wrist, took hold of his sword.

It was a knight. There was a red cross splayed across his tunic.

A Templar.

They did vouch for her, then. They did protect her. She expected horses to round the hillock. She expected one of the warriors to sweep her into his saddle and bear her to safety. She had news. The Yew was turning north, news that she had to get to their commanders at Mont Saint Michel as soon as possible. Suddenly, she cared.

No other riders came.

The Champion twisted his shoulders and rolled, just as his own sword point came down at him. It struck the frozen dirt. The Templar whirled to face the Champion's warriors. They stepped back, as had the villagers. Lil remained, though Peter's hands darted from her shoulders as he retreated.

Something was wrong.

The knight's tunic was filthy and frayed. His armor was dull. Links dangled from the cuffs like bracelets. He wore no helmet. His hair was a ghost of deep black. It was dirty and dull, wiry, wild.

She heard something rising above the rustling of the Templar's attacks, the last breathy moments of the villagers' gasps, and the bell ring of the Champion's sword against the stone, a sound that still swirled through the thin, frozen air. It was Peter. He was mumbling in Latin. He was praying, crossing his chest rapidly and pinching a roughly carved crucifix so tightly that his fingernails were dead white.

Then, from the crowd, two words from either corner, shouted, overlapping one another.

"Demon!"

"Dead!"

The Champion stood but buckled, gripping his knee. Lil did not see a wound. He must have smashed his leg against the stone. His warriors went into action, but had no plan. They jumped separately at the Templar, who swung deftly, dispatching two within a blink. They fell, one's chest splayed open and the other staring at his ropy, steaming organs as they tumbled from his torn gut.

The Templar leveled the sword against the third warrior, who parried two heavy blows, wincing at their force. His polearm splintered and, with the third attack, snapped. The Templar thrust the sword forward. The warrior turned to run, and took the blade into the soft side of his lower back. The Champion's last warrior shuddered and, as soon as the Templar freed the blade, fell in a heap.

The Champion tried to stand. The villagers gripped their tools and ancient weapons. The Templar faced them all. He faced Lil.

He was a demon. His skin was tight and cracked, brownish gray like that of an ancient corpse pulled from a bog. There was some expression to the fallen blue eyes and the muscles of the face, but tortured and sad. His jaw was gone and his upper teeth sliced away, all left on some quiet, burnt battlefield to the east. The cut went to his throat, where the top of his windpipe was tattered and dry. Silent. There was blood on his mantle, pinkish brown blotched all about the red cross.

The demon relaxed, then tightened his grip on the sword. He stood in a practiced stance, even an expert stance.

The Champion hobbled forward and, with a roar, launched from his good, straight leg. It was a futile attack. The demon leaned and gripped the Champion as he passed, flinging him hard into the side of the hillock. The Champion hit the frozen dirt and groaned.

Peter's prayer was now a yell, but it had no effect. The villagers seemed unready for this. They watched the priest and the demon, back and forth, waiting for the demon to sizzle with holy fire. Instead, the demon stepped forward and seemed ready to strike the priest down, indeed intent upon it as if it had not been Lil, or the Champion, or the sheep, or anything but the death of this priest that had lured him from his grave.

The knight glanced at Lil. In that moment, that brief moment when the gaze touched her, a breeze died against her back and a fat snowflake fell between them. When the Champion's groan fell to silence, Lil heard something else. Tuan's voice. She remembered the old man's last words to her before she left, heading south as he had commanded.

"Why?" she had asked.

"Find Martin. You will know him when you see him. Take him home."

She breathed, gathering air for the word, hoping that she could utter it before the demon struck.

"Martin," she said.

Peter's prayer ceased. The priest looked at her. She had said the name, she realized, in a scolding tone she might have used against a dog.

The demon stopped, looked from the priest to the girl again, and flexed his fingers. He seemed about to strike once more. She said it again, more certain yet softer.

"Martin."

She was not sure what was happening. Her world spun as she flew over the beast's back. He gripped her. He did not smell of death, but rather reeked of sweet char smoke, like burning syrup. Despite the look of him, the skin of his neck was soft and wet.

The Templar ran. She, hanging from his back, saw the villagers. They were surprised, yet somehow not, that a demon would carry her away from them. So, she thought again, a Templar watched over her. But this was a thing of the Yew. She was certain of it. Tuan had not warned her of that.

Dead or not, Martin moved with incredible speed, bounding over the pastures, darting between hillocks, down the slopes and into the snowy pastures.

✠

115 | J.P. MOORE

"Where do you take me?" she asked.

They sat in a small forest clearing, upon stones. The wind blew in the trees above them. They were quite sheltered. Their fire, though struggling, provided heat enough to let Lil forget that they were on the edge of winter. Snow had not reached this far inland, though the ground was frozen. The night sky was clear.

The fire was a crude thing. Martin had erected it for her. He did not need it. He had brushed away what leaves and needles he could, those that were not frozen fast to the ground, then piled bracken and twigs. He spent what seemed hours striking small bits of flint against the rough chain mail of his arm. When a spark jumped, he reacted with an almost childish excitement. He fanned the dying thing with his hands. This happened several times until luck brought a breeze into the clearing to aid his efforts. The pile then ignited. He presented the flame to her with outstretched arms, with pride. Then, he alternated between feeding wood into the small dancing beast, walking in ever wider circles to collect more fuel, and just standing still in different corners of the clearing, listening and watching.

Lil saw some nervousness. He could not stay still, she guessed. Something seemed to be eating at him, itching. Activity seemed to dispel it.

She looked into the fire. Perhaps he waited for her to sleep. She could run, of course, but was not sure if she should. This was Martin, certainly. What did Tuan know of this creature? Had he been alive when Tuan had given her the order to find him? Had it now gone wrong? She could not destroy him. She did not know the first thing of fighting, let alone fighting one of the Yew's dead. And Martin had proven himself to be an impressive specimen. He fought expertly and traveled impossibly fast. They had bounded across Brittany. It should have taken them all night to cross the distance they had crossed in a mere hour.

"Do you mean to feed me to the Yew?" she asked.

Martin shook his head.

The darkness, the shadows—sometimes she could not see his wounds. He looked like a whole man in those moments.

Lil sighed.

"We flee, then," she said.

Martin nodded.

"We flee the Champion," Lil continued. "We flee the villagers."

She had trouble looking at him. His edges blurred in her vision. She felt a pain in the bulge on her head whenever she tried to see the details of his face, his form. There was something in him that pushed at her, as if they were two polar ends of lodestones, repelling.

"The Yew marches north," she said, then paused. "Do you flee from them as well?"

Martin looked at her, then nodded.

This was strange, she thought. She knew that some of the Yew's soldiers were mindless, while others were not. That there could be division and dissent, that one would have cause to flee—she did not understand that. Tuan might have. He knew much of the Yew's forces, but had not discovered the secrets that would bring victory.

She turned to easier mysteries, as if there were a list and she was striking them out as they were solved.

"Why did you come to Brittany?"

Martin shrugged. She moved to another.

"Did you kill the sheep?"

Martin nodded.

"Did you command the wolves?"

He shook his head.

Lil sighed.

"How did you come to Brittany? Why did you leave?"

She was not sure these were the correct questions to ask, but felt that she needed to know more. She was not sure if it was trust, or her own curiosity about her mission.

"You ran," she said. "You ran from your comrades."

Martin did not respond.

"Did you run from the Yew?"

He looked at the fire before shaking his head. A frightening possibility struck her.

"You did not want to leave," she said.

He might still serve the Yew. The task that Tuan had given her had seemed harmless enough, but now put her in league with the enemy. She shrank from Martin, from the fire, but halted as the cold of the world beyond leveled against her back. The mission—the task to take him home, whatever that meant—might set a chain of events moving out of her control. Then she remembered that she had not looked for

Martin. Tuan had sent her into Brittany, to the mouth of the Loire. There, Martin had found her. And by chance, it seemed. He had been separated from the Yew and brought to her. Tuan had seen something.

Lil swallowed hard and shuddered in the breeze. She looked at the icy stars, and spoke.

"Tuan sent me to find you."

Martin snapped to attention. He looked at her, leaning forward, somehow imploring with his dead eyes.

"You know Tuan," she said.

He nodded like a child accepting a treat.

Tiny flames consumed twigs at the edges of the fire, curling them. The fire's heat now barely reached her, as if an impenetrable cold had settled in front of her. She gathered into herself, inched closer until she could feel the fire on her feet.

"He told me to take you somewhere," she said. "Sort of a riddle, really."

She laughed, then felt foolish for it. "Tuan and his riddles."

She looked again at Martin, whose face was now exposed in the light of the fire. He was grotesque, a broken thing. But so, she thought at that moment, was she.

"I am to take you home," she said. "Do you know where that is?"

Martin sat back, looking aside. Was that disappointment? Did he not remember? If that were true, what was she to do? Thoughts of destroying him returned. This was a test for him. If he remembered, then he was still an ally. If he were so far gone as to have forgotten, then he was an enemy. He was out of his own control, useless.

He looked about, then. Something descended upon him. She could see the glow falling from the sky, the stars, anointing him with realization. His eyes narrowed and she pictured him smiling, a handsome husband. A father. All of the things that Tuan had described. The master had described black hair, blue eyes and, oddly, a square jaw. Perhaps all part of the riddle.

Martin snatched a spent piece of char from the edge of the fire and, brushing away bracken and leaves beside him, exposed a flat stone. With crude, almost childish movements that seemed so strange from a being that had bested the Champion and his henchman, he made lines. Martin beckoned Lil to his side.

She recognized the shape in the dim light. It was a map, rough but recognizable. A line separated the Angevin holdings from France. A dot sat northwest of Paris, near the coast. Martin pointed to that dot with some hesitation. She wondered if he had misgivings about trusting her.

She understood. It was his home.

Or, rather, it was the home of someone he had been. Thus the whole exercise seemed somewhat flat, something of a fraud. The truth of home, of France, of all life, was no more real in these times than those rough black lines upon a stone.

Home. Life. These were ideas that the living impressed upon a cold, dead surface. When men and women were all gone, as it seemed they would be, then none of this would exist.

It reminded her of something Tuan had said. They were in a scriptorium. Monks worked at their parchments all about them.

"It is a struggle," he said. "It is a struggle between the living and the dead, between ideas and emptiness. There is no God, no heaven, no holiness without the living."

"You're a heretic," she said, smiling.

"I am no such thing."

She realized now that it had been about something else, something that made much more sense to her now.

The world, he was saying, was a human invention.

"That's your home," she said.

Martin nodded.

She looked at the crude map and, making her best guess, made a line.

"The Loire runs here," she said. "South of us. Not far."

He nodded again and pointed a shriveled finger at a spot along that line.

"You left the Yew there," she said. "You came by the river. The river put you...here. Now, we are here."

Lil looked at the stars again. She could not read them. She never could, and distrusted those who did.

"So," she said, looking about them. "We go northeast. Which way is that?"

Martin shook his head. He pressed his palms together and rested his broken cheek upon them. Lil blinked, staring at him a moment to decipher his meaning.

"We sleep," she finally said.

Martin nodded.

It was a restless night for her. The ground was hard and cold. Martin kept the fire lit, but it did not chase the sounds of the wilderness. There were howls, rustles, breezes through dead leaves that clung still to their branches. Time passed in fits between spells of dreamless sleep and wakefulness that was, in fact, much more like a dream.

She did not see Martin sleeping at all. He sat, staring at some far point in the distance.

Chapter XI

There was a pile of feathers on the map of France. He was roasting a bird. She was not sure how he had caught it. He had constructed a spit over the fire, and the bird was a glistening thing in the flames, a twig rammed through its body and coming out of its mouth. Its fat dripped into the embers, which flared and popped. She realized that she had not eaten since the morning before.

Lil relished every bite, leaving nothing but a broken skeleton. Martin had taken some shreds, but slipped them into his mantel rather than eating. She realized this with some surprise, and then chided herself. Of course he did not eat. He was saving the meat for her.

With the sun still low in the sky, Lil thought about the season, shivered, and gauged the direction. Martin was already striking out to the northeast, hacking at dense underbrush with a thick tree limb. Their progress was slow. Vines and branches tugged at them. The brier was thick.

She noted tufts of black moss on some of the trees. Stripes of black shot through their curling bark. Splits exposed the worm-eaten meat of the trunks. There was a smell to it, something like rot and sulfur. Martin pointed at these deformed things, then at her. Did he mean to say that she was so deformed? No, she realized. He worried about her.

"I do not suffer from the plague."

Martin cocked his head, as if confused.

She wondered if Martin brought the plague. Perhaps the forest reacted to him. She had seen such signs of plague when traveling with Peter, but further to the east. She had been close to the sickness many times, but had never contracted it. Peter, on one trip, showed bruises that, within a day, disappeared. Since then, he had offered services to many in the last fits of sickness. He seemed, now, to be immune as well.

Would a desperate hunter come into these woods and bring the sickness back to his village? Would it then spread through Brittany?

Would the Yew then march through these lands? All because she had not yet killed Martin.

Once they reached open ground, Martin would lift her onto his shoulders and bound across the plains. Would each of his footfalls, she wondered, plant the pest into the dirt?

Or, she guessed, it was just a matter of time before the plague spread to every corner on its own. The Yew, after all, was again marching north. Perhaps it had turned west, toward Mont Saint Michel or even to cross the sea to Britain.

Martin looked at the sky to check the sun. It was still early morning. Looking back, Lil judged that their path was as straight as they could make it.

She wondered why Martin had left the Champion's sword. They might have moved more quickly through the woods. As it was, he broke tree limb after tree limb clearing their path, forcing them to pause while he foraged for suitable replacements. She closed her eyes against her own doubt. Yes, this was a soldier of the Yew. Yes, she may be walking to her death, or worse. But she was alive now. If the Champion had not killed her, then the villagers would have.

She felt a prickling in the tips of her fingers, an urgency, an itch to break and run for cover. It was the sort of feeling she sometimes had before a vision. The forest seemed to feel it as well. The forest was not quiet. Clicks and calls, rustles in the fallen leaves—the place lived, but had the frantic energy of a forest before a storm. A tree to their left clogged with frightened birds seemed to be channeling a chaotic chorus. Shrieks and shouts. Small animals, visible only through the disturbance they created in the brush, darted across the path. Not running from Martin and Lil, as one might expect, but just running from something.

Martin seemed unfazed. Perhaps this was the world on the edge of the Yew. This was the frantic, desperate fringe of life that he knew well.

One call stood apart. A crow. Lil squinted. It sounded again, and she stopped. Further away, there was an answer of a similar character though lower in pitch. They were words—"caw"—rather than animal cries. Martin stopped and turned to her.

"Someone is watching us," she said.

Martin nodded and hefted the limb in his hands as if it were a sword, then regarded it with doubt in his narrowing eyes. She thought again of the Champion's sword, back by the hillock.

She was with a Templar, a soldier. No matter which side now held his allegiance, he knew how to fight. She had seen it firsthand. And he had ungodly, magical speed. In open ground, he was unstoppable. They would be gone. She had no sense, though, of the distance to the edge of the forest, to the wide plains beyond that would take them much of the way to the region of Martin's home.

Martin moved forward with some urgency, even anger, as he beat the forest from their path. Lil stood, shouting.

"Wait!"

There was no sense in hiding their presence. She realized that there may still be strategy in appearing ignorant of their pursuers.

"It's a trap," she said, forcing it through as loud a whisper as she could manage.

Martin rolled his eyes. This infuriated her. She reminded herself that she knew nothing of his trade.

"You mean to spring the trap," she said.

Martin nodded.

She stepped forward, and Martin thrust his arm across her path. It was as solid as a steel blade.

He pointed ahead of them. A man sat at the base of a tree. Lil knew him. He was one of the villagers, an older man with sagging, lumpy skin. Gray bristles sprouted from his chin. His eyebrows were wild. He was balding, but in a curious pattern. This man made a meager living shoveling trash of all kinds, whether dung from pens or vomit from the widow's tavern.

Lil began to whisper.

"I know—"

Martin cut her short with a threatening chop of his hand. He cupped his ear. She listened. Among the cries of the wood, the breeze in the leaves, she heard snoring. She watched as the man's chest rose and fell with that sound. Martin bristled, then, and pointed again. She saw a sword pressing down the grass at the man's side.

So, the village had pursued them. The Champion was near. He must have traveled all night.

Before Lil could even consider their next moves, Martin was darting silently from trunk to trunk. She lowered herself into the brush and peered over the twigs. In front of her, a spider spun a web. Intricate. Perfect. She peered through its panes. Beads of sticky fluid reflected a brilliant diamond version of the world.

The sleeping man muttered and smiled. He was dreaming. She was afraid of what Martin would do to him. Countless scenarios played in her head, one after another. She hoped for a vision, but nothing came. Her heart beat fast. Sweat began to rise on the back of her neck. Her breathing was too heavy to open herself. She felt nothing from the forest, and saw no crack in its facade that would allow her to peer behind and see.

She would know soon enough, for Martin was there, standing above the man. The man was disgusting, but was beautiful in contrast to Martin, whose cracked and stretched skin was gray like soot. Threads hung from the Templar's tattered mantle. His armor was in disrepair and showed rust. He was everything one expected of a rotted corpse left on a field.

Martin knelt, reaching for the sword. He stretched his fingers around the hilt, lifted, and waved the thing in the air. Then, without any warning, he drew back and swung. Lil did not see the strike. Martin blocked her view. She heard the fountain of blood slapping against the trunk. She saw the hairy bundle of the villager's head drop to the ground, between Martin's feet. He wiped the blade across the man's chest and pushed the corpse down with his foot.

Lil blinked. The spider drew one more glistening line from the edge of its web to the center. She was now more confused than ever. The man had been innocent. An idiot, to be sure, and she had no doubt that he would have killed her. But he was innocent. Here, now, was this demon, a soldier of the Yew. Martin had saved her, but had also now killed several men in front of her. Now, he had a sword.

The forest erupted. Cries and calls, animals rather than men. The kill had been almost silent, but a flock of fat black birds alighted from a nearby tree and, for a moment, filled the sky.

Martin motioned her forward with a quick gesture. She did not move. He motioned again, with more urgency. It was less likely, now, that she would be able to destroy him if she had to. He was fast, armed, strong. She closed her eyes.

Best, she thought, to follow him. For now.

Tuan had asked her to lead him home. Now, she followed him. She was of no use to him any longer, yet he seemed still intent upon protecting her.

Lil stood, opened her eyes and slowly stepped forward, placing her feet with care into the dry, noisy brush. Ahead, it thinned. Martin no longer needed to hack it away from their path. Just her luck—now that they had a sword, they had no use for it.

Except, of course, to kill.

Soon, they came to another clearing. It had a carpet of moss and a calming fragrance, something like flowers though there were none in bloom. The rest of the season was so hard, but this place was soft. Lil was pleased. Martin, however, seemed cautious. She realized that, for a soldier, even the most inviting clearing—perhaps the most inviting ones—must be dangerous places.

Martin gestured to the edge and began walking. She followed him around the border of the clearing, fixing her gaze at its center. A cloud of tiny flies swirled in a plank of sunlight above a fallen log that was breaking into mulch before her eyes.

The artificial calls, though less frequent, still sounded around them.

"Fools," she thought.

The villagers would now bring the plague back with them to southern Brittany, well ahead of the Yew. There was no telling where it would travel from there. So, the Champion, if that was indeed who chased them, would have put the plague in motion for the Yew.

Lil wondered if she would have chance to get word to the Templars. They would be in the best position to spread the news that the plague may be loose in Brittany, despite their best efforts to contain it. Unless, of course, Martin killed all of the villagers. This, she realized, was a possibility now that he was armed.

They left the clearing. The forest was denser. Even with the sword, they made little progress. Then, at its thickest point and with no warning, the forest broke. Lil and Martin found themselves on a thin strip of soft, muddy land between the trees and a field of brown, dead grass that was taller than Martin. The field stretched as far as they could see to their left and right. The Templar seemed just as confused as she. He rose to his toes to see if he could map any of the terrain ahead of them. He looked at Lil, then at the grass. She knew that they would have to push through it. It would be slow, but would be better than the forest.

Martin knelt, patting his back. Lil was pleased at the prospect of riding his shoulders. She had no sense of when she would next sleep or eat. She was tired and already famished. She leaned forward and placed her hand on his shoulder.

Everything went black.

She was moving backwards, taking long clumsy steps until she fell. Her head smacked the ground hard. Her arms were tight against her sides, lashed there by a rough rope. She heard steel, the striking of blades. She twisted, straining at the ropes. There was a sack tied tight at her neck. They were dragging her through the grass.

Then, she stopped.

"No!" she shouted. "Let me go!"

She thrashed and kicked.

A familiar voice answered, the head of the rabble at the village.

"Got you now, Witch. This will be the end of your—"

Then, a sickening crunching sound. A second later, a tug, and her arms were free. She reached to her face and clawed at the knot, tearing the sack from her head.

Martin was there, but disappeared into the grass. Beside her, the king of the rabble was dead. His throat was a gushing, bubbling gash. His eyes stared at her, shock in their wide, empty pupils. A bloody dagger lay in the dead grass beside a sliced length of rope.

Lil sat, taking the dagger onto her lap. There was sound all around her, rushing through the grass. Occasionally, she heard blades strike and cries of pain. She looked at the gray sky. Snow was falling—only a few flakes, but it seemed to be getting heavier by the second. She started to crawl back along the path that her body had made in the grass. She saw someone ahead, right at the edge of the forest.

It was Father Peter.

He looked about, but his gaze settled on Lil. He did not seem to see her, or rather did not believe that he was seeing her. He cocked his head in confusion. Lil, without thinking, rolled out of view.

She lay on her back, watching the snow. Why, she wondered, had she hidden from Peter? Had Peter meant to kill her?

Peter was in the grass, now.

"Lil!" he called.

She stood and tried to dart away, but slipped. Peter was there beside her.

"Come with me!" he said.

She turned.

"What are you doing here?" she asked. "How dare you? Are you here to kill me?"

She raised the dagger. Peter put up his palms and stepped back two steps.

"No!" he said. "Come with me! I can get you to safety."

"You can't save me," she said.

"That beast of the Yew can? Come. You and I can head west. We will go to Mont Saint Michel. We will alert—"

"No!" she said. "I must do something!"

It surprised even her to hear it.

Voices and blades came closer, then. Peter dove into the grass. Lil rose and ran from him. If they saw him speaking to her, they would kill him. She still believed Peter to be a good man.

The snow was now thick, beginning to show on the ground. Lil shivered and drew her thin robes close about her. She knelt, wondering if there were any way to get her bearings.

She smelled smoke. It seemed to come from everywhere. They were burning the grass. She could see the dark smoke and could now hear the roar of the fire. It would cut across the grass and consume her in no time at all. She stood again, running, pushing herself in panic, more frightened now of the fire than any man or demon.

Her head struck something hard. She had been looking at the ground. She fell back and blinked away the stars that clouded her vision.

Martin stood before her. He fought the Champion. He parried blow after blow, striking his own in between. The Champion was skilled. They battled back and forth. She knew that she only had seconds to decide. Would the Champion kill her if she aided him? What if she struck at the Champion? Would she be an accomplice to the Yew?

She closed her eyes, wishing to sink into the black. Then, after a moment, she opened them. She wished for a vision once more. She wanted to see both options spread out before her, their possible ends laid out for her to choose. It was the curse of the seer, to know so much as to be paralyzed by the prospect of a decision. Perhaps that is why it was easier for seers to live in hermitage, so far from any decisions.

Lil blinked. There were no visions. She looked at the dagger in her hand. The battling foes came closer. Martin retreated. Blows from the Champion came stronger and stronger. Martin may lose, she thought. His power was fading, or he was reserving it.

She had made a promise to Tuan. If nothing else, she realized, she owed something to him.

Lil scurried around the melee and raised the dagger against the Champion's back. He moved too quickly. She had no hope of piercing his armor. Martin gained on him now. The Champion was in retreat.

She lowered herself down on all fours. She closed her eyes.

The back of the Champion's legs touched her side. Then, a loud clang as Martin landed a blow. The Champion, stepping back, toppled over her. She darted forward from beneath his legs.

She rolled and opened her eyes. Martin scooped her up, and was running. Bouncing away, she saw the villager's sword sticking straight, impaling the Champion to the snowy ground. The hilt still swung back and forth with the force of the blow. The Champion, surprised, stared at the blade with his hands up, as if he had any hope of removing it. Then smoke drifted between her and the Champion, obscuring her view.

Chapter XII

They went north along the edge of the wasteland. They avoided settlements, though none they observed from ridges or the edges of dark forests showed any life. One leg of their journey ran along a road, and Martin showed some concern. Upon the appearance of a band of refugees, Martin led Lil to hiding behind a pair of stones jutting from an otherwise flat plain.

A priest stood at the fore of the column of refugees. His face showed resolute determination in his clenched jaw. Sobbing old women, rattling rosary beads in their shaking hands, followed him. Then, the rest plodded—men-at-arms, some bandaged, others smeared with blood or streaked with the black of char ash. Then, a handful of gaunt young women in jangling chains about their swollen, bleeding ankles shambled forward, resigned to choiceless progress, barefoot over the frozen ground. At the back, donkeys pulled carts piled with plague victims, supplies, possessions.

Lil wanted to leap out of hiding, to warn them to go back the way they had come. They would spread the plague. The panic welled up within her so fiercely that Martin covered her mouth.

The priest stopped. He raised his arms and a gnarled staff over his head and howled. The crones were stunned and then, composing themselves, mimicked his wail. The sound of it was horrific, though compelling to Lil. It soothed her panic to hear human voices, to hear something that was not wind, not cracking wood or the deep, sharp pounding of stone breaking in the heart of the world.

The men-at-arms were weary. Their shoulders fell at the alarm. They gathered their weapons and stood at something closer to attention than the mien of their exhausted march, but still quite far from any readiness.

The priest gestured, and five of the soldiers broke from the ranks, running toward the stones. Martin pulled Lil by the arm, yanking her from the priest's view. The calamity presented a hope. The night before, she had reiterated her promise. She had revealed her mission to Martin. She had, in a very real sense, set her course. But doubts lingered. She worried that she had acted in haste. And now, with soldiers approaching, she might have found an escape. She could dart out of hiding, yell and scream, and this priest and his soldiers would end her quandary.

Unless Martin defeated them. He had no weapon, but that had not stopped him against the Champion's men at the hillock, who were arguably more expert and refreshed than the haggard detachment that now approached. Sheer numbers, however, put the odds in the priest's favor. Unlike Peter, this was a priest who could protect her.

Or enslave her. Why were the women in chains?

Martin acted before Lil, still paralyzed in thought, could muster anything near a plan. The Templar scooped her under his arm and began to run. He would rely on his speed, then, to put the column of soldiers behind him. They might have crossbows, but it would take some time to bring them to the front. Lil had seen no horses.

Rather than allow Martin to decide for her, she twisted in his grasp. He looked at her, surprise in his eyes. She tried to keep a blank face, tried to act as if she were not doing anything, that falling from his grip was a matter of chance, or of uneven terrain.

Lil struck the ground so hard that her vision blurred and clanging filled her ears. Martin had gained such speed that she rolled for several seconds. He was quite far from her before he could stop and turn to recover her. By then, the five soldiers were nearing. Behind them, the rest of the column was now breaking to join the pursuit.

The first were upon her, grabbing her by the ankles and dragging. This was different from what she had pictured.

"No!" she shouted.

The soldiers, however, were not deterred. Rather, they looked at one another, each holding an ankle, and grinned.

A shout from the second wave of soldiers—Lil heard it, but did not immediately comprehend the words.

"How old?"

"Young," one of her rescuers replied. He looked at her, though there was no sympathy, no care in his glance. He regarded her as one inspects an animal in a market. "Sixteen. Seventeen."

"I'm fifteen," she said, and regretted it.

The soldiers smiled.

"Fifteen, then," one said. "Even better."

Soldiers crowded around her now. One carried chains. They parted for the priest. He was thin and old, with silver stubble on his cheeks. He smiled, flicking his tongue around a single black tooth. Pointing his staff at Lil, shaking as he held it there, he gave an order.

"Lift her skirt," he said. "Let's have a look."

"No!" she shouted again, rising to a kneel. "I am a seer of the Templars! You must take me to Mont Saint Michel!"

She lowered her hood, then, as if her deformity would be all the proof they needed. Rather than elicit awed gasps, however, it coaxed a scowl to the priest's face. He paused, then spat on the ground. Turning, he spoke over his shoulder.

"Have your way with her," he said. "Then kill her."

"No!" Lil shouted. "No! No!"

She scrambled backwards, bumping into boots. Hands fell upon her shoulders, tearing at her robe. She twisted, but they grabbed her legs, prying them apart. She strained, stiffening her body and gnashing her teeth. But there were too many soldiers, and they were too strong.

She shouted, again and again, unsure of the words she said. She did not even hear them. Her throat was raw. Her hoarse voice rose into a cracking, high-pitched whine, and then disappeared into a whisper.

The soldiers were laughing. They squeezed her ankles and wrists to the point of crushing them, but she felt no pain. They fought her stiffness, the determination that locked her hips closed, and broke her, spreading her legs wide. She felt nothing. The first soldier loosened his belt, let his armor fall. Nothing.

But she heard their laughter.

And, then, darkness. Had she died? Gone unconscious?

Was it a vision?

A shadow. A shadow had fallen, as it had behind the Champion at the hillock.

Lil dropped to the ground. Blades slid from scabbards. Soldiers flew. They flew, tossed like the scarecrows she had made as a child—clothes filled with dead leaves, tied at the cuffs, carried by the wind.

Martin.

He rammed his fists, his elbows, his knees into her captors. He gripped them by their necks, throwing them.

She would not doubt him again.

Night was falling. They had traveled a great distance. It was colder, windier. Though Martin slowed, he moved with some purpose, some familiarity. Lil was not sure how he could pick anything from this wasted place. The land was black. She was not sure if it was snow or ash falling from the sky. The smell was of rot and sulfur—she knew it from travels with Peter. But this was different. The world itself decayed, unleashing an unfathomable stench from beneath its skin.

They settled in the middle of a dead field, as if abandoning all concern for their safety. No one was near. Martin built a fire. Lil was surprised that anything, any twig or branch, was left to fuel a fire.

Martin produced dirty root vegetables and scraps of the morning's cooked bird from beneath his mantle. Lil ate these, appreciating the roots in particular for the slight water that they still held in their wrinkled, soft bodies. She spat sand for some time afterwards.

After the sun had set and the gray sky had gone black, Lil curled near the fire and closed her eyes. She fought away all thought, all memories of the day.

She had lived through many such days.

She woke in the morning, having passed the night in blissful, empty sleep. She did not feel refreshed. Rather, the night had been a blank time, a suspension of her life. She had withdrawn. No dreams, for which she was thankful. No visions. Just emptiness.

A light snow had fallen. Martin had collected it into a ball, which he gave to her, instructing her to eat.

"Good morning," she said.

He nodded.

She sat up, smoothed her hair, and began to eat the snow. It tasted like smoke, but filled her mouth with cold, glorious water.

Martin motioned her to stay, then ran off, disappearing down the slope of a hill.

Lil stood, surveying her surroundings. She was in the middle of an empty, dead pasture. A gray mix of ash and snow surrounded their camp. The new snowfall had hidden their tracks so that Lil was not sure from which direction they had arrived. The air was still, though wind howled high above, pushing the clouds with incredible speed beneath a solid gray sky. She heard nothing but the howl. There were no birds, no wild calls. Just the wind. Nearby, burnt stumps showed where a forest had been. In one place, a spent pyre taller than a man lay cold and black.

She looked about the campfire, searching for crumbs of meat from the night before. There was nothing. Martin's tracks were all about the site, buried to various depths. He had spent another sleepless night, pacing through the snowfall. Lil wondered if the lack of sleep had any effect on him.

She thought back on her brief exchange with him, moments ago. He had not seemed tired or drawn—no more, at least, than the night before. He had seemed to care, to treat her gently for the experiences of the day before. She was not sure what to do with this fact. Sympathy from one of the Yew's dead. Tenderness. Something about it turned her stomach.

She wondered about the time of day, and spent some time fixing the sun. Though bright, it was almost lost in the haze. It was low in the sky. Mid-morning, she guessed, though she questioned her sense of where the sun should be at the dawn of winter.

The Yew had marched through this pasture, she realized. Stumps. Wasteland. Its cart had crossed this very place. She thought she could see the ruts. She shivered, imagining the creak of the giant wheels.

Lil hugged her arms. She tried to imagine the place as it had been just the previous summer. Green and lush, this had perhaps been a field of barley. She saw it, then, creeping up from what it was now. She basked in the warmth, in the smell. Green barley waved, a great sea of it. A mill turned in the wind. A dog barked. A warm breeze carried the taint of manure and the tickling smell of a coming storm. Late evening. The sun was falling. Fireflies danced over the field. Glow worms were common in parts of France, but fireflies were quite rare. Yet, here they were, so dense in the drying barley that she feared their light would spark it into a blaze.

Lil blinked, and was back amidst the snow and ash. She bent over, bracing her hands against her knees as nausea swept over her and sweaty heat bloomed on her neck and back. She vomited water and bile, after which her stomach calmed and the cold penetrated to her bones.

She stood, suddenly afraid of being alone. Lil walked, following Martin's deepest tracks. His path weaved and bobbed. At times, it looked as if he ran. At others, he stopped and stood, facing nothing.

She was certain that he had a purpose, but found nothing of it in the spirit of his path. She sensed confusion.

Lil descended a slope, and saw his many paths winding between and within roofless remains of several structures, all clumped within a tight complex. This was a single farmstead. One ruin might have been a barn, another a home. The latter was nothing more than a stone hearth and low, broken walls. Smaller foundations might have been sheds or pens. She peered across this scene, trying to divine some order to Martin's paths.

"Where are you?" she asked.

There was movement in the barn. Martin was there, kicking at timbers and piles of ash that billowed into clouds. He moved to one corner, where the half-consumed frame of a long crate held only snow and ice.

The realization came, rising up as if out of the ground. Lil felt faint and nauseous once more.

She had brought him home. Her mission was done.

But it was not.

His home was as dead as he.

Lil was not sure what she had expected. Was he to have transformed back into a man? A Templar, resplendent in Crusader's armor? Part of her seemed to be waiting for that.

How foolish, she realized.

A cold wind shot across the scene, snuffing her nausea. She breathed deep, letting the air buttress her, and descended the slope. Martin moved from the barn to the home. She met him in between and stood in front of him, not knowing what to say. His eyes narrowed in anger. He clenched his fists.

"I'm sorry," she said. "Tuan told me to bring you here."

Martin brushed her aside and walked to the cinders of his home.

"I'm sorry," she said again, louder.

She followed him, though kept some distance behind him.

Martin stepped over charred beams, across the threshold. He ran his hand over the blackened stones of the foundation. The place showed remnants of life. Both Martin and Lil stood for a moment to see these, to absorb them. Perhaps, she thought, he was trying to remember them. A cooking pot, copper now showing patina, sat in the hearth. There were utensils—spoons, ladles and bowls. These were all about as if bandits had rifled through them. She noticed other refuse of his life. Cloth, half-burnt, perhaps bedding, in one corner. Snow had collected in its folds. Chairs, or rather suggestions of chairs in broken wood, leaned or had fallen away from a space once occupied by a table but now piled with thatch that, curiously, had escaped the fire.

The snow was falling again, intensifying, as if making the point that this was the last that the place would breathe with any life. It would be a buried ruin, an anonymous thing, its spirit broken from its structure forever. As with the stone circles that littered the landscape, some travelers would wonder but most would simply ignore.

No, Lil realized. There would be no travelers.

She felt something. A draw. A pull, much like the pull she felt at far more ancient sites. Those places had centers of power. She felt one here as well. She imagined a swirling funnel that pressed upon a single point. Here, it fell upon one corner, beside the hearth.

Martin distracted her. He had found a small carved horse, a toy. Kneeling, he held it in his palms as if it were a delicate, dying thing. He was calm, and regarded it in silence. His sadness, though, was a palpable, interfering presence. She concentrated, trying to block him out of her perception, annoyed and then feeling guilty for failing to comfort him. To provoke the last wistful memories from a soldier of the Yew—this was not why Tuan had ordered her to this place.

A familiar pain pulsed in the deformed ridge of her skull. She squinted, intent on focusing upon the heaviness in the air beside the hearth. Normally, she would turn away and explore the easier edges of such a space. Not this time.

The pain spiked. She reached for something to steady herself and, taking two steps sideways, leaned against the hearth. She did not feel the cold stone against her cheek. She had no sense, even, of the ground beneath her feet. Her whole body was numb.

The air in front of her twisted. Specks, yellow and green, dodged the falling snow.

Fireflies, she realized. She mouthed the word. She tried to speak it.

They swirled, multiplying until they were almost a single solid thing.

A woman.

The spirit of a woman, standing there. A memory.

Martin saw it now.

He walked toward the shaking, buzzing form that glowed so strongly in the snow that the flakes falling about it seemed to break into steam.

Lil pointed.

The woman's form wavered, fading in and out. She was dressed in robes, then not. She was young, then skeletal and old. She seemed to have something to say, but could not say it. This provoked some frustration to her face.

She looked at Lil, and then at Martin, who was now so close to her that he was nearly in front of her. The frustration spiked into panic. Lil could feel it welling up inside of her, the cry, the howl of death. A banshee's scream. As it rose in this woman, so it rose in Lil.

The woman's head fell back, her mouth opened wide.

It was Lil who made the sound.

The scream shocked the sky and shattered the last memories that clung to the remnants of Martin's home. It was the woman's scream, but it was also Lil's. It was the scream of rape, of death, of loss and neglect. It was the scream of the seer, lost from the world to wander in and out of time, knowing all but able to do so little about any of it. The snow blew from the walls of that column of sound as it launched into the clouds, which buckled with the blow. The whole valley shook. The snow died as the wail's echo bounced into the morning.

Lil brought her hand to her neck. There was a rough, fiery pain in her throat. Martin was on his knees, his hands outstretched. The fireflies, now dead, had fallen into a black and orange stain in the snow. There were many in Martin's hands. He regarded these much as he had regarded the toy horse—quietly, sadly.

Then, he launched into action. Lil was not sure what he was doing. He brushed away the snow and tore at the charred planking of the floor.

He stopped, staring down.

Lil approached and blinked. Stairs, hewn into the earth, descended into darkness.

Her mission was not over.

It had only just begun.

CHAPTER XIII

They found ancient torches under a layer of cobwebs and dust. Martin struck at his flint to light one and passed it to Lil. He took two others under his arms.

The space at the foot of the stairs opened before them. It was a natural tunnel, smooth and long, with stone formations reaching from the top and bottom to touch one another at small points in the middle. The path between the formations was clear.

An earthy smell filled Lil's nostrils. Mushrooms carpeted the floor before her. Martin knelt and, after examining one of these mushrooms, gestured to his mouth. Lil took one and smelled it. It looked and smelled like any mushroom that one would eat, though she knew that some were poisonous. The herbalism to discern which, however, was another hole in her seer's education.

She nibbled at the edge of the cap, not hungry though she knew that she should be. There was some grit in her teeth as she chewed. Then her hunger spiked as if out of nowhere, as if she had not vomited just moments before. She devoured the mushroom, then four more. They were large, with caps as wide as her face. Soon, her stomach was full. The mushrooms had little water, so she was now very thirsty.

One thing at a time, she thought.

Nothing guided them. She did not feel the presence of the spirit that they had seen. Martin, however, still seemed intent, seeking. He watched every direction at once and even turned several times to walk backwards, looking behind them. He did not seem fearful that they would fall under attack, but was rather looking for the spirit. Lil wondered who it had been, though she had her guesses. Tuan had said nothing of Martin's family or friends.

The toy horse, the home—Martin had married, to be sure. He had been a father. But this was odd for a Templar, even in these times.

The natural shape of the walls gave way to a hewn tunnel. A chipped mosaic passed under their feet. Roman—dogs and soldiers, women lounging and eating grapes. Decorations began to appear at intervals on the walls, between grooved columns with busy caps of stone leaves and fronds. Then, Martin stopped and Lil, who had been looking at the mosaic, looked up and gasped. In front of them, the face of a temple sat at the top of a short flight of steps. Statues of Roman soldiers with bulging muscles and spears, eyes with no pupils, stood at either side of the steps, guarding the darkness that lay behind four heavy columns. Above the columns, the wild face of the Green Man, the spirit of the ancients, cast an angry gaze upon those who would climb the stairs.

A small Templar cross in peeling red paint marked the riser of one of the middle steps.

This was a Templar place, but it had been much more before that. Lil knew that the gods of Rome mingled with others at the fringes of the empire. Hybrids of Roman and far older rituals had formed. Cults. She also knew that much of what the church practiced in Rome had risen from these strange philosophies.

They climbed the steps, passing between the columns and entering a round chamber cut into a giant vein of chalk. The floor was a pristine and intricate mosaic of interlocking ropes and gushing spouts of water.

Martin walked the edge of this chamber as if taking a strategic approach to a dangerous clearing. As he walked, he uncovered niches in the wall. In these, Lil saw marble statues. They were not statues of men and women in the typical Roman style. The forms were grotesque beasts. She had never seen creatures such as these, but had heard tales. Odd, she thought, for here were the demons of the Yew's cohorts crafted in marble ages ago. There was the eye that allegedly turned all in its gaze to stone. Then, she saw the demon with tentacles writhing from its mouth, its four clawed hands reaching forward and its bulbous eyes staring. Others, too odd and inhuman to fully decipher, stared from their dark alcoves. Some were lycanthropes, blended beasts. One was a cross between a man and a wolf, and bore some resemblance to the creature that the Champion had killed. Lil wondered at the connection between the Yew's demons and the Templars. Martin was the walking embodiment of both.

Martin lingered on one statue. It was like a wild man, a human form, wearing a loincloth and carrying a scythe. He studied it with some care.

Opposite the entrance, they arrived at an altar. The slab had depressions and grooves that Lil guessed were meant to capture and channel the blood of sacrifice. Behind the altar, a short cut in the wall led into a dark tunnel. They would have to crawl. Above, on the chalk, a drawing—it was out of place, in a different style. Lil squinted at it.

It was a crude sketch in charcoal.

A crowned man, a king or prince, gripped the head of a bearded man. Below that, Latin scrawled in quick hand: "Triumphant over the gates of death and hell, the just shall live amid the starry sphere."

Toothless leaned against the altar, staring at the words. Lil concentrated. She knew the verse. She knew it from Tuan. She had seen it even more recently, reading lives of saints in Peter's library.

"This is what Tuan wanted us to see," she said.

Martin turned to her, confusion in his eyes.

"I know this," she said. "This symbol, these words. These are both from…"

She tried to salvage the memory. There was a saint. A king holding a severed head. It came to her, then. She found it like finding a ring lost in a heap of clothes in a chest.

"Cuthbert," she said. "Saint Cuthbert. The head belonged to a foreigner. An invader. That is Cuthbert's crest."

Martin shrugged.

"Those are his last words," she continued, undeterred. "Don't you see?"

The Templar shook his head.

"Saint Cuthbert of Lindisfarne."

Lindisfarne, on the coast of Britain. It was one of the seats of the masters. Iona, Mont Saint Michel, many others. And Lindisfarne.

This was the message, then. Deliver Martin to Lindisfarne. Deliver him to the grandmasters so that they might divine his role in the end of the Yew. The demons, the room, ciphers in manuscripts, Tuan's knowledge of all that would transpire—a long, unbroken line of hidden history had brought them all to this point.

She did not want to be responsible for breaking it now. She would play her small part, as everyone did, whether they knew it or not. She would help to turn the page.

Lil took the torch from Martin, who was not expecting her to move so quickly. She ducked, crawling into the tunnel. Martin followed. The tunnel wavered between a natural chute and hewn corridor, braced with block and rotting timbers. At no point, though, could she stand. They crawled for a very long time. Thirst began to slow her. Finally, the tunnel opened to a dark emptiness. She had to fall several yards to land on a pebbly floor.

She could see nothing, but she could hear lapping water.

Without looking back, she ran toward the sound. Martin stayed close behind her. She felt the water before she saw it, as her shoes sank deep into loose stones. Soon, she was ankle deep in cold, clear water. She handed the torch to Martin and scooped the water into her mouth again and again. It was sweet and clean. She could not stop drinking.

Martin gripped her shoulder. She rose. He held the torch high, casting light about them. He pointed. She stood on the edge of an underground lake. Not far, a stake rose from the black surface. A rope reached from this pole to the prow of a boat, most of which was lost in darkness. The rope was taut. A current pulled.

Martin sloshed toward the boat. The torch soon revealed the full vessel. It was a small open craft with a single flat sail and a jib, and was meant to carry perhaps a half dozen passengers. He jumped aboard and lowered his hand for Lil. There were sacks stuffed into spaces in the fore and aft. Lil opened these and found dried meat and fish, torches, and full waterskins.

The current coursed around the craft. She pointed at the sail.

"Look," she said.

The red Templar's cross rippled across the face of the cloth.

Wind and current.

Martin pulled a loose end of the rope and the knot unraveled. The boat set off through the dark, its oars dragging. Martin lifted them from the water. The boat must have gained speed for that, but it was impossible to tell.

Martin dug a tinder box from the packs and lit a torch. It burned bright, widening their view. Lil saw that they drifted between hulking shapes. Stones, she thought, until they came so close to one that she could touch it.

They were ships. The cavern was full of ships, silent and tied fast, waiting. The bow of one came into view. It was not ancient, or the clime of the cave had preserved it. The wood was strong and smooth. She spied its name.

Sophia.

Others—*Baphomet, Sangreal.*

These were Templar names, Templar ships.

Martin was wide-eyed though exhausted, moving his gaze from one ship to the other as he lay in the boat. Lil wondered what thoughts might be crossing his mind. For the first time, she worried about him. He looked deader than he had at any point in the past two days. Any live person twitched or shifted, breathed. But for his eyes, he was limp and still. He was like the ships, empty and silent. Now, she felt sorry for him. She knew that she was hard and self-centered. She knew that she was best when she had nothing and no one to care for but herself. In the past weeks, she had worked a mission that Tuan had described in such terms that Lil felt the weight of the world upon her shoulders. She had taken it seriously, though had spent much of the time mystified as to how to proceed. Yet, she had completed the task. She would take the news of the Yew's turn north to the grandmasters at Lindisfarne. Martin would be key to their strategy.

But Martin was fading right in front of her. He had been a powerful being and an expert warrior. But he had lost a home and, she guessed, a family.

Yes, she realized. She was worried about him.

The boat drifted between the ships, as if those large vessels were arrayed in reception, in salute, their prows pointing at one another over the path of the small boat.

She and Martin would be tied together a bit longer, though she did not mind. She chided herself for ever thinking that she might destroy him, and regretted trying to escape.

"There is food in the packs," she said. "Water. Do you need anything?"

She knew the answer, but needed to do something. Martin turned his gaze to her and shook his head.

"Why don't you sleep?" she asked.

He did nothing but look back at her. His eyelids descended.

So he did sleep. Or so it seemed. She wondered if instead she were witnessing his death. His final death. Calm, quiet, and still. In sleep, perhaps, he found true death. Peace, if only for the moment.

She looked at him once more. She felt tenderness. It was not love. It was sympathy. Protection. It was almost maternal.

Lil remembered a day in her deep childhood, before she understood visions were separate from dreams, before she knew that she was different, before even anyone had caused her to recognize her deformity. She had not yet begun her string of residencies in countless monasteries, sometimes as student, sometimes as servant, sometimes as one to be abused.

Lil was with her mother. They sat in a rowboat, drifting down a sun-dappled stream. The ride was gentle and quiet, calming. It was, of course, very different from this ride through the cavern. This, however, was the closest she had ever been to that moment.

She dropped her fingertips into the water and felt it cool around her nails. She felt selfconscious for doing it, and was thankful that Martin's eyes were closed. The water was cold, invigorating if a bit slimy for all of the minerals that dripped from the cavern's ceiling. Still, the sensation was similar to that childhood moment when, drifting in a boat with her mother, she touched the surface of that long-gone stream.

Breaking the surface. It was like having a vision, or feeling certain feelings. The sympathy she felt for Martin, for example, was a foreign thing in this world. She was sure of it, and felt the tragedy of that fact. To just have that feeling in the world of the Champion, of insane priests—in a world that had Martin in it—was to invite something from another world.

There were hundreds of Templar ships. Lil could see nothing ahead, and knew that, were it not for the ships drifting by, she would have no sense of movement at all save for a gentle rocking back and forth, and the soft sound of water lapping against the hull.

She closed her eyes.

✠

The boat jolted. It had struck something. She opened her eyes, not sure if she were dreaming. Perhaps a vision. She was still in the boat. Martin was now standing, rigging the sail and pulling ropes. He worked the jib to catch the wind.

Sunlight floated on the surface of the water in an intricate web. It was brilliant. It hurt her eyes. They were outside. The sky was blue. She had not seen blue sky in months, but it was blue. Lil could hear waves crashing against stones. She imagined the spray on her face, but where they were, where the boat broke from the tunnel, was calm. She looked behind them. A large mouth of a cavern, somewhat hidden behind outcrops, must have led back to the secret berth of the Templar fleet. On either side of their boat, long spits of rock formed the banks of a gentle stream into the sea.

But they had struck something. Martin was now scrambling to catch the wind, which blew away from France. She thought that she could see Britain far to the west. North along that coast would bring them to Lindisfarne. That was the plan.

She trusted that Martin knew what he was doing. He seemed skilled, though was somewhat clumsy managing the ropes and sails. But air filled the cloth. In his intense concentration, in his activity, he seemed to be gaining confidence. He seemed to be satisfied.

They were pointed in the right direction and moving. She could hope for little more. The sail was taut with wind, though the red cross worried her. It said quite a lot to pirates and brigands. She might have been safer beneath a simple white sail.

The hull shuddered again, this time with a splitting, splintery noise. All was not well. She realized another possibility.

They were not hitting something.

Something was hitting them.

Lil looked at Martin, who was staring at the water. He did all that he could to hold the sail in place. He focused his gaze on a single point. Lil turned to see, as well.

They were breaking into the sea. The water was still calm, though it began to roll with deeper, darker swells. The wind grew, pushing the craft harder toward Britain.

Something slid beneath the water.

As a child in that boat with her mother, she had seen turtles. She had seen fish and slippery weeds. This creature had skin closer to a sea lion's, gray-brown and blotched. A whale, perhaps. It was enormous. The skin, however, was not smooth. It was studded with barnacles and spikes, hard ridges. It left an oily slick behind it. It had no shape, or it turned in such a way as to hide its shape. It looked to her to be a giant, amorphous thing. No whale. Appendages, horns, blades of shell-like bone—it seemed to be an accretion of the junk of death that sank to the bottom of the ocean. It smelled of salt and fish funk rotting in a low sunny tide.

She remembered. The Champion had spoken of sea monsters.

The Yew had summoned sea monsters to complete the circle about Mont Saint Michel. That was far to the south, but perhaps the Yew sought Martin. She looked at the Templar, who was now looking at her. He pointed at the packs.

Lil, nearly thrown out of the boat by another jolt, rummaged through the sacks for something, anything that might be a weapon. Meanwhile, Martin struggled with the jib and the ropes to keep the boat pointed at Britain. His energy was low. He fumbled with the ropes as if his joints were freezing. He stared, frustrated that he could not divine a way to tie a knot to hold it all fast.

There was nothing useful in the packs.

Martin pointed then at one of the oars. She jumped to it, but it was bolted fast beneath an iron clasp.

The beast broke the surface in front of them, its jagged hull-splitting edges making tiny whirlpools and frothy wakes as it turned. Their boat would not last long against its attacks. The monster slid about their side. They crossed its path. The monster reversed its course and came straight at them. She tried to hit it with the oar, but missed. It slammed again into the boat. The hull held.

The boat sped forward with a gust, gaining such speed that it left a deep wake. The breeze pushed Lil's hood from her head. Relief washed over her. She turned. Martin stood, triumphant beneath the full sail.

The demon was behind them. A gurgling roar lifted in giant bubbles from beneath the surface, well away from where the bony fins broke into the air. Either the beast was huge, or another had joined it. Whip-like tentacles shot from the sea, each covered with a thousand sawtooth-edged maws that were snapping at the air. The beast seemed to struggle to keep up with the Templar craft. Now that it had the wind, the boat glided through the water. Lil imagined it to be the same forceful wind that carried souls to the land of the dead.

She was wrong. The demon was gaining on them. It seemed to gather its energy into fits of movement, during which it closed the gap by a few yards and then held that distance, waiting to leap forward again. Soon, its tentacles would be within reach.

Martin braced his foot against the side of the boat and pulled with both hands at one of the oars. He strained so hard that Lil wondered if he would pull his arms right out of their sockets. But the iron clasp gave way first, and he nearly fell backwards into the cold sea. Gripping the oar in his hands, he stood and broke the thing over his left thigh. He discarded the flat of the oar and held the staff in his hands. It had a sharp point. He weighed it, tossed it up and gripped it over his shoulder.

A spear.

How would any but a warrior make such a thing work?

On the demon's next advance, Martin threw the weapon. The spear wobbled at first, then settled into a simple, smooth arc. It embedded itself into the monster's flesh. The demon lost much of its progress, then. Its tentacles, rather than whipping at the boat, gripped the staff that now protruded from its hide. The tentacles pulled the spear free. A milky, oily ichor gushed from the hole. The beast submerged.

Lil's joy, their victory, was short-lived.

Another creature surfaced on the port side. It came with such speed that Lil and Martin had little time to react. It smashed into the side of the boat. The hull continued to hold, but the force of the blow pushed the craft from its course. The sail deflated. Martin twisted the jib but could not find the wind.

The creature was on their starboard side, stopping, reversing, coming back at them. The sail filled, then. The craft shot forward, leaving the creature to cross their wake.

Martin tried each of the other oars, then. They would not budge, or he did not have the strength. He pulled at a bench, at the rails, at any piece of the boat that looked as if it might fly or break into a point. Nothing moved.

But the craft, now revived in the wind, carried them far ahead of the sea demon. The creature did not relent. It pursued, but could not advance or reach them with its tentacles.

Lil hoped, even prayed, that the wind would stay strong.

Chapter XIV

✠

Hours passed. Their situation remained the same, though the coast of Britain was growing larger as it rose from the gray sea. Britain was a beautiful thing, green and brown behind thin scraps of low misty cloud, the only clouds in the sky. The water was calm, though rose in tiny waves that split before the fast Templar craft, or died in white spray beneath the strong, steady wind. This stinging mist had soaked Lil's robes and reddened her cheeks. She tightened her hood with a fistful of its cloth below her chin. She shivered. Her teeth chattered. She wanted to lie on the floor, but water had collected there, black with the ashen mud of their trek through France. And she did not want to lose sight of Britain ahead and the monster behind.

Lil worried that the wind would die.

The demon was still visible, coursing at a steady speed behind them. Lil could almost hear the roar of the water parting about its mass.

Their boat would drift to a stop, or spin in a still, glassy channel. The monster would rush forward. Lil turned from the beast and planned to keep her eyes on the coast so that she would not know when to expect the final blow.

No, she thought. She would dare to hope.

She turned to considering how they would disembark. A dangerous moment—they would beach some yards from dry ground. They would have to wade into shore. The monster would be able to reach them with its tentacles. A horrible thought struck her, then. Perhaps it could pursue them on land. She imagined it with legs, or slithering on a roughened, calloused belly. If it were faster on land, it would be content now to remain a fixed distance behind them, conserving its energy for the real pursuit.

She could not mull over that, she realized. The fear made all of their efforts pointless. Lil passed a quick glance back to the monster. Had it lagged a bit? Was it now even further behind? She looked at Martin, who watched the coast, then returned to the question of the beach.

As soon as the boat stopped, she decided, she would jump from the bow, leaping as far as she could, and sprint. If the monster could pursue her on land, and there were no hope, then it would not matter if she expended all of her energy sloshing through the surf onto the beach. She would leave her robes behind, trust her warmth to the thin, worn shirt and pants she wore beneath, and hope that they might build a fire or find shelter and clothes.

This assumed a successful transit, of course. It assumed that the monster would not surge ahead and smash the boat, or carry it below with its tentacles. She worried that she tempted fate with such hope.

As she thought it, fate obliged.

The sail, taut and full to that moment, rippled just once. Martin turned toward it, concern in his eyes. The sail filled, and all was well for one second. Then, more ripples, large ones that began at the top of the mast and rolled to the jib, growing like ocean swells.

And then, without any more ceremony, the sail went limp.

Lil held her breath, as if inhaling would steal the wind. She looked back at the demon. It had paused, considering, perhaps unwilling to believe its good fortune.

Panic was rising in her gut. It halted her shivering, set her teeth grinding instead of chattering. It shot into her limbs, into her hands which went into such tight fists that her fingernails threatened to puncture her palms.

"What do we do?" she yelled.

The beast disappeared. It submerged. The water made a curious, almost comic plopping sound.

Lil looked at Martin, who stared at the water. For a long moment, nothing happened. Martin stayed still, holding the jib but not moving it. Was the beast gone? Had it retreated at the very moment of its victory? Lil looked back to the shore. It was close, but too far to swim. And, certainly, the cold would kill her. With no other options, however, she could still jump.

But the beast was in the water. Somewhere.

The sun was high in the cloudless sky. She felt a breeze on her cheek, though it was a nuisance, a tease. It barely moved the drops forming along the bottom of the jib, let alone the sail.

A thump—the sea monster brushed against the hull, as if trying to fix the boat's location. Lil yelped and braced herself by gripping the railing. The demon hit them again, harder. Lil looked at Martin, expecting him to have some solution. He was the warrior, after all. He had saved her several times, had caught and roasted meat for her. He had killed for her. He was faster than a warhorse, and had killed a sea beast with a spear made from an oar. This was not a fitting end for him.

A tentacle shot from the water, wrapping itself around the mast. Its slick, wrinkled skin drew taut as the demon pulled. The boat tipped. Lil strained to hold the railing. Water spilled into the craft. Martin pounded on the fleshy rope. It unwound, dented and bruised, and retreated. It was broken, flopping.

The boat leaned back to its center, several more inches of water now sloshing around Lil's ankles. The hull creaked, as if the boat would fall apart.

A second tentacle rose. It paused before whipping toward them, wrapping around Martin's waist. He pushed at it, as if pushing down pants. It held, even tightened. He looked at her, his eyes wide. Fear. She saw it. She squinted, curious.

Martin launched away from her. The beast held him above the water, his arms and legs outstretched. Lil rushed across the boat. He was dozens of yards away, but she hoped beyond hope that she might reach him.

The monster held him for a moment above the surface. Then, he was gone. The beast had pulled him into the sea. There was nothing but growing rings of ripples where he had submerged.

The sea calmed. The boat rocked in a lazy wave. The breeze stiffened, punching at the sail. Lil heard a sea bird. She saw it hanging above, wings wide, making little progress toward France against a wind so high that it did her little good.

She looked back to the water.

Nothing.

Lil sat and shivered, hugging herself in the cold.

She thought of crying, but the tears would not come.

She wondered what to do. She might continue to Lindisfarne, hoping that her story alone would be all that the Templars would need. She doubted that. She could try to save him, but had no idea how.

Was he gone? She was not convinced. Or, rather, the possibility of being alone was impossible for her to fathom. So many times in her life, under assault, she had wished to be alone. Now, for perhaps the first time, she was. Alone, adrift.

"Not real," she said.

A vision, or a dream—it must have been. She was alone, and she was never alone. This was not real. She would wake and Martin would be there, working the sail as they exited the tunnel.

Lil closed her eyes so hard that spiraling patterns and blotches of light filled her head.

The boat shook. A sucking noise sounded against the bottom of the hull. The sail rippled with a wild vibration. The boat began to spin. It went faster and faster. Lil braced her feet against the mast and pressed her back to the hull.

She opened her eyes.

The boat spun and dipped, its aft pointing into a whirling, widening funnel.

A whirlpool.

She clenched her jaw.

The boat fell upon its side. She watched as the mast broke and the water took the hull. She had no feeling of sliding into the water.

She screamed, then heard and saw nothing.

✠

She was submerged from her feet up through her hips. She gripped something in her fist. Wet pebbles. A pressure built in her chest and shot into her mouth. Lil coughed. A stream of salty warm water spewed from her.

A beach. The air was cold.

She lifted herself onto her elbows. She looked left and right. Black seaweed, pebbles, scraps of purple and ivory shells. Behind her, the surf broke and roared into giant waves that exploded in foam and mist. In front of her, the land rose in rugged green and gray folds from the beach.

But the land was alive. Grasses and trees.

Lil coughed again, this time producing only a mist.

Britain or France?

Then she remembered.

Martin.

She rose to all fours, looking again up and down the beach for him. Some wreckage lay nearby, but it looked old and weathered, half-buried. Perhaps she had been on the beach for years, and that mess of driftwood and rope was the Templar craft.

Crashing, rhythmic beats. She turned toward them, to her left. Four horses splashed through the shallow edge of the surf. She turned to her right, again. The wreckage—she might hide there.

She began to crawl, her balance reeling. Her lungs wanted air, but deep breaths caused pain to flare in her chest.

They were upon her before she made any progress at all. The horses surrounded her. She looked at the four armored riders. She could not see much, for harsh white sunlight framed them. It forced her to squint.

One of them spoke.

"Leave your helmets on," he said. "She may have the plague."

"I do not get the plague," she mumbled, certain that it made no sound. She went to say it again, louder, but broke instead into a fit of coughing.

The lead warrior shouted.

"What is your name?"

He waited for her coughing to subside, but the fit had left her hot and exhausted. She turned to face him. Water frothed about the horse's hoofs. The animal had a massive brown head with a white stripe down its nose. It blocked her view. She tried to look around the beast's nose, its simple, kind eyes. It stamped and shifted.

The rider wore a helmet, a white surcoat.

A red cross.

Templars.

She looked from one to the other. Bright armor. Pure, white cloth. Gleaming blades drawn, but now retreating from this girl who was no threat at all. Her hood was down. They saw her deformity.

"What is your name?" the soldier asked again.

She tried to speak but could not. Her name stopped short of the root of her tongue, lodged in the aching, swollen knot that was her throat. The Templars seemed annoyed. She thought that she heard sighs from beneath their helmets.

"There was another in your boat. Where is he?"

She planted her knees in the stones of the beach and rose to a kneeling position. Lil pulled the seaweed from her hair and looked down at her robes, wondering if she could wring out the water. She hugged her shoulders and planted her chin into her chest.

"She is cold," said another.

"What is your name?" their leader asked again.

"Lil," she said, but it was a whisper. She took a deep breath and forced the word through the blooming pain in her lungs. "Lil."

"Where is your companion?" the leader asked.

She did not know where to start. She could answer, of course, that a sea monster had taken him into the ocean. But there seemed to be some context necessary to understanding that. She tried to start at the beginning, but did not have the voice to pull it off. She managed only a single word, the first word in the story that had brought her from sweeping an abbot's cell to kneeling in the pebbles on a beach in Britain.

"Tuan…"

The single name, the name of a Templar master, had an effect. The leader dropped from his horse, walked through the frothy water and, motioning to another, grunted an order for a blanket. The subordinate obliged, and the leader draped the thick wool thing over her shoulders. She felt warmer, though her teeth chattered. The sound echoed, boomed, in her head.

"I am Stephen," the Templar said, removing his helmet. His light hair was plastered with sweat or sea water. He looked at her with ocean blue eyes. "We will take you to safety."

✠

The blue sky soon retreated behind gray clouds and mist. Lil wondered if the weather followed her. She was the focus, the goddess of torment and destruction. Was that why she did not get the plague, so that she could witness it all? She chided herself for thinking, even for a moment, that it all revolved around her. Indeed, she had been unable to complete even a single task, the only mission anyone had ever given her.

The one mission of her life was a failure. One could not be more insignificant in such a time that drew clear lines between heroes, traitors, and victims, even if all met the same end.

The Templars afforded her respect, or at least pretended to. Or, they were afraid of Tuan. The leader must have seen the boat. He may have seen Martin, perhaps closely enough to know that he was one of the Yew's. Respect, then, might not have been the right way to describe their willingness to escort her. Perhaps it was wariness, or curiosity.

Lil sat behind another Templar on a muscular brown horse. Her rump bounced in the back of the saddle. She had to shift her weight to keep the pain in her back and legs at bay.

They went for several hours in silence. Whenever she spoke, the knight driving their horse would raise his hand and, on more than one occasion, actually ordered, "Silence." He had a young voice. Perhaps he was not many years older than she. There was a time, she knew, when only nobles could wear the surcoat and mantle of the Templars, a time when the organization was strict, the monastic rule solid. Now, the Templars struggled to preserve their order. Those who might have been squires or, at best, sergeants in the ranks of the order were now knights. They were immature and ill-prepared. The order itself had split into factions along old disagreements and ethnic boundaries. There were now many masters, all of different ideologies, and a whole council of grandmasters rather than a single head of the order.

One led them all, a French knight who, some said, had proof of direct descent from Merovingian blood, but he had but a fraction of the power he and others of his office had once wielded. Decentralized, all but abandoned by their pope, the order took what refuge it could in defensible cathedrals and monasteries. Indeed, the whole faith had fallen. Each church was a religion unto itself, so that Father Peter had as much sway as the pope. Tuan had groaned on the state of affairs, and the youth who wore a knight's mantle in front of her exemplified all of those complaints.

This knight, like Lil, grew weary of the trip. At a certain point, a point at which Lil thought a meal was long overdue, the young knight's head began to bob and his body leaned. He was falling asleep. Lil was frustrated and scared, for she knew that horses were not always predictable beasts. A darting animal, a clap of thunder, and the horse would buck them both onto the rocky beach. She needed the knight to remain in control. He could do worse, she guessed. He could reach into his pack and wolf down a snack without offering her anything. Heaven help him, she thought to herself, if he woke only to do that. Still, what honorable knight of the order would fall asleep in his saddle? Tuan would have asked the same question, and ordered the correction, with but a gaze, a sharp look from his small eyes.

No, she realized, she was not important. Her new guardians found it interesting that she knew Tuan's name. They took her north as a curiosity. More proper, perhaps—she was their captive, rather than their charge. Perhaps they would reunite her with Tuan, or with others whose names she had forgotten but who would remember her and her deformity. Unless that, too, was assuming too much. Why remember her? She had news. The Yew turned north. Certainly, though, they knew that by now.

It was not about her at all.

And so, the November rain came because it was November. It did not come because of her. Perhaps the Yew was not far behind, and it would be snow and ash and, then, the end of all of this. She could change nothing, do nothing. Better to still be sweeping a humble abbot's cell. No doubt, that monastery was destroyed, its abbot dead or fleeing to a hermitage where the desert fathers had invented his creed and the monastic rule in the shadow of great stone pyramids. No doubt, Lil would have been dead by now had Tuan not rescued her, but dead was not such a bad thing to be these days.

They traveled north. The beach became rugged, the pebbles giving way to stone slabs. Ahead, cliffs rose against the party. The Templars knew this place, their horses walking a well worn path. They turned from the beach. The horses picked their way up a rocky slide, into a thick wood. It was not at all like the dead forests of France. Though eerie in its own right, it was refreshing. Its energy was wild, alive. She inhaled, listening to raindrops smack against trunks. The trees were yews and other evergreens. It was not as cold here as she thought it should be, though she was thankful for the blanket that the leader had given her.

Where was Martin? She realized that she had not considered him since leaving the beach. She wondered why she had forgotten him. Now, his absence was a sudden and painful void in her gut. Leaving the beach, she felt as if she were leaving him. If he were to jump from the trees now, would he carry her away from these knights? Would he kill them, or join them? Would they destroy him, even if they saw the faded cross on his surcoat, or the one on his shredded mantle?

She half expected one of these knights to remove his helmet and reveal that he was Martin, alive, his jaw restored. She would perhaps need a moment to recognize him, but she was sure that she would. She knew a look in his eyes, dry and deflated as they were, that was curious and impatient, hardly what a Templar master like Tuan would have tolerated. She wondered, then, how good of a Templar Martin had actually been. To be a good warrior monk was to be more than a good warrior. It was a severe life.

Lil sighed. She smelled something burning, and with it a sulfur tinge of the wasteland. She shivered, thinking that the Yew was near to crossing the channel. Or, perhaps it already had. The others did not react at all. She realized that she could wish the smell away. It was in her imagination, then. It weaved through the fresh smells of the forest on the edge of winter. She heard the crack of the Earth's stone, the pop of fires, blades sliding from scabbards, the growls and calls of animals twisted by the black magic of that tree. These were memories, things of vision that danced through the reality in front of her.

A vision was coming. She let it, though she feared losing control and falling from the horse.

She felt cold water all about her and heard its rushing. It covered her, clouding her eyes. It tossed her, its gurgling currents chaotic and rough.

She saw Martin. He slammed his fists through the water into the great brown shape of the monster. It squeezed with its tentacles, breaking him. Still, it relented. He had beaten it. It let him free to drift, his limbs loose in the water with the other dead things of the sea. The foam, the shells, the bones of fish and sunken ships—Martin landed like Lil as so much flotsam. But the water wound through coastal cliffs, carrying him inland. Darkness fell.

Skulls with horns, things deformed, watched with empty, airy gazes. They cried like children—inconsolable, breathless. They were a chorus of bitter sadness, of world wrenching disappointment and pain.

The water receded. The crying went with it. Cold cavern air filled the void. She heard distant dripping against stone, and the whistling rush of subterranean winds.

The horse tripped. The knight woke. Lil gripped his shoulders to steady herself. Their path now hugged the slope of a gentle hill, which rose to their right but was a cliff on their left. She peered down the drop, into a dimple in the land. Far below, a pool glimmered in the white sunlight. She shivered, the memory of the cold water of her vision still receding from her skin and muscles.

The young knight leaned again, so dangerously that she feared that he would fall. She tapped his shoulder, but it did not rouse him. She shook him. When that had no effect, she reached around his front and tried to set him straight. Her hands slipped. Wet and warm.

Blood.

Lil yelped. The young knight twisted, revealing a crossbow bolt protruding from his neck. Stephen turned. All that she could think was that the stub arrow was a fine thing, even an expert specimen, with pure white feathers cut into a straight shaft. She let him fall from the saddle.

Men in gleaming chain beneath solid blue surcoats descended the slope to her right. They moved at a steady, confident pace, their swords drawn. Stephen yelled, pointing his own blade at them as if his men would or even could charge through the trees to meet them. Instead, however, Stephen spurred his horse into a trot. The two others followed. Lil's horse tried but was slow, dragging the dead Templar by a stirrup.

Attackers appeared on the road ahead, readying crossbows. Stephen's horse reared. The first of the ambush stepped from the slope onto the road and began to hack at one of the horse's legs. One of the Templars fell.

The attackers were swarming about her horse now. One thrust his sword into the dragging Templar. He was already dead. Then, the brown horse bucked, kicking and thrashing. Lil tried to hold on, not sure if it mattered what happened to her now. The horse, flailing, tossed her from its back. She had some sense of flying, rising from the melee. Like a rising ghost, she saw a moment of the battle unfold. Stephen rode forward, his blade held high, as crossbow bolts raked through the horses.

Then branches whipped at her back. Fragrant needles closed over her eyes and filled her mouth. Her head slammed into a thick limb.

Chapter XV

She woke staring into a dead man's eyes. Lil recoiled, then braced against the pain that exploded in her head and back. She moved her limbs, then, and turned her head.

She lay in two feet of icy water, her head propped against a fallen tree, lucky that she had not drowned or frozen to death. The dead man was a fresh corpse, one of the attackers. His throat was slit, a bloodless white gash. She wondered if he would rise, a British Martin, and carry her into the midlands.

It was not quite night, though the heaviness of day's retreat was gathering in the air. Lil knelt, turned away from the corpse, and looked toward the sky. She was in a bowl, a round valley full of water. It was the pool she had seen from the road. She guessed she had fallen down the closest slope, but she could not be sure. Peering up, she did not see the road, but fog was obscuring the slope above, thickening as she watched.

Salt filled her mouth. She thought it was blood, but realized that it was water. This was a tidal pool with a fine, slimy silt beneath the black surface. It smelled like spoiled eggs. Nothing grew here. Looking, though, she noticed rotting posts arranged in two lines. A walkway had gone over this place, perhaps eons before. The posts rose several feet above the pool's surface.

The heaviness in the air—it was not just the coming night. Some other feeling tingled in her cheeks. The pain she felt masked the deeper sense she had of this place. It was a sacred place, perhaps a sacrificial place. In ancient times, priests of the tribes would have offered broken weapons, gold rings, perhaps even human sacrifices. Many such places had long since receded or evaporated, leaving squishy bogs or no trace at all. Not this one. Its spirit remained, though it had starved for a sacrifice for centuries.

Until now.

She looked at the corpse and, without knowing why, pushed his head and arm from the log, which was in fact a fallen post, and let him float. He went, following the line of the posts until his torn blue surcoat snagged on something below the surface.

Lil sloshed forward, stopping now and then to listen. She heard nothing from the slopes. The fog descended, forming a low ceiling of cloud mere inches above her head. The light was dying.

The posts led to the mouth of a cave. The ruins of the walkway ended in a wider arrangement of posts that may once have supported a platform. The water flowed right into the cave. The opening was circular. The stone looked like wet sand, with ripples and folds. She knew the sight of it, or rather felt the residue of her earlier vision. Her mind tugged at where the memory should have been but uncovered nothing, as if pulling a bucket from a well but finding only the severed end of the rope.

A faint light emanated from the cavern. It was greenish yellow, the color of the fireflies.

It did not matter what she did next, she guessed. She was already a sacrifice to this pool of some marshy ocean god. Perhaps she was already a spirit walking, and this was her tunnel to the land of the dead. Her vision of Martin had, instead, been a premonition of her own death. And that was Martin's mission—to lead her to his world. He was her reaper.

The light, she realized as she entered, came from nowhere in particular, or came from the surface of the walls itself. It drew outlines of the space around her. A tunnel led straight. Strange formations studded the walls. She knew them. She had seen them. They were skulls with horns. Deformed creatures. Yes, this was where she was to be entombed.

Lil reached, touching a skull.

It felt like stone. She realized, then, that they did not have horns. Rather, it was the accretion of centuries of dripping mineral. The form was indeed a skull, but the horn was a stalagmite. The flowing stone had encased the whole thing in a phosphorescent skin.

The skull was tiny. Others were just as small. These were children. The ancient priests had sacrificed children.

She gasped, putting her hand to her mouth as she heard her surprise echoing down the length of the tunnel multiple times. As she walked, her small steps grew to sound like roaring waterfalls. The smell, the salt and rot of the ocean, seemed equally multiplied. It was almost unbearable. Lil lifted the neck of her soaked robe to cover her mouth and nose. The robe, too, carried the stench.

The glowing intensified ahead as the floor rose out of the water. Each echoed sound, each breath, set an odd feeling flaring in the bulge on her scalp, as if the strange tissue there gathered the energy of this place. This was a gateway, a passage to the other world. Here was Lil, standing on the doorstep. Dead children and broken things had shed their forms and wandered in line down the tunnel to that distant island where spirits lived forever. They had passed long ago. She was not sure if the energy she felt was the residue of their passing or something else—a more recent death.

Martin.

She had also died. She believed it. Her short life was over, having passed all of its milestones of abuse and failure. Here was death, come to her without judgment, ready to welcome her.

Lil stepped from the water. Bones, bent swords, and broken broaches backed up against a sharp rise in the stone. They formed a gentle ramp to this higher landing, and the wider tunnel beyond.

Water streamed from her, falling back to the bracken behind her. The phosphorescence was bright enough to see details in the walls. Priests had carved swirls and other shapes into the stone. Lil felt these, finding that the touch of this world softened the light for a moment. She could trace her own shapes, then, on the slimy walls. Her glyphs disappeared within seconds.

She walked, the echoes of movement forming together into a rushing, mind-numbing hum in front of her. Her tough-soled shoes were gone, and she had to balance herself on the slick floor. The smell of the sea thinned, replaced by a cold and musty whiff that had a tinge of sulfur but was metallic and energized, like the smell before a thunderstorm.

Lil imagined this smell to be the last breaths of the world.

She was cold. The wet robe clung to her body. Goosebumps rose on her flesh. She could not help but shiver. This did not help her balance, and the sound of her chattering teeth became like countless tiny hammers on the walls. She closed her lips, which only confined the deafening sound to the inside of her skull, aggravating the tingling.

Still, the prospect of what lay ahead excited her. It was pleasant to think that she would join spirits. She would slough away her body, leave it to be entombed in the stone of the wall. Her deformity would disappear beneath the drip of stone. In the next world, she would not need her clairvoyance.

A cavern opened before her. It took the breath right out of her lungs. She remembered her father taking a hammer to a round stone, cracking it in two. She was very young. Inside, faceted crystals lined a round cavity. It was the only memory she had of him. She could not remember his face, but she remembered the sight of that rock twinkling in the sun. So, she stood in a cavern that was lit across its entire distance, as if the phosphorescence coming out of the tunnel were carried from one faceted crystal to the next, all the way around, all the way across. She was inside the stone that her father had presented to her. Her gasp, which still lingered, was the only sound. It had broken a heavy silence, beat it back into the other world as it bounced within the circle over and over.

Straight ahead, in the center of the room, a flat stone floated in the air. Something, a heap, lay upon it. She was not sure what it was, but it was part of the mystery. She exited the tunnel, and was surprised to step into water. She looked about her. The bottom of the cavern was a pool that reflected the ceiling. The water was warm, almost hot. The stone, then, was not floating in air. Rather, it was the top of a formation that broke the surface of the water. She noticed posts, then, much like the posts in the tidal pool. This walkway had stretched from the tunnel to that flat stone.

She beat back her disappointment. It was the way of the ancient priests who worshiped in this place. They manipulated the senses to make people believe. Still, was that not just as good as actual magic? Magic, like all perception, might be a thing of the mind. That, she felt, did not diminish it.

Lil grabbed the nearest post. It was soft. The ancient wood, the wood that had been touched by many who had already left for the isle of the dead, crumbled in her hands. As she went into deeper water, she relied on those posts to keep herself afloat. They were spaced to be just beyond her reach from one to the other. She was no swimmer. She had never learned, despite spending her earliest years near water. But Lil managed to thrust herself from one to the next, paddling in between. She crossed the space and reached the center of the cavern, the round stone platform. It was a natural formation that, she guessed, the ancients had chiseled away to make an altar, a doorway to death.

Her bare feet slid on the submerged side of the stone as she tried to climb. She managed to lift her elbows over the edge. Using these for leverage, she reached the surface. Lying on her back, looking at the ceiling, she thought that the crystals were like stars. They were thick in some parts, thinner in others. She followed them down with a gaze and saw the tunnel leading back to the living world. The water mirrored the tunnel's mouth, which therefore looked like two circles joined.

Lil turned to the heap beside her. She took a moment to realize what it was. When she did, she was surprised that she did not react. It was a body, its skin taut and clothes in tatters. It wore armor.

"Ancient." Though she whispered, it nonetheless echoed, dying as a hiss on the edges of the cavern.

This was, she guessed, the last to cross from this world at this place. The last, that was, before her.

Her gaze went up to the bony shoulder, which protruded from the mail. The body was wet. She saw the gray skin of the neck and, reaching the skull, drew a sharp breath. The sound of her gasp now echoed so loudly that she barely heard herself say the name.

"Martin."

Then, the tunnel roared.

✠

Water gushed from the tunnel. The tide, she guessed. Then she realized. This place would flood. She would have to go back against the current. Lil was not sure if it was the right thing to do or not, but did not have a choice.

How to move Martin?

Lil slipped from the stone into the water. She pulled at his arm, but could not move him. His armor—even if she could move him, he would sink straight to the bottom of the pool.

She scrambled back onto the stone and looked at him. Unbuckling his boots, she uncovered his feet. Then, lifting his surcoat, she loosened his chain leggings. They were stiff and rusted, but she managed to remove them. The surcoat came away, but she had more trouble with the mail hauberk. She managed to slip the armor over his head.

By then, however, the water had risen to the surface of the stone and was just beginning to creep above it. The water poured from the tunnel's entrance in a strong, steady stream that eddied about the tallest crystals and the posts.

She looked at Martin in the phosphorescence of the cave. In some parts, his skin looked almost supple and alive. In others, however, broken skin revealed scraps of muscle and white bone. His arms and legs showed every tendon, every striation of limp, deflated muscle, through his stretched skin. Ears, hair, the horrible wound—he was a lifeless corpse. Gone. This was the warrior who had danced and leaped in battle against the Champion, against the mad priest's army. He had raced across Brittany at inhuman speed. Fear, sadness, curiosity, and intelligence had all crossed his eyes. Now, he was so much wet leather and fiber. He was nothing more than refuse.

But it was the tide. It was the sea monster. It was the world itself that had left Martin at the doorway to final death. It was circumstance—not in the sense of chance, but a true architect of events—that had brought Lil to him.

She might finish her mission, then. She could say that she delivered him to Lindisfarne. No, she vowed, she would not die here. She would bring him into the sun.

Lil dipped back into the water. It was now cold. Her hands and feet went numb. Martin's body was drifting as the water climbed higher over the surface of the stone. She pulled him from post to post. This went well until she neared the mouth of the tunnel. The current was strong. It forced her away as she neared the tunnel. Martin drifted from her. She struggled to hold him, and was not sure how she would carry him through the current. She might return for his belt, but, looking back, she saw nothing of his clothes or even of the stone. The water had covered it all.

Lil sighed. This, then, was the end. Perhaps luck was with her, and she might wait out the tide. She would be unable to tread water for long. The cold would do her in. Might Martin keep her afloat? He already seemed to be sinking as water seeped into his tissues.

She began to struggle, her chin dipping below the surface as her legs dashed in tiring fits. The numbness left her wondering if she were moving at all. The current would take her corpse back to the world, or leave her with Martin in the cavern. Perhaps there were countless bones at the bottom of the pool, lodged in faceted formations or reduced after centuries to silt.

The water had risen several feet in the tunnel. The posts were gone. The smell of bracken blew from the cavern and the salt filled her mouth. The light from the tunnel was dimming as the water rose, darkening the cavern. Soon, she would lose sight of the tunnel's entrance altogether.

A noise—it echoed, but was a rhythmic sloshing at its source. Lil shouted. The noise stopped. She shouted again, and the sloshing began again, coming quicker. Orange light flickered in the tunnel. Fear rather than relief gripped Lil. Was it the blue-clad attackers come to finish her?

Two forms stood in the tunnel's entrance. They wore helmets, had swords drawn. She could not see their surcoats in the dark.

A rope came to her, then. She lashed it to Martin.

"Pull!" she yelled.

They did.

One of the men took Martin over his shoulder and, without protest or seemingly any thought, bounded back down the tunnel.

The rope flew back to her. She took it in her hands. A yank, and she was moving against the current, which pulled at her arms so strongly that she was afraid she would not be able to hold it. Within seconds, however, the soldier gripped her wrists and pulled her free. He took her onto his shoulder, like his companion had taken Martin, like Martin had once taken her, and fought the current. It had risen to his knees. He had to stop several times. The water continued to rise until it was up to his waist, halfway to the ceiling of the tunnel.

They were near the exit. The water flooded the bones, the skulls with their horns. The tiny skeletons of children were gone beneath the black surface. The water drowned the glyphs on the walls. It buried the broaches and the bent swords. It did not take Lil or Martin. It did not take these soldiers, who braved against it and brought them both into the waning light of day.

They were Templars.

Lil saw them once she was standing on dry ground, shivering. She saw them arrayed on the slope above her, hundreds of them, a full banner of white surcoats with red crosses, flowing mantles, helmets and drawn weapons. Two approached her.

Stephen.

The other was an older man with a gray-flecked beard and a nose that had been broken once. His eyes were dark. She knew this man, but could not remember his name.

"Lil," he said.

"Where is Martin?" she asked.

"That is Martin?" the older Templar said.

"Yes."

He blinked, then gathered his composure.

"He is safe," he said. "Though there is no life in him."

"I must see that he gets to Lindisfarne," she blurted. "Tuan has ordered it."

The older man sighed and squinted.

"Do you remember me, Lil?"

She closed her eyes for one moment to calm herself.

"I do," she said. "All but the name."

She did remember him. It was not a lie. He was a comrade of Tuan's. He and Tuan had fought in the Holy Land. Many of their comrades had died. They had dug on the Temple Mount and quartered in the ancient stables. Tuan said that they had seen and done things that none would believe.

"Cedric," he said. "At your service."

Cedric bowed, though it seemed silly in this place and time to offer such courtesy. But that was what a master Templar did. And these, she realized, were the Templars who would protect her from this point forward.

Hundreds of them, though Martin had done it all by himself.

"I must get to Lindisfarne," she said, speaking at Cedric's thinning hair. "I have news."

Cedric stood looking into the distance, surveying the slopes as if more attackers might arrive. Perhaps he was fighting anger. He clenched his jaw. She saw the muscles bulge. She had to admit that, no, she had not been as gracious as she should have been. His men, Stephen—they had saved her. Twice. They had vowed to protect her, to deliver her to Lindisfarne. She continued to act, however, as if they required explicit instruction. They knew Tuan, and perhaps Martin, better than she.

"What is your news?" Cedric asked.

"The Yew marches north. Martin is a key to its defeat. Tuan thought so. The Yew marches here, or will lay siege to Mont Saint Michel."

Stephen stepped forward then, and looked at Cedric. The old man closed his eyes and took a long, deep breath.

"What is it?" Lil asked.

Stephen turned to Lil.

"Mont Saint Michel?" he asked.

"Yes," Lil said.

Stephen swallowed hard.

Cedric, his eyes still closed, spoke loud and slow, as if addressing the tide or the clouds rather than Lil.

"Mont Saint Michel has already fallen."

Chapter XVI

The days blurred as the army marched north. An army—that was what it was. It seemed as disciplined as any she had seen. Still, Lil now understood some of the frustrations that Tuan had voiced about the Templar initiates. They were much of the army. They were green, their training disorganized. They were not devoted to the rule of the order. They completed the holy stations without, it seemed, wide attention or attendance.

The initiates were not idle. While some knelt in prayer to observe the offices, other busied themselves with carpentry, blacksmithing, or foraging. With many armies, there were more craftspeople, entertainers, and even whores than soldiers, so that an army was sometimes like a traveling circus. There were no such hangers-on here. Being a holy order, their appetite for entertainment was thin. The initiates had at least conquered their baser hungers.

Such a force, she realized, was rare in these times, even though it was small by most standards. The Templars had not gathered such a force in decades. They were all but shattered in the Holy Land. Tuan had spoken of it many times. The focus, the strategy of the order had changed by necessity. Small bands conducted nuisance raids, or single knights set out on the field of battle to do what damage they could, to inspire the rabble to fight against the Yew. Perhaps Martin had been meant to be such a Templar.

Day after day, they marched and camped. The routine of the army's work, the schedule of the holy orders, the weaving rhythms—boot steps in British dirt, then the pounding ring of the blacksmith's hammer—lulled her into losing a sense of time altogether.

She spent much of that time silent and sullen, staring at the ground, worried that she was squandering an opportunity to appreciate an unspoiled, unconquered country. When she was not riding, she slept in her tent or sat vigil over Martin. He lay alone in a tent, tended by hospitalier nuns who rubbed salves into his skin to keep it moist.

"Sometimes," one told Lil, "he moves. He jerks his arms. He hears soldiers outside of the tent speaking of battles and he thrashes. Other times, he is every bit a corpse."

Lil had not seen any such movement. She thought, on one of her vigils, that his forehead twitched, and then she wondered if it was just a trick of the flickering candle. They had shrouded him all the way up to his nose. Several more inches, and she would have believed him to be dead, shrouded for burial. The mere fact that his eyes, his wild black hair, were uncovered, reminded her that there may still be some life in him. She wanted to pull the shroud away from him, to look upon his wrinkled gray body. She wanted to think that he would be ready, at any moment, to rise and protect her.

She also began, however, to understand that this man who had already been gone was now gone again forever. The only protector she had ever known had left her to her own devices. She vowed to be more careful.

Trouble, Lil feared, had a way of finding her.

✛

She did not believe that she deserved their attention, the honor that the Templars paid her, as if she were a general or a noble. Indeed, they treated her with such respect, referring to her as a seer rather than a deformed witch, tending to her needs with food and drink, and respecting her tent at night. In fact, a guard stood outside the flap. He stood all night, as far as she could tell. After only a day, she went without covering her head.

The guard allowed only servants to enter. They brought great piles of food—choice cuts of meat, the last of the vegetables—on silver trays. She wondered where an army stored such trays and utensils as they traveled, and felt guilty about leaving any scraps. After the guard refused to take anything from her, she entreated the servants to tell the cooks that she would not require so much food upon such finery. It made no difference, and the food she left, she guessed, made for the best-fed hounds and pigs in the entire history of armies.

She did not often see Stephen, who rode with a cohort of knights who took orders from him, and in turn delivered these orders to sergeants. The handsome Templar with the fair hair visited her once at Martin's tent. The hospitalier nuns released their rosary beads, cleaned and stowed their implements, and then filed out of the tent. Stephen, alone and unarmored, looking like an aristocrat slumming in simple pauper's clothes, stood by her side. He prayed, or meditated, or gathered his thoughts for some time before speaking.

"This is Martin," he said.

"Did you know him?" Lil asked.

"I did not. I knew Tuan for a short time. I spent several days at Mont Saint Michel, having delivered an order from Lindisfarne. I served as Tuan's aid during that time, as I awaited his reply to carry back across the channel. I was happy to do so. He spoke of Martin so often and with such praise that I was surprised that I had not known him."

"What's happened to Tuan?" she asked.

Stephen shook his head.

"I do not know."

Lil, whether craving the connection or comforted by the kind tone, felt that she could speak about the demon that lay before them.

"Martin protected me," she said. "I thought of destroying him, but Tuan had given me a mission to find him, to bring him home. I didn't know what that meant, but I know now that it ends at Lindisfarne, whether this is all that he is or not."

Stephen nodded.

"We will see that you complete your mission, out of respect for Tuan and his affection for this man. And, his affection for you."

She looked at Martin. She thought again of his body, frail and gray, floating in the water of the cavern. She felt uncomfortable then, queasy and hot. She wanted to discuss something else.

"Who attacked us?" she asked.

"It is hard to say," Stephen replied. "The Yew has caused a stir even here in Britain. The king's sons, Richard and Henry the Younger, vie for control. King Henry was kind to us, so we are a target to both would-be usurpers. They march with no insignia, no coats of arms. It could have been either of them."

Lil sighed, then thought of Tuan again.

"Did he ever speak of me?"

"Who?"

"Tuan."

"No," Stephen said. "Not while I served him."

Lil bowed her head and closed her eyes. Of course he had not.

"But, I am told that he was not himself," Stephen continued. "He did not live up to his reputation. He was distracted, disorganized. I had assumed it was because of Martin, but that was not the whole of it. One of the captains told me that he was not the same since sending a girl to the south, a girl who had been important to him."

Stephen looked at her, kindness in his blue eyes.

"A seer," he said.

She was ashamed to note how handsome he was. The heat of that shame bloomed in her cheeks and ears.

"No matter what has happened to him," Stephen said. "Know that you were important to him."

She knew that he referred to Tuan, though it could have been Martin.

✠

When the army moved, she rode alongside Cedric, he on a brilliant white war horse that was the tallest animal she had ever seen. The soldiers had dressed a spry, mischievous pony for her. It had a curious shape—fat around its ribs, but with very thin legs. It was brown splotched with white. They apologized, but she was pleased to ride the animal.

Cedric spent these rides inquiring after her wellbeing, and even seeking her insights and advice on several occasions. There were many conversations about strategy and the quirks of the Yew's demons. Though there were some veterans in the ranks, none had been as close as she to the Yew's forces. Still, she and Peter had only seen them once, and from a far distance through smoke.

None except for Cedric, she would learn. She was trying to understand how Mont Saint Michel could have fallen. The best she could determine, it had only been several days since she had left Peter, since her vision of the Yew's turning north. Then, the enemy was still at the Loire. Then to now—it was not enough time for the slow-moving beast to bring a full siege to Mont Saint Michel on the northern edge of Brittany. And the fortress would have sustained even such siege for some time.

"The plague has changed," Cedric said. "Or, the foul tree has unleashed a second pest upon us."

"What do you mean?" she asked.

He closed his eyes, as he had at the tidal pool.

"Were you there?" she asked.

Cedric nodded, then opened his eyes.

"Foul beasts," he said. "Beasts like wolves. The sea creatures were at our backs, making escape all but impossible. The water churned with them. Then, the wolves..."

He trailed off, his dark eyes flitting, as if he were seeing the enemy all about him. Lil furrowed her brow, not sure what to make of this moment of weakness from a Templar master, a man who had trained to detach himself from his emotions.

"I think I know these creatures," she said. "There was one in Brittany. Like a wolfhound, but monstrous."

"Yes," he said. "Black fur, like the bristles of a brush. And the stench...the stench of the plague. I had only just arrived. I was expecting to rest and train, to send knights east against the Yew. I did not expect the wolves. They poured onto the beach. They did not care about the tide. They swam the channel. We killed hundreds of them, but it did not seem to matter. They kept coming. They were strong, but not impossible. It was their numbers, and..."

"And what?" she asked.

"Their bite," Cedric said, then swallowed hard.

The air had been still and cold. A breeze now flew low through the dead grass of the plain and whistled through bare branches. Cedric closed his wet eyes against it.

"We thought it was over," he said. "The wounded then went into fits and fevers. Thick black hair grew through their skin, starting at their shoulders. Their faces drew long. One morning, they were gone. They were all gone. We searched the island, but they were gone. They pounced during the morning service in the chapel. They were waiting for us. I and two others escaped. The sea demons did not even pursue us. I soon learned why, for one of us was afflicted."

He paused. The breeze punched at them.

"I killed him," he said.

"What of the other?" she asked.

"He went mad. He is in Lindisfarne, where he rambles in a cell. He shouts at night, howling like the wolves. I do not know what they will do with him."

Lil looked at her pony's mane as she considered this. The wolf the Champion had killed, then, had been the harbinger of a new detachment of the Yew's forces, and another legion that sustained itself by claiming its victims. Lycanthropes. Werewolves. Lil had heard of such in tales of rude peasants who worked the mountains above the Black Sea.

Cedric's past weeks, she realized, were as tumultuous as hers. She felt the need, then, to tell him all that she had seen and done. He interrupted the thought. He took a deep breath through his nose, stretched his shoulders, and, having regained his commanding posture and voice, spoke.

"You must have a story," he said. "But it is not yet time to tell it. The grandmasters at Lindisfarne will want to know all about you, and how you came to bring a soldier of the Yew to Britain."

She swallowed hard, then, and debated about the question she wanted to ask. She decided that there was no reason to refrain.

"Was Tuan still at Mont Saint Michel?"

Sadness fell over Cedric's face and sent a jolt down Lil's spine. Her stomach turned.

"No," he said. "But..."

"But what?"

"He had departed earlier, very soon after I arrived."

"So he is at Lindisfarne," she said.

Cedric shook his head.

"Iona," she continued.

"No," he said. "Master Tuan, my friend—he sent himself into White Martyrdom."

Lil was not sure how to take this news. She pictured Tuan climbing into a boat and letting the surf take him into the sea, to deposit him where it would. From Mont Saint Michel, the current might have taken him to Britain. Or, he was drifting in the open ocean, far to the west, where the ancient god of the sea drove a chariot pulled by white horses, leading spirits to the isle of the dead. No oars. No food. No water. Just himself in the boat—a leather currach by tradition—armored, wearing his sword. Did he leave with faith in her? Did he believe that she could complete the mission? Perhaps that is why he left. Or, he had given up. Surrendered. She would never know.

Lil felt tears in her eyes and could not remember the last time she had cried for sadness or pity. It was not just Tuan. She had spent a month or more at Mont Saint Michel. Certainly, the servants, the nuns, the children of the tradesmen—all of the people whom she had known but who now seemed so distant—were gone. She was certain that they were dead. Or worse, they stalked the countryside in another form.

"Hell is no place beneath the ground," Cedric said. "It is here and now."

This was the judgment.

"Where do we go from here?" she asked, thinking aloud.

Cedric turned to her. She felt some affection for him, then. She was not sure if it was his emotional reaction, or his ability to stifle such reactions, that led her to look on him as a protector.

"We take this army to Lindisfarne," he said. "We bring you and your dead one to the grandmasters. You tell them everything you can about how you came to be here. I believe that they will be most interested. From there, I do not know where you go. I cross the channel with this army, the largest army of Templars to take the field in some time. We will land, and march south to Mont Saint Michel or wherever the Black Yew takes root. We will fight in winter. We will fight in mountains or forests."

"How can you win?" she asked. She did not mean to insult him. She felt embarrassed, but Cedric reacted as if it were a legitimate question. He shrugged.

"You must understand," he said. "If we win, then we have secured something of a future for ourselves as an order, for the living, for the church. If we lose, then a new world order descends, a world without Templars, perhaps without the living. All will be as it should be. We do what we are meant to do."

He looked at her, then.

"You see," he said. "It is a kind of martyrdom. Just as Tuan set himself adrift, so do I, and Stephen, and these knights, though some do not have the training to understand. We apply our practice to reach an end that we do not yet see, and which we cannot understand. All practiced life is martyrdom. It is choiceless movement forward."

"Martin was one of yours," she said.

"I knew Martin. Martin is dead. The corpse that accompanies you is a different creature."

"I'm not so sure," she said.

"If you are right, then he would understand what I do."

✠

Lil had become so enmeshed in the schedule of bringing Martin to Lindisfarne, that she was somewhat shocked to reach the place. They were heading east along the coast. She had noted the turn, and knew that they must be getting close. She did not believe it when she saw it.

"That is Holy Island," Cedric said, pointing. "The grandmasters sit in Lindisfarne Priory. We may not be allowed across the causeway."

Lil could see nothing of the island's details through the mist. Holy Island was just a darker gray shape upon gray. There was nothing on the route to announce its importance, just a small fishing village. She remembered, then, that the army with which she marched was announcement enough.

They made camp near the dirt causeway leading to the island, and waited. Lil lost count of the days—days of continuing the routines without the marching, so that her vigils over Martin's body consumed most of the time. She had few conversations with Cedric or Stephen.

The hospitalier nuns were silent as they practiced their art over a body that did not respond. They no longer spoke of his thrashing, or reactions to conversations. Lil witnessed no movement at all. She wondered if this was just the natural end of the debilitation that she had observed as they traveled through France. He had diminished, it seemed, with each step. Or, this was the result of trauma that had come with his fight against the sea monster and the abuse of an angry tide. Or, it was something else altogether. This last possibility intrigued her. The idea inspired some kinship. She often felt that something else lived in her head, expelling visions as waste or some toxin into her body. She wondered if Martin was perhaps a similar kind of creature—a body, an insignificant thing, playing host to something greater that had now left him.

The ebb and flow of the tide added a new kind of schedule to the offices of prayer, to the routines of camp. The waves measured seconds, never ceasing. There was no other sound to the place at most times. In summer, she guessed, there were gulls. In another era, perhaps pilgrims or tradesmen gathered to cross the causeway. In this time, on the edge of winter, there were just the waves. When the waves were closer or farther, twice each day, she could determine the nearness of the offices, and whether or not the causeway would be accessible. She hoped, in the first days, to hear news whenever the causeway surfaced. The expectation faded.

The nuns followed their own routine. First this balm, then that. This prayer. Then that. And other things, over and over in a cycle that repeated itself through the night, through even the regular offices of prayer. They worked under a different rule.

Meals continued to come at the appointed times, but she was absent for most of those deliveries. She returned to her bed on one night to find seven meals in various stages of warmth and even decay lined around the inside of her tent. She asked the guard to have them removed. He would not enter the tent while she was there, but nodded. When she next returned, they were all gone and the tent had been sprayed with perfumed water. She wondered if the pigs and the hounds had gone hungry for two whole days.

Occasionally, rumors flowed through the camp. On one of these, men mustered, fearing a large scale attack by the blue-clad soldiers whom Cedric believed were Prince Richard's men. One had died in a small probing raid, leaving behind a seal of Henry the Younger. This, seeming too obvious, led Cedric to suspect Henry's brother. Lil did not care about the politics of any place, let alone a place so insignificant to her as Britain. She remembered Martin's map on the stone, crude lines that meant nothing at all, especially now. Did the Yew conceive of any boundaries but those presented by water or mountains? Did it consider different tribes and kingdoms? It had organization—cohorts and captains—but probably regarded the living as one big thing to be defeated, to be consumed.

On one day, the fog began to clear and Holy Island appeared. Lil could see monks and Templars moving about the place. The monks, especially, moved as if their deliberations mattered. They were like bees on a hive. She continued to watch, and noted a detachment of horses charging down the causeway. Six war horses came, their riders carrying long banners. She lost sight of the detachment as it wound through the camp, though the alarm was noticeable.

"Odo is here!" soldiers shouted. "The grandmaster is here!"

Even the nuns spoke of it, their whispers like steam from tea kettles on the edge of boiling.

"Odo meets with Cedric!"

"Odo is here."

"Grandmaster Odo wishes to see the girl."

"Odo...Odo...Odo."

The message evolved. Odo would visit Martin. He had met with Lil, though she had not left Martin's side. He would lead them against the Yew, which was now only a day's march south. That was impossible. She was surprised that the Templars would spread such rumors, but not at all surprised that the hospitalier nuns engaged in mongering. They were famous for it.

Stephen appeared at Martin's tent with two knights who did not look familiar. They must have been from Lindisfarne, for their armor was recently polished and did not carry the dirt of a long march. Lil did not raise her eyes or turn to greet Stephen. Rather, she nodded as he entered.

"That is Martin," Stephen said to the two knights, who mumbled something. Then, he addressed Lil. "Cedric has summoned you."

Cedric, the man who had spoken to her from his horse about his friend Tuan. Cedric, the Emotional. Cedric, the Defeated Survivor of Mont Saint Michel, had sent Stephen to retrieve her, to carry his summons. She smiled.

✠

Odo was tall and regal. He wore a close-cropped beard, which Lil had thought was in violation of the rule. He was not armored, but wore the mantle and surcoat. He sat in an ornate throne of dark, ancient wood. Lil recognized the symbols. Some were swirls and slashes, like those on the wall of the tidal cavern, while others were unique to the Templars. Their sum, however, conveyed a message that Lil did not understand. Odo drew what authority he could from it, adopting a straight though relaxed posture. He looked from that seat as if he had sight of all of the happenings of the world, and any that caught his attention should feel fortunate.

Grandmaster Odo was a French knight, as all of the grandmasters before him were. He claimed direct descent from Merovingian kings, whom history had hinted, through an interpretation of apocryphal gospels that angered the church to no end, were descended from Jesus himself.

But these were interesting times. So, not only was there a council of grandmasters rather than a single man, but a monk in austere grey robes and scapular stood behind him. This was surprising, given the church's certain rejection of Odo's claims of descent. This monk had a big angular nose that shot straight from between tiny dark eyes before plunging toward his thin lips. His chin carried the point, giving his entire face an elongated look. He had the wrinkles between his brow and along his mouth of one who frowned more often than he made any other expression.

Cedric was there, standing in audience to Odo. It was Cedric's tent. He was not the only knight. Templar knights, no more highly ranked than any on the field or bearing any additional regalia, flanked the grandmaster. They were his personal guard.

The throne, the guard, the stern monk—all of these were out of place in Cedric's tent. Cedric had a cot and a writing desk piled with scrolls. Nothing else. There were no rugs, tapestries, or pillows. These filled Lil's tent.

Odo spoke, his voice nasal and high.

"This is the girl, then."

He brought a cloth to his nose and sneezed with such violence that Lil thought the tent's walls would billow.

"Yes, Grandmaster," Cedric said. "The one whom Tuan prized."

Lil squinted, still unwilling to believe that she had meant anything to Tuan at all.

"The one who brought the soldier of the Yew among us," Odo said.

"Yes," Cedric answered.

"Why did she do that?"

Cedric looked confused, but composed himself.

"You will remember, Grandmaster, that Brother Stephen reported on Master Tuan's wishes. Tuan had ordered her to seek him. I do not know why, but Tuan worked closely with Grandmaster Declan in this."

Odo looked to the monk, who nodded. Lil thought this odd.

"Yes," Odo said. "Declan has many plans that he does not share with me."

Lil cleared her throat, then spoke.

"I believe that Martin is a key to defeating the Yew."

Silence filled the tent. Cedric closed his eyes. Stephen's eyes darted between Lil and Odo. The monk raised an eyebrow. She had spoken out of turn, she realized. Odo had not addressed her. She wondered now what would happen.

"Careful," she whispered. "Careful."

"You are a seer," Odo said, squinting, as if realizing that she was in front of him rather than just a topic of conversation. "What have you seen?"

Odo smiled, as if proud of his cleverness. Lil swallowed hard.

"I don't command my gift," she said. "It comes on its own."

The monk spoke, then. His voice was loud and clean, as if he were addressing a congregation.

"The grandmaster asks what you have seen."

"I saw the Yew turn north, toward Mont Saint Michel."

"A lot of good that does us now," Odo said.

"I couldn't have stopped the wolves. I didn't see those. But I have seen Martin. We seem..."

"You seem what?" Odo asked, leaning forward.

"Tied together. Tuan must've foreseen it. He sent me south to find Martin. But Martin found me instead. It's all so..."

"Go on."

"It's all so impossible."

Odo looked at her for a long moment, during which all were silent. He had kind eyes, but Lil was not sure how intelligent he was. It seemed humorous to him, rather than meaningful. Perhaps she underestimated this grandmaster. Or he was irrelevant, a figurehead. Perhaps the others on the council—this Declan, for example—wielded more power, with more insight. But in Odo's gaze, which continued on and on, she saw some understanding. He was coming to a decision about something. He opened his mouth to draw a breath and speak.

There was a commotion outside, shouts from a distance that drew closer. All looked up, including Odo, who swallowed whatever he was about to say. Lil wondered if the army were under attack. Were Prince Richard's men arrayed at the edge of camp? Had the Yew crossed the Channel?

A boy burst in, trailed by two sergeants who reached for him.

"Stop!" yelled Odo, his eyes betraying his own surprise at the commanding tone in his voice.

Cedric rested his hand on the hilt of his sword. Stephen had already drawn his blade. The Templars in Odo's retinue, however, stood still, as if nothing were happening.

The boy was not even a squire, but a servant or perhaps even an urchin making a few coins or earning a meal by performing small jobs in camp. His clothes were dirty with a day's work. He looked familiar to Lil.

"Begging your pardon," he said.

"Release him," Odo said. "He looks harmless enough."

The grandmaster, though, glanced at the knights. He looked at Stephen and Cedric, and seemed relieved that they were ready to fight.

The monk had not moved. He was like the statue of some lesser saint crafted by a novice sculptor who had not yet mastered the difference between serene and bored.

"Begging your pardon, Master Odo," the boy stammered.

"Grandmaster Odo," the monk said.

"Apologies. Grandmaster Odo. The mother of the hospitalier nuns begged me to come to you immediately, and to let nothing stand in my way."

Lil noticed Odo looking to the monk once more. The monk tendered a tiny shrug.

"What is it?" Odo asked.

"I...I came as quickly as I could," the boy said. "She told me not to stop for anything or anyone, not even the guards—"

"What is it?" the monk bellowed.

Lil now recognized the intruder as the servant to the nuns, an orphan they had rescued from some dire fate and a boy with whom she had never spoken but felt some kinship for his circumstance. He looked between the monk and the grandmaster and stammered, as if unsure of whom to address.

"Are we under attack?" Odo asked. "Are we out of food? Has the ground opened and swallowed the army? What is it?"

"No...no, Grandmaster. None of those things."

Odo let loose an exasperated sigh.

"Spit it out!" the grandmaster commanded.

"The dead one, Master. No, Grandmaster. The dead one, Grandmaster."

Martin, Lil thought. Something has happened to Martin. Her heart beat in her skull.

"What?" she asked, not caring if she had breached some ancient but meaningless etiquette by speaking out of turn.

The boy looked at her.

"He is awake," he said.

The word went past Lil, leaving no impression at first. He could not be awake, for he had not been asleep. He had been dead. He had been dead since before the day she met him.

Awake. What did that even mean?

"Alive," she said.

"Yes," the boy answered. "He is alive. He stands."

"Is he restrained?" Odo asked.

"No."

A murmur traveled the room, then.

"He is quite calm," the boy said, his voice betraying how strange he thought the notion sounded.

Lil went past him, then. She was the first out of the tent, but heard the others following.

Martin was alive. Awake. Whatever it was, he was back. And he was at Lindisfarne. Choosing him instead of the Champion, following him, bringing him to his home, leading him to the fleet, rescuing him from the cavern—she had not failed.

She could see the hospitaliers' tent. She slowed as she neared it. The crowd behind her slowed as well, perhaps wanting to see what would happen to her before they braved any approach to this beast. The flap was parted. She could see him. He was draped in the shroud that had covered his body. He stood, though bent. One of the nuns was speaking to him. He was nodding his ruined head as if taking simple instructions, as if there were nothing at all odd wandering about in the world. Lil stood still for a moment, and then entered the tent.

Book III: The Martyrs' Crusade

Chapter XVII

The rest of the world did not exist. That, Toothless guessed, had been the idea. Britons had perhaps settled Holy Island as a shamanic retreat in the dim past. Then, as most such retreats often did, it became a Christian monastery. Now, he and the howling man in separate cells, side by side, were making it a prison in fact. There was no rest of the world. There were just the two cells—wet and dark, each furnished only with a bucket and a pile of decaying straw. And the howling Templar, who between baying at some moon that only he could see and sputtering in noisy, disturbed sleep, spat words and phrases that meant nothing to Toothless.

"Fangs of the polluted blood!"

Toothless remembered battling the sea monster. He remembered forcing every last bit of strength into a ball in his chest—he had felt it pulsing there as he beat his fists through the black water—and releasing it in a great thrashing that forced the monster into retreat. Then, a wild current swept Toothless to the tunnel, leaving him on the floor of the cavern.

And that was death. He was sure of it, and learned to be happy for it. Time did not pass. There was only darkness, emptiness. He was desperate, at first. It was not at all what he had imagined of death. But it became comfortable. It became preferable to running with Lil, or serving the Yew.

Still, he could not help but feel that there should be more to it. The church extolled an afterlife that was quite like life in the material world. They persecuted any who suggested otherwise. The Yew had promised everlasting life. The frightening possibility, though, was that life would end into a void, a complete lack of any consciousness at all. To think that there might be something in between, an observable emptiness—it had not crossed his mind.

Now, though, he was risen. Again. He was much weaker, as weak as a living man. He felt tired, though no amount of stretching or shaking his head would bring more life to him.

The Yew must also be weak, he thought. The Marian Cloth had nourished it, but it had spent that power on the wolves and sea monsters. Cedric had explained the fate of Mont Saint Michel before Grandmaster Odo ordered Toothless to the cell. The Yew's priests and captains perhaps gambled that Mont Saint Michel would house whatever greater relic they sought—blood, they had said.

Yes, he remembered it now. In the ruined priory, they had discussed blood.

Had the Yew recovered the blood? If not, what accounted for Toothless' rise? But he was so weak. Toothless shook his head once more, wishing that he had a jaw to gnash. He wanted to press molars together so hard that they would crack, that he would see stars and swirling patterns, that he would go unconscious.

"...wild ivory eye! Six plus four times twenty plus five..."

Toothless shook his head, then pressed against the sides of his skull to settle the debris and scraps of tissue that rattled inside. He knew those numbers. Yes, he had memorized them and even written them. They were of the cipher that had led the Yew to Mont Saint Michel, that Toothless had produced in the ruined priory. The man in the cell beside him, then, was a Templar who had trained in the same answer.

The Templar was not a soldier of the Yew. Yet, he shed his memories as Toothless had, as any of the risen dead had.

The man howled, then, until his voice was raw and Toothless imagined blood spewing from that dry mouth. It went on for long minutes, attracting the attention of guards. Toothless heard the mechanism of a heavy lock across the pitch black room, and looked through the bars of the window on his cell door. He saw the outlines of three men enter the room. One was heavy, slow. He shouted in a low, almost drunken voice. A man at arms, perhaps. Perhaps not even a Templar.

"Shaddup! You can scream all you want. You're not getting out!"

The other two were slighter, shorter.

The soldier lit a torch in a wall sconce, and Toothless closed his eyes against the light. When he opened them, he saw the two slight men—they were monks—conversing as the guard dragged a table and three chairs from the hallway. One of the monks was younger, with smooth, unblemished skin, a proper Roman tonsure, and tiny black eyes. He was thin, so thin that Toothless wondered if his mission were to starve to death. The other was older, with a long face and an angular nose. The monks separated, the older standing aside as the younger finished arrangements—two chairs on the opposite side of the table, one on this side. The guard lumbered toward the dark hallway. He closed the door, and stood inside of it, before it, so that his fat head would block the view through the window.

The older monk spoke. His Adam's apple bobbed, though Toothless could not hear the words through the howling. The young monk gestured. He was a tangle of thin limbs, awkwardness. Toothless imagined him as an errand boy for a den of thieves.

The older monk nodded, unrolling a leather pouch onto the tabletop. Implements gleamed in the torch light. Probes, hooks, saws. They bore decorated handles and intricate, scrolling etching in the metal. Only a demon would devise such things, Toothless thought, and only to sate some sadistic appetite.

A lull in the howling, then, and Toothless heard the older monk's voice. He was half way through a sentence, his clear voice ringing in that moment from the stone of the chamber.

"...take care of this nuisance."

The guard stepped forward, and the screams began anew. The guard fumbled with keys, trying several in the lock before Toothless heard the click as the howling Templar took a breath. The prisoner screamed, then, but swallowed it with a gulp. Shuffling and some whimpering came from that cell, then nothing. The guard stepped from the cell, brushing his hands upon one another to punctuate a simple message.

"All done," he said.

The old monk nodded.

"Now get the other," he commanded.

Toothless saw the guard's face in his window. It was a meaty face on a very tall man. It seemed as if every bone of that face were swollen or had been broken—his cheekbones, his jaw, his brow. A scar ran across his forehead, giving his thin eyes a permanent look of frustrated confusion. His teeth were crooked. One of the incisors was longer than the other and had made, over the course of this man's rude life, a dent in his bottom lip.

The guard opened the door. Toothless expected to be invited out, but he should have known better. The guard stepped forward and gripped him by his upper arms, lifting him from the floor. He backed out of the cell holding Toothless, who could not react. Toothless knew that he was not strong enough to defeat this animal, who now turned as if carrying something putrid and disgusting. Of course he was, Toothless realized.

The guard lowered Toothless into the chair across from the older monk. The younger monk, seated beside his companion, shaved a quill over a beaten and thick volume bound in leather. The curled cuttings dropped onto the pages with audible smacks.

The guard produced four chains. He attached these to rings sunk into the floor. The other ends were manacles, which he clapped around Toothless' wrists and ankles.

"Now," the older monk said. "Let us begin."

The younger monk wrote with furious speed.

"This is Brother Ethelred," the older monk said. "He will transcribe all that we say. I am Brother Francis. You may call me Brother. At times, I will ask you to call me Father. At other times, I will ask you to call me names that will be uncomfortable for you to say, but you will relent. It will be unpleasant. Unpleasantness is necessary to what I do."

Francis' gaze followed the drop of his nose to his hands, which were clasped atop his tools. He must have realized, then, that his script—for that is what it was—was not appropriate for this meeting.

"Of course," Francis said. "You cannot call me anything. You cannot speak. Much of our time together may, as a result, be... awkward."

Still looking at his hands, he motioned to Ethelred, who handed a rolled parchment. Francis undid the red wax seal, and read aloud.

"I, Brother Francis, acting on the request of Grandmaster Odo of the Poor Fellow Soldiers of Christ, the Knights of the Temple of Solomon, and with the blessing of the Holy See, to discover and drag vile heresy into the light of Christ's redemption, do open these proceedings in the name of the Father, the Son, and the Holy Spirit. I invite you, Brother Martin of the aforementioned order, to engage with me in this Crusade."

Francis set the parchment aside and placed his hand upon it as if a wind would blow it from the table. Toothless squinted at the implements between them. Ethelred scribbled. The guard shifted his weight, then leaned back upon the door, which creaked under the strain.

Francis turned, his profile looking like that of some exotic bird, and spoke to Ethelred.

"Are you ready, Brother?"

Ethelred dipped his quill, turned from his book, and nodded. He had an earnest, almost eager look on his face.

Francis brought his gaze to Toothless. "Tell me," he said, "why you think I have brought you before me today."

Toothless returned the look. He wanted to rest, even to sleep and dream. Better yet, he wanted to return to the blissful emptiness of the prior days. What would it take, he wondered, for that guard to smash open his head, end his existence once and for all? Probably not much, though the chains kept him from even that.

After several moments of silence, Francis sighed.

"Do you understand what I have read, and what I ask?"

He patted the parchment. Toothless nodded.

"Brother Ethelred," Francis said, still looking at Toothless. "Put a quill and parchment before him."

Toothless let this unfold. He had no choice. Ethelred rose and scurried to his pack which lay against the wall beside the guard. He fetched a bottle of ink and a quill, then stuffed a roll of parchment under his arm. He returned to the table and spread these before Toothless. Ethelred then worked at arranging these, then dipped the quill.

"Yes," he said. "There we are."

Ethelred returned to his seat. Toothless looked at Francis, then lifted his hands as high as the chain would allow. They did not rise above his thighs. He did it again for effect. The clang of the chains snapping taut echoed down the hallway beyond the door. Francis sighed again.

"Well," he said. "I shall have to ask you very simple questions."

Francis stared at Toothless for a long moment. The guard shifted his weight again, and then smacked his lips as if preparing for sleep. Ethelred looked up from his page, curiosity in his eyes. He looked at Francis, then at Toothless, then back to the page, as if the silence had led him to wonder if the two were still in the room.

"On October 21, in the Year of Our Lord 1180," Francis began, "you fought in a battle southwest of Paris. Is this correct?"

Toothless was not sure. He squinted at the memory. Yes, the battle. He died in that battle. He nodded.

"Brother Ethelred, please indicate that he has answered in the affirmative."

The quill scratched against the page.

"Your master, Brother Tuan of your order, entrusted you with the defense of the relics of that place and, through bravery on the battlefield, the morale of townspeople and soldiers. Is this correct?"

Toothless nodded. Ethelred wrote.

"You failed in both, did you not?"

Toothless squinted.

"The enemy overran the region," Francis continued. "Some relics were saved, but others were not. Many of the living, many of them soldiers, including you, were impressed into the ranks of the Yew. Is this true?"

Toothless paused, remembering the march of memories away from his ruined body. He remembered Aine and Emer, about whom he had not thought since standing in his home, his farm. Memories, even those of his more recent second life, were indistinct and hazy. He wondered if ale or wine would help, or if the capability of memory were now fading. A shambler. How much longer?

"Brother Ethelred," Francis said. "Please note his second delay in responding."

Toothless nodded, then wondered why he had responded to Francis' prodding.

"You are nodding to indicate that you failed in your mission."

He nodded again.

"You served the Yew, then, through most of the month of November, separating from the Yew somewhere on the banks of the Loire and arriving in Brittany by the end of that month."

Toothless nodded, thinking again of the memories of his wife and daughter, of the flight of their ghosts from his corpse on the battlefield. Was Emer looking at him? He did not remember her face.

"How many innocents did you kill in your service to the Black Yew?"

Toothless was not sure of the meaning of "innocents," or how he was expected to answer. If with fingers, he did not have enough.

"Five?"

Toothless shook his head.

"More than five?"

He nodded.

"More than twenty?"

He nodded.

"More than one hundred?"

Francis had adopted an astounded tone. Toothless was not sure if it were genuine, or employed for effect.

One hundred? Perhaps. Toothless shrugged.

"We shall say, then, that you have murdered one hundred, and may God have mercy on your soul."

Toothless wanted to ask how many innocents Francis had tortured. Or were the implements for show?

"I must now turn to another line of questioning, though I must admit some lingering shock at what you have confirmed. We will return to that, but let us now proceed to the issue of Brother Tuan. He trained you. That is a question, in fact."

Toothless nodded. Tuan. What had happened to him? Was he here?

"Would it surprise you to know," Francis said, as if hearing Toothless' questions, "that he is among the missing? That he set himself adrift in White Martyrdom? Would that surprise you?"

Toothless blinked. His shock was not of surprise, but of sadness. He had assumed that the master was dead, that he had fallen, perhaps in the same battle as Martin. Tuan had lived, but what did it matter? He was gone forever, now. Again. Men did not return from White Martyrdom, except in the lives of saints and in legends they resembled. Still, Toothless was not surprised that Tuan had set himself adrift. He shook his head.

"Did you know Master Tuan trained under Grandmaster Declan?"

He must have known at one time. Why was it important?

"Did you?"

Toothless shrugged.

"Are you saying that you did not know, or that you did not consider it important?"

Toothless shrugged again.

"If only you could speak, though given your deeds I tremble at what you might tell us."

Francis closed his eyes for a moment, opening them halfway through his next question.

"Did you train under Grandmaster Declan?"

Toothless shook his head.

"Did you ever meet or converse with Declan?"

No, again.

"Did Master Tuan ever discuss Declan in your training?"

Toothless shrugged.

"Think hard on that."

He shrugged again.

"Did Master Tuan ever discuss Grandmaster Odo in your training?"

A knock sounded at the door, then.

"Hold!" Brother Francis shouted, raising his palm. He turned to Toothless. "Do you sense where these questions lead?"

Toothless shook his head, which only seemed to enrage the monk. Francis paused, perhaps to steady himself, though he grew agitated with each second. He could not remain still, but shuffled his feet over the grit on the floor. Ethelred did not seem at all surprised. It had all happened before, Toothless guessed. It was all chronicled in that book. The two had seen and done so much that they were not at all impressed to be seated across from the walking dead. In some way, all of their victims were walking dead.

"I assert," Francis spat, "that Grandmaster Declan engineered the surrender of a Templar to the enemy. I say that he may be a traitor, and that you may be complicit with Master Tuan and Grandmaster Declan in this abomination against your brethren and your church."

Toothless returned the accusation with a blank stare. He felt some anger, then. Some energy. It welled up from the depths of his empty gut. It seemed to grow. He felt it spreading within in, a prickling power.

Francis opened his mouth to continue, then stopped. He straightened in his chair, and looked at the devices in front of him. He reached for one, grasping it without touching any of the others, as if they were fragile.

"This," he said, wielding a clamp. "This I use to pull nails from fingers."

He replaced it, choosing another.

"This one...this is a short blade, dulled at the end here. Do you see? It does not cut my skin, but with enough force it slices cheeks and noses. But this...this is my favorite. This is called 'the pear.' I designed it myself. Shall I explain how it works?"

It was a rhetorical question. He held up a metal device the size and shape of a large pear, as its name suggested. It was adorned with fine, careful carvings. Delicate, even. On end, the end of the twig if it were a pear, the flat handle of a key protruded. An angel's face, like the face on Toothless' lost sword, looked with stern eyes from the key.

"I insert it into a cavity. Any will do, though some produce more pain than others. I turn the key, and...do you see how it opens? Imagine what that will do inside of a person. Do you see how, when none of these other tools will work, this one does?"

The device creaked, spreading open like a blooming tulip.

"Ethelred," Francis continued, "must be careful to keep up with the ramblings. And there must be witnesses." He motioned to the guards. "The pear leads to confessions, but then often leads to silence."

Toothless looked at these implements, and the others that remained untouched. All were polished to a bright silver gleam. Did Francis mean to scare him with these? Certainly, the monk knew that Toothless felt nothing. That he was already dead. That he could not even speak. What could Francis hope to accomplish?

"Enter!" Francis shouted.

The door opened. Another guard, as big and dumb as the other, stood in the doorway. Toothless then understood, for this second guard led Lil into the room.

Lil, no doubt enticed through some lie, was quick to understand what was happening. She turned to run, but the guards blocked the door. The first guard stepped forward and grabbed her just as he had taken Toothless. She fought. She kicked and thrashed. But he was too strong.

It took both guards to close manacles around her wrists and ankles, and so to chain her to the wall, her arms and legs pulled apart.

The anger spiked in Toothless. But it was not just rage. It was power. It was wakefulness. He tried to stand. The chair shot from behind him. He landed on the floor, and then rose to his knees. The chains held fast to the stone.

Lil remained silent, her mouth clamped shut. She exhaled, panicked, through her nose.

"Ah," Francis said. "This witch is important to you. And so, I was correct. Whatever shred of humanity remains in you bends to her. Ethelred, note it."

Ethelred had not stopped writing.

The guards chuckled.

Toothless tried to calm himself. Every dusty fiber, every dried strand in his body, now hummed. He felt that he could run as he had run through France. He felt that he could kill hordes as he had killed in France. He worried that it was a flash, something that would not last. Every second that he waited, however, it continued to grow.

Francis chose a small bit of metal from his array of tools. It was a probe, styled as a miniature shepherd's crook but with sharp points at both ends. It was a brilliant, gleaming thing in his hand. He held it with the finesse of an expert Arab surgeon.

"I often start with this one," he said. "Small punctures, at first. Normally, these are not enough to reveal what I need to see. Then…"

He motioned with the probe, as if scratching at something in the air.

"Then," he continued, "I dig. Then, the hook. I pull flesh, like a falcon pulls flesh from its prey."

Lil began to whimper through her closed mouth.

Toothless crouched, hugging his knees.

"You understand the feeling of this," Francis said. "You understand the power. At first, I did not."

He paused, looking at Toothless and adjusting his grip on the crooked probe.

"I do now," he said.

CHAPTER XVIII

Abell sounded, distant but strong. At first, Toothless paid no heed. The guards, however, exchanged glances.

"Now," Francis said. "You may be ready to confess to treason against your order. You may be ready to indict Grandmaster Declan and Master Tuan. This, however, is not the time. I will not hear your confession until I am certain that you are absolutely ready."

He took two steps toward Lil. Toothless flexed his fingers.

"This means," Francis continued, "that she will have to scream for a little while."

Shouts in the hallway—the guards looked at one another, then at Ethelred.

"We have to go," one said.

"You will go nowhere," Ethelred replied. "You will guard the door."

"We are under attack."

Before Ethelred could respond, before the bell could ring again, before Francis could take any more steps or the attackers—whoever they were—could advance one more yard, Toothless raised his arms. The manacles on his wrists shattered. He stood and kicked one foot forward, knocking the table back upon Ethelred. The chain to his ankle snapped. Francis' instruments fell, tinkling on the floor.

The guards were moving on Toothless now. Ethelred scrambled from beneath the table. Toothless lifted his other leg, breaking that chain and planting his knee into the first guard's groin with a sickening crunch. The guard fell, his hip shattered.

Toothless took the guard's blade. It was no greatsword like the one that he had prized, but it was a blade. The power flared. It brought the sword into him, making the blade part of him, just as it had when he had taken the blade in the forest and lopped away a peasant's head, and when he had fought the Champion.

Two quick swings and the second guard was down, spouting blood from cuts in his chest and neck.

Then, Toothless had Francis by the neck. The monk smiled as he released the crooked probe, the sound of it hitting the floor lost in the shouts and the bell beyond the door. Something else—the Templar in the other cell began howling again, voice high and hoarse.

Toothless thrust the sword deep into the monk's gut, ramming up from his belly, all the way through his chest. It sounded like breaking a gourd, and was no harder.

He dropped the corpse to the ground. Toothless felt the warmth of the blood on his arm. He felt as alive as when he had killed for the Yew, when he had slaughtered those of the village of the Marian Cloth. His hunger became so strong and sharp that he nearly turned on Lil. She met his gaze. He stopped himself.

Lil whimpered. She pointed her chin. Ethelred was out the door, tripping down the hall, brushing by an approaching form.

"What goes on here?"

Stephen entered the room and, seeing Toothless, unsheathed his sword and took a defensive stance.

"Demon!" Stephen shouted.

Toothless was not sure what to do. Lil shouted. The sound of her voice, loud yet familiar, both distracted and calmed him.

"Stop!" she yelled. "Stephen!"

Stephen looked at her out of the corner of his eye.

"Speak now, Lil. In two moments I attack this beast, and one of us dies."

"Martin saved me! The monk is the villain."

Stephen blinked, flexing his arms.

"Explain," he said, looking at Toothless but addressing Lil.

"Guards brought me to this room claiming that the monk required my gift. But he ordered me shackled to this wall. He came at me with those implements. He meant to torture me."

Laughter, girlish giggling, rose from the cell as the afflicted knight reacted to whatever insane thoughts rattled his mind.

Toothless stared at Stephen's eyes, looking for even the slightest hint of an attack. Stephen seemed ambivalent about doing anything at all, perhaps wishing that he had not stepped into the room.

Cedric rescued him. The master entered, then. He placed his hands on his hips and said a single word.

"Well."

Stephen lowered his sword and stepped to Cedric's side.

"The seer," Stephen said. "She claims that Brother Francis was going to torture her, and that Martin saved her."

Cedric looked at the corpses on the floor, then at Lil.

"Tell me," he said.

"Please," she replied. "Release me first."

Cedric looked once more over the scene, then sighed.

"Brother Stephen," he said. "See that Brother Martin is armed. I want him on the field now."

Toothless was surprised. Stephen bristled.

"Master Cedric," he said. "I must object. We do not know what he will do."

Additional soldiers—Toothless counted six—entered the room. They stopped just inside the doorway, as soon as the scene greeted them.

Lil then spoke, almost under her breath.

"Do you want to win?"

Cedric almost interrupted her.

"Brother Stephen, I have ordered it. Grandmaster Declan has ordered it. Master Tuan would have ordered it."

"Master Cedric," Stephen said, his voice betraying some uncertainty.

"I am now weary of this discussion," Cedric snapped. "Remember your place and your practice. You have an order."

"Yes, Master Cedric."

Bitterness laced Stephen's words, and he narrowed his gaze.

"Escort Brother Martin," Cedric said to the soldiers behind him. "Find him armor. And a greatsword. He is most gifted with a greatsword."

Stephen blinked.

"And a helmet," he said. "Cover the beast's...face."

He scowled on the last word, as if unwilling to use it.

✠

Toothless stepped into the orange light of dawn. He wore fine polished chain and a surcoat so new that he could imagine its smell. He carried a serviceable greatsword, the only in the Lindisfarne armory. He wore a helmet that covered his face, so that as he walked he felt the confidence of blending in with the Templars. There was no denying that he was different from them. He was flush with a power that they would never know, and that had come to him at the cost of his life.

The power. Something had happened. The Yew must have taken something. A relic. Lives. Something. It would stand him in good stead.

The soldiers escorted him to a ridge overlooking the causeway. From here, he could see across the channel to the mainland. Men fought on the beach, there. Templars, their backs against the water, engaged a long, thick line of soldiers in blue surcoats. Embankments and, between them, wooden fences separated the attackers from the Templars. The enemy stretched up and down the beach. They were numerous enough to draw the Templar line thin. Richard's men—the soldiers escorting Toothless were sure that they were Richard's men—would soon flank. That would be the end.

Still, the attackers showed some disorganization. The Yew's captains would have ordered an assault straight through the center of their line. Toothless could see where Longinus would have concentrated his force, a brief thinning where the enemy was confused over whether to move toward the flank far down the line or continue to throw their assault against the embankment. Toothless could sense their fear. Their number was large, but they began to question the mounting dead. He could see it in the whole line, as if the indecisiveness at this small point sent shudders up and down the rest of the assault.

Cedric was on the ridge with Toothless. He stood beside another man, whose head was shaved to gray stubble and whose square face and calm gray eyes surveyed the same scene. He was powerful and tall, like the champion in Brittany though of a different mien. He barely moved at all, except to exchange brief words with Cedric. No doubt, these two men thought on the welfare of their soldiers. The Yew's captains had no such need.

Toothless realized, then. Declan. Formerly a master in Ireland, he was now one of the many grandmasters who sat on the council. He had been Tuan's teacher. Toothless could not imagine it. Despite the wrinkles and gray stubble, Declan barely looked old enough to teach Stephen, let alone Tuan.

Declan caught his gaze and, with two fingers, motioned him forward. Cedric looked at Toothless as well, saw the greatsword, and introduced him.

"Martin. He was a student of Tuan's."

"Indeed," Declan said. His voice was low and sonorous. It vibrated through Toothless' trunk. He looked Toothless up and down. "I hear that you killed Brother Francis."

Toothless was not afraid. He was certain that the act was punishable, though not in any way that mattered in his own world.

Declan turned to Cedric and smiled.

"I almost killed him once or twice myself," Declan said. "Are you ready to fight, Brother Martin?"

Toothless nodded.

"Show us," he said, "what you can do against these attackers. They are not the peasants and rabble that you are used to fighting. They are trained. And beware of distinguishing yourself too mightily. News of your deeds and of the murder of Brother Francis will spread quickly. Blades may come at you from both directions, down there."

"There," Cedric said, pointing at the beach. "There he is. The horse."

Declan looked at the battle. Toothless squinted. Smoke now rose from the woods beyond the melee. The Templar ranks were thinning, but a man on horseback rallied them.

"That is Odo," Declan said. "He is a fool. He has powerful friends. He means to be rid of me. There have been many attempts on my life. Francis was one his servants, or perhaps Odo served Francis. No matter, Odo can blame much on you. He can use you to topple me, to kill Cedric, to destroy Tuan's legacy."

A boy ran to them, then. He was thin, sandy-haired. He delivered a parchment to Cedric, and stood twisting his legs, waiting for a response. Cedric peered at the parchment, then sighed.

"It is as I feared, Grandmaster Declan."

"Say it."

"The bulk of my men are mustered from their camp on the eastern shore, and can be here very soon. Their weapons, however, are already stowed aboard the ships. The armory is nearly empty."

Declan looked at the boy.

"They are to gather whatever implements and tools they can," he said. "Anything that can be used as a weapon. And they are to march immediately. Take the message now. We have nothing to write it, and no time to find something. Brother Stephen approaches?"

The boy nodded.

"Yes, sir," he said. "Brother Stephen is but a minute behind me, perhaps longer, for I ran as fast I could. He is..."

"What?" Cedric asked.

"He is quite angry at fighting alongside the..."

Cedric waited, but the boy did not finish the sentence. Toothless, helmeted, may have appeared as just another knight to the boy. Cedric looked between Toothless and the boy, then laughed so loud that the battle might even have paused to learn what could be so humorous.

"Very well," Declan said. "Run as fast as you can—even faster—to deliver the reply. Tell the captains that it comes directly from me."

Cedric smiled as the boy ran off, stumbling.

Declan stepped closer to Toothless.

"I knew to trust Tuan," he said. "So, I trust you. Are you ready to fight this day? Are you ready to defend your brothers and reclaim this order from corrupt and evil men?"

Toothless nodded.

"Are you ready to cross the water, to attack the beast that has robbed you of your family, of your life?"

Toothless nodded again.

"I am ready to follow you. Cedric is ready. The brotherhood, the whole world of the living—we are all ready for this terror to end."

He paused, looking back to the battlefield. It would not be long before the Templars buckled. If they did, Richard's forces would claim the causeway. If they crossed and established a beachhead, there would be no dislodging them. They would reinforce, and push Cedric's army into the sea.

"Lead us, Brother Martin," Declan said. "Lead us as we embark on the Martyrs' Crusade."

✠

Toothless and Stephen traveled the causeway in a wagon meant for straw or plague victims. Two ponies navigated the mud, their hoofs squelching, as an ancient driver whipped them with a green pine branch. The driver was drunk or blind, or some other quality that, in any less afflicted world, would have precluded his participation as a driver. But he whipped the ponies, and they seemed to know their way.

The water of the channel between Holy Island and the mainland rippled with a stiff, cold wind. The sky, gray and flat, threatened snow. The sound of the battle was crisp and thin through the cold. The tide was beginning to swallow the causeway.

Toothless looked across the wagon at Stephen, who stared back with a scowl on his face, his blade unsheathed and sitting across his thighs. His blue eyes leveled upon Toothless. Stephen was ready to strike.

The battle raged ahead. Odo was still at the center of line, tall on his steed, directing the defense inside the fences and earthworks. The forest and brush just above the beach were burning, and the wind pushed that wall of smoke inland. Still, the attackers poured from this fire with no pause, wave after wave. It had a rhythm, like the creaking of the wagon or the rocking of Stephen's blade as he, with nervous energy, patted it against his armored thighs. A command, shouted from the center of the Templar lines, traveled up and down the beach. Richard's men answered with their own cries. The whistle of crossbow bolts replied, then grunts, shouts, ringing steel. Then, it all began again.

The Templar dead formed a wall behind the line. It held back the rising tide in the center of the line. As if the channel were not enough of a barrier to retreat, there were these corpses, their faces telling all who might run to turn around and make the deaths worth something.

The defenders would have seen the wagon. They were looking for reinforcements. But here were just two Templars riding in a slow wagon, lounging as if they rode from one market town to another. The enemy must have seen them as well, and must have been bolstered by it. Could the grandmasters muster no more than that? Where, everyone must have thought, was the army that had marched from the south and now camped on the far shore of Holy Island? They did not even assemble catapults, crossbowmen, or ballista to cover the causeway. Only fifty or sixty Templars delayed a force of countless more.

Toothless clenched his fists in his stiff, new gloves. Yesterday, even during the night, he was barely able to move his hands at all. He turned to Stephen, who still stared at him with distrust and caution. Toothless shifted his gaze between the Templar and the beach.

The wagon was almost there, but was mere minutes too late.

The Templar line broke.

Toothless was not sure what was happening, at first. He saw blue surcoats crest the earthworks. These attackers fell to swords and pikes, or fell in among the Templars only to be beaten into the sand. But the attackers kept coming. Richard's men overpowered the Templars. Blue surcoats were now behind them, flooding to the flanks. Odo's horse reared and he disappeared, thrown from the beast's back. The ponies pulling the wagon stopped, then. The driver muttered something unintelligible through his swollen purple gums. The ponies would not budge.

Stephen looked at Toothless.

"I will be at your side the whole way," he said. "I have no qualms about lopping off your head if you so much as cut the hair of a Templar."

Toothless held Stephen's gaze. The Templar dropped from the wagon.

Richard's men had taken the opening of the causeway. The Templars were divided with no way to retreat. The first of the attackers advanced up the causeway and pointed at Stephen, then charged. Stephen, however, was ready, and dispatched him with a slice across his chest. Another approached. Stephen thrust his blade into that man's gut. Four more were on their way. Now, Toothless determined, was his time to enter the fray.

He leaped from the bed of the wagon, high over the driver's head, feeling the wind carry him. He looked forward, wondering if he might sail right into the fires. He felt that he could, or that he could continue on to the horizon. Toothless shook his head as he descended, landing in the muck.

Fighting, then, was like any task, any practice. It was like copying letters from a manuscript. It was like memorizing a cipher. It was like the offices of prayer, or any rhythm. He moved fluidly, swinging that blade—inferior to his prized blade, to be sure, but formidable in his hands. He could sense the amazement growing among the attackers, as one by one they fell away from him to land, broken, in the mud. The tide rose, but Toothless fortified the causeway with the dead flesh of the enemy.

Snow began to fall, or it was ash from the fires. The wind shifted, bringing smoke. The battle had changed, first by the breach in the Templar line and now by Toothless. Stephen watched, paralyzed, wonder on his face. Toothless was, for once, thankful that he had been unable to speak, unable to express how foolish they had all been.

Brother Francis, for assuming that Toothless could be commanded. Stephen, for assuming that he could do anything to answer whatever Toothless decided to do to anyone. Now, an ungodly, angry power flowed through him. He chose how and when to apply it.

It was judgment, again.

He knew that he would have to choose. When all of Richard's soldiers had fallen, would Toothless continue on to the Templars? And Cedric? Would he destroy the entire army? He saw this playing on the horizon as he swung his blade. He saw the death spreading from this place—like the plague, but more decisive, more immediate.

"Return to me."

The Yew.

Toothless was not sure whether its roots had spread beneath the channel, or if it connected to him through his anger, through the slaughter of these men. It sounded distant and weak.

"Return."

It pleaded.

Toothless had now advanced to the line and was climbing atop one of the earthworks, beating back Richard's men. Stephen was behind him. A group of Templars rallied at his rear. The line reformed. They cheered Toothless, though they had no idea who he was. This was what Tuan had trained him to do from the start.

"Return."

Toothless could return. He could cleanse this island of the living and return at the head of his own army of dead. He could reclaim what was his as the true heir of the Yew.

Yes, he thought. Its heir.

He looked into the smoke, watching the scenes unfold. He saw Lil, cowering under his blade. Aine and Emer, their ashes swirling in the raging hot air of their funerary fire. Tuan, drifting and dead on the open sea. The master had seen something of the future, but had he seen this? What, Toothless wondered, was he now meant to do?

He stopped. Richard's men retreated from him. Some engaged Templars around him, avoiding him. Toothless looked at his hands. They were covered in blood. It was soaking through the leather, drenching his skin and bones. His surcoat was red, and gore clotted in the links of his armor.

He was mighty again. Transcendent. He should not have left the Yew. He should have claimed the Cohort of Ruin and marched at the head of the Yew's army to bring the end of the world.

Yes. He would have to kill the Templars. He would have to kill Cedric and Stephen. And Lil.

Fury and smoke surrounded him. One of the attackers charged. Without even realizing that he was moving, Toothless batted him down with a short, sharp swipe of the greatsword.

Had Lil pulled him from the cavern, he wondered, only to hasten the end of the world?

Whatever his mission, he had considered it a failure. He had thought that he was free to die, to leave the doomed world behind. She had retrieved him.

Toothless stood, alone and still, wrestling with doubt. It was as palpable a foe as the sea monster, or the Champion, or Richard's men.

Five of the attackers surrounded Stephen. Two Templars were with him. They fell. Toothless, without thinking, bolted into the melee. After pushing Stephen to the ground, he swung his sword in wide, slashing arcs. The attackers were no more.

Toothless reached for Stephen's hand, surprising himself, for his thoughts told him to strike at the Templar. Stephen paused, trying to stand but slipping. Toothless reached again. Stephen took his hand.

He could kill Stephen now, Toothless realized.

Richard's men retreated. The fire, however, had grown so thick that they perished. A few ran back to the line, screaming. The Templars were waiting for them.

"You broke them," Stephen said. "By yourself."

Toothless looked about him, through the smoke and the snow, through the blood. He sensed the Yew's voice retreating. He felt his energy dipping with that retreat. He thought of Lil, and wondered if he would be able to put her under his blade.

"I will follow you," Stephen said, and knelt before the soldier of the Yew.

Chapter XIX

Toothless sat on a hill overlooking the eastern shore of Holy Island. The snow had ceased, having just dusted the ground. The sun was setting behind him. Night had already descended over the channel, over the Yew's conquests.

He had not heard the voice since the day's battle, but he could feel the presence. He could feel it in the rock beneath his feet, in the wind, in the low, dark oppression that was the cloud-shrouded night sky. It was as if the Yew had grown to such a height that its limbs stretched over the entire world.

Six ships sat anchored just beyond the surf below him. The beast-like barges had sails emblazoned with the red cross. He wondered if these were the ships from the cavern. On the prow of one he thought he spied the name *Baphomet*, but it was too dark and distant for him to be sure. Even at this late hour, men loaded the ships with supplies. The army, camped out of view, was preparing to embark. A thousand knights, perhaps more—it was the force that had brought him to Lindisfarne.

Toothless heard footsteps behind him. Three figures approached. Cedric, Declan, and also Lil. Toothless was annoyed, but stood and faced them, thinking that he at least owed the girl some respect. There was something about her, her deformity, her clout at such a young age. There was something in the dim aura around her, a shifted color and a shimmering brightness, as if she were a walking relic.

Cedric extended his hand. He offered a wineskin.

"Go on," the master said.

Declan nodded.

"You'll be wanting this," the grandmaster said.

Toothless took the skin. It sloshed, full of something. He uncorked it and brought it to his nose, as if he could smell.

"Drink it," Declan said. "We did not come by it easily."

Toothless poured it into his open gullet. Sweet, smoky spirits filled him.

Whiskey.

He sat then, nearly collapsing as the warmth covered him like a fine linen shroud. He wondered where on an island of monks and Templars one found whiskey. Toothless' cheeks ached with drunkenness. It had come with the first gulp.

"We must speak with you," Declan said.

Toothless nodded. He remembered Emer falling to all fours and making noises like a frog, laughing. He yelled at Kennocha for nipping at the girl's hands and feet as she did this. Emer cried, and Aine took the girl in her arms.

He stared past Declan, past Cedric, who was now sitting across from him. He stared past Lil, who stood behind Cedric. Toothless looked for the western horizon, but saw only the outlines of stone and trees darkening in the descending night.

"Odo is dead," Declan said.

This had no effect on Toothless. The grandmaster had been a fool. Of course Richard's men had killed him.

"And Master Tuan is gone from us," Declan continued.

Toothless blinked. Tuan, barking orders, drilling him in the field with the favorite greatsword. That gravelly voice instilled the ethic of constant practice.

"I did not consent to his White Martyrdom," Declan said. "His only failing was his pride. You sent him away."

Toothless looked at the grandmaster and shook his head.

"Do not protest," Declan replied, kneeling beside Cedric. "All is as it should be. Had you not left the order, you would likely be a mindless marcher or a sacrifice in the Yew's fires. Or, perhaps, a captain in the ranks of the Yew. He saw a different future for you. This future. Before you left, even before you went with him to Ireland, he confided in me. He saw something of what you are now."

Toothless looked at Cedric, who stared at a twig in his hands, a twig that he broke again and again into tiny pieces. Toothless then turned to Lil, who shook her head as if to say, "I saw nothing." He was not sure what to make of that.

"Why do you think we let you go?" Declan asked. "Why do you think we settled you on that farm? Did he see the death of your family? Did he see the loss of your jaw? I do not think so. He saw something to lead him to an understanding, through his pride, that he had to let you go. He nearly stopped it. He nearly sent you away to Jerusalem. I would not let him, because I believed in his vision more than he did."

Declan paused.

"His lack of belief in himself," he continued, "ultimately led him to seek purification."

Tuan, the round old face, the wisdom—a man that age had every right to sit back from his failures and let the world walk on without him. He had every right to retreat, to spend his time with a garden or with children. He had earned the right to cancel his obligations, to declare them paid or null and to challenge any who would doubt the balance of things. Tuan, however, considered that he still owed an enormous debt, all because Toothless had abandoned his own obligations.

But was that foretold? Was it part of some plan? Perhaps there was still a role to play, some way to make it right. His power had peaked. Though it had not ebbed just yet, he felt the impulse to wander, to shout at the sky and wail at the memories that haunted him.

Declan and Cedric began talking strategy. The six wide ships would carry the thousand soldiers across the sea. The crusade would land in Normandy and march south, gathering what support and supplies it could. The Yew was rooted in Mont Saint Michel. Its forces spread over Brittany. If it was to be the last march of the Templars, then so be it. Lil stiffened at this discussion, particularly during their grim forecasts for Brittany. Apparently, no word had come from that peninsula. They all anticipated the worst.

Toothless stood, unable to ignore the itching that ran up and down his spine. The whiskey was gone. He threw the empty wineskin to the ground. It had afforded him only a very small number of memories, and had therefore done little to make him feel more alive. He feared he was beyond that.

He wandered away from them, down a slide of stones. Away from the ships, away from the shore altogether. Cedric, Declan, and Lil paused to watch him go, though the men resumed their discussion after only seconds. They did not seem concerned. They did not know the questions he considered. They did not understand that he still conceived of destroying them all.

Toothless roamed the night. The temperature had risen. Thunder sounded in the distance. This was odd on this night on the edge of winter, with the earlier snow shower still on the ground.

He drew comfort from the howling of the Templar who had occupied the cell beside him. He could not hear this man now, of course, but knew that he shouted up at the bright moon that was now threatened by gold-rimmed clouds. He could feel those shouts. They rang in the stone beneath his feet and shuddered in the trunks of bare trees. Perhaps they traveled all the way to Mont Saint Michel, to the scene of their genesis, like salmon swimming back to the place of their hatching.

Another fork in the road. Another choice. It had been a choice to leave the order and marry Aine. It had been a choice to leave the Yew. A choice to follow Lil. A choice, this day, to fight the forces of Prince Richard. Where did regret and uncertainty fit into the traits that the Yew felt necessary to preserve in its sentient soldiers? Why had the spriggan not cut doubt from him? Perhaps it was better to become a mindless shambler.

That would happen whether he desired it or not. The choice before him now: save the Yew and destroy everything on this island, or participate in an uncertain crusade against the Yew. At the end of all of the discussions, he realized, he was their only strategy. He could not imagine how he could be strong enough to destroy the tree, or even approach it. Winter would not affect the Yew's forces. And the Templars assumed that they would cross the channel without incident and make the long march without tiring or losing men to the cold. Had the enemy been mere living men—Richard's men, or even a rabble—Toothless would not have recommended the assault. They were settled into a fortress.

The Martyrs' Crusade.

They discussed strategy and made plans, but they agreed to die. Declan and Cedric believed that the outcome, whether victory or defeat, fulfilled some heavenly plan. They had forgotten, it seemed to Toothless, that they would all end up serving the Yew and hastening its cause.

He stepped from the trees, into a field with frozen furrows. He walked over these, into an empty corral, to a stable. Horses—he could hear them breathing and grunting. They reacted to him with nervousness, as they had in Brittany. He could see their light, their life glow, flickering in the wooden stalls.

At the far end of the stable, a boy slept beneath thick blankets on a pile of straw. Was it the boy who ran errands between Declan and the army? Or was it the servant of the hospitalier nuns? It did not matter. There were countless orphan boys from the continent and elsewhere, in slavery or living as wild things in the woods. This one was important now, and could be forever more, as the one whom Toothless found at that moment, and who could have been, perhaps, the first to join him.

Toothless had no sense of how he would do it. He would first kill the boy, of course. A strangling. That would be the best. He believed that he would then know how to raise the boy from the dead. The Yew could do it. So should he be able to do it.

The thought of the Yew frightened him, and he braced for the voice. It did not come.

He looked back at the boy, who twitched in some dream and turned beneath the wool. Toothless imagined the sharp musty smell of the blankets.

He had been at this place in Brittany. There, a young man and woman barely out of childhood had stolen away to the stables. They made love. Toothless stood over them in the dark, watching their life glow mingled into a shapeless form, and he thought he could kill them, raise them, and take the whole of the peninsula as his own kingdom. He had thought of bringing that army to the Yew as a peace offering. Some force, drifting on the same chorus of dead voices that had deafened him in the village of slaughter, forbade him. He sated his blood lust on sheep.

Toothless blinked.

Now, there was no such chorus. Only the nearing thunder.

He extended his hand, reaching for the boy's neck. A pang of guilt shot from his gut, forcing him to pause. He withdrew.

Barking and growling. He turned. He expected to see wolves, but instead saw two small hounds, not at all informed as to what they were getting themselves into. They sensed something, though, for they bared their teeth.

The boy shuddered and sat up, forcing Toothless to take a step into the shadows. The dogs continued, low growling deep in their throats and the hair standing tall on their backs. When they barked, their bodies shot back an inch or two, ground they made up with quick steps toward Toothless. They would not enter far into the stable, however, before the growling built into barks that sent them back out the doorway.

"What?" The boy's voice was high and sleepy. "What is it?"

He was much younger than Toothless had thought. Perhaps he was no more than five years old, maybe even younger. A moment before, the boy had been seconds from death. Now, he was an innocent, indestructible thing.

Like Emer had once been.

Toothless leaped from the shadows. The boy gasped, but Toothless did not look back. The Templar launched over the dogs and ran into the night. They did not chase him, but barked on and on. He ran until he could not hear them, until the moon disappeared behind clouds and the rain began.

✠

The rain smacked against his numb face, running down his open throat and washing the blood from his skin. He ran through flashes of lightning, across Holy Island, through the waist-deep water of the channel, to the mainland. He ran across the battlefield. The corpses were gone. The forest's red embers, uncovered by his boots, sizzled and went dark.

He ran beyond the fire, beyond the rain, before stopping on a low rise, woods behind him and a plain reaching before him. There were lights below, far ahead, almost on the horizon. A village or a farm—the lights drew him like a moth to a flame. He could cross that plain and reach those people, those prey, in no time at all.

No, he thought.

He turned, his foot smacking against a stone. Toothless looked. A foot or two toward the forest, another stone. Then, another. A line of rectangular stones led back into the woods. The stones were smooth and ancient. He saw them as blank spaces in the glowing light of the brier. He followed them. They ended not more than fifteen yards into the forest, at a clearing.

There, a circle of stones like he had seen in France lay still and cold before him. The lightning flashed. The stones were wide panels, rounded and chipped at their tops. They were as tall as men. Their shape reminded him of cowled monks, so that Toothless imagined a ring of druids or saints staring at something in their center, something that he could not see.

Toothless walked the circle multiple times. He examined each stone from top to bottom in the lightning. They were bare of markings and lichen. Stopping, he looked about and up. Lightning revealed still images of a few falling drops. The rain was catching up to him. Steam from the doused fire poured onto the scene, staying low.

Strange things happened in such places. They were gateways. He knew it. He remembered the strange vision of fireflies at the circle in France.

He leaned against the inside of one of the stones, sliding down to sit. Looking across the center, he saw the stones on the opposite side when the lightning flashed. Toothless was not sure if he needed to sleep, but it felt good to sit. It felt good for the growing rain to drench him. He still felt powerful, and at the same time still felt the creeping sensation of losing himself, of becoming a shambler. He needed only Breakneck and Curdle by his side, and all would be as it had been.

This was good, he thought. He could think and plan.

Toothless closed his eyes, just for a moment, to center his thoughts.

He did not open them again until morning.

It was still raining. He did not hear any thunder. The stones stood as silent sentries around the puddle of brown water that had collected in the center. The circle was a dozen or more yards across, perhaps double the size of the one in France. He half expected the stones to sink inwards in the uncertain, soupy ground. Toothless looked at the low, solid gray sky. It gave no sign of brighter weather in any direction, though he could not see far.

Toothless wondered what had happened here—what ceremonies, what promises and oaths. He thought, as he had once before, about the men who made such places. There was no telling who they were. Perhaps they once lived on the plain below the forest, and the men who now made the light were far descendants. He then imagined the Yew in this place, taking root in the center and filling the whole circle. He wondered if such things like the Yew sprouted from places such as these. Did the stones make or mark the place as sacred?

There was a rustle in the woods to his side. He reached for the hilt of his sword behind his head. He found it there and pulled the greatsword from its straps, laying it across his lap. A figure appeared. Robed in blue, the intruder was not tall enough to be a soldier or a monk.

It was Lil.

The rain intensified, and was now running from the edge of her hood in streams. She was hunched, holding her robes tight at her neck.

She saw him. She stopped but was calm, as if expecting to find him. She looked at the stones, and at him. Relief replaced the tension on her face and in her frame. Her shoulders relaxed. She smiled. Toothless was afraid of moving, afraid that the blood lust would grip him and that he would kill her without a thought. He had felt it once before, when they had arrived in the land of his farm. On that morning, Toothless had left her at the fire, sure that he would strangle her if he remained. She had answers, then, whether she knew it or not. He had needed her. Where would he be without her?

Perhaps he would have rampaged across Brittany and gathered the army that he now considered. Perhaps now he would be at the head of the Yew's legions, crossing the channel, close to Lindisfarne anyway. And then what? He had asked the question before. When all of the judgment was done and all the living were dead, what would happen to him and his memories?

"It's not safe for you out here!" Lil shouted through the rain.

He did not answer her. In fact, he turned away from her.

"It's not safe!" she repeated. "Odo is gone. Francis is gone. But they had friends."

Toothless looked at the puddle at the center of the stone circle, at the explosion of raindrops on its surface.

"Stand up!" Lil continued. "Don't you understand? They're looking for you!"

He wanted to ask how she had found him. He was concerned. If she had found him, then they could. Then he remembered that she was a seer. Perhaps she had followed some sense, some vision to this place.

"The army sails in two days," she said. "They need you. Come back with me."

She seemed to have more to say, but she stopped. He still made no reply. Toothless did not even move, except to shift his gaze from the puddle to the stones on the opposite side of the circle.

Lil knelt in the mud and leaned against the stone closest to her. She huddled into herself in the cold rain. Streaks of blonde hair were plastered to her cheeks. The water dripped from the end of her small nose and puddled in her lap.

Toothless closed his eyes.

It was dark and the rain had stopped, when he opened them again. The sky was clear of clouds. He saw bright stars and a full moon. They cast a yellow light to the gray world.

Lil was asleep, still kneeling and leaning. Toothless shook his head at her persistence, though he was not sure why he thought she would have left. He would now have to face killing her, or would have to control the beast within him. He could get up and run, but she would find him again. He was sure of it.

Lil gasped. She stood. She looked at Toothless. Lil sighed, frustrated, and shook her head. Her robes were still soaked, though she did not shiver. In fact, she opened her robe. He turned away, not wanting her to catch him staring at her.

"It's warm," she said.

Though he could not feel the temperature, Toothless sensed the humid heaviness in the air. Lil's breath did not cloud in front of her. The air around the stone circle grew thick into fog. It twisted and swirled in shapes like the symbols on the wall of the cavern by the tidal pool.

Toothless looked back at Lil. She pressed her body against the inside face of the stone. She breathed hard. She closed her eyes. Was she having a vision? Or dying?

Toothless stood and took a step toward her. Then, however, something in the corner of his eye distracted him. A small glowing point, it floated about the base of a stone at the far side of the circle. Yellow green light, flitting in and out. Another appeared, and then several more, all around that stone.

Fireflies.

They described tangled arcs. After some seconds, their arcs brought them toward one another, toward a single point. They met and lightning flashed. They burst into a dizzying, swirling horde.

They next gathered into a tight cloud around the stone, perching on its edges, so that it had an aura like a living thing but far brighter. It was a stronger light than the moon. The wall of fog surrounding the stone circle reflected this glow.

Then, a dog.

Toothless blinked, even reached for his eyes to rub it away. He did not believe that it could be possible. A snout and eyes, one ear standing and one flopping—Kennocha peeked from behind the stone. She bounded into the circle, splashing into the puddle and dropping her shoulders, ready to play. A ghost. A memory. Toothless' eyes narrowed in the closest thing to a smile that he could manage. Kennocha ran to him. She jumped upon him. He thought that he felt her paws on his thighs. Toothless reached down, but his hands passed through her.

More movement. He looked at the stone. Kennocha tore off to his right to bark at Lil.

Four soldiers walked from the stone, then. Toothless raised his blade. They pointed, feigning concern and taking mock stances, then laughed, slapping one another's backs. They approached and extended their hands. He knew them. He had trained with them. They were brothers, and they were long gone, long dead.

His father came out then and, though limping, led his mother by the elbow. They were dressed in some finery, his mother wearing the necklace that she had always claimed came to her from some distant Viking heritage, and which he had seen her wear but once or twice. It was a thick thing with twisted strands, a gold rope. His father wore a tunic with intricate stitching at the edge of the skirt. The wedding, Toothless remembered. That was how they appeared at his wedding.

A child from his youth dodged the soldiers and his parents. He was a fat boy. Toothless could not remember his name, but felt the sun and breezes, the exhaustion, as they ranged through forests and fields.

"Can Martin come out to play?" the boy asked.

And then many more, stepping from behind that stone, one after the other. Tuan moved among them, smiling, heading straight for the soldiers, making them uncomfortable. Their joking ceased.

Stranger memories—the priest who had whipped Toothless' knuckles for dropping the host. Toothless was a little boy. The priest rapped his knuckles until they were bloody. He still held the green sapling branch in one hand. It leaned on his shoulder like a ceremonial sword. He stood to one side, nodding. Also, the blacksmith with lewd eyes who, when Toothless was a young man, stared at him. He stopped his ringing hammer whenever Toothless passed. The smith turned up dead one morning, his throat slit.

Many of them were now strangers. They wanted to be recognized, but Toothless could not muster the memories. They passed glances between them, as if bored or disappointed. After some moments, they fidgeted along the edges of the circle.

The crowd grew, pressing in on him. Those nearest him were smiling, congratulating him. They jostled to get close to him. He began to feel breathless, as if he even breathed. It was panic, or sharp nervousness. He was not sure. What was he to do? Was he to walk away with them? Or to run from them? Was he to drive them back to the land of the dead?

He dropped his sword and covered his face.

Silence, then.

Toothless looked up from his palms. The crowd had parted. The ghosts now stood in two groups, their attention locked on the stone at the end of the path they had created.

Aine.

She was the same glory that he had seen at the fair in Ireland. It was not long ago, but it was forever. Her robes flowed about her confident, graceful steps. She looked at him. Dark hair framed her kind but keen eyes. She walked to him. He took stumbling steps forward, then increased his gait into a jog. The faces turned to follow him as he crossed the center of the circle. They were all smiling. Tuan nodded. His mother held her hands together at her heart.

Aine raised her arms. He embraced her. He could smell her hair and feel her soft warm cheek against his neck.

Silence again, then. He opened his eyes.

Darkness.

He held no one. Around him, no one.

Lil inhaled and coughed as if she had been drowning.

Toothless unhooked his arms and looked at his hands. As he comprehended the emptiness, he dropped to his knees, splashing muddy water. He looked left and right and saw nothing—no figures, no fireflies, no fog. He looked up. The clouds were gone. The stars and moon were quiet, still, far.

He yearned now for death more than he had at any point. He felt the emptiness now, so wide and loud. The memories had been here, and were now gone.

All of them.

Lil breathed and gasped again.

The stone ahead—Toothless squinted. A dim afterglow still shimmered there. Something moved behind it. He dropped to his hands.

A little girl.

Emer.

She peered around the edge of that stone and smiled, waving pudgy fingers at him. Then, she was gone.

Toothless rose to his knees. Putting his face back into his palms, he sat upon his heels. The emptiness within him yawned wide. The stars hummed. The Yew's roots crept and cracked as they groped below him.

A hand touched his shoulder. It was Lil. She was still breathing hard. She was wheezing. Tenderness bloomed in her wet eyes. She looked at him for a long moment. He did nothing but look back at her, trying to write the features of her face—asymmetrical, below her misshapen head—into the void. Lil opened her mouth to speak. She paused a moment, as if unsure. Then, she took a breath.

"As long as we remember them, they live."

Tuan had said it.

"Do you see?" she continued, kneeling beside him in the water. "Death can claim none of us until the very last one of us is gone."

Toothless looked at the stone. It was dark and silent.

He stood, then. He took two steps, pausing to wait for Lil. When she rose, he walked to the edge of the circle, to his sword. He took the blade and slid it through the straps on his back. He did not need to motion to her. She walked forward to join him.

The two returned to the beach and waited for the causeway to Holy Island to rise from the water. They lit a fire and sat in silence, as they had in France.

Toothless' thoughts swirled with memories. Aine walked to embrace him. Emer peeked from behind the stone. Anger welled up within him. Their faces were already vague.

The Yew's march, he vowed, would end.

Chapter XX

✠

The six vessels—*Baphomet, Hiram Abiff, Sangreal, Sophia, Merovingian, Hugues de Payens*—plied the rough seas between Britain and the continent. Each carried two hundred men and their supplies. Their hulls drafted low and their sails strained hard at the rigging for the weight. Thankfully, the wind was strong and steady. A small force of armed and armored knights remained on the deck of each ship in the event of pirate or other attack, which had not come. Nearly two days, and the cruise had been uneventful.

They aimed for Normandy. There had been much discussion about how to best cross the channel. If the ships sailed in a tight though conspicuous group, Cedric worried, the Yew might learn of the passage and set a gang of sea monsters in ambush. The whole enterprise would be done before the army would have even had a chance to land. Declan, however, wondered at the wisdom of breaking the fleet into a wider group. It would delay the march. The situation on the continent, he said, was probably deteriorating, and winter would be harsher than in Britain. Spreading them out, he asserted, would also be leaving each to its own. A single lost ship would be a catastrophe to this already small army. No matter the arguments, Declan carried the day.

Army—the collection of men in the bellies of these six ships barely deserved the title. Toothless knew that, even if green, these were Templars. A single one was worth twenty regular men at arms. Richard had sent a sizable force against them on Holy Island. A few score Templars had held the beach for some time. They had much hope that Toothless would somehow be able to turn the tide in any battle, as he had against Richard. He had no way and no desire to tell them that his power was in decline. Whatever the Yew had achieved to wake him and imbue him with strength, was waning. He had no way to express that his worry over becoming a shambler far outweighed any concerns he had for the coming battle. He ignored any concern that, once back in the sphere of the Yew, he would turn on the Templars as he almost had in Britain.

Lil had stopped him, through no effort of her own. She stopped him by being numbered among the possible victims. Francis had been right. She did mean something to him. There was some connection between them.

But Lil was not with them, now.

Toothless stood on the aft deck of the *Baphomet*. Lil, he imagined, still stood on the beach. The two of them, alone, the distance growing between them, wondered when they would next meet. Their fates, their missions were linked. So he guessed, the Yew stood at one extreme of his world, Lil at the other, and Toothless reached to both of them from the center.

He was sure that much would happen between this moment and any possible reunion. Lil would go with Declan and the remaining grandmasters to Iona or some other seat. Toothless, Cedric, Stephen, and the bulk of the fighting order would attack the Yew. In some ways, Lil was in more danger than he was. Though Toothless had killed Francis, and Odo had perished in the battle against Richard, that faction was still strong. It must have made evil bargains to secure its power. How else, Toothless wondered, could a monk like Francis have earned the trust and service of a Templar grandmaster? For centuries, the church had only tolerated the Templars. In recent months, however, the order had become a fashionable target of blame in Rome and in the royal courts of Europe. Odo, weak and desperate but ambitious, must have bridged this chasm to reach the darker corners of the church, where men like Francis perfected evil arts and waited for the call to use them. Enormous amounts of money must have changed hands. Many would have an interest in the alliance.

Declan would be a target, as would Cedric and the army. This was another reason behind Declan's assertion that the ships sail together. Roving pirates on the payroll of corrupt churchmen or Odo's lackeys could have taken any single ship without any of the others knowing. As a close fleet, however, they not only presented insurmountable numbers to any such attacker—though a small fleet, it was the largest of its day—but they also moved with speed that would allow them to land as one group in Normandy and march south, preserving as much of the element of surprise as possible. Were they to launch separately, they would have to land much closer to Mont Saint Michel.

Standing on the aft deck, Toothless looked west. Night was falling on their second day. Most of the men slept below decks. Sailors worked the rigging. No more than ten armored knights kept watch. Also on the aft deck, Cedric and Stephen pored with a dozen other captains over a map. A weak lantern cast a dim orange glow over the scene. They plotted strategy, moving their fingers in lines as if that were all that it took to move armies. They discussed friendly towns, towns where they would find supplies and additional soldiers. They also discussed towns that had become fortresses ruled by crazed men. Their fingers did not stray too far south or east, for that would take their march into the plaguelands.

Toothless looked into the ship's wake. Algae glowed, faint and green in the churning water. The wind was strong. He heard not only the snapping sail of the *Baphomet*, but also sails and clanging pulleys of the ships behind, only the closest of which he could see. The *Sangreal*, a black shape leaning in the falling night, was not far. Fog, night—these were good. They would hide the fleet's passage.

They sailed east, and planned to turn south at the coast, but not so close to the beach as to be seen. They would soon make that turn. By next daybreak, they hoped, the fleet would be nearing Normandy.

He looked west, past the ships, to the British beach, to Holy Island—things he could not see. Lil would be watching the surf. Beyond her, over Britain and Ireland, to the far ocean—there, Tuan drifted in his currach. Toothless wondered at what lay beyond. Riddles and ciphers made dim references to a land of plenty, shores first touched by Norse raiders and Irish monks. The tale of Brendan, for example, had been of particular interest to Tuan. Maybe he was not dead, then. Maybe he had found this western land, the land of everlasting youth.

Toothless closed his eyes. Behind him, Cedric and Stephen were arguing. The other captains remained silent, perhaps sensing what Toothless felt, that Stephen was impudent, challenging his master for the sake of challenging. Tuan would never have allowed such open defiance. And the question seemed trivial—whether to take a higher or a lower road out of a village in the northernmost reaches of France on the odd chance that they should land there instead of in Normandy. Toothless guessed that Cedric need only to declare an end to the discussion, much as Declan had ended the discussion on the formation of the fleet. Cedric could render a decision, and that would be the end. Instead, however, the master Templar entertained the younger captain's sparring.

To take the higher ground, Cedric argued, would provide them the ability to survey their surroundings. A lower road, Stephen argued, would preserve the secrecy of their march. So, they went back and forth arguing variations on these two positions. The rest of the captains, Toothless noticed, were beginning to exchange bored glances.

Toothless wondered if he should weigh in. He could point at the lower road, which was his preference. He would be able to convey, perhaps in gestures, that speed and secrecy would be their best tactic. Who cared what lay about them, if they were to speed south?

He had, however, no interest in turning from the sea. It was not just squinting to see the ships, or Lil, or Tuan, or beyond to lost memories. Something was not right. The creak of the hull, the whipping of the sail—they seemed to speak with some urgency, some anxiety. The *Sangreal,* now closer, showed no such issue. The life glow of the guards wandered the deck of that ship. Sailors leaped through the rigging. That was all.

Then, the *Sangreal* and, now visible, the *Sophia* behind it, peeled away. The *Baphomet* turned the opposite direction. North, he realized. The *Baphomet* was turning north. It was leaving the fleet. Did the knights and crew on the other ships see? Or could they not see? Perhaps his own sight enhanced due to his gifts as a soldier of the Yew. Perhaps the living could not see through the night and the fog as well as he.

He waited a moment, expecting some correction. Perhaps this was planned. Perhaps the *Baphomet* would round to the back of the fleet. He leaned, looking at the wake, which straightened. To his left, the dim glow of land slid into view and then settled at the starboard side of the ship.

North by northeast. Steady. The rest of the fleet disappeared from his sight.

Toothless turned then, and forced his way between two of the captains. The conversation ceased. Cedric raised an eyebrow. Stephen, caught in mid-sentence, sighed the remaining breath with annoyance. Toothless pointed at the map, where six markers showed the ships in the channel at the turn of the line—east, then south to Normandy.

Toothless rearranged the markers to show what was happening, then pointed to the starboard side of the ship. Cedric and the captains squinted. A single light—a fisherman's late campfire, or some other encampment on the beach—slid from fore to aft not more two hundred yards off the deck. It took but a second for the Templars to realize the situation. At once, without any orders, they moved across the deck, to the pilot at the wheel near the center of the ship.

"Who pilots this ship?" Cedric asked.

Stephen paused before answering.

"I believe word went through the parishes to muster able-bodied seamen."

"Dammit!" Cedric snapped. "Richard has manned these ships, or worse! Odo and Francis!"

"You!" Stephen called to the pilot. "Turn this ship south!"

The pilot did not move except to steady the wheel on a northerly course.

"Turn the ship now," Cedric ordered.

Stephen motioned the nearest watchman to his side. There were but three armed knights, the rest at other corners of the ship. Toothless, Cedric, the captains—none of these men carried a blade.

The pilot flexed his shoulders. Toothless saw it, and was not sure if the Templars did. In a flash, this man crouched and then leaped into the air, twisting as he flew overhead, and landed behind them. The watchmens' lanterns turned upon him. He wielded two short daggers, one in each hand. The blades were curved like crescent moons. He released his robes to reveal tight-fitting shirt and pants. His skin was dark, and his frame thin, athletic. Toothless realized that this was not the body of a man who spent most of his day in labor aboard a ship, and most of his night bathing in ale.

"Hashashin!" Cedric hissed.

He had served in Jerusalem. He, perhaps better than anyone, knew the Persian assassins. Toothless had only heard tales of the mysterious army that fought their wars, and the wars of any who paid them, by such unconventional means as those now arrayed against the Templars. Too small a force to face its foes on the battlefield, the Hashashin had become expert at espionage, subterfuge, and disguise—skills that were valuable to men like Odo and Richard. Indeed, Richard was known to have consorted with such men.

More of these men descended on ropes from the rigging. Before even Toothless could react, battle was underway on the decks as the assassins, each armed with daggers like the first, assaulted the Templar watchmen. It turned badly for the knights, as each of the Hashashin wielded their daggers and performed acrobatics with such expert skill that many of the Templars were disarmed within seconds. As soon as the heavy arming swords clanged to the deck, the Hashashin kicked them across the boards and into the ocean.

The watchmen fell, one by one. Two of the captains then succumbed, arching their backs at dagger strikes into their kidneys before dropping to the deck, their bodies flopping and spouting blood like landed fish. Toothless backed away with Cedric and Stephen. The watchmens' lanterns were gone, and he could not distinguish attacker from Templar among the auras before him.

Stephen did not seem to understand this dilemma.

"Attack!" he shouted. "Damn you, Martin! Attack!"

Toothless glared at the Templar, but Stephen was scanning the darkness before them. They were near the table, by the lamp. Their shadows descended into the darkness of the deck. The sail was loose, flopping in the wind. The *Baphomet* drifted. Toothless feared they would grind into the beach.

The Templar watchmen were defeated, either dead on the deck or floating in the channel. Toothless heard pounding, which he traced to the hatch into the hold. The hatch was in the fore deck. It was locked.

A dozen attackers. They were on the verge of capturing a ship of over two hundred Templars.

Cedric and the remaining captains moved by his right side, along the starboard deck. With Stephen, they formed a tight circle. The Hashashin were not far behind. They whirled and leaped into the light, but the captains, wielding what weapons or implements they had gathered from the deck, fought them back. Toothless looked about and, when he found no weapon, turned toward the sound of a whistle from the captains. Stephen handed him one of the attacker's curved daggers. Toothless weighed the weapon in his hand and, nodding in satisfaction, stepped forward into the dark. His joints were stiff, his instincts sluggish. Though his power faded, he knew that he was still a formidable foe.

The hull shuddered. Rocks. Toothless widened his stance in order to balance himself. The ship leaned, then slid away from the rocks with a violent motion. The lamp fell from the map table. It burst, its fuel igniting across the aft deck. Fire blazed upon the ancient wood of the deck, sending shadows up the length of the ship. Flames climbed the rigging and touched the loose sail, which burst into a fiery pennant flying far behind the mast. It was a beacon. Would the other ships see it and come to rescue them, or were they, too, under assault?

It only lasted seconds. Once spent, the sail drifted away in black strips. The fire died on the deck as well, though smoke was puffing through the seams in the planks. Flame lit thin columns of smoke that poured through tight portholes and carried screams to the stars.

The fire had spread to the hold.

Toothless could see the Hashashin creeping among corpses on the deck. The assassins would have made good captains for the Yew. Below, men burned. Some of their corpses would be useful. Most of the watchmen on the deck could rise again. Here then, was the beginning of his army, and a ship to carry them if he could stop the fire. Perhaps one hundred marching dead from the two hundred who died below, plus a corps of captains ready to lead thousands—it was a start.

He shook the thought from his head.

The Templars, he guessed, were not able to see in the dark and the smoke. Toothless, however, watched the auras of a pair of Hashashin walking back along the starboard rail, approaching the Templar position. The assassins crouched as they moved, holding their daggers low, ready to strike up into their prey.

Toothless launched at them, taking one of the assassin's heads in his left hand and slamming the man's face into the railing. The assassin went limp, dropping into a heap on the deck. Toothless sliced with the dagger then, cutting the throat of the second assassin. Blood sprayed in a circle as the man spiraled to join his comrade.

Toothless gathered the dropped daggers. The Templars, he thought, might need them. He turned to the circle of knights.

He did not quite see what happened next. There was a flurry of movement in the smoke between him and the Templars. A dark shape rose before him and barreled into him. As he fell back, the daggers flying in all directions from his still-cradled arms, he was nothing but surprised. Was he that weak? He landed on his rump, cracking the fire-weakened deck planking, and slid several yards in blood.

The smoke was now thicker, swirling all about the Templars. The Hashashin seemed part of that smoke. They moved in and out of it as they approached the Templars from all sides. They were like ghosts, phasing in and out of existence. Had the Yew already enlisted them, creating yet another type of soldier? Perhaps the walking dead, even the sentients, were primitive compared to what the Yew actually planned to unleash upon the world.

No, he thought. He looked at the assassins' corpses in front of him, the one with the smashed face and the other, blood still dribbling from the slit on his neck. They were just men. They were no more powerful than the limits of life would allow them to be.

The Templars swung into the smoke. The Hashashin dodged and feinted. Toothless wondered—where was the patience and studied practice? Who had trained these knights? The Hashashin, on the other hand, showed immense discipline. They were focused on a single objective, that of killing their prey. They seemed unfazed by the prospect of dying. Indeed, they seemed cured of the fear of death altogether, as if death were the natural end of their mission.

The Martyrs' Crusade had embarked, Toothless thought, on the same notion. But only Cedric and Stephen seemed to display the steel and discipline to see it through. The other captains were breaking. Panic was beginning to bloom in the center of their defensive circle.

Toothless shook his head to clear his thoughts. He stood, his legs unsteady. He braced against the railing and turned again to the Templars. The Hashashin were now gathered on the edge of the defensive circle, probing, preparing to strike.

Cedric was clutching something. A small pouch no larger than a child's fist. He held it as if it were key to his survival. A weapon, Toothless thought, though he could not imagine what it could be.

There would be no answer. The boat shuddered again, leaning, throwing the starboard side high into the air. The Templars and the Hashashin slid away across the deck. Toothless gripped the starboard railing in the crook of his arm and, peering over the side, saw the fire reflecting off the surface of jagged rocks. The side of the boat split, and the fire leaped into the night. The *Baphomet* disgorged burnt crates and sacks, charred corpses. These smoldered on the rocks. The ship cleared the shoal and leaned back into its starboard side. The yawning hull now swallowed sea water. Steam billowed.

Toothless flipped over the railing. The dark water enveloped him, taking him down, kissing him and whispering cold promises of eternal oblivion. He remembered that the Loire in France had made similar promises. Icy silt, silky and soft, laying over him. But it was not to be.

He burst through the surface, facing the ship, which now bubbled and sank, the last of its flames dying in jets of steam. As they died, so too did the light, and the boat disappeared into fog and darkness.

Toothless spun, looking for some sign of the shore—a dim glow of life, the campfire, anything. He found the small point of the fire, far and flickering. Fixing his gaze some degrees to its left, to its north, he gripped a broken plank from the *Baphomet* and began to kick.

The Martyrs' Crusade, his crusade, was not over.

Chapter **XXI**

The morning came, borne on a cold wind from the east. As the sun rose, the wind shifted so that it pushed against Toothless as he trudged down the beach. The sky was a gray thing that had no depth. It threatened snow.

Toothless was not sure where he went, and so was quite thankful to find Stephen, Cedric, and three knights some distance down the beach. They huddled around a crate that they used as a table. They described plans as they had on the deck, as if a map were before them. There was no map, though they all seemed to see the lines and points that they conjured with their shivering fingertips. The knights must have survived the inferno in the belly of the ship. If so, it must have been as close to hell as they had ever stood. They were courageous, or lucky.

They did not respond to his arrival with anything more than a nod. Their reaction was so limp, and their appearance so sudden, that Toothless wondered if he were dreaming. He realized, though, that the three surviving knights were too anxious to afford him any welcome. They were now thrust into positions of prime leadership, though the army they now led was gone, landing somewhere to the south—or dead, having suffered some similar attack. Toothless, it seemed, was not enough of a comfort to soothe them.

The discussion wound through various points, but returned to the topic of their location. Flanders, Stephen asserted. Cedric argued France. It did not matter in any tactical dimension, thought Toothless, though the resolution of this argument might provide some definition to their plight, whether correct or not. Perhaps they needed this. They wore wet clothes and were in danger of freezing to death, yet insisted on arguing the point. The three knights stood aside, almost whispering to one another, as if wagering on the outcome. Disagreements between Cedric and Stephen, then, had become sport.

Cedric had found a scrap of cloth, sail cloth or some other, and was wearing it like a mantle over his shoulders. It was greased, and repelled the water that sprayed from the surf or condensed from the fog. The droplets grew on his shoulders and, once too large to stand, rolled down his back. Toothless could not imagine the thing keeping the master any warmer, though it did afford him some additional status.

Another item—beneath the makeshift mantle, he still gripped the leather pouch that Toothless had observed on the deck of the *Baphomet*. Cedric now wore it around his neck on a leather cord. His knuckles were white and his fingers as still as dead sticks, as if the cold channel water and the icy wind had frozen his fingers closed about the bag. He seemed about to whip it from beneath his mantle, lay it on the crate as some item of status, some trump that would silence Stephen's impudence once and for all.

Instead, he spoke.

"This ends. We march south."

After an hour or two, they reached the fisherman's camp, the light of which Toothless had seen from the deck of the *Baphomet*. The fire still glowed, but the camp was abandoned. Cedric, Stephen, and the three knights gathered over this meager heat to warm themselves, but it did not seem to be effective. Carcasses of large fish, filleted and gutted, lay in a heap. The Templars sucked and gnawed scraps of frozen meat from these. Toothless wondered if it would only make them hungrier, but then realized that it also added hours to their stamina. Still, as they departed the camp and the hunger grew in the guts of Toothless' companions, they became quiet.

After some hours of silence, one of the knights launched into near-manic rants. He swore that he saw the five remaining Templar ships just offshore. There was nothing, nothing at all. The knight continued for some moments about feasts that would be laid out for them just beyond the next set of dunes, or the celebration that would ensue when they cut the Yew, which he described as a sapling, from its roots. He went quiet, then, only to renew his monologue at unpredictable intervals.

The rain began to fall as soon as night touched the eastern horizon, and they stopped to make camp. Dark clouds barreled from the north, as if intent upon joining with the smoke of the Yew's march to the south. The rain was just a heavy drop or two at first, intensifying as more and more fell, pocking the sand and exploding against the rocks. The knights, already drenched, set themselves to the task of stripping branches from sapling trees to make a shelter. Cedric's makeshift mantle was now the covering to a crude lean-to. It became heavy with ice, though, as the rain mixed with sleet and billowy snow.

Cedric, Stephen, and the three knights shivered as Toothless stood watch. Toothless passed the time by dragging a sharp-edged stone down a straight limb, green and supple, to create a point. He had little training in how to wield such a stave. It had no balance to be thrown, but its point would pierce skin. He felt better with a weapon in his hands as he stood watch. None of the Templars were armored. While the ice and snow provided some relief from thirst, both their hunger and the cold weakened them. Even Cedric and Stephen showed signs of breaking. They had short conversations in wakeful moments between fits of sleep, but could come to no useful strategies. They spent most of those moments staring at one another, or into the distance, with worry in their eyes.

Toothless was worried as well. Each scrape of the sharp stone against the soft wet wood sent vibrations through his arm that angered a flaring sensation, a familiar itch. He turned to the sky and felt the impact of the rain against his face. It ran down his throat, into his lungs.

He could feel a shambler's howls gathering in his gut.

He ached, feeling pain in his joints and his head. He ached for memories. Toothless wondered what it would take to get ale, but knew that it was too late. To drink ale now would be to open doors on empty spaces. The memories were gone. His wife, his daughter—he remembered seeing them at the stone circle on Holy Island, but that was all. Nothing else. He remembered seeing his parents and Tuan. He remembered nothing of them before that moment.

He held the stave in his hands and took a defensive stance. He wanted to swing it, like a blade, but knew that he had to jab. It was better than nothing, he thought.

Why, he wondered, had he retained his training? Why was he still a warrior when he had forgotten everything else about his life? The chant of the spriggan, when they had first lifted him from the battlefield, had worked away his soul. The black priests sang to the same effect, as well. The song, the magic of it, had widened the wound through which leaked his memories. The Yew, however, held fast to what it needed in him. It still did. Those empty spaces, those places where memories had once pooled, were now dry and empty. The Yew moved to fill them.

That, he realized, was what made a shambler. When all the humanity was gone, one was nothing but a vessel for the Yew. One was a marionette dancing to the whims of another thing. The black priest had said that Toothless was special, that he shared something with the Yew. Toothless no longer believed it.

He also had no idea how to manipulate the dead into minions. Just as he had failed as a Templar, as he had failed to protect his family, as the Martyrs' Crusade was failing, he would fail as a leader of the dead. How to raise them, how to control them—he had no answers.

The howl was burning at the edges of his throat like bile. His open neck would be like the mouth of a trumpet and he would scream at the rain and, above it, the stars. He would scream at the memories that had fled. He would scream at the Yew. He would scream at the chorus of the dead that screamed, itself, below everything. But he could not join that chorus, for he still stood in the world.

He brought his hands to his throat, covering his wound. He stumbled away from the camp.

"Where goes our watch?" Stephen asked.

There was no answer. Stephen did not seem to care.

Toothless left the beach and climbed a small ridge of slippery rock and frozen mud. The thin aura of struggling brush, buffeted by rain and wind, spread before him. He walked forward, still stumbling.

He could not hold back the sound now. It rose up through him and vaulted from his open neck. It was like a horn, like a trumpet. But it was a baleful note. It came out of him quite out of his control. He fell to his knees and had to grip the sides of his head for fear that his skull would explode. The pain was unbearable. He tried to cover his throat, but the howl blew his hand away. The sound was coming from deep within him, the rush of air through emptiness. It trailed off, dying in rasping whimpers at the top of his chest.

He fell to his hands, exhausted. Then, it rose again, balling in his stomach, streaming up through his throat, bringing him back to his knees.

The howling went on this way for what seemed like hours. The rain and snow fell from above. The ground, below, received it. In between, Toothless, the dead one, screamed.

When it passed, it had left him little more than a corpse in the brush. He struggled to move and managed to stand. He was stooped, leaning against his knees to keep from collapsing. Toothless wanted to feel his heart pounding in his head, sweat beading on his skin. He wanted to heave for breath. None of this happened.

Then, he noticed a sound. It had been answering his calls for some time. It came above the rain, from further inland. It was coming closer.

Snapping and growling. Savage barks through fangs. Howling.

He had brought the werewolves.

Toothless reached for his stave and, crouching, looked left and right. He was not sure if he would see the aura of the wolves, whether they had any life or not. None of the Yew's dead cast an aura, but Cedric had described these beasts as if they had shifted from living men rather than risen from the dead.

He remembered that the Champion had destroyed one of these wolves, and that he had done it with nothing more than a rock and his hands. Their strength was in numbers, in speed. If they came at him in a pack, he was sure that they would tear him to shreds.

Ten, twenty yards in front of him—he could not be sure—he heard slobbering, sniffing. He heard it to his right as well. They were smart, coming from two directions, but it seemed a small number. They drew closer. He heard grunting. But it sounded as if there were just two beasts. And perhaps they were not wolves—wild boars or badgers.

Then he saw their auras. The one in front of him moved low through the brush. It was long and lean. Its shoulder blades rose high above its bony back, almost like wings. Its eyes glowed an unholy red. They were lenses into the evil that had taken the beast's brain. The wolf had been a man, perhaps even a Templar from Mont Saint Michel.

Toothless glanced to his right. Another, a bit father off.

Both stopped at Toothless' slight movement. Crouching, holding his stave, he tried to remain still.

The one in front rose, its ears perking. Toothless did not breathe. His heart did not beat. Still, this beast heard something. Did it also hear the voice of the Yew? Or the chorus of the dead?

The two wolves, if they communicated at all with the sounds they made, could fix his position. The closer one, the one ahead, was the immediate threat. Toothless flexed his fingers around the stave and stared down the beast, watching for movement from the other out of the corner of his eye.

The rain and snow fell heavier.

The beast in front charged. Toothless tried to remain calm. The one on the right did not move. Toothless waited, flexed his fingers once more. As the thing leaped, Toothless rolled back, holding the stave before him. The beast landed right on the point, which sunk into its breast. It shuddered, letting out a pitiful whimper, a whimper like a simple dog getting stung on the nose by a bee. Toothless let the stave go, and it and the beast flew over his head. The stave snapped when the wolf landed, though not before sinking even further. The wolf stumbled and fell.

Toothless rolled, looking for the other. He could not see it, though he caught a flash of movement. The second wolf was retreating.

Toothless rose and made straight for the camp. He was not sure he was heading in the right direction. The sound of the rain obscured the sound of the surf. Then, he found a ridge and, looking down, saw the Templars. They had managed to get a small flame going beneath the lean-to. Toothless could see their faces in the orange light. They were awake, conversing. Strategy again, he thought. Questions of strategy were a luxury. They were five men with a weakened soldier of the Yew, trying to survive in a winter storm. And werewolves might now stalk them. What strategy could there be but to run?

Toothless broke into their meager light. They barely looked at him. Unable to express urgency with his face, he pumped his hands up and down to entreat them to rise.

"Up," he wanted to say. "Get up. Get up!"

"I think we need to leave," Stephen said.

Toothless nodded, pointed south along the beach, and kicked their fire away.

Moments later, they were walking through the rain and snow.

✠

They marched through the end of the storm, which ranged from freezing drizzle to outright blizzard. Morning came, cold and gray like the day before, bearing the same threat of snow. Toothless could sense that they were tired. Even Cedric and Stephen seemed close to stumbling. But they had to move. The second wolf, and perhaps more, were still ranging.

Stephen spouted, as if to raise morale, the names of all of the towns on the way to Normandy. Toothless wondered, where were they? And if they reached them, would the towns be dens of wolves and shamblers? If so, then the Templar army, wherever it had landed, would be surrounded and pushed into the sea. And then Britain, Iona, the whole world. Perhaps Stephen had the same thoughts, as his monologue trailed into silence.

The Martyrs' Crusade seemed to be finished. For his part, Toothless knew that he would not join his wife and daughter, wherever their souls had fled. If defeated, he would cease to be. Or, his broken soul would be sent to atone for its deeds. If, indeed, the notion of a soul was true at all. Lil had tried to tell him that life after death came through the memories of others. But was that all? The ghost of Aine—just his own memories?

To the west—sniffing and grunting. Cedric heard it as well, and knew what it was.

"Find rocks or logs," he said. "Anything to use as a weapon."

They scattered across the beach. The three knights found a pile of debris which yielded three planks of wood. Toothless found a large oval rock. Cedric and Stephen worked to split a log of driftwood into two clubs. Its cracking, however, made a loud, dangerous sound that silenced the wild noises beyond the beach for a moment.

The three knights were moving to rejoin the group when the beast struck. It nearly flew from the summit of a tall dune. It was long and lean like the one the night before. Its skin was black, with hair thick about its shoulders and rump. Foul slime trailed from its panting mouth. It fixed its red eyes on the three knights and plowed into them, knocking two aside with thrashes of its heavy neck and gripping the third in its jaws, crunching. The Templar screamed and gurgled before the wolf tossed him far to the side.

The knight was dead. Would he rise again as a wolf? His corpse was nearly broken in half. Toothless wondered, then. Had the beast just rendered judgment? Had it just chosen to destroy this man instead of letting him serve with the Yew?

The wolf did not hesitate, but turned on the other knights. Both

of them were just now rising. It approached one of them, snapping at
the air around him as the knight swung his plank. The third Templar
was now on his feet, slapping his plank against the beast's back
with no effect at all. Cedric and Stephen ran down the beach, now.
Toothless moved up behind them.

The werewolf paused, then lunged forward, gripping one of the
knights by the chest. The Templar screamed as the beast whipped
him back and forth. He landed somewhat near Toothless. The man's
chest was a bloody mess, but he was not dead. He would perhaps
become one of the wolves.

The third knight moved to run. The wolf growled and lunged
forward, sinking its teeth into his thigh. The knight tried to pull
away, a terrifying scream rising from his throat. The wolf dug its
black clawed paws into the sand and pulled with jerking motions of
its shoulders. The punctures on the knight's legs grew into gashes.
The knight fell to the sand, still screaming.

Stephen and Cedric were on the beast now, pounding it with their
clubs. The wolf cowered and winced under those blows. It slinked
about and found a break, bolting away from them. Running just
several yards up the beach, it spun about, its muscles flexing beneath
its scarred gray skin. It bared its fangs in fury, barking and growling.
Slime flew from its lips. Its red eyes pierced the misty rain.

It barreled into Cedric, knocking the master from his feet.
Cedric gripped the pouch around his neck. The cord broke. With
no expression at all, Cedric looked for his club, which he had
dropped. He reached for it as if it were a simple thing, in a harmless
situation—a farmer reaching for a dropped hoe, or a blacksmith for
a fallen hammer.

The wolf seemed to smile, then struck.

It held onto Cedric's upper arm, its fangs deep into his bicep.
Cedric barely winced but stared down the beast, which did nothing
but hold the bite, as if meaning to do nothing but infect the master.
The only feeling that seemed to cross Cedric's face was sadness.

Stephen and Toothless attacked the werewolf. Stephen whipped at its
legs. Toothless smashed the stone into its skull again and again. It released
the master, who scrambled back away from the melee. The wolf was now
flat on the ground, trying to crawl, whimpering. Black red blood seeped
out from gashes and cuts all over its body. It was a pitiful thing.

Stephen kicked and cursed, lost in fury over the wound that Cedric had taken, a wound that would no doubt turn him into one of the beasts. Toothless stepped back, his arm aching from throwing the weight of the stone against the wolf. He was tired. He could barely move.

Now, Stephen yelled as he stomped on the wolf's neck and chest. He planted his boot into the beast's skull. There was a sickening crunch. The werewolf, who had been one of the living, perhaps even a Templar, sighed in one last gasp before blood and slime spewed from its mouth.

Legends from rude tribes on the shores of the Black Sea spoke of silver weapons, prayers, and spells. It had taken only a rock, a log, and a boot to kill the thing.

✠

Cedric had managed to sit. He held his wounded, bleeding arm in his lap. Also there, the pouch that he had worn about his neck.

"Martin," he said, his voice straining through pain and frustration.

Toothless looked at the two dead knights. The third lay in the icy, frothy surf, propped on his elbows, his screams having given way to whimpers in his throat. His legs jerked. The one with the wounded chest twitched as well. The sickness was already getting to them. It would not be long, Toothless realized, before Cedric succumbed as well.

Toothless still carried the rock. It glistened with dark blood. He dropped the thing. It thumped in the sand.

Cedric looked at Stephen. The two said nothing, but seemed to exchange some message. Stephen nodded.

"Martin," Cedric said again. He pinched the pouch between the thumb and forefinger of his good hand, and lifted it to Toothless. It seemed heavy, or painful. "Take this."

Toothless took it in his bloodied palm, where he had held the rock. The pouch was light, though it burned. He felt the warmth. He squinted at it.

"Open it," Cedric said.

Toothless inserted two fingers into the mouth of the pouch and pried at the drawstring. A relic's aura leaped from the opening, then. He found a small glass bottle, no larger than a large grape. Its glass was uneven and bumpy, as if discarded by the glass blower as a bad start on something much finer. The stopper was a simple age-blackened bit of cork. A rough brown film like dried paint peeled from the inside of the bottle.

It glowed like the Marian Cloth, though brighter. Indeed, the bag seemed to swell to contain its power. Toothless' eyes went wide as he tried to conceive of that power. He could feel it up and down his spine, though it did nothing for him. After a moment of looking at it, he felt the same pain in the back of his head that he had felt beholding the Marian Cloth. He turned away from it, and held it forward in his palm as if it were an unholy, impossible thing.

Stephen stepped closer and took Toothless' free hand in his own. He moved the dead man's hand to cover the small pouch.

"Guard this," Stephen said.

Cedric, gnashing his teeth through a spike of pain, strained to speak. "It is the Blood," he said. "If anything will aid you in battle, it will."

"Scriptures and legends," Stephen said. "The lives of saints—they all speak of armies taking relics into battle against demons. This is ours. Some say that it is the blood of Christ, brought to France by Joseph of Arimathea. Others say that it is far older than that. Some wonder if it is the blood of Adam. Declan hints that it comes from a past so distant as to be a different world."

He took the two ends of the broken drawstring and tied them back together. He pulled the mouth of the pouch closed. Then, taking the pouch, he draped the thing over Toothless' neck. His touch was soft, as if the pouch were an extension of the wounded master.

Toothless blinked. Had a Templar just given the holiest relic to a soldier of the Yew? One last memory came, as Toothless remembered what Tuan had said. It was not the things, the people who had crafted them or from whom they had come. Rather, it was the eons of veneration falling upon them like layers of silt at the bottom of a river, that gave them power. The living made holy magic with their devotion, just as they created everlasting life through their memories. The living were divine. The Yew aimed to steal that divinity.

Stephen looked into Toothless' empty eyes. The Templar captain had vowed to follow Toothless. Now, he would.

Chapter XXII

Toothless buried the dead knight, digging a hole in the cold sand with a piece of driftwood and rolling the corpse into the seeping puddle on the floor of the grave. The wind whipped the sand into his back. He did not feel this, but it made a rushing noise like wind through dry leaves.

The sickness spread through Cedric and the two wounded knights. The knights were both unconscious, now—one on the beach, his gaping chest wheezing and sucking air as his wounded lungs inflated and deflated. He would probably not live much longer, anyway. The other, however, was only lightly wounded, and had passed out in the surf. Both of the knights' faces seemed longer and darker. If Toothless were to strip their tunics away, he would not be surprised to find bristling hair growing in patches on their shoulder blades. Cedric did not yet shows such signs, but had begun to shiver and stutter.

Cedric and Stephen discussed how to handle the turn of events, as if Cedric's fate were not at the center of that discussion.

"The aff...afflicted," Cedric said. "They must die."

Stephen acted on this order, ignoring that Cedric was among the afflicted. Toothless turned away as Stephen smashed the skulls of the wounded knights with a stone. Stephen then buried his brothers.

That left Cedric, who had entertained Stephen's discussions long enough. He did not want to engage Stephen in yet another. He stood, in pain, near-retching. He walked into the surf. The waves beat at him, but he did not seem to feel the cold of the water.

He moved as quickly as he could, struggling past the line of the waves' breaking, out dozens of yards to where the sea was calm. He submerged, then, only to come up gasping seconds later. He took a single deep breath, exhaled, and submerged again. There was a disturbance on the surface, bubbles, and then nothing.

Like Tuan and the dead who had spilled from the *Baphomet*, another Templar was given to the sea.

Stephen did not speak. He did not even look at Toothless. Rather, he turned, his jaw clenched, and walked south. Toothless walked behind, reacting at first to every sound—every rustle beyond the beach, every splash in the water, every wild call on the wind. He worried that there would be more wolves.

Hours passed, and a night in a cold camp. Then, another day passed. They saw no one as they traveled. They passed no settlements.

Stephen did not break his silence, but fixed his gaze ahead of them.

✠

Stephen must have smelled the smoke. He sniffed at the air, and spoke for the first time in days.

"We must conceal ourselves."

They left the beach and found a path through the dunes that provided some cover. After some moments, they reached a river, wide and slow moving, emptying into the sea. To the left, it wound out of view, perhaps to some town or keep. It was wide enough to be navigable.

Toothless and Stephen crawled through sand and brush to the river's high bank. Peering through weeds, they saw a camp with a blazing bonfire across the current. They could see the tops of the tents. There were many. Toothless heard song. The evening meal. Cooking, eating, drinking. Stephen must have had the same realization. He licked his lips.

"Roasting meat," he said. He looked at Toothless. "You cannot smell it, can you?"

Toothless shook his head.

Stephen's gaze slid to Toothless' wound.

"You will have to stay as I go—"

"Don't move!"

They both turned in surprise at the rough voice. Behind them, four burly men dressed in furs and leather climbed the slope. They had hair all over them—long beards, long mops at the tops of their heads. They each carried small, rough-hewn wooden shields and rude-looking short swords that were notched and rusty. They were peasants, at best, but probably brigands. There was no way for Toothless and Stephen to escape, unless they dropped to the river below. They had squandered their opportunity to consider that, on surprise.

The four approached, two restraining Stephen and two reaching for Toothless. One of these, a man with a tattered red scarf slashed around his forehead, stepped back, shouting.

"A demon!"

The second, however, stepped behind Toothless and gripped him by the arms. The scarfed man drew a dagger and approached Stephen.

"You consort with this?" he asked, pulling Stephen's head back by the hair to expose the Templar's throat. "I should kill you. Or..."

He turned to Toothless.

"I should take the demon's head," he continued. "You should have maimed yourself, demon. That's what real men do, rather than fall into the hands of the enemy."

A voice came from below.

"What do you have up there?"

A thinner man appeared. He was short, though he wore the same furs and leather as the rest. His hair was cropped close but uneven, as if he had done it himself. Curiously, he was unarmed. Still, the four at the top of the ridge granted him some deference. Many more soldiers followed him, each reacting to Toothless in a different way. Some stopped, horror on their faces, refusing to go any farther. Others flexed their sword arms and prepared to fight. All knew what he was.

"These louts," the scarfed man said. "I was going to kill them. I was going to feed this one to the dogs."

He pointed at Stephen.

"But this one," the thug continued. "He is one of the Yew's."

The thin man looked Toothless up and down, then approached Stephen. The two wore nothing to signify their affiliation with the Templars, though an experienced man would recognize their cloth as coming from a monastery. Still, there was no explaining how one of the Yew's dead would be so far north, let alone wandering with a living man.

"What should we do?" the scarfed ruffian asked.

The thin man, looking at Stephen, spoke in a low, rough voice.

"This one is fit and strong," he said. "But that one is past his prime. Still, he is a soldier of the Yew. The priest will want to see them."

"I can't kill them?"

Disappointment filled the scarfed man's voice.

"No. Not yet, anyway. Take them to camp. Cover their heads.

And keep quiet about this. All of you."

"A shame," the thug said to Stephen. "You would have made a good meal for the hounds."

"He may still," the thin man added as he descended the slope. "He may still."

✠

Men laughed and cheered. Toothless heard brawling and shouts, as well. Some minutes into the blind march, however, children played and women gossiped. He wondered if there were refugees among the soldiers.

His face covered, Toothless would not appear on quick inspection to be anything but a living man. Still, a large number of soldiers had seen him. Though their reactions had ranged from steeliness to horror, he could not believe that they would keep quiet about the fact that a soldier of the Yew was now among them. Would Odo's faction have spies among these thieves and refugees? Or would the Yew hear, and send its minions to destroy this camp?

Toothless reached for the pouch, the vial of dried blood, which bounced against his chest. This only brought attention to it. The thug leading Toothless whipped away his hand and pulled the pouch, snapping its cord.

"I'll take that."

Toothless felt panic now. The Blood, perhaps for the first time in centuries, was now lost. He did not have it, and could not see it. What would the brigand do? If he opened it hoping to find coins but only saw a dirty bauble, he might throw it to the ground. Such things had a habit of losing themselves if they were not watched.

The popping and hissing of a fire rose above the sounds of the camp, which were now somewhat distant. The hoods came off, then. Stephen and Toothless stood beside one another in a large tent. A brazier with a blazing fire sat near the center of the space. There were some soldiers here, large men dressed in leather and furs, much like the men who had discovered them. The soldiers recoiled at the sight of Toothless. Swords slid from scabbards. The thin man walked in front of Stephen and Toothless, looking them up and down.

Stephen whispered to Toothless.

"Where is the pouch?"

Then, as if in answer, the thin man held it forward.

"What is this?"

It was open. Toothless could see the top of the bottle. The relic's glow radiated, as if the pouch held a ball of fireflies.

Stephen stammered over an answer.

"A personal item...a family relic, no doubt."

"A soldier of the Yew carries a family relic?" the thin brigand asked. "I find it doubtful."

A new voice—someone else arrived.

"What has Roderick brought me today?"

Toothless thought it a familiar voice.

"A man," the thin one, presumably Roderick, said. "A soldier of some sort."

"And?"

"His pet corpse."

The new figure entered. His robes were loose on his thin frame. His hair fell long from the back of his head in an unfashionable Irish tonsure. His voice had a character that Toothless now placed as scholarly. Toothless realized that he knew this man. He had seen him.

The newcomer was a priest. Toothless had seen many throughout his life and death. This one, though, he had seen recently. It was the priest from Lil's village, the priest who had stood with that crowd, Lil at his side, when the Champion displayed the dead werewolf. Toothless had been watching.

The priest looked at Martin with some revulsion, but then showed recognition. Then the priest turned to Stephen, and his face went sour. He glanced at the thin man.

"Leave us," he said. Then, he spoke louder to the rest in the tent. "Leave us! All of you!"

"That was not our arrangement," Roderick said. "I know what you know. That was the agreement. I do not make decisions without you, nor do you without me."

"Let me speak to these two," the priest said. "Then I will speak with you." The priest's tone softened. "Please," he said.

The thin man nodded as if he were forcing his neck to bend. He then left the tent, passing the pouch to the priest. The ruffians followed Roderick, their weapons still drawn. Toothless was now curious about the arrangement, but more concerned about what would happen next. Certainly, the priest recognized him.

The churchman approached Toothless and, standing mere inches from him, stared into his sunken eyes.

"You are the demon from Brittany," he said.

Toothless nodded.

"You took Lil. Is she safe?"

Toothless nodded again.

"She is," Stephen confirmed.

And that was all. The priest stepped before Stephen.

"How dare you come before me?" he said.

Toothless blinked with surprise.

"Brother Peter—"

"Do not call me 'Brother.' I swore that if I ever saw you again, I would kill you."

Peter turned his back on them and walked to the brazier.

"We have...a history," Stephen said under his breath.

"And you two come together before me," Peter said. "One is a personification of all of the demonic tendencies rooted in the other. Interesting. I truly never thought I would see you again, Stephen."

"Brother Peter—"

"I told you not to call me 'Brother.' What is this?"

He held the open pouch in his palm, and lifted the bottle between the thumb and forefinger of his other hand. Peter looked at it a moment.

"You would not believe me," Stephen said.

"Try me."

It was like a glowing bright star at the ends of his fingers. If they could only see the aura of such things, he thought. Father Peter seemed, at that moment, to come upon a guess. The right one. He gasped.

"This is the Sangreal! This is the royal blood! How do you come upon it? Do you, demon, intend to take this to the Yew? Stephen, I would not be surprised if you now serve the enemy!"

"Stop!" Stephen said. "You are rambling, and know nothing. We were here with Cedric. We come under Declan's orders. We come with Tuan's blessing."

"Tuan? Cedric and Declan? Do you mean to say that you are still a Templar?"

"I am," Stephen said.

"They forgave you?" Peter asked.

Toothless looked between them. There was a story here, but he was not sure he cared. Stephen, however, seemed to feel the need to fill him in.

"When I was younger," Stephen said, "I...transgressed."

"That is a word for it," Peter said.

"This man here was not always a priest. He was betrothed to a beautiful woman who took a liking to me. I made a...rash decision, which led..."

"Tell him," Peter said.

"Which led..."

"Which led her to take her own life," Peter blurted. "Cedric nearly booted him out of the order. Apparently, he did not. I am sure, however, that he wishes he had. I fell to such despondency that Cedric saw fit to place me with the brothers in Iona. So, here I am, now a priest. That is my story. I still do not understand how you come before me with the royal blood."

"I need food, first," Stephen said. "And water."

Peter stepped between them, to the flap of the tent, and passed a curt order to the guards outside. He returned.

"Thieves," he said. "All of them. But they are repentant men. I offered to give them sacraments. In return, they provide protection to this camp. Refugees. We wandered all the way from Brittany."

"How many of you are armed?" Stephen asked. It was Toothless' question as well.

"Between the bandits," Peter answered, "and the younger men under my charge, perhaps six or seven hundred. Enough to protect ourselves from the dangers at large in this part of the country. But you have seen the weapons and the armor. We are lucky the Yew has rooted for the winter."

The conversation between them, Toothless noted, was now easier, though Stephen was wary. Peter, however, was relaxing into a more comfortable voice. However, sadness—or exhaustion—weaved between his words. He sat on the stained, tattered rugs of the floor and entreated Stephen and Toothless to do the same, as if there were far stranger things to do in the world than converse in a refugee camp with a dead man and a Templar knight.

"I probably make a mistake in sharing our numbers with you,"

Peter said. "Who knows what you will do with that information?"

A bandit entered with a bowl of thin gruel and a mug of water. Stephen slurped the water down in a single draft and, waiting for the stew to cool, began to speak of the march with Cedric across Britain. He told of meeting Lil, and taking Toothless to Lindisfarne. He described the battle against Richard, and the plans against the Yew.

"A thousand knights," Peter said. "That is something, indeed."

"They aimed for the northern coast of Normandy," Stephen said.

He then spoke of Cedric's fate, of the fight on the beach. His voice broke several times during this part of the tale, and he had to swallow hard to keep his emotions from rising. Peter nodded through this, saddened by the news and also familiar with the beasts.

This led the two men to share other memories, memories of a time spent together with Cedric and other men who, like Toothless, were initiates or knights at one time but who were now gone. They spoke of things that seemed so familiar to Toothless, but which were so far from him now that he could not recover any details. He wondered, then, if Peter had been an initiate at one time. He spoke with some familiarity of the experience. Their camaraderie, now surfacing above the earlier animosity, seemed genuine, well-tempered by common experience.

Through this, however, Peter's eyes went sad, and his gaze would turn to the side, and he would return to the woman they had loved.

"That was before Esmerelda."

Or, "Esmerelda had thought that was humorous."

"What of Tuan?" Peter asked.

"No good news," Stephen said, shaking his head. "This one trained under Tuan."

"Martin," Peter said. "I know something of this."

Stephen raised an eyebrow at Peter's familiarity, but did not pursue it.

"Yes," Stephen said. "This is Martin."

"The one who is to end this terror."

"Yes."

Toothless blinked.

"He does not look like much," Peter said.

"You have not seen him fight."

"I have. He looks...weaker."

Toothless made no motion. He stared at the priest, who returned the stare for a moment before turning away, discomfort on his face.

"What of Tuan?" Peter asked again.

"He set himself adrift. He considered himself a failure."

"Or finished," Peter said. "I would prefer to think that he considered himself finished."

He turned back to Toothless.

"You were to be his last. You were to inherit his legacy and carry his lineage through these dark times. Perhaps you may yet do it."

Peter stared at Toothless, his eyes narrowing as if he were seeing something inside of the dead man's thoughts. He opened his mouth and took a breath before speaking.

"You have not failed yet."

Peter turned to Stephen.

"I will speak to Roderick," the priest said. "I will attempt to gain his support. If there are ships, I intend to send my people to safer shores. If I can convince Roderick that you fight against the Yew, perhaps he will lend a hand."

"I do not deserve this," Stephen said.

Peter stood and approached the tent flap. He paused before exiting. His head was hanging low, and a heavy sigh lifted his back.

"Stephen."

"Yes, Brother Peter."

"If we are lucky enough survive this, then I will make good on my promise."

"Which promise is that?"

"If I ever see you again, I will kill you."

✠

There were two kinds of bandit kings, those who wanted to hasten the end of the world in order to revel in the ruin, and those who wanted their men to feel pride and belonging, to be protected. The latter were closer to true leaders. They were flexible in their approaches. Banditry seemed a last resort for them, something that had to be done to meet their goal in a world that had little regard for those who went without. The march of the Yew had only crystallized men into their types, so that the revelers reveled even harder, and the true leaders found themselves facing even tougher choices. Roderick proved himself to be a true leader. He relented to Peter, and promised to argue the case for providing protection on the march to Normandy and perhaps even marching against the Yew.

"Some of my men will want to fight," he said. Stephen and Toothless listened from the tent. "I might as well."

Toothless pictured him—small, slight among the massive men of his band—arguing that in order to make their lives meaningful, he would have to send them into battle against what they had all assumed was an unbeatable foe.

So, Toothless was not surprised the next morning to learn that Roderick had made a compromise with his men. He and his band would march ahead, no more than a mile. This, Peter argued, was best for everyone. Roderick would need more time to soften his men to the idea of marching and even fighting alongside of one of the dead.

"Many have lost kin," he said. "Wives and children."

Roderick seemed pleased, however, to learn that Toothless had lost, as well. This might mean something to his men.

All of the Yew's soldiers, Toothless wanted to say, had lost loved ones.

Word went through camp to strike the tents and gather meager belongings. The men and women who followed Peter would now follow him down the coast to their best hope of survival, to Templar ships that would take them from the continent. Peter stood atop a stump and seemed uncomfortable addressing such a large crowd. They squinted at his obscure scriptural references, but found his message. Sighs of relief spread through the crowd in waves. Still, Toothless worried that Peter made promises that he could not keep. What if the army were not there? What if the ships had sailed back to Britain? What if the army had marched to the Yew without them, without the relic?

Not that Toothless knew what to do with the relic. The pouch, now on a new and stronger cord, hung again from his neck. Just as he had no idea how to raise the dead and bend them to his will, or how to retrieve his lost memories, he had no idea of what to do with the relic. Any relic that touched the Yew only made it stronger. Even if he could approach the tree, what would he—weakened and perhaps wounded, with hordes of demons and dead behind him—be able to do? He was thankful that he had no voice to express his concerns, for hope was the only shield that the living carried.

The first day's march carried a celebratory atmosphere. Children played instruments. They weaved in and out of the crowd as they blew rambling tunes through flutes or beat to odd meter on hide drums.

"They should keep quiet," Stephen said.

Peter hushed him.

"Roderick is ahead of us, and probably all around us. We are safe."

Toothless was not so sure.

The children, smiling and laughing, came even by him. They did not know him from any of the living, for he again wore a helmet. He recoiled from the children, unwilling to invest anything in them. He worried that they would soon be dead, or worse. All he could see was the face of the boy in the stable, the boy whom he had almost killed. Surprise and horror in that child's eyes was now a sharp memory. Toothless tried to remember Emer at the stone circle, but could only think of her fat fingers waving. He could not conjure her face.

Peter and Stephen spent the daytime discussing everything but strategy. One question, however, interested Toothless. It was a question that he had not thought to ask. Peter spoke of returning to his village after the death of the Champion and the failed hunt for Lil. No sooner had he reached the fields on the edge of that village when the black smoke whipped in from the east. The Yew appeared, ahead of the plague, now pulled by thousands of wolves in addition to the malformed beasts that strained at the taut ropes and chains. Toothless wondered how it was possible that the Yew could cross so far a distance in so little a time. It was not unprecedented. The Yew had swooped into France from the north. While Toothless served the tree, however, it crept under the labor of the beasts.

The Marian Cloth, Toothless realized. It must have accounted not only for the burst of power that Toothless felt in his trek across Brittany, but it must also have allowed the Yew and its forces to cross France with such speed. Did they fly? Or, did they disappear, only to reappear in another place? Or were they, like saints, appearing in two places at once? Like all such gifts of power, however, it was short-lived. Spent. So, Toothless weakened as well. Then, as the Yew settled at Mont Saint Michel and scoured Brittany for relics and lives, Toothless woke from his death sleep, feeling a new surge. Now that, too, had faded.

The celebration waned by evening, when the wind rose and the cold dug into them. Stephen commented on the smell of smoke as they stood in a forest clearing no more than a mile from the beach. It would be the center of their camp.

"I know that smell," Peter said.

"Do we avoid the towns?" Stephen asked. "We may find shelter in them, or aid."

"Or slavery," Peter replied. "Towns survive by raiding one another, and sending captives to fight for Constantinople against the Turks."

"Why do they not send an army?" Stephen asked. "We offered much aid in the Crusades."

"I do not think that the Jewish elders or the leaders of the Eastern Church would call it aid."

"I served in Jerusalem," Stephen said. "I know nothing of what happened in Byzantium."

"The pope is in Jerusalem," Peter said. "But he has no army, and has struck some deal with the Muslim leaders. The Turks are now free to look north. Constantinople is ruled by a child. I cannot expect them to do anything but muddle through their own crises."

Toothless considered this short-sighted. The Yew would reach them, as well.

Two of Roderick's men wandered into the clearing with warnings to douse fires and make a quiet camp. They had killed several werewolves on the southern edge of their march, and had murdered one of their own who had been bitten. That was the word that they used—"murdered." Stephen shook his head, while Peter greeted the news with a steely mien.

Toothless was not surprised. They were nearing the Yew's domain. Would his presence attract the Yew's attention? Would the ranging werewolves smell his dead hide on the wind? It was wise, he thought, to separate from the group for the night. He was thankful, for he did not feel the emptiness blooming or knotting within him, rising into a yell. Indeed, he felt calm. He could ascribe it to nothing in particular, but was certain that it would not last. Or, he feared, it presaged his final descent into mindlessness.

He walked through the camp, passing mothers and children, some men. They huddled over small fires that they would soon have to extinguish. Perhaps they hoped the heat to stay with them all night. They must have known better.

He wandered through quiet, empty forest. It was alive, though the auras of its life flickered. It feared the plague. It feared the fires. It knew that they were close. The energy bothered him, and threatened to ignite his own nervousness. It threatened to awake his howling. He was not unhappy to break from the trees, now far from camp. He stood at the tip of a valley that ran down, it seemed, from his feet. Perhaps Roderick's men slept in the brush before him. He did not see their auras. There were some lights at the base of a far corner of the valley—a farm, or a village. Perhaps they had a desperate night, as well. They could not fight the Yew, as slavers sent their able-bodied men to die in the Levant, their blood spilling into the thirsty sand.

He looked at the sky. Black smoke shrouded the stars and the moon.

The wind carried the call of the werewolves.

Chapter XXIII

Adozen of Roderick's men entered the camp the next morning. They came in pairs, carrying large crates of rough, splintery wood between them. More followed.

"Weapons," one said.

Roderick arrived behind them.

"Arm whoever can fight," he said. "Especially that one."

He pointed at Toothless.

"What is going on?" Stephen asked.

Roderick did not answer, but was looking into the forest.

"Wolves," Peter said. "They've found more wolves."

Stephen approached one of the crates and lifted a short sword, regarding it with disdain.

"Do you have anything better?" he asked.

"It will kill a wolf," one bandit spat. "Even in a Templar's hand."

Stephen let the insult pass, but stepped back from the crate and swung the sword. He nodded. He looked at Toothless, then at Roderick.

"Do you have a greatsword?" the Templar asked.

Roderick cocked his head.

"Do any of the men carry a greatsword?" he shouted.

One of the bandits stepped forward.

"Jack," he said.

"Where is Jack?" Roderick asked.

The largest man Toothless had ever seen, larger than even the Champion or any of the bandits, stepped forward. Another head or two and he would have rivaled Ruin in height. Indeed, something was wrong with him. He was a Goliath, with enormous hands and shoulders. His joints were swollen, and he walked with a stoop.

"Jack," Roderick said, craning his neck as if looking to the top of a tree. "You carry a greatsword."

Jack looked at the sword on his hip. He drew the blade, his one hand covering a grip forged and wrapped for two hands.

"That one," Stephen said, pointing at Toothless. "That one is most gifted with a greatsword."

Roderick paused. Toothless realized that the request was uncomfortable. To honor it, Roderick would have to disarm one of his men. The bandits looked on, concern on their faces. Toothless recognized Jack as the type who took a lot of abuse, but who was popular among the men. A mascot.

Jack spoke after only a moment's pause. His voice was higher than Toothless expected it to be. The words seemed to have trouble passing over his tongue.

"I will give," he said.

He offered the blade hilt first, over his massive arm, as if he were presenting it to a king. Toothless nodded and took the grip.

Toothless, Stephen, and a dozen of Peter's men received leather armor from Roderick's band. The armor was stiff, with rough metal studs. Toothless was happy to have it, though Stephen could not hide his disgust at the suit. The brigands did not notice, or failed to pay his judgment any regard.

They marched south with an equal number of Roderick's men, entering a dark wood of pines that draped the tops of low bushes with brown needles. After some time, Roderick motioned them to be quiet, and the march proceeded in silence. They stepped over the dry, dead brush. The brigands made no more noise than the light breeze. Toothless looked for the black moss. He did not see any. A good sign.

Roderick halted them. The forest had thickened around them, but Toothless could see a break in the trees not more than thirty yards ahead. Toothless heard nothing. No animals. No calls. Roderick crept to Stephen's side.

"They sit at the far edge of that clearing," he whispered. "They are asleep. If we rush, we might cover enough ground to take them before they are roused."

Stephen gripped his short sword and nodded. His armor creaked as he flexed his arms and legs. Toothless now worried that he would expend valuable energy reaching the clearing, and that he would have little remaining for the fight. It was better to kill them now, he realized, than to risk an ambush at night. And he recognized the value of his participation. The brigands about him were some of Roderick's best men. If they were to see him kill the werewolves of the Yew, they would take it to the others. That would be worth something.

Roderick stood. He raised his hand, waited perhaps for his heart to calm or the air to feel the way he needed it to feel, or for some instinctual moment that only a bandit king would recognize. All eyes were on that raised hand. And then, it fell. The group, nearly thirty strong, rushed forward. The pouch of the relic bounced against Toothless' chest. The heavy blade felt good in his hands. It felt powerful. He looked forward to swinging it. He felt no surge when he had killed the wolves days before, but wondered if that would change, if killing enough of them would sate him at all.

The attackers broke into the clearing. The wolves were at the far side, just as Roderick had said. Their heads bolted up. Their lips curled. Their growling filled the air. Some stood, shaking sleep from their heads, and braced or prepared to leap.

A whistling. The air filled with it. Toothless dropped to his knees. The bandits and Peter's men also dropped, looking at one another in confusion. Stephen and Roderick knelt on either side of Toothless. Wolves were falling and writhing, snapping at their backs.

Crossbows.

Wave upon wave of bolts. Other wolves came from the darkness of the forest, and they too fell in the hail.

Then all was quiet but for the whimpering of one wolf. A single bolt knocked it to the brown grass. Armored men appeared. Scores of them. White mantles, red crosses.

Templars.

"Who are you?" one demanded.

Stephen stood.

"It is Brother Stephen," he shouted. "I am here with Martin. We have the Sangreal."

A cheer rose from the Templar line. As word spread, that cheer rippled northwest through the forest, back to the beach, where tents sat on the sand under the gaze of five ships, anchored and still in the cold sea, their sails furled.

✠

The army was like a hive of bees kicked open. Men donned their armor and gathered in tight formations as the tents fell into the sand. Long rowboats ferried Peter's refugees to the five ships, which were alive with men in the rigging. None of the ships had fallen to Hashashin, or monsters of the sea.

Stephen wandered the ranks, promoting captains to replace those who had perished on the *Baphomet*. He was pleased with his selections, good men whom he had known. Many had trained with Tuan or Cedric, and so moved in earnest, with a thirst for vengeance.

Toothless, Stephen, and Roderick pored over a map of Normandy with the new captains. The wind whipped from Britain, across the channel. It threatened to blow the map right from the table, but they anchored its corners with round beach rocks.

The Templars had done just as Declan had ordered them to do. They had waited on the beach, defending their camp, and scouting the countryside. The map showed every sighting and skirmish—wolves, for the most part. It showed every abandoned farm, and noted the status of each town. Most of the settlements were ruined or occupied by slave traders. Straight to the south, quite far, the map showed a red circle.

"What is there?" Roderick asked.

A young knight paused his discussion of the map. He was every bit the classic Templar, the type whose departure from the ranks Tuan had bemoaned. He was young but disciplined and quiet, thorough in his tour of the map for Stephen.

"We encountered a demon," he said. "He was a giant with red skin. He carried a scythe. Do you know him?"

Toothless nodded. Ruin. It meant the cohort was near. His thoughts turned to Spoiler, then to Breakneck and Curdle. He had barely thought of them since his departure, since they had begged him to lead them. He was surprised to remember them.

"There is an abandoned farm there," the young Templar said of the circled settlement. "We believe the demon and his men to be camped there. There is no avoiding them."

Men. Toothless closed his eyes. They were no more men than the werewolves were.

"Any significant force between us and them?" Stephen asked.

The young knight shook his head. "Wolves, but they do not seem organized. Rogue packs, looking to add to their numbers. That is all. We have seen them in groups as small as pairs, all the way up to a throng that would fill this beach. They are easy to kill in small numbers."

"That is our experience as well," Stephen said, turning his glance to the side.

"I have heard," the Templar said. "I did not know Master Cedric, but—"

"That is enough," Stephen blurted.

"What of the plague?" Roderick asked.

"We saw some patches of the moss," the Templar said. "Not until we reached...here." He pointed at Ruin's red circle. "I imagine that it is thicker to the south, though spring and summer seem to be its seasons."

"The spores," Stephen said. "They bring the sickness."

"Spores?" Roderick asked.

"The dust that falls from the moss," Stephen said, staring at the map. "The spores bring the sickness. Spring and summer. We have nothing to fear in winter."

Roderick nodded. That was news to him, and would go far with his men. They had, to a man, already agreed to follow the Templars into battle. He would make good use of anything that would ease the fear and anxiety that nonetheless rose about their campfires at night.

"Then my men can march into the wasteland," he said. "We will swing to the south, and follow the Yew's path into Brittany."

"Yes," Stephen said. "The Yew must know that we are here. Your men, Roderick, may draw enough of the Yew's guard away from the shore for us to have a crack at Mont Saint Michel."

Toothless wondered at the plan. Did they believe that they would approach the Yew with a hatchet and bring it down?

"How will we coordinate the attack?" Roderick asked.

Stephen looked at him, as if the question were too simple. This bandit king, Toothless realized, was a warrior by circumstance. Toothless remembered fighting bandits—no specific battle, but a vague sense of their disorganization, their ineffectual bravado creating nothing more than chaos on the battlefield. Like the wolves, they were only dangerous in numbers. Stephen's answer, however, surprised him for its patience and deference.

"Coming from the southeast," he said, "your action is perhaps the most decisive in our plan. I leave the timing and the location to you."

Stephen motioned to a servant boy, who lifted a shrouded box by a thin metal handle. The cloth over its frame was thick, velvet. A cage, Toothless realized, as Stephen placed the thing on the table.

It rattled. Stephen lifted to the shroud, revealing two white doves, huddled into themselves and beside one another upon a twig. They were sleeping, purring.

"It is customary," Stephen continued, "to let one of these fly as soon as you ride into the attack. Assuming your men are able to occupy the Yew's forces for several days, and that you are able to draw them far enough away, we will have time to strike. We must factor the tide, however, for Mont Saint Michel is like Lindisfarne. It is an island for all but certain times of the day. I will give you this boy, and both of the doves. He trains them, and keeps them alive."

"Why two?" Roderick asked.

"They are quite fragile," the boy said.

"So, then," Stephen said. He looked about the table at his new captains, at Toothless, at Roderick. "We will take the farm of the red demon. We will march south on the Yew when the dove arrives."

Roderick cleared his throat.

"What if—?"

"If the dove does not reach us," Stephen said, "then we will decide how to proceed."

Roderick nodded.

"I am clear, then," he said.

He stepped back, muttering something about seeing to his men or seeing Peter off on the beach. Stephen looked about the table once more, perhaps waiting for Cedric to overrule him. A look of uncertainly flashed across his face. Cedric, of course, would not intervene from wherever his spirit now resided.

"To your preparations," Stephen said.

✠

The army took positions on two sides of the farm. Pens, shacks, and several other small structures surrounded a large barn. Stephen and Toothless watched from a ridge to the north of the plantation. To the east, mist-shrouded pastures led to a forest. There, Roderick's men waited.

Reports from scouts had been accurate. Sentients congregated in the barn, though the reports gave no description of the captain or any others. Toothless could see them coming and going through the dark morning, but was not close enough to recognize them. Hundreds of shamblers spread across the eastern pastures. He could not see them in the thick fog, but heard the last of their wailing against the rising sun. Hundreds of shamblers, a core of sentients—it was, Toothless guessed, a full though somewhat small cohort. He wanted to see the demon to prove it, and to confirm his suspicion that the Cohort of Ruin lay before him.

"We must give the order," Stephen said. "Roderick is ready to lead the assault."

Toothless lifted his hand and squinted at the stone structures below. Fog was thinning, revealing the frozen dirt beneath dead brown crops. Carcasses of livestock, of soldiers and workers, littered the place. Frost made their skin and hair look like stone.

Where the dead settled, the moss came and smoke filled the sky. Everything died. This had not yet happened here. The cohort was a garrison on the edge of the Yew's winter rooting, perhaps placed only days or so before to watch the northern frontier.

"Now," Stephen said. "We will lose the surprise."

Toothless was still, his palm still raised. Then, he saw the beast.

Ruin was asleep, lying on the thatch roof of the demolished farmhouse as if it were a bed. His rump sank deep into the space and his neck was propped upon the remains of the chimney. Ruin was somewhat gaunt, and quite scarred. Toothless peered at his hands, not sure which the demon had used to grip him. He looked for a wound, but saw nothing.

The demon had the potential of turning the tide. Roughly six hundred bandits, plus a thousand Templars—that should have been enough to handle a single small cohort encamped far from any aid and taken by surprise. The demon, however, could carve great holes in the attacking force. Toothless felt panic rise. He now had doubts in Stephen's plan.

Roderick's men would open the battle by marching against the shamblers. The sentients and the demon would wake to that attack. At that point, and not a moment later, the Templars would descend from the northern ridge. The plan depended upon numbers and surprise, as well as the finesse and bravery of two detachments of the Templar army. Templar crossbowmen, two hundred sergeants and others who had not taken the vow, watched a rutted strip of weeds that ran between the pastures and the plantation buildings. Any creature straying into that space would walk into a hail of bolts. An equal number of knights would lead the main assault from the ridge, but turn from that assault to attack the demon.

The rest of the Templar army would march on the barn, or work with Roderick's men to corral the remaining dead into the crossbowmen's field of fire. Stephen's only instruction for Toothless was to fight how and where he would, though to exercise caution over his and the relic's well-being.

"Stay close to me," Stephen had ordered.

Many questions remained. If the Yew knew of the army, then perhaps this was a trap. Other cohorts were near. Or, wolves were ready to fall upon the rear of Roderick's force. Spriggan might rise from the debris and the brush to hack at the invaders. Also, Toothless was not sure how Stephen had planned for the demon's destruction. Any error would mean the end of the Martyrs' Crusade, and so Toothless considered the whole enterprise somewhat haphazard. But there was little choice. Nearly decapitated by the assault on the *Baphomet*, the force had achieved much merely by having arrived at this place and time.

Toothless nodded. Stephen gave the order, which wound its way down the rear of the slope and across a half mile of forest, to Roderick. Toothless enjoyed determining the moment of the attack, but his hands and arms also itched for the thick of combat. He reached for giant Jack's greatsword, which was strapped to his back. The blade had required sharpening, and was a touch warped. It would do, though it felt heavy in his hands. He wondered how effective he would be.

Again, Breakneck and Curdle entered his thoughts. If he found them, if they had not perished on some battlefield in Brittany, would he be able to destroy them? What of Spoiler? Stephen had planned the total destruction of the cohort, which meant that none of the sentients would make it through the day.

"What is he up to?" Stephen asked, pointing across Toothless' view of the plantation.

Toothless turned to the east. Fog still covered the pastures. The shamblers were vague gray heaps in the mist. A column of black smoke rose from the far eastern edge of the field.

"This is not part of the plan!" Stephen spat, leaning forward.

"Why does he light a fire? He will alert the demon and the others before he has any chance to thin the ranks!"

Toothless squinted, not sure exactly what he was seeing. He looked at Stephen, who blinked, then turned his gaze back to the field. A tiny spot had lifted from the fog. It was a small dark thing, but it trailed an arc of black smoke. Then, there was another, and then scores.

Mushroom-shaped blooms of flame and smoke lifted from the pasture. In a blink, the fog was gone. Toothless still did not know what it was, or that the projectiles had even caused the fire, when the tinkling sound of breaking pottery, the impact of the first missile upon the frozen field, reached him upon the ridge. Then came the rushing, air-sucking roar of the flames. One after another, the things landed.

Roderick, whose men had seen their land put to the flame, now brought fire to the dead.

Whatever filled those pottery vessels, hurled by strong brigand arms, stuck to the shamblers and burned through their skin and dry muscle. Most of the dead were consumed where they lay, where they had howled all night wishing for the fate that now met them. The smoke drifted to the ridge. Stephen twisted his face in disgust at the awful sweet smell that Toothless could only imagine.

"The bandit is full of surprises," Stephen said.

Some of the shamblers fought through the flames. They were strange apparitions, fiery demons clawing their way through their fallen brethren to get at the bandits. Giant Jack was waiting for them. He smacked at them with an enormous club. He shattered them. Toothless saw flaming limbs and scraps of glowing hide exploding from each impact.

A thought struck Toothless. Were the shamblers making a choice to be destroyed by the fire?

"There," Stephen said, pointing back to the barn.

Movement near one of the doors—four purple-clad sentients left the barn and headed for the bandits. Toothless looked at Ruin, who remained asleep but was stirring.

Soldiers to a captain. Three more left the barn, and were approaching the pastures, and would soon enter the crossbowmen's range. Such soldiers signaled the presence of a captain, but where were the spriggan? Where were the other sentients? Breakneck and Curdle, hundreds of spriggan, hundreds more shamblers—that had been the cohort that Toothless knew.

"Now," Stephen said under his breath.

Thousands of bolts flew upon the seven sentients, knocking them to the ground. Two of the dead remained fallen, their limbs nearly cut from their jerking torsos. Five, however, rose again. Bolts prickled from them in such numbers as to make them look like a witch's cursing dolls.

Toothless looked to the east. The fires had consumed all that they could. The shamblers in the pasture had either met their ends on the side of Jack's club or had allowed the fire to take them. They were all gone.

The remaining five of the captain's guard entered the pasture. Three of the exploding projectiles arced from Roderick's line and burst upon the field. The sentients came through the flames. They staggered forward, flames igniting into jets from their joints as pockets of rot gas met the fire. Roderick's force was now pouring from the treeline. Hundreds of bandits rushed the smoking cinders to meet these five.

The weakness of the Yew. Toothless knew it, now. The Yew fought with plague and terror. Its captains and priests ambushed, choosing the time and place of battle, giving them ample time to bring the whole army to bear. Allowed to exercise such tactics, the Yew was unbeatable. The Cohort of Ruin, alone and surprised, was no match for even this small army of the living. Toothless imagined himself under such an attack. Had he been at the height of his strength, he might have made some difference. The closest he had come to fighting such soldiers had been his battle against Guillaume's band. That Templar and his men had attempted to lay ambush, to put the lesson into practice. Toothless had gotten the better of them. Today, however, Toothless stood with the living.

The lead force of two hundred knights now rushed the waking demon. They tossed heavy chains over him, attempting to strap him to the farm house. Large groups of knights held each end. Then, they lit the thatch. The demon screamed as white smoke rose all about him. His voice was enough to dispel the rest of the morning fog.

The Templars held against his thrashing as long as they could. The crossbowmen were shifting their aim. Roderick's force approached as well, flowing around each of the smoking piles of dead flesh on the pasture. The five sentients were all but consumed by flames by the time they met Roderick's men. They offered no meaningful fight.

Ruin acted quickly and, with a great howl, bolted up from his burning bed. The Templars lost the chains. Smoke billowed from the demon's charred back. Between screaming and patting at his burns, Ruin swung his scythe. The Templars took their first casualties. The detachment of two hundred became far fewer in those short moments. The crossbowmen, however, loosed a torrential fire that had Ruin shielding his face with his hands.

"Now!" Stephen yelled.

The order went from man to man across the back of the slope. Horns sounded to signal the charge that was already coursing in tight, disciplined formations down the hill and into the plantation. They surrounded each of the buildings and buttressed the force against the demon.

Ruin looked about him and then leaped over the knights, landing into a roll, screaming as the bolts pressed deeper into his burned flesh. He rose, bounding away to the south, followed by a large force of Templars. Blood glistened on his skin and marked his tracks on the cold earth.

Toothless rose and walked down the slope, no longer eager to swing his sword but thinking only of finding Breakneck and Curdle. He passed through the Templar formations, through the cordon around the barn. The smoke was thick but breaking as the fires of the bandits' missiles died on the pasture.

He reached the barn doors and threw them open. Four more of the captain's retinue, their heads severed from their still twitching bodies, lay amidst empty bottles and mugs. Sounds of struggle, blades striking, reached from beyond a wall of hay bales that ran three quarters of the width of the barn. Another of the captain's guard limped from the darkness beyond that wall. This one was mostly bones, like Longinus had been. Its left leg was ruined, its thigh bone like a dead and broken tree limb. Its sword arm hung by the threads of a ruined tendon. The shoulder joint was gone, smashed away.

Templars entered the barn behind Toothless. He lifted his hand to slow their advance. They obeyed. Toothless swung his sword at the limping guard. It fell, its head rolling into the darkness and its body collapsing into the dry straw covering the creaking planks of the floor.

Toothless pressed his back against the wall, and followed its edge as he crossed into the other side of the barn. He arrived just in time to see Curdle pull his short sword from Spoiler's gut. Spoiler, wearing a captain's mantle, shuddered but renewed his grip on his own sword. Breakneck stepped from the darkness and swung his ax into the captain's neck.

Breakneck, Toothless, and Curdle—between them, Spoiler had fallen. The captain was not gone yet. He turned to lay on his stomach. His head was nearly separated from his body. It fell to the side much like Breakneck's. Spoiler crawled toward his sword, which had spun some yards to the side.

Curdle looked up from the captain and saw Toothless, who was still helmeted and fully covered in new Templar chain. The other Templars followed close behind him.

Breakneck and Curdle dropped their weapons.

"Destroy us," Breakneck said.

Toothless stepped forward, lifted his sword high, and swung it down upon the struggling captain. He swung again and again, until Spoiler's head was fibers and grit.

Breakneck and Curdle stared at Toothless.

"Go on," Curdle said. "Destroy us."

Toothless gripped the side of his helmet and pulled it from his head. He let it fall to the floor. Curdle watched it land and roll, but Breakneck looked upon the ruined face and laughed.

✠

"Ingenious," Breakneck said, holding the round pottery ball in his hands. It was slightly larger than his fist.

"One lights the wick," Curdle said. "When the thing breaks, the wick ignites a flammable oil."

His hands made a motion to describe the resulting explosion.

"Carnage," Breakneck said. Then, arranging the thing before his tilted head so that he could peer down the wick's hole, he smiled. "I wonder what would happen if I drank from it."

Curdle smiled.

There was no shortage of ale. Toothless, Curdle, and Breakneck sat within a building devoted to the storage of spirits. Barrels gushed frothy ale to the ground. Open bottles evaporated their magic to the cold air. All that the three sentients had imbibed now leaked from their bodies. The bandits had taken much before departing on their march. Still, there was more to be had, much more in barrels stacked three or four deep against one of the walls. Full bottles of distilled liquor lined another wall. The Templars would drink none of it.

It was for the sentients of the Cohort of Ruin, all three of whom had killed their captains.

The ale brought no memories for Toothless. He had not expected it to. It did, however, bring a pensive, calm mood. Happy, he even dared to think at one point. Still, a nagging disappointment bit at the edges of his good mood. He was not sure what it was until Breakneck, without responding to any question or invitation, still staring at the bandit's missile in his hand, spoke of Spoiler.

"We were a dozen more sentients across much of France, and into Brittany. This was after you left." He blinked. "Spoiler was a fool. He marched us into fights without any sense. Most were destroyed. A fool. He squandered us."

"What you saw," Curdle said. "That was all. Just Breakneck and I, and a handful of the captain's guard. Spoiler. A few hundred shamblers. The demon."

"Even the spriggan are gone," Breakneck said. "We formed one morning to march, and they had gone. All of them. They knew."

"I did not understand why you left," Curdle continued. "But you, then the spriggan. I knew that there was some reason."

"We both knew," Breakneck said. "We would have gone with you."

Toothless looked at the mug in his hands. Yes, there were memories. He saw Longinus before him, falling into dust. He saw Breakneck and Curdle at the top of the tunnel by the side of the Loire, begging him to lead them. He felt the water of that river, and of the ocean off Britain, filling his emptiness with cold, gray blue sleep.

"I am done," Curdle said. "I remember nothing. Each life I take, that is the only face I remember. That is the only face I see."

Toothless looked up at him. Breakneck was nodding.

"I understand why the shamblers howl," Curdle continued. "I understand why they let themselves die in the fire. I am done. Whatever remains of life in us, we hold it so dearly. But we are dead."

Breakneck nodded again. Toothless returned to regarding the mug in his hands. The disappointment he felt, he realized, was that he had not been able to fight Spoiler. He did not deserve it. Longinus had been his. Spoiler had made Breakneck and Curdle understand the conundrum of the sentient servant, and so had belonged to them. Toothless now felt guilty for even hacking at him, for dealing the last blows. He wanted to apologize.

"Do we attack the Yew?" Curdle asked.

Toothless nodded.

"How?" Breakneck asked.

Toothless thought of showing them the relic. He thought of bringing it forth, holding the star in his palm as if the very sight of its aura would make them know something that he did not yet know: how to use the thing. Instead, he shrugged.

"The bandits," Breakneck said. "They will attack from one direction to lead some of the force away from Mont Saint Michel."

Toothless nodded.

"Then," Curdle added. "We attack. Not incredibly creative. But the Yew is weak. Cohorts are spread all across Brittany. There may be wolves."

Breakneck spat.

"The Yew's prized wolves!"

"Several cohorts sit on the beach," Curdle continued. "The bandits may draw one or two away. These are full cohorts."

"With spriggan," Breakneck added.

A pause fell over them. Toothless considered the battle. The relic. He vowed that it would all end, one way or the other. It did not matter to him, at that moment, how.

"We have something for you," Curdle blurted. He stood with an energy that made Toothless envious and darted into the darkness. Breakneck smiled.

"You'll like this," he said.

Curdle returned a minute later, a long bundle resting across his palms. He let the cloth spill out of his hands. It unrolled to the floor. It was blotched and water stained, stiff. Dust and fibers billowed as the cloth fell. Something heavy clunked to the floor in front of him.

Toothless looked to his feet.

The angel upon the pommel of his greatsword stared back at him.

Chapter XXIV

Toothless looked south, over the dirty sand that ran before him. Some distance ahead, the beach gave way to swampy salt flats that curved to the west. To his right, the cold gray water of the bay was calm, with only the occasional wave leaping into white mist. To his left, a thin forest of twisted trees struggled beneath the moss. All about him, black smoke wafted in thick ribbons, carried by a light breeze. The smoke also rose in three heavy columns along the southern horizon, making a high ceiling of black that washed the filtered sun into a dirty smudge of light.

Stephen winced at the smell. He pointed to the southwest, where the outline of a rectangular structure topped a great stone that jutted from the bay. It was barely visible.

"Mont Saint Michel," he said. "Two or three miles at the most. No doubt, the Yew can see us."

Toothless could see the Yew. The iridescence of its canopy shone even through the acrid haze. The glow rose from a break in the line of the cathedral's roof. Toothless realized that the building's tower was gone, removed or collapsed into the cathedral's crossing. Toothless pictured the Yew rooted there, where the nave branched into the wings at the foot of the priest's perch over the congregation. The finery, the architectural genius, the holy implements of the mass were all muddied by the vile soil of the evil tree and laced with the smell of its toxic breath. Insects left trails of rotting carrion on the pews. The werewolves drooled and urinated across the floor. Their feces piled in the corners. The slave demons who pulled the cart would be sleeping, huddled in the choir.

The skin of the island seemed to move, as if it were made of smoke or water rather than stone. Wolves. They crawled over the great rock, over the ruined village on its eastern shelf. Toothless could not hear their howling, only the whispering of the breeze and a distant and constant thunder that must have been the fires.

Three days before, one hundred Templars returned to the plantation with Ruin's head. Toothless had stared at it for long moments, its expression frozen in shock, even surprise. The Templars had left it on a stump. The cut through the neck was not clean, and so strands of muscle and scraps of skin hung down over the stump's edge. Blood had streamed to the ground, creating a moat around the stump's base before drying into a thick, purple sludge.

Ruin had been a demon, but also a living thing. Toothless was amazed at the fragility. Ruin had been invincible. He had been a being of otherworldly power, from some unknown place. At the end, he was flesh and blood. He had been alive, and now he was not. Perhaps he would return to his world, reconstitute into some other being. Or, his existence was done. His service to the Yew, to be sure, had ended.

The dove arrived on the very next day. Toothless had stepped into the harsh, cold light of winter morning. Hail had fallen and still piled in ruts and gullies. He had been drinking ale in the storage shed with Breakneck and Curdle.

"It is morning," Breakneck said, ending their session.

Curdle yawned. He actually yawned, though Toothless suspected that it was an ale-driven explosion of muscle memory.

Toothless walked toward the barn, stretching his arms over his head. He felt nothing for the effort, and brought his hands down. He approached Ruin's head. Hail clumped above the demon's ears and on the shelf of his brow.

The dove stood on Ruin's scarred scalp. The bird lifted its legs and cocked its head as if posturing for a fight, or a mate. Toothless realized that it tried to release a roll of parchment tied with a leather cord to its leg. He approached the bird and wrapped his hands around its softness.

He delivered to dove to Stephen, who was alone in the barn, eating. Stephen saw the bird and raised an eyebrow, as if surprised. The Templar took the parchment. It unrolled into a thin strip, almost a foot long. Stephen read, his eyes darting back and forth across the thin column. The writing was small and neat. Stephen smiled and paused on several lines, nodded on others.

"They have lost some men," he said. "They found wolves. But they ride at nearly full strength. They see four cohorts on the flats in front of Mont Saint Michel. They see many wolves on the island itself. The Yew roots in the cathedral, in the crossing. They believe that they can draw at least two of the cohorts. They will pull them southeast. We should march immediately."

They did, crossing Normandy without incident. They found werewolf corpses, and the mounds of twelve brigand dead. They found the smoke and the black moss. They passed one abandoned settlement after another as they marched Roman roads, or trudged new and impermanent paths into brush.

✠

Breakneck and Curdle joined them on the beach at the southern edge of Normandy.

"The Yew will know that we are here," Breakneck said.

Toothless nodded. Stephen had just said the same thing.

"It will be some time before the the cohorts can return," Stephen said. "Our scouts confirm Roderick's report. Two remain on the beach. One is called Squalor, the other is Pestilence."

"Werewolves?" Curdle asked.

"The wolves seem confined to the island." Stephen said. "We find this strange."

"I don't," Breakneck said. "The Yew trusts the werewolves. It doesn't trust the dead." He looked at Toothless. "That's your fault."

"Interesting," Stephen said. "I wonder if that may help us."

Toothless watched the smoke rise. The columns leaned as the wind grew and shifted. He looked at the island, then down at the relic hanging around his neck. He had not thought about the Sangreal and how he might use it. He realized that he was not hopeful. How could the Templars succeed? Dispatching one weakened cohort at the plantation was one thing. Storming the Yew on an island, with werewolves and two full-strength cohorts in between, and more cohorts likely on the march—this was another thing altogether.

"It is time for us to leave the beach," Stephen said.

He planned to move the army inland, march them south, and then turn west to assemble above the salt flats in front of Mont Saint Michel. Toothless had tried to express his concerns, tried to scratch

265 | J.P. MOORE

it onto their maps to make them see the tactics of the Yew—to drive multiple cohorts against an enemy's line, break it, and then flood through. He tried to explain that tactics like Roderick's—speed and surprise in flexible formations—would be more effective. They would have none of it. Stephen had not even accepted any of the bandit king's fiery projectiles.

"These are not Templar arms," he said.

With two cohorts in pursuit, Roderick's band had more of a chance than these highly trained soldiers. And Roderick's men had more experience. This would be the first major engagement of a Templar army against the Black Yew.

Stephen and Breakneck were correct. The Yew would know of their presence now. It would send a call across Brittany to the ranging cohorts. Two cohorts on the salt flats would become seven or eight, or more. The new arrivals would exploit unprotected flanks.

A thousand Templars would then join the ranks of the Yew.

Toothless wondered if he would let himself be destroyed, or if he would try to parlay the Sangreal into some bargain with the black priest. It would be dishonorable to do so, but he had enjoyed no monopoly over honor this season.

The army left the beach, joining the road beyond the dunes. They marched south and then followed the coast as it turned to the west. How many armies had traveled these roads? How many had marched back, in retreat? The Templar mood was somber. There had been much talk and much resignation over the idea that fate would place them where it would. One of the new captains had served in Jerusalem and beyond, and spoke of meeting a monk from distant Cathay. The monk knew nothing of Christ or the pope, or even the Crusades. He seemed to understand the Templars, though. He advised this captain to let himself go into the stream of life, to follow its courses and currents. To fight. To win, or die. They should resign to their fates, the Templar said.

But they would not die. They would serve the Yew. They would add to its cause. The Templars were realizing this, making pacts to maim one another if they fell.

Toothless thought on his own mission, his own reservations. Eternal life came through memories. So, the living must endure. He had no hope in their victory. He began to wonder what memories mattered if he were cast into oblivion.

He worried that he perpetrated a greater evil now than anything he had done before. They relied on him to fight, which he would do. They had no idea how weak he was, but they had faith. He was as weak, perhaps, as they. They relied on him to destroy the Yew. This hope might even carry them through the battle. They might defeat Pestilence and Squalor. They might cross the channel and climb the rocks, fighting off the wolves and the priests. They might find themselves standing beneath the buzzing, sighing needles of the Yew. Its anger would groan through its limbs. It would be summoning aid from across the land. These cohorts might even nip at the heels of the Templars as they entered the cathedral. There, Toothless would hold the relic in his palm. And do what?

He shook his head, and pulled his thoughts a few steps back to the battle. More immediate problems, he told himself.

The Templar order of battle was simple. Stephen and the captains dashed it off in a short meeting over the map. The two hundred crossbowmen would lure the enemy from the salt flats. Spriggan and shamblers, perhaps some sentients, would take the bait. The demons—Squalor with his gaze that turned men to stone, and Pestilence, reaching with his tentacles and four arms to fill his maw with warm flesh—did not provide corpses suitable for service, and so would most likely remain at the rear of the Yew's forces.

Once the dead neared the line, the crossbowmen would shift to the flank, revealing a long formation of knights. These would engage the advancing dead while the crossbowmen thinned the deeper lines from the side. And when, or if, the knights retreated, a second formation of knights would be ready behind them. Toothless, Curdle, Breakneck, and Stephen would fight in that second line of knights.

The endgame was sketchy, as if Stephen planned a strategy to unfold, or merely considered his men a diversion while Toothless fought singlehandedly across the flats to the Yew. The Templar army would break into small forces to destroy whatever pockets of the dead remained, and then wait on the tide to provide access to Mont Saint Michel. Crossbowmen would concentrate upon the demons, with the great eye of Squalor their priority. The army would form into a square to face the onslaught of wolves, as if facing cavalry.

It would have been an effective strategy against a bandit army, or even a force of Turkish regulars. Toothless felt it somewhat simple for facing two full-strength cohorts of the Yew. When the sentients joined the fray, directing the Yew's assault to capitalize upon weak points in the Templar lines, the plan would unravel. It did not, Toothless felt, put enough Templar strength to the fore. It did not use speed or surprise. He recognized, however, that there were few choices. The Templar army, which had ruled the battle at the plantation, was now outnumbered.

Doubts grew in Stephen, as well. He even wondered aloud if he should have let Roderick's men go, if the Templars and the bandits might have met four cohorts more effectively. Toothless shook his head. The pressure of four cohorts upon even that larger army would have been unbeatable.

The Templars moved northwest from the road, through a forest that had been preserved by the Yew, perhaps as a breeding ground for the plague moss. The battle was near, and the Templars' quiet and discipline impressed Toothless. Still, they eyed the black moss warily, despite the widespread word of its harmlessness in this season. None of the soldiers seemed to believe it. One of the Templars in the second line of knights, near Toothless, brushed into a gnarled black trunk as he stepped over a thorny bush. The moss on that trunk was dry and brittle. Broken bits fell to the ground. At that mere touch, the Templar almost panicked. He stopped right in the middle of the thorns. He twisted his neck, peering through his helmet to make sure that he was not stained by spores. He was not, just dry fibers. Stephen, marching beside the three undead, pushed the man.

"Stay in formation," he ordered. "The battle is not yet begun, and you break ranks."

The Templar mumbled an apology and bowed his head. Leaping from the thorns, he filled the hole in the line that had already moved yards ahead of him.

The army broke into a wide clearing. On the far edge, the trees parted. A wide path descended a shallow slope into the flats. The smoke was thick, clotting in the center of the clearing above a boulder that was as tall as a man. Beyond the flats, wolves moved over every inch of the gray pile of stone that was Mont Saint Michel. The broken cathedral lay at its top, and the ruined frames of a village squatted about its skirt. The green orange glow of the Yew rose from the shattered cathedral roof and bathed the island. The wolves began to howl.

Toothless could also see the two cohorts on the flats. They were stirring. Small groups of sentients—captains' guards and soldiers like Toothless, Breakneck, and Curdle—were gathering in the rear echelons. Spriggan teemed in the mud, conjuring their daggers. The small creatures would form the vanguard of the Yew's assault. Toothless feared that they would make impossible targets for the crossbowmen.

A nervous energy rose at the back of Toothless' open throat. It flared, there. A tickling, a buzzing. He recognized it. It had come before every battle as the power of the Yew washed over the field. Or, it was the energy of the shamblers, thankful to be doing something other than howling but saddened by the deeds that they would commit. It may have been the chorus of the dead, of the victims, the stream of their souls running beneath the ground, driven to swells and chop by the rumor of a new storm.

This was a holy place. The boulder's placement was no accident of a long-evaporated glacier. Ruins of standing stones, some jagged and some smooth, ringed the entire clearing. He was not sure if the characteristics of the place were lost on the Templars or not. Stephen, however, recognized something. He climbed to the top of the boulder. Crossbowmen surged around him to watch over the flats. He looked over the army that gathered in front of him. The knights filled the clearing and then some. The three dead moved to the center of this group.

The army had its energy, as well. Perhaps this contributed to Toothless' feelings. They were nervous and anxious. They fidgeted. They struggled to hold onto their training, and to the conviction that history demanded what was to come.

Stephen cleared his throat.

"Today," he began, then paused.

He stared at some point behind the crowd, some point on the southern horizon. Then, he began again.

"We have never carried the Sangreal into battle," he said. "The blood of our ancient father guides us today. It guides us to our fate. It guides us over broken land. It guides us through the memories of lost family and friends."

The army was now silent and still. Visors were raised, and quick nervous breaths filled the air. They slowed, however, into a meditative calm so that they were like long sighs from the mouths of these men. Toothless glanced at Breakneck and Curdle beside him. They listened, as still and as silent as the Templars.

"We carry more than the relic," Stephen continued. "We carry those memories. We carry this land. We carry all of history against the one who would vanquish us."

He pointed over the heads of the crossbowmen, through the break in the trees and over the flats to the Yew. The cohorts were moving. The crossbowmen looked back and forth, not sure if they should interrupt their master.

"If we lose," Stephen said. "The world ends. But we do not go without a fight."

One man shouted. Then another.

"We stand!" Stephen continued.

More shouting.

Toothless squinted. So odd, he thought, to rally Templars who had trained in such stoicism as to not require bolstering. But it was necessary, even genius. These men had seen and lost much.

"We do not go without a price! Today, we remember our families, our friends. We remember the land. We remember the world that was, the world we were sworn to protect."

Heads nodded and bowed. Many men made the sign of the cross. Toothless looked at the relic on his chest. The bag was dirty, creased. It said nothing of its contents.

"We fight for all of the living and the dead!" Stephen shouted. "God's Will be done, for today we bring the new world through our deeds!"

All at once, the Templars lifted their fists. They cheered. They were lost in bravery and recklessness. Toothless now wondered if it was wise. The plan required discipline. Now, he worried, each and every one of them felt as if he alone could bring down the Yew. Breakneck and Curdle appeared concerned, as well. Breakneck turned to Toothless, pursed his lips, and shrugged. He said something, but Toothless could not hear.

Did they even know? They had fought wolves. They had defeated a weakened cohort. Did they know the power of what now faced them?

The shouting subsided. A single voice rose from the ranks of the crossbowmen.

"They are coming!"

A sea of spriggan flooded the flats as both cohorts advanced. Behind, shamblers marched. The sentients remained with their captains and the demons. Squalor was there. The great round eye sat upon the cart that, though enormous, was a miniature of the Yew's massive land barge. The dented metal panel that covered its eye was bolted into the remnants of a brow, as if this single eye had once been part of a much larger thing. Pulleys and ropes formed a contraption that would lift the panel and unleash the demon's paralyzing gaze. And Pestilence stood on the opposite side of the flats. He was as tall as Ruin had been. His empty black eyes narrowed, pulling the greenish gray skin of his forehead taut. The mass of tentacles about his mouth whipped at the air, feeling with some sense unknown to the living and the dead, alike. His four arms reached forward.

"Form up!" Stephen yelled, and leaped from the boulder.

The army rushed into its lines, dispelling Toothless' concerns about their discipline. Perfect lines. The crossbowmen drew across the center of the clearing, just ahead of the boulder. Then, the first line of Templars stood just inside of the treeline at the bottom of the clearing. Some yards into the forest, the second line formed. Toothless, Breakneck, Curdle, and Stephen joined this line. Detachments of scouts watched the rear corners.

The warbling cries of the spriggan now rose into the clearing. Toothless also heard the shifting and squelching of the shamblers' feet through the mud of the flats.

Then, the voice of the Yew.

"Return."

Toothless looked at Breakneck and Curdle, who heard nothing. They looked ahead, Curdle gripping his sword and Breakneck standing with the ax leaning against his shoulder.

"Return to me."

Toothless felt the roots in the ground, deep, running over the voices of the dead. He looked up. The black smoke was like the canopy of the Yew, reaching over the world. He saw the green orange glow shooting through the sky.

The crossbowmen fired. A volley of bolts whistled into the flats. Spriggan screamed. The second line of crossbowmen stepped forward as the first retreated to load and wind their weapons. A second volley went. More screams from below. Each volley, and a hundred spriggan dropped. The Templars' aim was expert. Soon, though, the beasts would arrive in such numbers as to overcome the crossbowmen.

Toothless closed his eyes. Deep below the sounds of the battle, he searched for the chorus. He could hear the dead, distant and soft. The Yew's roots now separated each voice, throttling them one at a time.

He wished to be anywhere but here. He would open his eyes and be at the bottom of the Loire, or beneath the sea. Or, it would be long before, summer. There was a dog he knew. A wife and a child. He could not conjure the sight of them.

Toothless opened his eyes. Crossbowmen moved to the side of the clearing. Spriggan poured into the clearing, through the gate of trees. The knights braced to meet the beasts. Bolts now shot across the enemy lines.

The first of the shamblers reached the clearing. The first line of Templars engaged in a slaughter of spriggan. Toothless watched, however, as Templars in the line began to drop. Their companions did as they had been trained, hacking their fallen brethren. But that pause in the battle soon proved fatal. The Templar dead mounted as the onslaught of the Yew intensified. Spriggan were beginning to carry the corpses from the line before any Templars could reach them. Breakneck groaned.

"We must advance!" he said.

"No!" Stephen yelled. "Wait!"

He said it through clenched teeth, with angry eyes. It pained him to say it.

The line began to buckle. Men were beginning to panic, looking left and right, finding no one near them. Some began to retreat, while others tried to hold. Stephen closed his eyes for some seconds and then, upon opening them, abandoned the plan.

"Forward!" he shouted.

The second line, rather than wait for the battle to come with the first line's retreat, now marched forward. Breakneck cheered, though Toothless shook his head. The plan, though questionable, had been better than no plan at all. Now, they had no plan. Every Templar was on his own.

Still, Toothless was thankful to swing the greatsword. His greatsword. But his mind was not in the fight. His gaze fixed on the broken cathedral through the trees. Spriggan died beneath him.

Shamblers fell before him. The sword cleaved. His limbs were tired. He marched and fought, thinking of nothing at all.

"Return to me."

The attackers turned, retreating down the slope. The Templars shouted in celebration, and Stephen ordered the pursuit.

"Follow them!" he shouted, again and again. "Follow them!"

"No!"

It was Breakneck.

"No!"

Toothless blinked. Stephen was passing him. Breakneck was a step behind, with Curdle.

"We can't move forward!" Breakneck yelled.

He was right. The Templar army rushed down the slope, into the flats, right into fresh troops of the undead. The Yew had drawn the Templars out of the forest, feinted just as the Templars had planned to do.

Toothless gripped Stephen's shoulder and spun the Templar captain to face him. Breakneck and Curdle came to Toothless' side.

"You have just lost this battle," Breakneck said.

Stephen, still looking at Toothless, spoke.

"There is no win or loss. We march to our destiny."

There was no endgame, Toothless realized. There was no need to discover the workings of the relic. Stephen had not meant to reach the island at all.

The Templar turned and bounded down the slope, leaving Toothless, Breakneck, and Curdle alone in the clearing with broken corpses of both armies.

"They will need all the help they can get," Curdle said.

Breakneck shrugged. The two followed the Templars.

They, too, were resigned to destruction.

Toothless looked at the greatsword in his hands. It was slick with gore. He was exhausted, and had been unconscious of that until this moment. The Yew itself, though it fielded a strong army, was weak. And so, Toothless was weak. He was not sure how much longer he could fight.

The relic around his neck continued to chide him, confounding him. He opened the pouch and collapsed to his knees. The glow nearly blinded him. It caused pain to spike in the back of his head. He turned away from it. Below, on the flats, the battle was raging.

Men and spriggan screamed. It sounded so distant. All there was in the world was here—the relic, and the Yew.

Toothless was connected to the tree. He could feel the roots below the ground. They reached up to him. He alone heard its voice. He was bound to whatever demonic spirit inhabited that tree. By destiny or by design—perhaps he would never know. But it was a fact. There was no strength in him because there was no strength in the Yew. He would only be strong if the Yew was strong.

He placed the relic back in the pouch and struggled to stand. He walked forward, down the slope. The Templars had lost their formations. Each was an individual warrior, fighting for his own destiny. They were no longer an army, no longer capable of winning the battle.

Breakneck and Curdle fought shamblers now. The two from Ruin fought well, but the enemy would soon overwhelm them. The two demons were close, waiting to pounce. Shamblers now climbed Squalor's cart, ready to lift the metal lid. Pestilence licked his lips and snapped at the air. And there were the wolves on the rock. The Yew was pleased with the harvest, and was ready to end the fight.

Toothless stepped forward, heading toward Curdle and Breakneck. The battle was now a confusion of spriggan, sentients, shamblers, and Templars. Toothless swung his greatsword at whatever crossed his path. One of the dead stood directly before him, wearing the purple of a captain's guard. The enemy lifted a tall polearm. He jabbed it at Toothless, who parried as best as he could in such tight quarters and then managed a strong, fast swing. The enemy caught the greatsword in the crook of the polearm's blade. The jolt of the strike shot into Toothless arms.

The sword felt suddenly lighter.

Toothless looked. A jagged edge, halfway down the blade. The sword had broken. The angel's face at the pommel was now scarred and corroded.

The end of the blade lodged into the enemy's throat. Toothless, still dumbfounded, gave the soldier a kick to bring him to the ground.

He looked again at the remains of his greatsword. Without another thought, but with a sharp pang of sadness, he dropped it to the mud. Toothless ran forward, moving as fast as he could. But he was tired, tripping through weeds and the soupy ground.

Breakneck, now only a dozen yards ahead of him, fell.

Curdle shouted.

"No!"

Curdle reached to help his fallen comrade, parrying blows from shamblers at the same time. They sensed, or were directed, to the treason. Toothless limped forward.

Breakneck's chest was split. His skull was smashed.

He was no more.

Toothless heard ringing in his ears, and saw blinding light.

"No!" Curdle yelled.

It sounded far, divorced from the vision in front of Toothless.

He stared for a moment, then reached to the ground and found the handle of Breakneck's ax. Toothless took the weapon, then grabbed Curdle by the back of his leather shirt. Toothless yanked, pulling Curdle to the ground.

The ax, lighter than the sword, was awkward to swing at first. But once at home in his hands, it sang through the air with a precision that Toothless admired. It struck into the shamblers, severing their limbs and heads, slicing their torsos.

Pestilence joined the fray, crossing Toothless' path, heading for the center of the Templar line. To the left, pulleys creaked as the lid over Squalor's gaze lifted.

Toothless did not look behind him. Before him, between him and the island of the cathedral—nothing. He looked at Curdle, who was cowering beside him. Toothless lifted him and pushed him.

They ran forward. They crossed the salt flats. The tide was low, and so they waded to the island. The Yew's forces surrounded the last of the living behind them. Stephen would die. Toothless did not look. Stephen was ready to die.

The first of the wolves met Toothless and Curdle at the base of Mont Saint Michel. The beasts growled and postured. They leaned into their haunches, ready to pounce. They howled, and others swarmed to them.

But they did not attack.

Toothless and Curdle walked carefully among them, through the ruined village. The wolves clogged the alleys, but parted to make way for the last of the Cohort of Ruin. They leaped to the burned and broken roofs, or snaked among each other in a writhing mass of growling and fangs, muscle and scarred gray skin.

"Return to me."

Toothless looked to the cathedral, to the glow of the Yew. He and Curdle climbed the stone. He moved under another's power, the confidence in his steps growing, his strength growing. The Yew's power increased at only the prospect of his return.

Would he lead the army of the dead? Could he?

He pulled at the pouch, breaking the cord.

Noise behind him. He turned. The cohorts now streamed across the channel. They were marching to join him. Remnants of the Templar army stood on the beach, confused and stunned, wandering among their fallen, or among the pillars of stone that had been their comrades, but who had caught Squalor's gaze.

The black priest stood in the cathedral's doorway, between the massive and broken wooden doors.

"Come," he said.

Toothless entered the cathedral with Curdle close behind him. It was just as Toothless had imagined—ruin and desecration, wolves and the laborers of the cart, and there the Yew, its massive trunk sitting in the crossing atop a pile of its black dirt, roots spiraling and plunging into the cracked floor, into the stone.

The acolytes to the black priest chanted.

Toothless stepped to the soil. The demon of the cart, the beast with the scroll and the quill, crossed his arms over his massive chest. He looked at Toothless and nodded.

"You have returned," the demon said.

Shamblers filled the western wing of the cathedral. They moved toward Toothless, toward the black priest. The priest brushed by Curdle, and joined Toothless before the Yew.

"Give me the relic."

The priest extended his palm.

The gray demon of the soil raised the eyebrow over his one good eye. Toothless looked to him. A strange light flashed in that eye. A smile tilted the corners of the demon's mouth. He knew something. He saw something. Toothless held the Sangreal in his palm. The pouch fell away and the light of the blood filled the shade of the tree.

Shamblers now poured to the edge of the crossing. Their footfalls were a chaotic rhythm at first, but then settled into a measured march. They marched in place, shaking the stones of the cathedral, rousing the sleeping laborers. Streams of dust and grit fell from the ceiling.

"Go on," the demon said. "Do it."

Toothless gripped the Sangreal and moved his fist toward the dirt. The black priest reacted then, taking Toothless' arm.

"What are you doing?"

The demon of the cart roared. The shamblers leaped forward, howling and moaning, shattering the last of the gray and dirty stained glass set high into the walls, and billowing the tapestries and banners that fell as threads from the rafters.

Toothless spun to face them. This, he thought, was the end. They trampled Curdle, whose shouts fell in the beats of their boots.

Toothless closed his eyes.

He heard a scream.

He wished again for the water, for the end.

But it did not come.

He opened his eyes. The corpse of the black priest lay in shreds at his feet. The shamblers were marching in place again, waiting. They had tracked the priest's blood about the floor, and stamped it now into the rock of Mont Saint Michel. Their breathy moans were a chant. A word.

"Toothless. Toothless."

"Do it," the demon said again.

Toothless plunged the Sangreal into the sap and mud. The Yew's roots groped for it, wrapping around his arm. He let his fingers open, and the relic fell from him. He heard the chorus of the dead. They sounded from each stone, from each particle of smoke. Each drop of the priest's blood vibrated. Power flew through Toothless, rising into his fibers, his muscles. He was strong again. He was mighty.

He could rule the world.

The gray demon of the cart spoke.

"We will follow you," he said.

The shamblers' march intensified. Curdle crawled from beneath their feet, looking at the ruin of the black priest, looking at Toothless. Curdle's jaw went agape. He gasped.

"You are alive!" he said.

"We will follow you," the demon repeated. "Or, you will set us free."

Toothless climbed upon the mound. He stepped into the sticky mud and approached the Yew. He led the army of the dead. The demons bowed. The shamblers marched for him. Sentients would bow to him.

"Join me," the Yew said. "We shall render judgment."

The chorus of the dead shrieked. It was his name. Over and over. They were prisoners beneath the Yew's roots, which knit into a cage that pressed them into the bowels of the Earth.

They were the shamblers. The members of the chorus were the voices of the shamblers.

Judgment. Destruction.

The end of the living.

And with them, the end of memories.

Toothless blinked.

The end of memories.

He stood beside the trunk of the Yew. He looked at its brittle bark, aglow with new power that would now conquer the world. He looked into the cracks, into the humming pillar of energy that wound up through the tree's core and spilled like a fountain through its needles.

No, he thought.

Toothless lifted the ax of Breakneck, the ax of his companion. He lifted it high and the crowd sighed. The demon of the cart smiled.

Toothless swung. The ax flew with the might that now filled him, the power of the Yew brought against its own bark. He swung again and again, and the green orange light spilled from the breaks. It filled the cathedral. The demons, the dead—they shielded their eyes and bowed their heads. The chorus of the dead ceased one voice at a time, one by one flinging into the heavens, onto the wind, to freedom and blissful oblivion. The great trunk collapsed into itself. The branches fell. The roots curled. Toothless felt the water of the sea, the water of the end, flooding over him.

✠

Declan looked at Lil. She did not return the stare, but watched the ships moving slowly into line far off from Lindisfarne, deep in the gray mist of the channel.

"They go to die," Declan said. "Judgment has come."

Lil was not shocked, though felt that she should have been.

"What if they win?" she asked.

He did not reply.

"Martyrdom," she continued. "Not very fair to Roderick's men."

Declan turned away from her.

"Roderick knows."

Declan wasted no time, and ordered preparations for a small party—himself, several high-ranking knights, and Lil—to travel to Iona. Plans must be made, he said, to save important records. They went over land, a trek of six days in a small caravan of wagons. The trip was much longer than it should been. Snow and rain hampered their progress.

Halfway through the rugged interior, Lil began to feel queasy. The deformity on her skull started to throb, and she had a rippling blur clouding the lower right corner of her vision. She tried to rub it away, so often that her eye teared and the skin of her cheek and temple became red and raw. She could not eat, and began vomiting yellow bile. At night, she was so still and silent in sleep that Declan confessed to worrying that she had died.

They took a small fishing boat across the channel to the monastery at Iona. The pilot was an old man, the skin of his limbs white with salt crust and his face bristling with gray whiskers. He regarded Lil with disdain and fear. He must have witnessed the plague, once. He must have assumed that it had gripped her. He worked the sails with frantic nervousness. The wind could not fill them tight enough.

As soon as they landed, a pair of hospitalier nuns went straight away to appointing an empty monk's cell with all that they needed to care for Lil. The cell was a crude mound of rocks, barely tall enough for the nuns to stand. Lil was not quite conscious, but was aware of a knight carrying her through the monastery grounds, past gray stone walls and through silence cut only by the squelch of his boots in the mud. When she saw the cell, she thought of the tent in which the nuns had cared for Martin.

The nuns stretched Lil onto a makeshift bed of planks, covered her with a cloth, and pressed cold, wet sponges into her temples, into her hair. She thought of Martin's dead skin. She wondered how they fared at Mont Saint Michel.

The nuns cared for her ably, trying to keep her comfortable rather than having any plan to cure her. They whispered about the plague.

It seemed to be a point of argument. Did she have bruises? Was there blood in her vomit? She wanted to tell them that she did not get the plague, but she could not form the words.

She thought that she heard Father Peter at one point. A dim form placed a gentle hand upon her head. Was that him?

The one sensation that was clear, that stoked her nausea and counted out the time of the day for her, was the feeling that she was still in the fishing boat. It was a gentle though dizzying rocking, back and forth, unceasing.

In the middle of one night, she woke with a searing pain in her head, as if a blacksmith had hammered a white-hot rod into the bulge on her skull. She sat up screaming, pressing her temples with her palms to keep her head together. Her voice died as it climbed into silent agony, forcing her throat open as one of the inquisitor's implements of torture would. She needed to inhale, but the breath kept coming out of her. As it dwindled, the scream returned, cracking at first but settling into a solid roar. The two nuns grabbed her by the shoulders and lowered her to the planks. They were not sure what to do with her. She was thrashing from the pain in her head. Tears leaked from the corners of her eyes. She had quelled the screams, but her teeth gnashed so tightly that she feared they would shatter.

Something was leaving her. It was not a power, or a part of her. It was a shroud lifting. Lil opened her eyes. The sky had cleared, the sun had risen, and the light pouring into the cell was blinding.

Through blurry tears, through her pain, she saw a form. It was the woman who had appeared at Martin's hearth. She stood at Lil's feet, then glided to her side. Lil could see her silhouette, but nothing more. Then, the spirit leaned over her, its hair falling to Lil's chest. A palm to Lil's cheek—the pain lessened, then.

Lil saw the woman's face. Strong lines, caring eyes. A bright woman. Powerful. She was Martin's wife, and exactly the kind of woman Lil wished herself to be.

A voice. It was the spirit, though her mouth did not move.

"It is done."

Lil's lips parted. She blinked, and looked through the spirit of Martin's wife. She saw nothing beyond—no vision, just the rock walls of the cell and the white light of the morning sun barreling through fog. She knew without seeing what the spirit meant. The army had fought. It did not matter whether they had lost or won.

"Go to him," Lil said.

The nuns froze.

The spirit leaned closer, placing a kiss on Lil's forehead.

"She speaks," one of the nuns whispered.

"Go to him," Lil said again.

The spirit disappeared.

Lil sat. The pain, the nausea—all of it had gone.

Her mission, the task that Tuan had given, had ended.

✠

The Yew was dead, and so Toothless was dead. He could not move. Scraps of humanity, whatever the Yew had left, smoldered. With each second, they dimmed.

The insects of the Yew spread over Mont Saint Michel, feasting on the corpses of werewolves and shamblers. Curdle and all of the dead were free. The demons and the spriggan were gone, left to descend back to their dark homes beneath the rock.

All but Toothless.

But the living did not know that a glimmer of life remained in him. They treated him as a fallen hero, with care and honor. They wrapped his body in a Templar mantle. They carried him to the flats, to the edge of the rising tide. Roderick, leading but a fraction of the band that had departed the abandoned farm, saluted him. They placed Toothless in a boat.

Only Stephen spoke. The captain, rather the master, led the boat beyond the gentle surf. He stood over Toothless, speaking to him in a shivering whisper. Toothless heard none of it. He heard only the wind above him, and the last of the chorus of the dead, which weaved a wistful, ghostly tune.

Stephen leaned in.

"I will tell Lil," he said. "We will remember you. All the world will remember you."

He kissed Toothless' forehead.

"Go," the Templar said, and pushed the boat. "To Tuan. To Cedric. To your sleep."

281 | J.P. Moore

Toothless watched the sky, the pink and orange of the sunset toward which he now drifted, toward which the current of the shore took him. Shocks of blue and purple, and the first stars. The smoke was gone.

The boat seemed to move by itself, unaffected by the waves. It turned west, to the open ocean. With great effort, Toothless lowered his eyes. A figure, there. He did not believe the sight, but she was there, walking the surface of the water, pulling the boat.

He smiled, or felt that he smiled. He felt his jaw, felt his lips.

Aine stopped and turned. Her hair fell about her shoulders. Her robes billowed in the evening wind. She smiled back at him, her eyes alive with love and relief. The setting sun shone through her specter. She held Emer, then, and leaned over him, placing the sleeping toddler on his chest. Emer, without waking, crawled toward his face, nestling her smooth forehead into his neck.

Her breath was hot on his skin. Her wild curls, touched by the salt breeze, tickled his cheek.

ABOUT THE AUTHOR

J. P. Moore writes in New Jersey, which is a long way from the settings of his novels and stories. His fiction examines worlds on the brink of ruin, in which only unlikely heroes are left standing.